Praise

"Timothy Hallinan's *The F*
a Hallinan novel: indelible,
of hold-your-breath suspen
the *New*

"Ever since Dashiell Hammett introduced us to Sam Spade in 'The Maltese Falcon' 83 years ago, hundreds of writers have adopted his formula, flooding the bookshelves with wisecracking private eyes who work both sides of the law, disrespect authority, icily stare down gun barrels and conceal an immutable code of honor beneath a cynical outer shell. This can get awfully tiresome, but every now and then a writer comes along with the imagination and skill to make the whole thing feel fresh and new again. That's what veteran crime novelist Timothy Hallinan has accomplished with his latest series of novels featuring Junior Bender, full-time Los Angeles burglar and part-time private eye-style fixer for the city's criminal element.... An intricate high-stakes plot, a compelling subplot and heart-pounding suspense."

—*Associated Press*

"Timothy Hallinan's affable antihero, an accomplished thief but inept sleuth named Junior Bender, makes a terrific first impression in *Crashed*.... Bender's quick wit and smart mouth make him a boon companion on this oddball adventure."     —*The New York Times Book Review*

"If Carl Hiaasen and Donald Westlake had a literary love child, he would be Timothy Hallinan. The Edgar nominee's laugh-out-loud new crime series featuring Hollywood burglar-turned-private eye Junior Bender has breakout written all over it... A must-read."     —Julia Spencer-Fleming,
*New York Times* bestselling author of *One Was a Soldier*

"Junior Bender is today's Los Angeles as Raymond Chandler might have written it. Tim [Hallinan] is a master at tossing out the kind of hard-boiled lines that I wish I thought of first."     —Bruce DeSilva,
Macavity & Edgar Award-winning author of *Rogue Island*

# Little Elvises

**Also by Timothy Hallinan**

# Little Elvises

A Junior Bender Mystery

## TIMOTHY HALLINAN

*For Ken and Mike*

o o o

LITTLE ELVISES

Copyright © 2012 by Timothy Hallinan

Published by Soho Press, Inc.
853 Broadway
New York, NY 10003

Library of Congress Cataloging-in-Publication Data

Hallinan, Timothy.
Little Elvises : a Junior Bender mystery / Timothy Hallinan.
p. cm.
HC ISBN 978-1-61695-277-8
PB ISBN 978-1-61695-279-2
eISBN 978-1-61695-278-5
1. Thieves—Fiction. 2. Private investigators—California—Los
Angeles—Fiction. 3. Mystery fiction. I. Title.
PS3558.A3923L58 2012
813'.54—dc23    2012033883

Interior design by Janine Agro, Soho Press, Inc.
Illustration by Katherine Grames

Printed in the United States of America

10 9 8 7 6 5 4 3 2 1

# 1

## All That's Admirable in Law Enforcement

From behind his little pile of crumpled Tootsie Roll wrappers, DiGaudio said, "We can make you for the Hammer job."

The Tootsie Roll wrappers were the only thing on the table, now that police stations are no-smoking zones. I've got nothing against health, but if there's anyone in the world who needs a cigarette, it's a crook in a police station.

"I'd emit an outraged squeal of innocence," I said, "except I don't have to. I didn't do the Hammer job."

DiGaudio scratched his cheek. I could hear the whiskers under his nails. "I'm going to extend you a courtesy I usually don't offer career criminals," he said. "I'm going to believe you."

I would have pushed my chair back but it was bolted to the floor. I said, "This is too easy."

"You think? Well, you're right. See, it doesn't matter whether you did it. What matters is that we can make you for it."

I was *already* not happy. Since I'm a career criminal, to use DiGaudio's description—and we might as well, since it's accurate—I rarely have scrapbook moments in an interrogation room. But now we were in new territory, even for me. It didn't matter whether I did it?

Just to test the depth of the tar pit, I said, "I have an alibi."

DiGaudio folded his hands over his continental belly, a belly big enough to have a capital city. I could remember when he was a trim-waisted patrolman with laundry-scrubber abs and a three-pack-a-day nicotine habit. When he made detective, four or five years back, he'd traded cigarettes for calories, and now he looked like something you might toss a peanut at. "You probably oughta call the people you were with that night," he said. "Just, you know, match your memory with theirs."

This was *especially* not good. Generally speaking, even the worst cops don't intimidate witnesses.

"The Hammer job," I said. "As I recall, there was a gun involved."

DiGaudio nodded. He had a cop's eyes, eyes that had seen so much they looked frayed. For the moment, he used them to check out an interrogation room he'd seen a thousand times. He'd put me in one of the nicest in the Van Nuys station. Had a floor and everything. Looking up at a corner of the ceiling, he said, "Special circumstances."

"You know that's not my style," I said. "I mean, assuming that I steal things in the first place is a laughable proposition, but even if I did, I wouldn't be dumb enough to use a gun. As pretty much everyone knows."

"Sure," DiGaudio said. "Everyone knows that you don't steal stuff, since you've never actually been convicted of stealing stuff, and everybody also knows that if you *did* steal stuff, you'd be too smart to go in strapped. Because of—what was that phrase? The one I just used?"

"Special circumstances," I said.

"That was it. And if you got made for robbery under special circumstances, especially against people like the Hammers, who demand and receive the very best in law enforcement, him being a circuit court judge and all, and her a little old lady, weighs about eighty pounds, getting pistol-whipped, you'd probably be looking at twenty years." He reached into the inside pocket of his Quintuple

XL sport coat, courtesy of the local Tall Porkers outlet, and brought out a couple more Halloween-size Tootsie Rolls. "Want one?"

"I'll get by without it," I said.

"I wouldn't have given it to you anyway." He tugged the twists at the ends of the paper wrapper. "I like two at a time." He popped the first into his mouth and unwrapped the second, parking the first one in his right cheek. The wrappers fluttered down onto the little pile on the table.

"DiGaudio," I said. "Are we being recorded?"

"You crazy?" His teeth were stuck together but the words were understandable.

"Just checking. Let's review. You threaten to make me for a robbery you know I didn't pull, and you've intimidated the three people who could verify my alibi, which you know is straight, and you keep bringing the conversation around to special circumstances, just to remind me that I don't want to be here. My guess is that we're working our way toward an act of generosity on your part."

For a count of ten, or twenty if you've had a lot of coffee, DiGaudio gave all his attention to chewing his chocolate cud. Tootsie Rolls demand a lot of chewing. When he'd gotten the candy soft enough so he could pry his teeth apart, he said, "My name mean anything to you?"

"Sure," I said. "It's a synonym for all that's admirable in law enforcement."

He waved a fat hand, the back fringed with black hair, in the direction of his left shoulder, meaning *earlier*. "Beyond that."

I said, "Philadelphia in the fifties. Imitation Elvises. Handsome Italian kids with tight pants and big hair."

He gave me a rich brown grin. Tootsie Rolls are a truly awful color. "How the hell do you remember that?"

"Rina," I said. "My daughter."

He squinted over my shoulder. "You got a daughter? She proud of her daddy?"

"Hey, fatso," I said, "I haven't punched you in the face yet, but that could change."

DiGaudio flushed, and the worn-out little eyes got even smaller. "Any time," he said. "Here or anywhere."

"You start it, you'd better be ready to finish it." I was past caring about anything he could do to me, legally speaking.

He passed a pink tongue over his brown teeth. Whatever he found there, it seemed to calm him down. "So, your daughter. What's she got to do with—"

I gave myself a three-heartbeat break to get my voice under control. "She's thirteen," I said. "But she's in an accelerated program, and she wrote a paper called 'The Distorted Mirror' for some class they didn't have when I was in school."

"'The Distorted—'"

"Mirror. About the way American pop culture imitates itself, the way it stamps out little tin copies of anything original that makes money. The example she chose was all the Little Elvises from Philly who were churned to the surface in the wake of Elvis Presley."

"*Churned to the surface.*" He burped. "Colorful phrase."

"It's Rina's. So after Elvis you had all these junior goombahs, all these Bobbies and Billies and Frankies and Fabios and so forth, popping up on *American Dance Hall* and selling lots of records for about six weeks each. And the guy behind them all, according to Rina's paper, was somebody named DiGaudio."

"Vinnie."

"Oh, please," I said.

"No. Really. Vinnie. Went by Vincent because, well, because who wants to be called Vinnie? But anyway, it was Vinnie DiGaudio, Vincent L. DiGaudio, who found all those kids and made them stars—"

"Shooting stars, Rina calls them."

"Because they went by so fast, right? But they all made a bunch of money, and Vinnie managed to get most of it into his pockets."

"As interesting as this is, sort of a tiny-print footnote to the pop music history of the fifties, I'm not sure what it has to do with the Hammer job."

"Act of generosity," DiGaudio said. "Remember?"

I may be slow sometimes, but I'm not dead. "Vinnie DiGaudio," I said. "He's a relative."

"My uncle. My dad's brother. Family, you know? We're Italian, family means something."

"I've never understood why all the non-WASP groups think they own the concept of family. Italians, Jews, Chinese, Latinos—they've all got real *families*. Like WASP families are just groups of people who are close to each other in the phone book."

"Look at 'em on TV," DiGaudio said. "They come downstairs every morning and shake hands."

"Mobbed up?"

"Say what?"

"Your whatever-he-is. Is he mobbed up?"

DiGaudio wiped at his upper teeth with the tip of his index finger and then checked it out. "Italian?" he said. "In Philly? In the music business? Why would you think he was—"

"And he's your *uncle*?"

He said, "How far back in the conversation would you like me to go? Did you miss most of it, or just bits and pieces?"

"I just want to make sure you're telling me your uncle is mobbed up. At least now I know we're not being taped."

DiGaudio spread the pork chops he used as hands, his imitation of someone being reasonable. "You always this suspicious? You miss a lot in life, you go around suspecting everybody all the time."

"You know," I said, "if I go to work for you and the word gets around, I'll be lucky if there's enough left of me to identify."

He looked so surprised his eyes got bigger. "Work for *me*?"

"Okay. What am I missing?"

"See, suspicion, it's a poisonous thing. You think I'm looking to force you to do something for me, and all I'm doing is bringing you a piece of business."

"Business."

"We know—and by *we* I mean a very small number of my colleagues—we know that you do sort of lost-and-found detective stuff for people on the other side of the fence."

"It's good it's a small number," I said, "because they're wrong."

"There's Wattles, who's like an executive thug," he said, holding up a finger. "Three-Eyes Romero, the Valley's leading car-chopper. The Queen of Crime herself, Trey Annunziato." He had three fingers in the air. "You tell me what these three people have in common."

"Good accountants?"

"*You*," he said. "They got you in common. They all had a little problem and they all went to the go-to guy for crooks with problems. You. Junior Bender, boy crimebuster." He pulled out another Tootsie Roll. "It's like that distorted mirror you were talking about. You're a crook but you're the crooks' cop, too."

"Okay," I said, "just to see if we can't wrap this up before we both die of old age, you're saying you won't make me for the Hammer job—which I didn't do—if I help your uncle, the Philly music crook. And I'm saying to you that the whole thing about me, that stuff about solving crimes for crooks, it's wrong. And even if it were right, and I really did solve crimes for crooks, I'd need to know exactly what your uncle needs help with, because I won't get anywhere near murder. If I were doing it at all, that is, which of course, I'm not. So what's his problem?"

DiGaudio said, "Murder."

# 2

## An Original Void

The month's motel was Marge 'n Ed's North Pole at the north end of North Hollywood. The advantage of staying at the North Pole was that even the small number of people who knew I'd lived in motels since my divorce from Kathy would never figure I'd stoop that low. The disadvantage of staying at the North Pole was everything else.

Generally speaking, motels have little to recommend them, and the North Pole had less than most. But they made me a moving target, and I could more or less control the extent to which anyone knew where I was at any given time. I'd been divorced almost three years, and the North Pole was my 34th motel, and far and away the worst of the bunch.

I'd been put into Blitzen. In an explosion of creativity, Marge 'n Ed had decided not to number the rooms. Since Clement Moore only named so many reindeer in "The Night Before Christmas," Marge 'n Ed had pressed Rudolph into service and then come up with some names on their own. Thus, in addition to the reindeer we all know and love, we had rooms named Dydie, Witzel, Tinkie, and Doris.

Doris wasn't actually being passed off as a reindeer. She was Marge 'n Ed's daughter. Marge, who grew confidential as the evenings wore on and the level in the vodka bottle dropped, had told me one night that Doris had fled the North Pole with some-one Marge referred to as *Mr. Pinkie Ring*, a pinkie ring being, in Marge's cosmology, the surest sign of a cad. And sure enough, the cad had broken Doris's heart, but would she come home? Not Doris. Stubborn as her father, by whom I assumed Marge meant Ed, whom I always thought of as *'n Ed*. Ed was no longer with us, having departed this vale of sorrows six years earlier. It was probably either that or somehow orchestrate a global ban on vodka, and death undoubtedly looked easier.

The string of Christmas lights that outlined the perimeter of Blitzen's front window blinked at me in no discernible sequence, and I'd been trying to discern one for days. They sprang to life whenever anyone turned on the ceiling light, which was the only light in the room. I'd tried to pull the cord from the outlet, but Marge 'n Ed had glued it in place.

"YouTube-dot-com," Rina said on the phone. "Y-O-U-Tube, spelled like *tube*. Aren't you there yet?"

Something unpleasant happens even to the most agreeable of adolescents when they talk to adults about technology. A certain kind of grit comes into their voices, as though they're expect-ing to meet an impenetrable wall of stupidity and might have to sand their way through it. Rina, who still, so far as I knew, admired at least one or two aspects of my character, was no exception. She sounded like her teeth had been wired together.

"Yes," I said, hearing myself echo her tone. "I've managed somehow to enter the wonderland of video detritus and I await only the magical search term that will let me sift the chaff."

"*Dad.* Do you want help, or not?"

"I do," I said, "but not in a tone of voice that says *I'd bet-ter talk really slowly or he'll get his thumb stuck in his nostril again.*"

"Do I sound like that?"

"A little."

"Sorry. Okay, the interview is called 'Vincent DiGaudio Interview.' Have you got that?"

"Slow down," I said. "Did you just ask me whether I can follow the idea that the Vincent DiGaudio Interview is called 'Vincent DiGaudio Interview'?"

"Oh." She made a clucking noise I've never been able to duplicate. "Sorry again."

"Maybe I'm being touchy," I said. "Thanks. Anything else?"

"Not on video. I'll email you the links to the other stuff, the written stuff. There's not much of it. He doesn't seem to have wanted much publicity."

"Wonder why," I said. I figured there was no point in telling her I was going to be getting involved with a mob guy. She might worry.

She said, "But the FBI files are kind of interesting."

"Excuse me?"

"Somebody used the Freedom of Information Act," said my thirteen-year-old daughter, "to file for release of a stack of FBI files on the outfit's influence in the Philadelphia music scene. Since DiGaudio's still alive and since he never got charged, his name is blacked out, but it's easy to tell it's him because a lot of the memos are about Giorgio. The files are on the FBI's site, but I'll send you the link so you don't have to waste time poking around."

"The FBI site?" I said. "Giorgio?"

"Wake up, Dad. Everything's online."

Was I, a career criminal, going to log onto *the FBI site?* "Who's Giorgio?"

"The most pathetic of DiGaudio's little Elvises. Really pretty, I mean fruit-salad pretty, but he couldn't do *anything*. Tone deaf. He stood on the stage like his feet were nailed to the floor. But really, really pretty."

"I don't remember him in the paper you wrote." I was taking a chance here, because I hadn't actually read all of it.

"I didn't talk about him much. He was so awful that he kind of stood alone. He wasn't an imitation anything, really. He was an original void."

"But pretty."

"Yum yum yum."

"Thanks, sweetie. I'll check it out."

"You can look at Giorgio on YouTube, too," she said. "Although you might want to turn the volume way, way down."

"Let me guess," I said. "It's under 'Giorgio.'"

"Try 'Giorgio Lucky Star.' That was the name of his first hit. 'Lucky Star,' I mean. Little irony there, huh? If there was ever a lucky star, it was Giorgio. If it hadn't been for Elvis, he'd have been delivering mail. Not that it did him much good in the long run, poor kid. Anyway, search for 'Giorgio Lucky Star.' Otherwise you're going to spend the whole evening looking at Giorgio Armani."

"Is your mom around?"

A pause I'd have probably missed if I weren't her father. "Um, out with Bill."

"Remember what I told you," I said. "Whatever you do, don't laugh at Bill's nose."

"There's nothing wrong with Bill's nose."

"Just, whatever happens, next time you see Bill's nose, don't laugh at it."

"Daddy," she said. "You're terrible." She made a kiss noise and hung up.

It was okay that I was terrible. She only called me Daddy when she liked me.

I've had more opportunity than most people to do things I'd regret later, and I've taken advantage of a great many of those opportunities. But there was nothing I regretted more than not being able to live in the same house as my daughter.

**I'd wanted to** stay in Donder, but it was taken.

"Donder" is a convincing name for a reindeer. "Blitzen" sounds to me like the name of some Danish Nazi collaborator, someone who committed high treason in deep snow. But Donder was occupied, so I was stuck with either Blitzen or Dydie. I chose Blitzen because it was on the second floor, which I prefer, and it had a connecting door with Prancer, which was unoccupied, so I could rent them both but leave the light off in one of them, giving me a second room to duck into in an emergency, a configuration I insist on. This little escape hatch that has probably saved me from a couple of broken legs, broken legs being a standard method of getting someone's attention in the world of low-IQ crime. And as much as I didn't like the name "Blitzen," there was no way I was going to stay in Prancer. It would affect the way I thought about myself.

Blitzen was a small, airless rectangle with dusty tinsel fringing the tops of the doors, cut-outs of snowflakes dangling from the ceiling, and fluffs of cotton glued to the top of the medicine cabinet. A pyramid of glass Christmas-tree ornaments had been glued together, and then the whole assemblage had been glued to a red-and-green platter, which in turn had been glued to the top of the dresser. Marge 'n Ed went through a lot of glue. The carpet had been a snowy white fifteen or twenty years ago, but was now the precise color of guilt, a brownish gray like a dusty spiderweb, interrupted here and there by horrific blotches of darkness, as though aliens with pitch in their veins had bled out on it. The first time I saw it, it struck me as a perfect picture of a guilty conscience at 3 A.M.: you're floating along in a sort of pasteurized colorlessness, and *wham*, here comes a black spot that has you bolt upright and sweating in the dark.

I have a nodding acquaintance with guilty consciences.

When Andy Warhol predicted that everyone in the future would be famous for fifteen minutes, he was probably thinking about something like YouTube. What a concept: hundreds of thousands of deservedly anonymous people made shaky, blurry videotapes of their pets and their feet and each other lip-synching to horrible music, and somebody bought it for a trillion dollars. But then all this idea-free content developed a kind of mass that attracted a million or so clips that actually *had* some interest value, especially to those of us who occasionally like to lift a corner of the social fabric and peer beneath it.

*Vincent DiGaudio Interview* popped onto my screen in the oddly saturated color, heavy toward the carrot end of the spectrum, that identifies TV film from the seventies. Since I was going to meet DiGaudio in about forty minutes, I took a good look at him. In 1975, he'd been a beefy, ethnic-looking guy with a couple of chins and a third on the way, and a plump little mouth that he kept pursing as though he had Tourette's Syndrome and was fighting an outbreak of profanity. His eyes were the most interesting things in his face. They were long, with heavy, almost immobile lids that sloped down toward the outer corners at about a thirty-degree angle, the angle of a roof. His gaze bounced nervously between the interviewer and the camera lens.

Vincent DiGaudio had a liar's eyes.

As the clip began, the camera was on the interviewer, a famished woman with a tangerine-colored face, blond hair bobbed so brutally it looked like it had been cut with a broken bottle, and so much gold hanging around her neck she wouldn't have floated in the Great Salt Lake. ". . . define your talent?" she was saying when the editor cut in.

"I don't know if it was a talent," DiGaudio said, and then smiled in a way that suggested that it was, indeed, a talent, and he was a deeply modest man. "I seen a vacuum, that's all. I always think that's the main thing, seeing in between the stuff that's already there, like it's a dotted line, and figuring out what could fill in the blanks, you know?" He held his hands up, about two feet apart, presumably indicating a blank. "So you had Elvis and the other one, uh, Jerry Lee Lewis, and then you had Little Richard, and they were all like on one end, you know? Too raw, too downtown for nice kids. And then you had over on the other end, you had Pat Boone, and he was like Mr. Good Tooth, you know, like in a kids' dental hygiene movie, there's always this tooth that's so white you gotta squint at it. So he was way over there. And in the middle, I seen a lot of room for kids who were handsome like Elvis but not so, you know, so . . ."

"Talented?" the interviewer asked.

"That's funny," DiGaudio said solemnly. "Not so dangerous. Good-looking kids, but kids the girls could take home to meet Mom. Kids who look like they went to church."

"Elvis went to church," the interviewer said.

DiGaudio's smile this time made the interviewer sit back a couple of inches. "My kids went to a *white* church. Probably Catholic, since they were all Italian, but, you know, might have been some Episcopalians in there. And they didn't sing about a man on a fuzzy tree or all that shorthand about getting—can I say getting laid?"

"You just did."

"Yeah, well that. My kids sang about first kisses and lucky stars, and if they sang about a sweater it was a sweater with a high school letter on it, not a sweater stretched over a big pair of—of—inappropriate body parts." He sat back and let his right knee jiggle up and down, body language that suggested he'd rather be anywhere else in the world. "It's all in the book," he said. "My book. Remember my book?"

"Of course." The interviewer held it up for the camera. "*The Philly Miracle*," she said.

"And the rest of it?" Di Gaudio demanded.

"Sorry. *The Philly Miracle: How Vincent DiGaudio Reinvented Rock and Roll.*"

"Bet your ass," DiGaudio said. "Whoops."

"So your—your *discoveries*—were sort of Elvis with mayo?"

"We're not getting along much, are we? My kids weren't animals. I mean lookit what Elvis was doing on the stage. All that stuff with his, you know, his—getting the little girls all crazy."

The interviewer shook her head. "They screamed for your boys, too."

He made her wait a second while he stared at her. "And? I mean, what's your point? Girls been screaming and fainting at singers since forever. But you knew if a girl fainted around one of my kids he wouldn't take advantage of it. He'd just keep singing, or maybe get first aid or something."

She rapped her knuckles on the book's cover. "There were a lot of them, weren't there?"

DiGaudio's face darkened. "Lot of what?"

"Your kids, your singers. Some people called it the production line."

"Yeah, well, some people can bite me. People who talk like that, they don't know, they don't know kids. These were *crushes*, not love affairs. The girls weren't going to marry my guys, they were going to buy magazines with their pictures on the front and write the guys' names all over everything, and fifteen minutes later they were going to get a crush on the next one. So there had to be a next one. Like junior high, but with better looking boys. Girl that age, she's a crush machine, or at least they were back then.

These days, who knows? Not much innocence around now, but that's what my kids were. They were innocence. They were, like, dreams. They were never gonna knock the girls up, or marry them and drink too much and kick them around, or turn out to be as gay as a lamb chop, or anything like guys do in real life. They were dreams, you know? They came out, they looked great, they sang for two and a half minutes, and then they went away."

"And they did go away. Most of them vanished without a trace. Are you still in touch with any of them?"

It didn't seem like a rough question, but DiGaudio's eyes bounced all over the room. He filled his cheeks with air and blew it out in an exasperated puff. "That ain't true. Some of them, they're still working. Frankie does lounges in Vegas. Eddie and Fabio, they tour all over the place with a pickup band, call themselves Faces of the Fifties or something like that. They're around, some of them."

"And Bobby? Bobby Angel?"

"Nobody knows what happened to Bobby. Somebody must of told you that, even if you didn't bother to read the book. Bobby disappeared."

"Do you ever think about Giorgio?"

The fat little mouth pulled in until it was as round as a carnation. "Giorgio," he finally said. He sounded like he wanted to spit. "Giorgio was different. He didn't like it, you know? Even when he was a big star. Didn't think he belonged up there."

"A lot of people agreed with him."

DiGaudio leaned forward. "What is this, the Cheap Shot Hour? Even somebody like you, after what happened to that poor kid, even someone like you ought to think a couple times before piling on. Who are you, anyway? Some local talent on a TV station in some two-gas-station market. I mean, look at this set, looks like a bunch of second graders colored it—"

"This is obviously a touchy topic for—"

"You know, I came on this show to talk about a book, to tell a story about music and Philadelphia, about when your audience was young, about a different kind of time, and what do I get? Miss Snide of 1927, with your *bleep*ing jack-o'-lantern makeup and that lawn-mower hair—"

"So, if I can get an answer, what are your thoughts about Giorgio?"

DiGaudio reached out and covered the camera lens with his hand. There were a couple of heavily bleeped remarks, and then the screen went to black.

"My, my," I said. "Touchy guy." I glanced at my watch. DiGaudio lived in Studio City, way south of Ventura Boulevard, in the richest, whitest part of the Valley. I had another thirty-five minutes, and the trip would only take fifteen. I typed in *Giorgio Lucky Star.*

And found myself looking at fifties black-and-white, the fuzzy kinescope that's all we have of so much early television, just a movie camera aimed at a TV screen, the crude archival footage that the cameraman's union insisted on. Without that clause in their contract, almost all the live television of the fifties would be radiating out into space, the laugh tracks of the long-dead provoking slack-jawed amazement among aliens sixty light years away, but completely lost here on earth.

Even viewed through pixels the size of thumbtacks, Giorgio was a beautiful kid. And Rina was right: he couldn't do anything. He stood there as though he'd been told he'd be shot if he moved, and mouthed his way through two minutes of pre-recorded early sixties crap-rock. Since the face was everything and he wasn't doing anything with the rest of himself anyway, the cameras pretty much stayed in closeups, just fading from one shot to another. No matter where they put the camera, he looked good. He had the same classical beauty as Presley. Like Presley, if you'd covered his face in white greasepaint and taken a still closeup, you'd have had a classical statue, a cousin of Michelangelo's *David*.

But unlike the sculpted David, who stares into his future with the calm certainty of someone who knows that God is holding his team's pom-poms on the sidelines, Giorgio had the look you see in a crooked politician who's just been asked the one question he'd been promised he wouldn't be asked, in the athlete who's been told he has to take the drug test he knows he's going to fail.

Giorgio was terrified.

# 3
## In Some Cases, I'd Give You a Discount

The house looked like a box designed to hold four eggs, a pyramid, and part of Niagara Falls. Hung irregularly with windows the way some people put up pictures, it was an exercise in geometrical schizophrenia, squares connected to rectangles and triangles and parallelograms and irregular trapezoids and other useless shapes, plunked down on a view lot. Maybe nine thousand square feet, one story high, meandering drunkenly over half an acre. It was a burglar's nightmare. Just finding your way back out would be a challenge.

The door was yanked open by a grim-looking, artificially black-haired, defiantly elderly woman as tall as I was, with a protruding chin-mole on the left side of a protruding chin, NFL shoulders, and severely muscled calves beneath her black skirt. The calves looked like they'd evolved to hold the planet still while she walked. Her hair was drawn back into a tight bun and further restrained by a hairnet. The overall effect was the apple-bearing witch in Snow White on steroids. She banged the door against the wall, glared at me, grunted as though the worst suspicions of a long lifetime had just been confirmed, turned her broad back, and started to hike down the hall. I followed, and she said, without looking back, "Close it."

I shut the door while she waited for me, tapping a booted

foot, and then I followed her for what seemed like ten minutes across a pale wood floor that zigzagged through rooms of all shapes, any one of which would have done fine as a living room, until we reached a semicircular space with an enormous window, a single molded pane of curved glass that stretched the length of the rounded wall to reveal the lights of the Valley glittering expensively below. Beneath the glass was a curved sofa in white leather, exactly the same length as the window. And dead center on the sofa, behind a curving coffee table in bleached wood, was Vincent L. DiGaudio.

Grandma Atlas ushered me into the room, announced, "Your mistake's arrived," and stepped aside with the air of someone who's completed an unpleasant task.

DiGaudio was a lot wider now than he'd been when he did the YouTube interview in 1975. Like a lot of guys who've run to fat, he'd been told that dressing in black from head to toe would make him look like Fred Astaire. His hair was dyed the same black as the woman's, a dead black that ate light without reflecting any. He'd also grown a little soul patch. It clung uncertainly to his lower lip, like a misplaced comma.

"You don't look like much," DiGaudio said without getting up.

"You get what you pay for."

He replayed the sentence, half-moving his lips. "I ain't paying you nothing."

"We'll discuss that later. Could you ask Frau Blücher here to get me something to drink? A Diet Coke or something."

"That stuff will take the chrome off a bumper."

"Then it's a good thing I'm not a 1957 Chevy."

"What I mean, we don't got it. We got fruit juices and natural sodas, got a bunch of kinds of bottled water."

"Whatever's easy," I said.

"What's easy," the woman said, "is you stay thirsty."

"Your mom?" I asked DiGaudio. "Or a rental for the evening?"

"Hey, buster," the woman said.

"*Buster*?" I said. "You allow her to call your guests buster?"

"This is Popsie," DiGaudio said. "Popsie can call you whatever she wants."

"You're the one who has to live with her. Water, out of the tap, would be fine."

Popsie said, "*Psssshhhhhhh*," with a disgusted shake of the head and barged out of the room, towing a vast amount of negative energy behind her. I half expected to see all the metal objects in the room drag themselves in her wake.

"You don't want to fuck with Popsie," DiGaudio said after the door closed behind her. "She used to wrestle. WWF, no less."

"What'd she call herself?"

"Hilda, the Queen of the Gestapo."

"And this qualified her for what job description?"

He shifted his bulk, tried to cross his left leg over his right, and failed. He brought the leg up again, grabbed the calf with both hands, and forced it into place. "What do you care?"

"Just making conversation. Why'd she call me your mistake?"

"Popsie's got strong opinions. Figures anybody Paulie sends will be a fuckup. She thinks I should just sit around waiting for the cops to come and get me."

"Before you tell me why they might come and get you, let's do a fact check. This isn't free."

He brought up a heavily ringed hand. Primed by Marge, I checked for a pinky ring, and found one. The man was a cad. "Scuse me?" DiGaudio said. "Correct me if I'm wrong, okay? Paulie's got one of your nuts in a vise—"

"Paulie?"

He opened his mouth a couple of times but nothing came out. He wasn't used to being interrupted. "My nephew," he finally said. "Paulie."

"Jesus. Vinnie, Paulie. *Popsie.* Where are Vito and Sonny? Why not just hang some neon in the window, MOBS R US."

He shook his head, just a general rejection of anything I might have to say. "Like I was saying, Paulie's got one of your nuts in a vise, and what you're trying to do is keep the other one out."

"What I'm trying to do is walk away from this with an even number. But I have some rules about what I do, and here they are: No mob guys, no murder cases, and no freebies. I've had to break One and Two just to get here tonight, but I'll be damned if I'll break Three. If you want to talk for more than sixty seconds, if you want to tell me about your problems with the cops, I need five thousand in my hand. In cash. If you don't want to pay, I'll walk out of here, and Paulie can do whatever he wants."

He'd lifted his chin to look at me better, and I could see all the work that had been done to keep him looking younger than the seventy-five, seventy-six years old he had to be. He'd been lifted, sanded, scrubbed, buffed, peeled, and Botoxed until the face under the dead black hair looked like it was made from some misguided new synthetic, *Sim-U-Life* or something. "You think I got five thousand just laying around?"

"Sure," I said.

The plump little mouth pursed, so there were some muscles the Botox hadn't reached. "You any good?"

"I'm fucking fantastic. And, no, I won't give you referrals."

He said, "Pfuhhh," and I realized it was a laugh of sorts. "Guess not. Okay, say I give you the five. Then what?"

"Then you explain what's going on and I tell you whether

I can do anything about it. If I can't, I give you half of the five back and go home and wait for Paulie to show up with his vise. If I *can,* you give me more money whenever I ask for it, up to about fifty thousand, depending."

"Fifty?" He cracked his knuckles so emphatically I got sympathetic joint pain in both hands. "Depending on what?"

"On how tough it is. On whether I have to kill anybody. Generally speaking, I prefer not to kill anybody."

The door banged open, and Popsie barged into the room with a cheap plastic glass in one hand. She'd filled it to the brim, and as she shoved it at me, water slopped onto my forearm and down the front of my trousers. Then she wheeled around and stalked out.

"Of course," I said, watching her, "in some cases, I'd give you a discount."

He grinned at the stains on my pants. "Ahhh, she's okay."

"Yeah?" I said, and I leaned over the coffee table and poured water in his lap.

"What the *fuck*," he said, trying to get up, but his left leg was stuck on top of his right, and even if it hadn't been, he was too bulky to rise without pushing off with his hands. He got the foot on the floor and then sat there, breathing at me.

"Keep the help under control," I said. "And give me the money. I'm not having fun, and I'm not going to go on not having fun for much longer without getting paid for it."

"Jeez," he said. "And Paulie thinks you're soft."

I said, "Money."

He opened a drawer in the coffee table. "You didn't have to get me wet."

"You'll dry."

He had a stack of hundreds in his hand. "I don't know about this."

"You see the gun in my hand?" I said. "Am I threatening you? I'd just as soon go home."

"Sheesh," he said, flipping the stack of bills with his thumb. "Is it okay if I talk while I count?"

"If you can."

"Oh, back off. I was counting money when you were still messing your pants." He licked a thumb and started dealing hundreds onto the table. "Guy got killed in Hollywood three nights ago. You hear anything about it?"

"Is this what we're here to talk about?"

"Nah," DiGaudio said. "I always kick off a conversation this way."

"Then keep counting." I watched the stack grow. "Where?"

His hands didn't slow at all. "Hollywood Boulevard."

"Somebody got killed on Hollywood Boulevard? Boy, that hardly ever happens."

"I don't know if he got killed there." He was up to twenty-seven hundred, hands moving fast and sure. "He got found there. Six thousand block, pretty crappy block even for Hollywood. Might have been killed somewhere else."

"Who was he?"

He looked up, the stack in his left hand, a single bill in his right. "English journalist. Scum hound, wrote for the rat rags, the ones with the two-headed babies on the front page. *Bat Boy Graduates from Princeton*, *Maharishi's Face on Mars*, that kind of shit. Name of Derek Bigelow."

"Friend of yours?"

"Sure, same way I'd make friends with a herpes wart."

"And?"

"Hold on." He dropped the last five bills onto the pile. "And what?"

I picked up the money. "And what's it got to do with you?"

He looked at me as though he'd just realized he'd been speaking a language I didn't understand. "What it's got to *do* with me? They're going to arrest me for it."

"Did you do it?"

"Are you sure you're any good? 'Cause, I mean, what kind of question is that?"

"Humor me. Did you?"

"No. But, I mean, would I say yes? What're you, furniture?"

"Then why are they going to arrest you for it?"

"*There's* the question," he said. "Finally."

I waited for a good slow count of three. "Want me to ask it again?"

"For five thousand bucks? Sure."

"Why are they going to arrest you for it?"

"Because I was *going* to kill him. I was going to kill him tonight."

# 4

## Christmas for Suicides

"Louie," I said into the phone as I navigated a tight curve, which seemed to be the only kind they had up here. "I need to talk to you."

"Everybody needs to talk to me," Louie the Lost said. "Whole world's got questions, and I'm like Mr. Answer Man. Phone's ringing off the hook."

"Well, let it ring. Meet me at the North Pole in fifteen minutes."

"Awwww," Louie said. "Not the North Pole. Place is like Christmas for suicides. Hey, good name for one of them bands, huh? Christmas for—"

"It's great," I said. "I just met the guy who could manage them." There were bright headlights in my rearview mirror, coming up fast, faster than I'd normally drive the twisting streets above the Boulevard. "Fifteen minutes. I'm in Blitzen."

"That's so cute," Louie said. "Marge try to give you Dydie?"

The headlights were blinding. I angled the mirror down and said, "See you there," and then dropped the phone onto the passenger seat.

And the car rammed me.

I was taking yet another sharp curve, to the right this time, and the impact caught the left rear fender, swinging my car halfway around. I spun the wheel in the direction I'd been shoved and gunned the accelerator, and the car jumped the curb on the right and plowed eight or ten feet up an ivy-covered slope with a Norman castle on top of it. For a moment, I was afraid I was going to roll, but I kept accelerating and cranking the wheel to the right, and then I was heading back down through the ivy to the street, and the car that had hit me was already a hundred yards past me.

But it was turning around, making an ungainly three-point turn, and I could see why it had hit me so hard. The damn thing was a Humvee.

Since I'd essentially made a U-turn, I was facing back uphill, toward DiGaudio's house. If I'm going to be chased, I'd rather be chased uphill, where I can get some muscle out of the eight-cylinder Detroit behemoth of an engine Louie wedged into my innocent-looking white Toyota. I downshifted and punched the accelerator again, leaving rubber on the street, the tail of the car whipping around as I straightened up and followed the yellow cones of my headlights back up the hill I'd just come down. A couple of mail-boxes whipped past, and then it was a tight crook, almost a hair-pin, to the left, and there was nothing to the right except fifty or sixty feet of vertical chaparral, and I found myself grateful that they hadn't rammed me there, or I'd be waving at coyotes as I plum-meted past them, hoping to land in somebody's swimming pool.

Over the sound of my engine, I heard the souped-up roar of the Humvee, eating the distance between us, and its headlights briefly swung into my mirror and then out again as the road took another turn, right this time, and I ran it as fast as I could without losing the pavement and fishtailing hopelessly through the flimsy guardrail and out into space, hoping that the Hum-vee's high center of gravity would force it to slow down, and then there was a hump in the road and I was briefly airborne and even before my tires hit the asphalt again, I saw the bright lights behind me.

Closing fast.

I own three Glock nine-millimeter automatics. They were neatly boxed up, wrapped in oilcloth and safe from rust, inside the storage lockers I keep in Burbank, Hollywood, and down near the airport. I had an electric screwdriver with me, but it was in the trunk, and it seemed unlikely that I'd be able to locate an outlet even if I managed to get the damn thing out without getting killed.

Tight to the right again, scraping the guardrail this time, fighting the urge to brake, and instead dropping the car into second as the road took a dip down, the San Fernando Valley glimmering off to my right, and suddenly on the left a little street called Carol Way opened up—a little earlier than I'd anticipated—and I slammed on the brakes, spun the wheel left, and jammed the accelerator again, a half-formed image of a driveway assembling itself in my mind even as I passed the yellow diamond-shaped sign that said DEAD END.

Carol Way was steep and narrow, just a series of drop-dead curves and suicide switchbacks that snaked along the side of the hill, a testimonial to the greed of some contractor who wasn't going to let a virtual cliff-face prevent him from carving out a few lots. The Humvee wasn't in my mirror yet, but I could see its lights sweeping the brush as it made the turns behind me, stabbing right and left through the darkness like a giant's flashlight. They'd slowed a little now, having seen the dead end sign. They probably figured either that I'd made a bad turn or was planning to back into some driveway and wait with my lights off as they rolled past.

But I wasn't depending on a driveway I could hide in. I was depending on my burglar's memory.

I slowed, too, resisting the urge to look at the rearview. I'd see their lights without looking at the mirror, and I didn't want to be blinded. But I needed them to be able to see me if this was going to have a chance of working.

And then there they were, accelerating behind me and closing the gap, and I heard a cracking sound and something whistled past my head and punched a spidery hole in my windshield. I would have zigzagged, but Carol Way was too narrow now, barely wider than my car, so I just put my head down and ransacked the lighted curbside as it slid past, and *there it was,* the first Whitley driveway, and I accelerated past it to the second one and cut the wheel right, too fast, slamming against the curb and banging my head on the roof of the car, but I got it under control and powered up the driveway that pointed to the top of the hill, to the Southern colonial mansion I'd broken into about six months ago.

And behind me, the Humvee made the turn and slowed, taking the narrow drive at a sane speed, because, after all, where could I go?

*Around* was where I could go. The Whitley's driveway was a big U that ran behind the house, past a gravel parking area smugly populated by a Lamborghini and a Bentley, and then swung left and went straight back down the hill to Carol Way again, and within eight to ten seconds, that's where I was, tires hitting high C as I pushed the car's weight downhill, seeing the Humvee's brake lights in my mirror, stuck partway up the second driveway, and knowing that there was no way it could get up and over the loop behind the house and back down again in time to catch me before I could turn off and lose myself in the web of streets that crisscross the hills above Ventura.

I thought for a second about pulling in somewhere and waiting for them, then trying to track them to wherever they'd go to report, but then I looked at the bullet hole in the windshield and chose the better part of valor. I went home.

# 5

## A Nice Reduction of Port Wine

I said, "He said, 'Some asshole shot him before I could.'"

"Lemme get these pronouns straight," Louie the Lost said. He was doing something mildly disgusting with his tongue to the end of a new cigar. Someday I'm going to videotape it and show it to him, and he'll never do it again. "*He*, the first *he*, the one that's doing the saying, that's Vinnie DiGaudio, and the *him* who was shot, that's the Brit reporter, Derek something—"

"Bigelow."

"See?" Louie said, lipping the cigar in a way that made my whole face itch. "See how much easier conversation is when you use names? As I understand it, Vinnie DiGaudio told you that some asshole, we could call him X if we wanted—"

"Let's not."

"That some asshole shot Derek Bigelow, ace reporter, before he, Vinnie DiGaudio, could get around to it."

"I couldn't have put it better myself."

"And you didn't," Louie said. He was rummaging his pockets for matches. "And that the cops are going to come looking for him, Vinnie, I mean, because he told a bunch of people that he was planning to kill old Derek."

"Exactly."

"He tell you why he wanted to kill him?"

"Ah-ah," I said. "Pronouns."

"Why he, Vinnie DiGaudio," Louie said, releasing the words into the air in precisely bitten syllables, "wanted to kill him, Derek."

"No. Said it shouldn't matter, since he wasn't the murderer. But that I should work fast because pretty quick somebody's going to talk to the cops about him, Vinnie, yakking about wanting to kill—oh, hell, you know who he wanted to kill."

Louie had given up on his jacket and shirt pockets and was now searching his pants, the unlit cigar sticking out of his mouth like a miniature Louisville Slugger. "Always a good way to work up to offing somebody," he said. "Tell as many people about it as possible. Buy an ad if you got the budget. Maybe a skywriter."

He started looking around the room, his ponytail bobbing. Louie was short, wide, and darkly Mediterranean, and if his face had been a house, his forehead would have been the living room, since it occupied about half of the front of his head. For a while he'd worn bangs, but he had a natural curl in his hair, and the bangs flipped up at the ends with a twee effect that made him look like a hitman for the Campfire Girls. Recently he'd grown his hair out and pulled it back with a rubber band in the ever-popular dude-tail so beloved of tiny music executives in pressed jeans. He gave up on searching the motel room, probably because he couldn't stand to look at it anymore, patted his shirt pocket again, and said, "Got a match?"

"Here."

"You know, my wife, Alice, she's been working with this broad who teaches people how to get things done," he said, and took a deep drag, looking cross-eyed at the coal. "Alice, she's got problems with what she calls *completions*, meaning everything gets kind of half-done and then it lies around the house until I straighten things up and then Alice gets all crazy because she can't find stuff. Like she'll open all the bills and organize them

alphabetically or by color or size or how she feels about the store
they come from or some other fucking thing, and then she'll tear
a bunch of checks out of our check book and then she'll go on a
cruise. And a week later, we're getting late notices and she's yelling about how I can't leave stuff alone, and I'm messing up all her
*systems*."

By now Louie's head was so wreathed in smoke I could
hardly see him. "So she hires this broad, and for a hundred fifty
bucks an hour, the broad tells her—good thing you're sitting
down—to make lists. I coulda done that for free, but it wouldn't
have meant nothing. But, see the problem with lists is that you
gotta organize shit in order of *importance*. Otherwise, you keep
adding stuff to the top of the list, and before you know it, your
list says stuff like *Go to K-Mart for Michael Bolton CD* and
*Don't forget kibble,* and you find yourself sitting in your car,
listening to Michael Bolton with a trunk full of kibble, and you
learn that you can cross off number three on your list, because
*bang*, somebody just capped your journalist."

I said, "Michael Bolton?"

He took the cigar out of his mouth and regarded the cylinder
of ash on the end with the kind of satisfaction God probably felt
on the Seventh Day. "For Alice. See, the thing is, this kind of
lets you off the hook about your rules, don't it? Because you say
no murders, but this guy DiGaudio, the reason he's pissed off is
because he *didn't* commit a murder."

I said, "He gave me money."

"Yeah?" Louie waved the smoke away. "You in the giving
vein?"

"You've been going to your extension course. *Richard
III*, right?" Crooks have more time than most people for self-
improvement, but Louie was one of the few I knew who took
advantage of it. This year it was a seminar on Shakespeare.

"Yeah. Wouldn't miss it. Good old Richard, nothing stopped him. We're in the third week on the histories."

"Aren't the histories tough?"

"Naaahhh. They're a snap. Kings are just crooks with better hats."

"I always had trouble keeping them straight," I said. "All those Richards and Henrys."

"No problem. But tell me something, how the hell do you multiply and divide with Roman numerals?" He sucked long and happily on the cigar and then used the little tool he poked the cigar tip with to scratch the surface of the table. "Let's say Richard III and Henry VIII and two dukes stick up a place, some minor palace, okay? They get, I don't know, CCCMMXXXVIII shillings or so. Then they gotta divide that by IV." He scratched the problem, division sign and all, on the table, and regarded it. "I mean, come on. Look at that."

I said, "It probably came down to who had the biggest gun." I pulled out the stack of bills DiGaudio had given me and divided it in half by eye, then tossed it to Louie, who picked it up and dropped it into his pocket. "That should be twenty-five hundred. Count it."

Louie was looking at the long division problem again. "I trust you."

"In the interest of accuracy. I mean, it looked kind of cool, splitting it that way, but suppose I got it wrong? Suppose you only got twenty-one hundred?"

"Make a deal with you," Louie said, tapping the pocket with the money in it. "You can count it and divide it up again if you were wrong, or I can count it, and we keep whatever we've got, no matter how it turns out."

"You're on."

Louie pulled out his share, folded the hundreds around the

index finger of his left hand, and flipped through with the thumb and forefinger of his right, so fast I couldn't follow. When he'd finished, he said, "Okay," and put the money back in his pocket.

"What do you mean, *okay*? How'd it come out?"

"I didn't say I'd tell you," he said.

"Fine." I slipped my share of the money into the pocket of my T-shirt. "So here's the deal, here's what I need help with. And there'll be more money, assuming we both survive."

"Sounds good." He looked down at the small round table with the Roman numerals division problem scratched into it and said, "You know these people are really crazy."

"Which people?"

"*These* people. Marge 'n Ed. The people who put this place together." He gripped the table by the circumference and rotated it until he'd turned it halfway. Screwed to the edge was a small rectangular brass plate I hadn't seen before. Engraved on it were the words, *For good elves only*. "Whaddya suppose they do with the bad elves?" Louie said. "Hang them up in stockings in front of the fireplace and smoke them like hams? Make 'em listen to NPR?"

"What's wrong with NPR?"

"Oh," Louie said, screwing up his face, "just spare me all that fucking *concern*, okay? All that sensitivity. All those guys named Noah."

"Do you want to hear what I need help with, or would you rather foam at the mouth?"

"Sure," he said sourly. "But next month, stay someplace better."

"Okay. First, I need to know everything anybody's saying about Bigelow's murder. Anything, I don't care how stupid it sounds. Second, I need to know about the Hammer robbery."

"That the judge?"

"Yeah, and his wife."

"Stinky Tetweiler," Louie said.

"Why? Why Stinky?"

"Jade. They took a fucking bulldozer full of jade. All sorts of carved jade from various centuries that were renowned for people being really good at carving jade. Stinky's the place you'd take that kind of stuff."

Louie the Lost never ceases to amaze me. Since he destroyed his credibility as a getaway driver by losing his way in Compton after a diamond robbery—a bunch of jacked-up white gangsters in a Cadillac with a million in ice in the trunk, and half the black population of LA staring in through the windows—Louie has turned into one of the premier telegraph stations of the LA underworld. If he doesn't know it, nobody does, and if he can't find a piece of information, it's buried deeper than Vladimir Putin's conscience.

"Is there a third?" he said. "You said first and second. Is there a third?"

"Well, I'd like to know who tried to kill me tonight, and how they knew I'd be up in the hills when the only people who were supposed to know were Paulie DiGaudio the cop, Vinnie DiGaudio the crook, and me."

"I got a feeling about that," Louie said, getting up and giving a friendly pat to the pocket with the money in it. "My feeling is that you'll get another look at them next time they try."

**Louie was out** tugging on wires or whatever he does when he's finding stuff out, and I drove over to a little coffee house on Ventura that had its own computers and would sell you half an hour online to go with your pumpkin-butternut squash latte. Sure enough, there was an email from Rina with a couple of links to the FBI site.

Feeling nice and anonymous on the shop's computers, I clicked on the links and got images of a bunch of really ratty looking documents, badly typed and with all sorts of stuff handwritten diagonally in the margins, liberally crossed out with black marker all over the place to protect both the innocent and the guilty who had good lawyers. The memos detailed a series of wire taps involving Eddie "The Moose" Salerno, one of the Philly big guys from the fifties, and Sammy "The Ferret" Weiss, a lawyer who was clearly not of Italian descent but had been honored with a nickname anyway. What they were talking about was money, naturally, in this case money given to radio stations to play records by Giorgio and also Bobby Angel. After a moment, I recalled that Bobby Angel was the kid who was mentioned in the interview, the one who disappeared. Rina was clearly right—despite all the rows of XXXXXs, it was obvious that these two salamis were talking about DiGaudio.

*Thing is,* The Moose was quoted as saying, *that fuckin' Bobby Angel, he can sing a little. So the stations, you know, they're okay with it. But fuckin' Giorgio, they're getting sued because people are breaking their fingers hitting the buttons to change the station, when the fucking record comes on, you know, they're steering into trees, they're running over grandmothers.*

Weiss had responded, *Not in the towns where he's been on the TV. Where he's been on the TV, kids call up and ask for the record. Forget radio, Eddie, radio is last year. The TV is where it's going. We got to keep getting the kid on the radio just enough to get him on the TV, and then everything takes care of itself. The girlies look at him, and it's all good, they drive the radio station crazy with calls. And we gotta get the contract, Giorgio's contract, away from that jerk XXXXXXXXXX.*

*So break his fingers,* The Moose said.

*Not my department,* Weiss responded. *Anyway, XXXXXXXXX has a few other kids who bring it in, too. What we got to do, we got to get them all, which means we got to get XXXXXXXXX under control before Caponetto and them get hold of him.*

Caponetto? Oh, yes. *Caponetto.* The Philly Mob Wars. I'd forgotten about the Philly Mob Wars. Caponetto had won, if you figure that having Eddie The Moose cut into pieces in the kitchen of a restaurant, sauteed with a nice reduction of port wine sauce, and served as a surprise course to some of his partners counted as a win. And, apparently, DiGaudio's stable of dreamboys was one of the bones the big dogs had been tussling over. My reaction could be summarized in one word, *Hmm,* and a question: did they get to DiGaudio or not? Was there a chance he *wasn't* mobbed up?

But good Lord, all that was fifty years ago, I thought as I powered off. Who cares any more? Both mobs had been vaporized in the war and its aftermath. No way a gang tug-of-war over someone called *Giorgio* was connected to any of this.

And I remained certain of that right up to the time I pulled to the curb at the Hollywood Boulevard address DiGaudio had given me—the address where Derek Bigelow had been found—and discovered that the Walk of Fame star where old Derek's body had been dropped had one of those old-fashioned record players on it and that it said in brass type, GIORGIO.

And feeling like my luck had just turned very, very bad, I took the money out of my pocket and counted it. I had nineteen hundred dollars, and Louie had walked away with thirty-one hundred.

# 6
## Alahar the Alien

B. Harrison Tetweiler III wasn't your garden-variety crook. For one thing, most crooks—if you don't count politicians—aren't born rich. Stinky had been conceived dead-center in the unending river of money that flowed from the invention of the perfume strip. It's safe to say that without Stinky's family, global fragrance sales would be substantially lower and it would be possible to sleep in the same room as a copy of *Vanity Fair*.

Stinky's legend said he'd tried to lead the straight life of a worthy heir, had tried to diversify the perfume strip industry into niche markets such as paperback aromatherapy books, fried chicken ads for a national chain, and, most memorably, celebrity sweat. He'd somehow gotten hold of a T-shirt that had belonged to Tom Cruise, and he hired a chemist to create a molecule that smelled precisely like the cloth that had once brushed against Tom's armpits, and then he inserted the strips into a few million copies of *Entertainment Weekly* as a come-on for people who might like to subscribe to the Stars' Sweat of the Month Club.

He'd already lined up a year's worth of media personalities, mostly people who were at a point in their careers where they were waiting in vain for a call from *Celebrity Rehab*, but it was not to be. Stinky was served with a cease and desist order by the Church of Scientology, which claimed that a person's "biological fragrance" remains mystically connected to, and is thus a part of, the person's Operating Thetan, whatever that is, and Stinky's business was nipped in the bud.

Thus embittered, people said, Stinky turned to a life of crime. A tragic story of decline.

And eyewash, start to finish. Stinky was as crooked as Brillo and always had been. He'd been kicked out of the Cub Scouts for paying another kid to climb a rope for him, and that was what Oprah might call a life-defining moment. He'd set foot on the slippery slope, and the first thing he did was steal a pair of skis so he could get down it faster.

And now, what with crime paying really well, he lived in his own shining city on a hill, a three-story, mostly-glass Rubik's cube in Encino, not far from Vincent DiGaudio's spiky dodecahedron. It was 12:30 A.M. by the time I pulled up the driveway, but the lights were blazing away. Stinky rarely went to bed until he'd read the morning papers.

The door was opened by the latest in a long line of wasp-waisted Filipino houseboys, maybe the fifth one I'd seen over the years. Rumor had it that Stinky underwrote American tours by entire folk-dance troupes from the Philippines, encouraging the most light-footed and narrow-waisted of the boys to overstay their visas and move in to help with the dusting. Later, when he'd succumbed to the hunger for novelty that is the Mark of Cain on all human males, there'd suddenly be a new dance troupe performing down at the Shrine Auditorium, and the former Boy of the Day would be set up with either a donut shop or a florist outlet, depending on which way the kid faced, so to speak. There were supposed to be reunions up at the house on the anniversary of the overthrow of Ferdinand and Imelda, with a dozen or more of Stinky's formers grilling plantains and whipping up *adobo* while the others argued over which doilies to put on the table.

Stinky was in the all-beige living room, sitting at a primly distressed table of white oak. In front of him, on a square of green felt, was a wooden box full of rubies and emeralds, just sitting there the way some families might display a box of shells picked up on their last trip to the beach.

"How absolutely ripping to see you, Junior," Stinky said without getting up. "Just ripping. Bearing up all right, are we?" Stinky was born in Tarzana and had spent a total of maybe ten days in London, but he ate a lot of scones.

"I still have two legs," I said. "Nice rocks."

"Aren't they," Stinky said. He picked up ten or twelve and let them trickle through his fingers. They made a disappointingly prosaic clatter as they landed, but they threw off a lot of fire. "Lot of stories collected here, I'd imagine, old boy. Good jewels trail stories behind them. Volumes of stories."

"And if it's all the same to you," I said, "I'd just as soon not hear them."

"Ahh, Junior," Stinky said in his best disappointed-Sydney-Greenstreet mode. One of the things about Stinky was that he was Sydney Greenstreet if your eyes were closed and Alahar the Alien if they were open, what with the tiny nose and big, slightly sloping eyes. Like Vincent DiGaudio, Stinky'd had some work done, a couple of lifts that had yanked his entire face up like he'd been grabbed by the hair for the Rapture. The surgeries had smoothed everything, tilted his eyes at the corners, and made him look like someone who'd just moved to California from Roswell, New Mexico.

"Ahh, Stinky," I replied, pulling out a chair and sitting. Stinky smiled to the extent that his various lifts permitted, and pulled the box of stones about six inches closer to his chest.

"What is it, then? Have you something for me? Oh, and can I have Ting Ting get you anything?"

"No, thanks," I said. Ting Ting hovered discreetly for a moment and then ushered himself out in a way that made it clear that there was a flower shop in his future.

"Ting Ting?" I asked. "Isn't that one of the TeleTubbies?"

"Lightness of spirit," Stinky said. "That's what I love best about Filipinos. Lightness of spirit. So buoyant, so unlike the leaden animating energy of the Anglo-Saxon."

"I've heard they float really well."

"Not to cut things short, old bean," Stinky said, "but I'm on a bit of a tight lead. Show me what you've got."

"Actually, it's question time," I said.

"Is it?" he said, turning the friendliness down by about 30 percent.

"Carved jade," I said. "Seen much lately?"

"Ah," Stinky said, scratching his nose. Stinky didn't know he touched his nose when you shot him in the heart, and I wasn't going to tell him. "Might have done," he said cautiously. "Yes, might have done."

"All those Chinese craftsmen," I said. "Craftswomen, too, I suppose. Digging away by candlelight at those smooth green stones with their sharp little tools, coughing their lungs out from the dust. Dying at their tables, the hand extended uselessly, the gouger or whatever it was, dropping one last time from their lifeless fingers—"

"They wore silk masks over their mouths and noses," Stinky said. "I assume you have a point."

"Carved jade," I said. "Didn't I already say that?"

Stinky didn't reply, just sat farther back in his chair. He had a ruby the size of a mammoth's molar in his hand, and he turned it between his fingers without looking at it.

"See, some was stolen recently," I said. "Jade, I mean. From a judge, no less. Terrible thing, when a judge can't even collect carved jade any more without attracting the attention of brutes. Did I say he was a judge?"

"You did." He clicked the stone against the table and then glanced down to make sure he hadn't distressed the wood any further.

"So, as you can imagine, there's a lot of effort being put into finding the miscreants who kipped the jade and slammed Mrs. Judge around with their big old automatics."

He went after the tip of his nose again. "And if I *had* seen some lately?"

"Well, I'd think it would be really imperative to keep even a hint of it from reaching the constables. I mean, I've heard directly from them that they're under a lot of pressure."

Stinky pushed his lips out like somebody trying to speak French. "And if I hadn't seen any?"

"Same thing. Really, if someone were just to *suggest* to the cops that bits and pieces of the judge's collection had passed through this house, I think it would be hard for even Ting Ting to get the place clean enough to withstand a really sincere search. And if they didn't find the jade, you know how hard they'd look to find something else." I reached over and picked up one of the stones—a ruby, cold and slippery—and Stinky's eyes followed my hand until I dropped it back into the box. "For example," I said.

"The Hollywood Reservoir," Stinky said dreamily.

"What about it?"

"I wouldn't be at all surprised to learn that you've been found floating there, face-down, some day." He tossed the ruby back into the box. "What do you want?"

"Names."

"And what do I get? And don't give me that bushwa about not going to the cops. Of course, you don't go to the cops, but what do I get in the future?"

"What do you want?"

"A job," he said, not sounding even faintly British. "At some point in the future, I designate a target, you hit it, and I get the proceeds."

"All the proceeds?"

"One hundred percent."

"Just so you understand, Stinky, if I take the deal, there will be an absolutely unbreakable chain leading from me back to you. Just in case it turns out to be a double-dodge and the room is full of cops."

He smiled. "I'd expect you to make arrangements of some kind."

I smiled back. "And I won't disappoint your expectations."

"All right," he said. "I'll give you a name. But you're not going to like it." And he did, he gave me a name.

And I *didn't* like it.

# 7

## Hell Is Sometimes Defined as a Complete Lack of Hope

The name Stinky gave me was enough to make me think about going to the Wedgwood Apartment House and staying there for a year or two, just ordering Chinese and pizza in, and waiting for someone to die.

Number 302 at The Wedgwood is my rabbit hole. The monthly change of motels is an effective way of avoiding most trouble, since most of those who might want to damage me live outside the law, and despite Hollywood's love affair with brilliantly twisted criminal masterminds, the majority of crooks can charitably be described as slow learners, people who have trouble finding even someone who stays put. The motel scheme has the added advantage of looking like it's my method of hiding out. Once someone who's looking for me figures out the motels, he probably thinks he'll have me in his sights. In fact, if I ever *really* need to hide out, Number 302 at the Wedgwood is always waiting.

No one, and I mean no one, has ever been there.

In the 1920s, Western Boulevard (as its name suggests) had marked a western margin of urban Los Angeles. West Los Angeles, Beverly Hills, and Brentwood were just dirt roads and chaparral at the time, and since Los Angeles's moneyed elite has, by and large, tended to live on the western edge of things, the area around Western Boulevard was home to some extraordinary apartment buildings, art deco monuments to gracious living that had once housed Mae West and Wallace Beery and other members of the posse of privilege.

But Los Angeles moved west, and Western Avenue stayed put, and these days the old luxury buildings had mostly been chopped up into smaller places to house Latinos and other recent arrivals. Three of them, though—the Wedgwood and its sister buildings, the Lenox and the Royal Doulton, called the "China" apartments because they'd been named after prominent makers of china—had been bought by syndicates of Koreans, who left the outside of the buildings looking sadly shabby but restored the living spaces to their former grandeur. From the outside, the China buildings were indistinguishable from their sadly declined sisters, but inside they were monuments to 1920s elegance. This approach had the advantage of giving the landlords control of dazzlingly beautiful and extremely expensive apartments with very low property taxes.

A twenty-year lease on Number 302 is held by a Korean con woman named Lee Cha-Young, who is known to some of her friends as Winnie Park. Winnie owed me a very, very big one, and 302 was the way we evened things up. I paid the rent, she had someone maintain the papers while she languished in a Singapore jail, and I had no legal connection with the place at all. I went there only two or three times a year, doing hours of aimless circles and double-backs to identify anyone who might be behind me. I was certain that no one had the place mapped.

Given the reputation and the advanced age of the person whose name Stinky had provided, a year or two at the Wedgwood seemed like a prudent move.

Except that it would have kept me from Rina. She couldn't come to me, and every time I went to her there might be someone waiting. I weighed the alternatives as I drove down the hill from Stinky's. On the one hand, protecting my neck; on the other hand, protecting my relationship with my daughter. At the last moment, I turned toward the North Pole.

**A sudden silvery** dazzle in the web of cracked glass surrounding the bullet hole in my windshield grabbed my eye as I turned into the motel parking lot, drawing my attention away from the cute wooden hitching posts with the reindeers' names on them that had been set up at the front of every space, and making me look up.

The lights were on in Prancer. My unoccupied adjoining room.

Right. Given the day thus far, an ambush made perfect sense for Act Three. I hadn't hit the brakes yet, so I just kept going in the hope that whoever was up there either wasn't watching the lot or didn't know what my car looked like. I headed left and pulled around behind the building, into the Parking Area Whimsy Forgot, just asphalt and painted lines, completely devoid of seasonal creativity.

There was no Humvee parked back there. That was something.

I backed in between a couple of more or less parallel lines, cut the motor, and leaned sideways until my cheek was resting against the cool glass of the window. Okay: Paulie DiGaudio the cop, leading to Vinnie DiGaudio the gangster, leading to the Philly mob, leading to a murdered Brit journalist, leading to a talentless Italian Adonis named Giorgio. And then the other wing of the structure: DiGaudio the cop, leading to the Hammer robbery, leading to carved jade, leading to the city's foremost recipient of exotic stolen goods, Stinky Tetweiler, leading to. . . .

I shivered. I couldn't even bring myself to *think* the name.

And now there was a light on in Prancer. A room I had strategically left dark so it would look unoccupied.

Maybe I *should* go to the Wedgwood.

Los Angeles is your basic urban forest. By and large, we gambol unharmed in its asphalt glades, resting in the shade of the giant concrete trees, avoiding the thorns, the poison oak, and the occasional carnivorous plant, keeping an eye out for the things that are bigger or faster than we are and have sharper teeth, or things that can see in the dark, and most of the time we tuck ourselves safely into our little nests at night without even a flicker of gratitude for the fact that we're still alive.

But once in a while we blunder into a web. The webs are everywhere, mostly set too high for normal folks to worry about. They've been built for those who are reaching too far, those who are on financial tiptoe, those who are perilously stretched or dangerously ambitious and defenselessly vulnerable. And at the center of those webs are the city's spiders, each of their eight legs resting on a different strand, waiting for the tug that brings the fangs out, that prompts the scuttle and then the silk, and that ends with the prey conscious but immobilized, trussed, paralyzed, pumped full of digestive juices, being eaten from the inside out. Probably with a laugh track.

The name that Stinky had given me belonged to the biggest and most voracious spider in Los Angeles. All I could hope was that I hadn't yet tugged on his web, because he could eat me and all my ancestors on both sides of the family tree, stretching ten or twelve generations back, and not even burp.

But there were lights on in Prancer.

I considered my options. Florida sounded nice. Or Akron, Ohio. Who'd look for me in Akron? On a smaller scale, my Glocks sounded good, but they were locked in storage facilities that wouldn't open until tomorrow morning.

So look on the sunny side. I had surprise in my favor.

Or maybe not.

Maybe I was on a completely shady street. Maybe I'd been dead for half an hour and just hadn't noticed yet.

See? I asked myself. Things could *too* be worse. I was alive, and life is meant to be confronted. The thing to do was just march up those stairs on tiptoe, kick open the door very quietly, and boldly peek inside for a trillionth of a second, with one foot stretched out behind me so it could bear my weight when the bullet plowed into my chest. That way, I wouldn't hit my head on the railing as I went down.

I always feel better when I've decided on a course of action.

The electric screwdriver from the trunk may have been useless, but it felt good in my hand. I eased the trunk closed and headed around to the front of the building.

The North Pole, beneath all of Marge 'n Ed's sprayed-on snow, blinkie-lights, and red-and-white candy-cane froufrou, was your standard joyless LA motel: a stucco oblong with the approximate relative dimensions, and the architectural interest value, of a giant brick. Since there were two floors, it was higher than it was deep. The doors on the second floor opened onto a high-railed balcony that ran the entire length of the building, reached on either end by a wooden stairway, home to an expanding universe of termites who probably all had their own problems. In the middle of the building was an elevator in which a great many cats had urinated freely.

At 2:20 A.M., Prancer was the only lighted room. Everyone in the place was asleep. Holding my breath, I tiptoed up the stairs, clutching onto my unplugged electric screwdriver.

As I hit the top step, I smelled cigarette smoke. The fear in my gut uncoiled a bit. No professional hitman was going to sit around smoking while waiting for the victim to pop in. And, I asked myself a bit belatedly, what kind of professional hitman would leave the damn light on in the first place? A professional hitman, I decided, who could possibly be intimidated with an unplugged electric screwdriver. I tiptoed past Prancer's door, which was about half an inch ajar, and got to Blitzen without getting shot. Marge 'n Ed had exchanged the noisy old mechanical locks for the almost-silent electronic ones that read a slipped-in card. I inserted the card, heard a muffled click, and pushed the door open.

Blitzen welcomed me with its light-hearted holiday fragrance of mothballs, dead cigarettes, and damp carpet. I left the door open behind me just in case, and moved flat-footed, gliding as best I could across the sticky rug, to the adjoining door that opened into Prancer. I pointed the heavy electric screwdriver in front of me with both hands, figuring I could lunge and stab with it if I had to, lifted my right leg, and kicked the door in.

A shrill scream split the night.

**"This stuff isn't** free, you know," Marge said, mopping vodka off the bedspread. "Not to mention the fucking door." She had the smoldering filter of a cigarette screwed into the corner of her mouth, and she'd pulled her mouth to the left to get the smoke away from her nose.

"Yeah, well, I rented this room," I said. "And when I rent a room, I usually rent it empty. I figure if someone turns out to be in it, I've got grounds for complaint."

"It's just me, for Chrissakes." She unwound another twenty feet of tissue off the roll of toilet paper in her left hand and went back to blotting the bedspread. "It's my motel."

"That's probably how Norman Bates felt."

"Who? Oh, never mind." She sat heavily on the wet bed. "How do I start?"

This was not turning out to be my day. "How do you start what?"

She pulled the cigarette stub from her mouth between thumb and forefinger. "Honey, you been here a while."

"Eight days," I said. Marge had obviously been here a while herself. The economy-size jug of generic Vodka, Old Igor's Private Stock or something, was half empty, and the ashtray, which was shaped like an elf's boot, complete with pointed toe, was half full. And, now that she'd stopped vibrating all over the room, I could see that Marge looked terrible. Long streaks of black mascara ran down her cheeks like skid marks, and her nose was as red as, well, Rudoph's.

"Eight days," she said. She dropped the cigarette butt into the boot and wadded up the vodka-soaked tissue and tossed it onto the rug. Then she shifted to her left, away from the wet spot. "And we talked some, you and me, and I seen you in and out at all hours, not like somebody lives a normal life, with a job and all, and if Ed was here, Ed, he'd say, *That boy's up to something.*"

"Wish I'd met old Ed," I said. I wanted to go to bed.

Marge swiped her index finger beneath her nose and then wiped the shiny finger on her pants. She was wearing a sort of matador's jacket, short in the butt, and black trousers that ended at mid-calf. Her shoes were thong sandals ornamented with gold plastic sequins the size of quarters. The sequins were kind of heartbreaking, for some reason. "You learn," she said. "In this business, you learn. You learn to tell who's checkin' in with a body in the trunk, who lives half a mile away with the little woman but needs a place where he can bring littler women, who's just staying one more night somewhere on the way down, who's got a bottle of pills and plans to take them. You gotta pay attention, otherwise it's not fair to the maids. You don't want these poor girls from Panama or Salvador opening the door on something that'll keep them awake for the rest of their lives."

"Guess not."

"So you're not in the regular world. You're not a cop because you don't smell like a cop. You work nights, but irregular. I figure that makes you some kind of crook." She held up a hand as though to ward off a vehement protest. "I don't give a shit," she said. "As long as you're not, you know, hurting kids or something, and you don't smell like that, either. What you smell like is a burglar."

"What's your sign?" I asked.

Marge's eyebrows went up. "Aries. Why?"

"Just wondered maybe if you were the same sign as I am, and you'd seen the horoscope this morning. I missed it, and I'd really like to know what it said."

"What are you?"

"Cancer."

"That was Ed's sign," she said. She wiped her nose again and accompanied the gesture with a sort of memorial sniffle and two blinks. "I always read it."

"What did it say?"

"Hold on." She squeezed her eyes shut and screwed her face up so her features looked like something being sucked into a whirlpool, and then she said, "Something about turning challenges into opportunities."

"I am positively awash in opportunity," I said. "And listen, it's nice to know you've been thinking about me, but I'm just a normal, everyday—"

"Doris is missing," Marge said. "I haven't heard from her in a couple of weeks, and today I went by the dump she lives in with Mr. Pinkie Ring, and the place is clean. I mean, clean. Closets are empty, nothing left in the medicine cabinets, floors swept, even the kitchen cleaned, just *scrubbed*, everything scoured in nine directions like they were afraid of fingerprints."

"Marge," I said as a great wave of weariness washed over me. "It's probably nothing. They probably—"

"Except," Marge said. Then she said, "Wait a minute," and poured a slug of vodka, put the glass down, held up a finger meaning *hang on*, shook out a cigarette, lit it, leaned back against the pillows, and said, "Her glasses. Except for her glasses."

There was no way I could continue to stand. I sank onto the end of the other bed, Prancer being equipped with two, and felt the room tilt and spin slowly. Hell is sometimes defined as a complete lack of hope. From the top stair of the front porch of hell, I said, "And she needs her glasses."

"Blind as a—" Marge said, and then she sobbed once, got it under control, hit herself in the face with her forearm to blot the tears, swallowed, and said, "Blind as a bat. She can't find her own feet without them."

"And you think I—"

"I think you're a *mensch*," Marge said. She wiped her eyes again. "I was married to a mensch for thirty-seven years, and I know one when I see one. I go to the cops, they're going to ask how old Doris is and I'm going to say, thirty-two, and they're going to say, Lady, she can go anywhere she wants. She doesn't have to check in with her mom."

"Well," I began.

"And look at these." Marge dug into a purse the size of a saddlebag and came out with two color snapshots. She dealt them at me, giving each of them an expert, Vegas-worthy flick that carried them from one bed to another. I picked them up and found myself looking at two shots of the same couple.

The female was clearly the issue of Marge's loins, if the pronounced nasal apparatus and the long upper lip were any indication, but the man was a complete mystery. In one shot, he was shading his eyes from the sun, and he'd tilted his hand down until nothing showed but his mouth, and in the other, he'd turned his head away at the last moment, creating an interesting modern abstract where his face should have been.

Not good.

Marge said, "Tell me about that."

"Okay," I said. "I'll think about it. Go away now. Go to bed. Get some sleep."

And she did, with the purse hanging from her shoulder and the bottle tucked under her arm. I heard her stumble once on the stairs going down, but she obviously grabbed the railing in time, and there were no other indications of disaster. She didn't even drop the bottle.

I went back into Blitzen, closed the connecting door to try to keep out the smell of the smoke, and lay down on the bed, thinking about turning challenges into opportunities.

## 8
### We're Still Going to Get into Trouble

The recently widowed Mrs. Derek Bigelow had baby-fine, flyaway blond hair that the morning sunlight was exploring with obvious enjoyment and attractive results. She'd yanked the hair into a long golden rope and twisted it on top of her head and then stuck a fork through it, handle first.

"We're not gonna stay long," Louie the Lost said sympathetically, "what with your loss and all, we'll be out of here in no time, Mrs., uh, Mrs.—"

"Ronnie," she said. "My—my loss?" Her nose wrinkled in a way that made me want to lean over and smooth it, possibly with my tongue. Ronnie Bigelow was, to put it briefly, quite fine. Even with a wet sponge in her hand, even smelling of some sort of household cleanser that was heavy on the bleach, and wearing an old T-shirt that said FINAL ANSWER? above a pair of ragged jeans that could have been a hand-me-down from the Ancient Mariner, Ronnie Bigelow was fine enough to make me wish I kept a diary, just so I could write something about her.

"You know," Louie said, "Mr., uh, I mean, Derek—"

"Oh," Ronnie Bigelow said. "*Derek*." She leaned against the side of the front door to her apartment in West Hollywood, a neighborhood where she was probably the only female on the block. "You seem like a nice little man, and I don't want to shock you, but Derek was a twenty-four karat shit, and I haven't really given him a moment's thought since the police told me what happened."

Louie threw me a helpless glance, and I let him flounder. "You were—I mean, you were, um—"

"Married," Ronnie Bigelow said. "Yes, we were, and I've been trying to figure out *why* ever since I woke up next to him on my first abysmal morning as Mrs. Bigelow." She closed her eyes for a moment and then opened them again. "Surely," she said, "at some time in your life, you've done something hopelessly, irredeemably, irremediably, unrecoverably idiotic, haven't you?"

"Well, sure," Louie said. "Lotta times."

"And your tall, silent, nicely muscled friend?" She lifted eyes the color of lapis lazuli up to my face. "Haven't *you* ever—"

I said, "Suggest something."

She looked up at me, wrapping me in that lapis blue, for the span of a couple of accelerated heartbeats and then one eyebrow went up a sixteenth of an inch, and she stepped back and held the door open. "Come on in," she said. "I'll make some coffee."

**"He was mean** when he was drunk," she said, plonking three blue-and-white Chinese-willow cups onto their saucers, "and boring when he was sober. He had the personal hygiene of a truffle. There was no woman he ever met, *ever*, that he didn't make a pass at. He had terrible taste in clothes. He had British teeth. Sugar?"

Louie and I took our coffee black and unsweetened, and it was pretty good. The apartment was basic but neat and bright, with blond wood Ikea furniture and rugs of a slightly overstimulated robin's-egg blue. The long wall in the living room was floor-to-ceiling books, always a good sign. The titles were eclectic with a slight tilt toward biography, and not all of women, which I took as another good sign. No matter how militantly we may be either male or female, it's no stretch to admit that the world has seen interesting specimens of both sexes.

"I don't mean to be personal—" I said.

"Why not?" she said. She looked down at her bare feet as though she'd just bought them and hadn't made up her mind about them yet. "I was insanely drunk, and I thought his accent was cute. We were in Las Vegas. He told me he was a novelist, working on a book written from a woman's perspective, and he was being devoured by insecurity about whether he was capable of carrying it off. *Devoured* was the word he used, and I was drunk enough to think that sounded sensitive. I'm a fool for sensitive." She regarded her feet for another moment and then gave them a resigned-looking nod of acceptance. She said to me, "Are you sensitive?"

"I sand my fingertips."

She gave it a moment's thought, which was more than it deserved, and said, "Why?"

"Certain kinds of locks," I said. "Certain kinds of locks require an elevated sense of touch."

Louie waved a hand to interrupt the confession. "So, your former, um, this guy you—"

"My deceased better half?" Ronnie Bigelow asked.

"Yeah. Him. Derek."

"Is there a question there somewhere?" She turned to me. "And why are you interested in locks?"

This time, Louie literally leaned in between us. "Derek, he made his money writing for those little rags you read in line at the market, right?"

"Ah, well, that's an interesting question." She sipped her coffee. "Here's what he would do. This is how Derek Bigelow eked out a living. He would scuttle along the bottom of the sea of life, down where all the shit eventually winds up, looking for something that would cause pain to some people and give a cheap thrill to some other people. The people he would cause pain to were generally rich and famous, and the people to whom he would give a cheap thrill couldn't afford an expensive one. They're almost all women, and nothing lifts their poverty-stricken little hearts like learning that some rich, glamorous movie star has gained three hundred pounds and is living on an intravenous supply of coconut milk, or that *this* female sitcom star is gay and secretly married to a transsexual NFL tackle, or *that* country music star has three children of, ahem, mixed race, chained to the wall of some tar-paper shack in North Carolina. Cancer, mastectomies, secret sex-change operations, plastic surgery gone horribly awry. In other words, stuff that demonstrates that misery, despite all the evidence to the contrary, actually *does* get its claws into the people who have everything."

"Pay much?" I asked.

The question almost brought a smile. "Aren't you quick. No, it doesn't. And Derek had an expensive nose, in addition to his other vices. He went through a lot of money, without—I could add, if I were that kind of person—without directing much of it at me."

I said, "What's Ronnie short for?"

She reached up and touched the fork jammed into her hair as though she wanted to make sure she'd used the sterling. "Veronica. What name is hiding behind Junior?"

"Junior," I said. "It's my name. My dad was named Merle, and he wanted to name his son after him, but wasn't going to hang *Merle* on me, so he called me Junior. Veronica's a pretty name."

"A little long," she said. "There's something about a fourth syllable—"

"I really hate to break in on all this," Louie said, "but I'm sure you got a lot to do."

"Not really," Ronnie Bigelow said. "I've exhausted the thrill of scouring. Have you had lunch?"

"I haven't even had breakfast," I said.

She looked at me as though I'd just told her I was scheduled for a heart transplant and I was too busy to go. "Oh, that's not good. Breakfast is the most important meal of the day."

"I keep hearing that," I said, "and I'm sure it is, to the people who eat it."

"This money thing," Louie said.

"So." She looked at Louie but pointed at me. "He's quick, and you're focused. Is that how it works?"

"He's focused some of the time," Louie said.

"Well, then," she said. "It's interesting that the police didn't ask me about this."

"About the additional opportunities for income?" I asked.

"Of course. It should have occurred to them, shouldn't it? Here he is, Derek. He developed damaging information about people with money. That's what he did for a living. He had the ability to get that information into supermarket lines all around the world with nothing more than a keyboard and an Internet connection. So he could take it two ways, couldn't he?"

"Sure," I said. "How often did he take it the other way?"

"Often enough to keep his nose running," she said.

"For example."

"Okay. Thad Pierce, you know Thad Pierce?"

"That series," Louie said. Louie watched a lot of television. "*Black Lightning* or something."

"Right, *Black Lightning*. Thad Pierce is the nation's top-rated stud. Mister Cool-Tattoos-Ultra-Macho-Series-Star. Well, Mr. Pierce is a big fan of *America's Next Top Model*."

Louie said, "So? Me, too."

"But he's *really* a fan. He's such a fan he has a stenographer take down every word spoken in every show and turn it into a script, and then he invites a bunch of the guys over and they act it out. In costume."

Louie said, sounding dismayed, "Awwwww. You mean, like dresses?"

"And bikinis and the occasional thong panties. And they take a lot of pictures."

I said, "Ouch."

"Derek got a bunch of them. The pictures. Bought them from one of the guys, one who wasn't getting any work and had borrowed too much money from the wrong people. And Derek was faced with an ethical dilemma, wasn't he? Hand the pictures over to the publishers of a rag that'll pay him five, six thousand for them, or have a chat with Thad Pierce, who will part with ten or twenty times as much."

Louie says, "Or maybe have him killed."

"In Thad Pierce's case, he went with the money. But, see, Derek was good. He knew the secrets of being a successful blackmailer. He knew instinctively how much to demand, and he never, ever went back for more. But you're right, of course. If Derek threatened the wrong kind of people, there was always the possibility that they'd choose the cheaper option of just, you know, beating him to death."

"That's how he died?" Louie asked.

"According to the police, fourteen broken bones," Ronnie Bigelow said. "They left him eight teeth. A closed-casket funeral was strongly recommended." She put her cup down and said to me, "So, then, how about an early lunch?"

"Okay," I said. "But we have to make a stop first."

o o o

**"Hollywood," she said,** looking out the window. "If this is glamour, you can keep it." Louie had gone back to pulling on wires, and Ronnie and I were stuck in traffic on Hollywood Boulevard, not too far from the stretch of sidewalk where Derek Bigelow had washed up, extravagantly fractured, on Giorgio's star. "I was so horrified when I first got here. Hard to imagine it was ever anything but awful."

"In the thirties," I said. "It was really something in the thirties."

"Hmmm," she said, glancing at my left hand on the steering wheel. "What's your wife like?"

I said, "She's recently divorced."

"Oh, my. I'm sorry. Well, no, I guess I'm really not."

"You're forward," I said. "Has anybody ever told you that?"

"If I were a man," she said, "you'd describe me as *decisive. Goal-oriented.* Something like that. And no one has used the word *forward* in years and years. Would it be out of line for me to ask what happened? With your marriage, I mean."

"According to the laws of polite discourse in the twenty-first century," I said, "women are allowed to ask any man any question that comes to them at any time, and a man who doesn't answer it is marked for life as emotionally unresponsive."

"I wish someone had told me that years ago. What happened?"

"We were too different, I guess. And we got more different as time went by."

She put her feet up on the dashboard. "I've always thought differences make for more interesting relationships. What's the fun in being with somebody who thinks all the same things you do? It'd be like watching a TV channel that doesn't show anything except your own home movies."

"There's different, and then there's different. If we'd had any less in common, it would have been an interspecies marriage."

"But that's vague, isn't it? There's always a main issue, a specific issue. With Derek and me it was that he was a shit and I wasn't. What was it with you?"

"I suppose it was mainly my job."

The light changed eight or nine cars ahead of us and we went through the inevitable urban pause while several drivers tried to remember how to get their foot from the brake to the accelerator. When we were finally moving, she said, "Which is what?"

"I steal things."

"What *is* it with me?" she asked. "I go from a blackmailer with a terrible prose style to a thief."

"I think you're getting ahead of yourself."

"Oh, pshaw," she said, actually pronouncing it. "Don't pretend. You know what's going on."

"Yeah, I suppose I do."

Ronnie leaned forward and fiddled with one of the sandals decorating my dashboard. She had painted only the smallest toenail on each perfect foot, just a tiny dot of color at the border between foot and not-foot. "Tell me at least that you only steal from the rich."

"Okay."

She put an elbow out the open window. "That's a little better."

"They're the only ones with anything worth taking. What are you going to steal from the poor? Aspirations?"

"It's not going to make any difference," she said. "Whatever you tell me, however awful, it's not going to make any difference. We're still going to get into trouble."

I said, "Glad to hear it."

**"Exactly what are** we doing here?" Ronnie asked. We were picking our way up a concrete walkway to a peeling clapboard bungalow on a street folded in between Hollywood Boulevard and Sunset. The neighborhood hadn't been fashionable seventy years ago and still wasn't. The lawn looked like it hadn't been watered since the Hoover administration.

"We'd be breaking in," I said, "except that I've got a key. Although we could still break in, if you'd like to get a feel for it."

She slowed down, looking dubiously at the bungalow, which was rapidly approaching shack status and looked like the place where dark waits for night to arrive. "Who lives here?"

"Right now, probably nobody. Until recently, it was occupied by a guy who wears a pinkie ring and the daughter of the woman who owns the motel I'm living in this month."

"That sentence opens up so many questions I can't even figure out which one to ask."

"All will be revealed," I said, climbing the three cement steps to the front door.

"When?" She was behind me, but hanging back, and I didn't blame her. The bungalow practically rippled with unhappiness.

"At lunch." I keyed the door and pushed it open, and was greeted by the stale, old-paper odor of an uninhabited house. "Coming in?"

Marge was right: The place had been cleaned with a suspicious amount of energy. I could even see the tracks left by a handheld vacuum on the couch cushions. The house had been rented furnished and the furniture was still on hand, so if it ever came down to hairs and fibers, traces probably lingered here and there, but not for want of trying to remove them.

"I need the bathroom," Ronnie said. "I always need the bathroom when I'm someplace weird."

"I'm sure it's sparkling clean," I said. "Probably down the hall."

"Spooky houses," she said, going down the hallway, "are spookier in the daytime."

The living room walls had been painted a bad-mayonnaise yellow, and most of the light in the room was absorbed by a floor of dark-chocolate linoleum with a pumpkin swirl in it, probably laid down over the original oak floors back in the fifties, when the first thing people did when they bought an old house was to wreck it. In the dining-room, the toxic yellow walls gave way to pink-patterned wallpaper in a vaguely Aubrey Beardsley nouveau-decadent pattern, printed on what looked like aluminum foil. A dusty, cobwebbed chandelier in wrought iron hung over the round Formica table. Three chairs were pulled up to the table while a fourth, missing a rear leg, loitered drunkenly against the wall. The effect was depressing beyond measure.

"Hey," Ronnie called. "Come look at this."

I went down the hall and found her standing at the doorway of a bathroom that had a quarter of an inch of water on the floor. "You went in *there*?" I asked.

"It was dry when I went in. This happened when I washed my hands. I turned on the water, and all of this came out of the cabinet under the sink."

The day got even dimmer. I said, "Oh, no."

"Oh, no what?"

"Let me look at the kitchen," I said. I didn't want to, but I had to. Ronnie followed me back down the narrow hallway and grunted at the sight of the dining room wallpaper as though someone had punched her in the stomach. In the kitchen, I went down on one knee in front of the sink and opened the door to the cabinet beneath it. Then I said, "Shit. Shit, shit *shit*."

"What? What is it?"

"Same reason the bathroom got wet." I pulled the door all the way open and showed her the drainage pipe that ran down from the center of the sink. It ended abruptly about eight inches above the bottom of the cabinet. "The traps have been taken."

"The traps?"

"You know. That elbow-bend in the pipe that's always under a drain. It's there to catch anything valuable, rings or anything, that might fall down there."

"But why would anyone want those?"

"He didn't want the traps. He wanted whatever might have been in them. Hair, for example. Anything that might have had DNA on it."

Ronnie took a couple of steps back, looking around the room as though transparent forms were writhing in the air. The house chose that moment to creak. She said, "Can we leave now?"

## 9

## Three Guys Away

"Trenton, New Jersey," Ronnie said, and then swallowed. "A great place to be from and a terrible place to go back to." A few scraps of steak clung to the bone in front of her, a steak that had disappeared while I was still buttering bread. I'd never seen a woman eat that fast. My former wife, Kathy, would still have been salting it.

I cut the second piece out of my veal chop. "And you left Trenton because?"

"Because I could." She looked around the restaurant, Musso & Frank, one of the oldest restaurants in LA, and practically the only place I ever eat in Hollywood. "Do you think anybody would notice if I picked up the bone and just sort of chewed on it?"

"Most of these waiters have been here since the King of Spain owned the state. They've seen it before."

"Good." She grabbed it in both hands.

"Okay, so Trenton wasn't hard to say goodbye to. What was the cue to kiss it off, though?"

"Another bad boy," she said. The light from the window that opened onto Hollywood Boulevard fell across her face, deepening the blue of her eyes and revealing a dusty little constellation of freckles scattered across the bridge of her nose. "I've got this problem with men. I only like the dangerous ones. If I had a pet, it'd be a coral snake."

"And the guy who got you out of Trenton—"

"Was Donald. Donald had green eyes and he liked other people's cars. We left Trenton in a Porsche at about 3 A.M. By the time we got to Chicago, we'd also been in a Corvette, in that sweet little Lexus sports coupe, and a Jaguar. Oh, and an Audi. The Audi was for comic relief. As things turned out, so was Donald."

My phone rang. "Audi," I said. "Donald. Hold the thought and gnaw on your bone."

"Yeah?" It was Paulie DiGaudio, from the cop branch of the family, returning my call.

"Your uncle's putative victim," I said. "He was doing some blackmailing."

Ronnie looked across the table at me, but she didn't stop picking at the bone.

"That's interesting," DiGaudio said. "Kinda opens it up, doesn't it? Gives us some more suspects, besides Uncle Vinnie, I mean."

"I thought you'd like it. Do you happen to know whether Bigelow was blackmailing your uncle?"

"Let's pretend you didn't ask that."

"Fine. I don't suppose you've got a cop I could borrow."

A sound that might have been a chortle, if I'd ever heard a chortle to compare it to. "You gotta be kidding me."

"Hey, he's *your* uncle."

"You're it, Bender. Maybe you want a license plate run or something, I could handle that. Check a reverse-directory, something like that, no problem. But if you think I'm calling attention in the department to my uncle the crook, you're nuts."

"Okay," I said, getting to the actual reason for the call. "I need to know whether there's a current driver's license issued to someone living at an address in Hollywood. Or any license listing that address in the past five years."

"This have anything to do with Vinnie?"

"It's what I'm working on," I said.

"Okay. Address."

"One-four-six-seven Florence. Zip is probably 90068."

"Got it. Couple of hours."

"And listen. Don't put any cops on this, no matter what name turns up. The blackmailing thing, well, there could be dangerous people involved, and I don't want to be walking around with my fly open, not knowing that some cop has already been knocking on doors and asking questions."

"Yeah, yeah." He hung up.

"That was *extremely* interesting," Ronnie said. She had the bone in her right hand and a small piece of meat between the thumb and forefinger of her left. "That was a cop, right? First you asked him for something he wouldn't give you, just to let him say no, and then you got what you really wanted. And everything you told him was true, but it was also a total lie. The address, which is where we just were, has nothing to do with Derek because it was about your landlady's daughter. So this cop is out getting a name and he doesn't have any idea why."

I nodded. "And?"

"And he feels like he won the conversation."

"I'd shrug modestly, but I need practice."

She looked at the piece of meat between her fingers, popped it into her mouth, and said around it, "And then there's the fact that you're a crook but you seem to be working for cops. I know there are cops who work for crooks, but I didn't think it worked the other way around. And while I'm on this topic, I probably should ask you why you're interested in Derek in the first place. I would have asked back at my apartment, but you distracted me."

"Well, you distracted me, too."

"See what I mean? It may be true, but it's not an answer." She eyed the veal chop on my plate. "You going to finish that?"

"I've barely started it."

"That's not an answer, either. Yes or no?"

"Every last ounce. And then I'm going to take the bone home and have it bronzed."

"Jiminy. So what's the deal? What are you, a crook or a cop?"

"I'm a burglar. That's where my heart is, as people say these days. But once in a while, I help out other crooks who have a problem, who got ripped off or something and for obvious reasons can't go to the cops. It's a sideline, sort of. And now I've got a cop pressuring me to do a favor for him, or he'll put me in jail for something I didn't do, and the favor involves the fascinating question of who killed Derek. And the woman who owns the motel I'm living in at the moment thinks something has happened to her daughter and asked me to check it out. And my waist is thirty-two and my inseam is thirty-four. How'd you get from Chicago to LA?"

She pulled the bread basket over and rifled through it. Before we left the apartment, she'd replaced the fork through her hair with a chopstick, which she deemed dressier. The way she ate, it was surprising she didn't have a whole table setting in her hair. "You're more interesting than I am," she said.

"To you, maybe. Chicago is what, about seventeen hundred miles from LA?"

"That's one way to look at it. Are you hoarding the butter?" I pushed it over to her. "Another way to look at it is that Chicago is three guys away from LA. After I chased Donald off, in Chicago, I got kind of hooked up with DeWayne, and you *know* he had to be hot to overcome a name like that. Do you think some names are hot and some names aren't?"

"Definitely."

"Yeah? How do you feel about Ronnie?"

"I like Veronica better."

"You and everybody else, except me. And, I've got to tell you, you've got more to overcome in the name department than DeWayne did. I mean, *Junior*? What's the least hot name for a woman?"

"Tillie. So, DeWayne. What did he do, run numbers?"

"DeWayne was a dealer. The straightest, most organized dealer ever. Never touched anything more stimulating than chocolate. Had a six-state route and ran it regularly. Like a milkman, but with dope. And he was gorgeous. If there'd been a dope dealer's calendar, he'd have been Mr. January to get everybody's year off to a good start."

"But the relationship didn't last," I said, cutting into the veal chop and watching her eyes follow my hands. "Did his beauty fade tragically, or what?"

"Actually, I developed a weensy substance abuse problem. I got to the point where I needed four lines to tie my shoes. And it finally hit me that DeWayne, with his infinite stash, probably wasn't the ideal companion, so I split. We were out on his route, in Taos, New Mexico. He had artist clients there. Artists do a lot of dope, did you know that? So when this guy Leon wanted to paint me, I took my suitcase out of DeWayne's car and started posing."

"Leon, he do dope?"

"Leon didn't do anything except downers, and I hate downers. That was his appeal, that I didn't want his dope. How can you just sit there and talk with all that nice food in front of you? Some poor little calf lived and died in a tiny wooden pen so you could have that chop, and you're not paying any attention at all to it. Do you think if I told you all about how they raise veal, you'd lose your appetite and give it to me?"

I cut a chunk and put it in my mouth. "Not a chance." I pushed the plate toward her a couple of inches and then snatched it back. She put half the bread away with a single bite. "So, to recap," I said, "it was Donald from Trenton to Chicago, DeWayne from Chicago to Taos, and there you are, sober in the desert, posing for downered-out old Leon. *Girl and Sand*, something like that."

"I could have been a piñata for all you'd recognize me. Leon was heavily abstract. What he wanted to paint was the *energy field*. Everything and everyone had an energy field, he said every day of his life, and he said it very slowly, too. When he looked at me, what he saw was something that looked like the northern lights, if the northern lights were made of string cheese."

"What colors?"

"Whatever he had the most of. Anyway, some guy from Vegas came to Taos and saw Leon's stuff in a gallery, and it reminded the guy of neon. So he asked Leon to come to Vegas and design some abstract neon for a casino he was building, a casino with a kinda modern-art theme, and Leon saw a chance to paint *real* energy and he jumped at it. And the fourth night we were in Vegas, I bumped into Derek in the bar at the Venetian, and Derek did that number about, you remember, the novel from the female perspective, and eighteen hours later we had blood alcohol counts high enough to make us flammable, and we were married. And Derek towed me to the city where Fate awaited him, which is to say, LA."

"If you'll excuse a personal comment—"

She pulled the chopstick out, and her hair tumbled down over her shoulders. "It's about time."

"Your affections seem to be, um, short-lived."

"Oh," she said, running her fingers through the spill of gold to untangle it. "I'm terrible. I might as well be a guy. I even eat like a guy. And you, you eat like Miss Manners is sitting on your lap."

"I always think this might be my last free meal, the last one I ever eat outside of prison. So I take my time with it."

She stopped, her fingers trapped in a snarl of hair. "Oh. Oh, that's awful." Then she gave her hair a hard tug and squinted at me. "Unless it's bullshit."

"It is. Sorry."

"No problem, but it'll cost you." She grabbed her knife and fork, leaned across the table, and sawed off about a third of my chop. "I'm going to be eating now, so you talk."

"Same old story. I'm your normal, everyday burglar, but better. I broke into my first house when I was fourteen. I've never been caught, never been charged, because I'm careful. I change the way I go in, I work different hours and different neighborhoods, I steal different kinds of stuff, so I haven't got a trademark the cops can trace. I know a lot about a lot of things, so I can usually recognize value when I see it. If you had nine pieces of good costume jewelry and one real piece, I'd take the real piece every time. In the personal column, I married my high school sweetheart, but I couldn't change into who she wanted me to be, which was an insurance salesman, and we split up. On the other hand, we managed to produce my daughter, Rina."

"Sweet name," she said. "How old?"

"Thirteen."

"Ooooohhhh. The entrance to the hormonal wind tunnel. How's she handling it?"

"So far, so good. She hasn't hit the stage yet where the entire world seems like a personal imposition. I'm sure it's coming, but so far she can still look at me without sneering."

"Does she know what you do?"

"Sure. I don't lie to her, ever."

"What's she think about it?" She was chewing, but I could translate.

"It worries her. The idea that something might happen to me. Kids are pretty conservative. They rebel, but they're not good with uncertainty."

"I guess. I never minded it, but in our house, uncertainty was in long supply. We might not have had enough money to make the rent or buy dinner, but we always had plenty of uncertainty." She put her fork down and brushed her hands together. "And that's enough of that. I have to save some of the tragedy for tomorrow. It'd be terrible to run out of tragedy on the first date."

"One more question. Other than hanging with bad boys, what do you do?"

"Whatever I want. I devote one hundred percent of my energy to doing exactly what I want. When I was a kid, I looked around at all the people who worked for a living, and it seemed to me that the living they were working for wasn't worth the work they were doing. If I *have* to work, like if I run out of money or I'm between guys or something, I tend bar. It's a good portable skill that pays pretty well, and since you're a thief, I'll also admit that it has a high skim potential. I don't need much, just a place to sleep and some books. Derek had a wad of money in our joint account, courtesy of Thad Pierce, so I'm okay for a while. When I'm not, I'll go back to mixing cosmopolitans and flirting with drunk guys. And then I'll quit again."

"Sounds good to me."

"For now, anyway. It's cute to be poor when you're young. Lots of art about it, operas and everything. It's not so cute when you're old." She rested an elbow on the table and cupped her chin in her hand. "So," she said, "your place or mine?"

I actually had to think about it for a moment. "Neither. Not yet."

"What *is* this?" she said. "A scruple?"

"A daughter. I haven't been with anybody since Kathy and I broke up, and if you and I make the transition, I'm not sure how Rina would take it."

"And you'd tell her," Ronnie said, "because you never lie to her."

"Exactly."

"Unbelievable," she said. "I finally meet a *good* bad boy, and I can't have him."

"Well," I said, "not yet, anyway."

# 10
## Might As Well Live Outdoors

"Nobody called you," Popsie snarled through a two-inch crack. Looking at the one visible eye between the door and the door frame, I revised my estimate of her age upward: she had to be in her mid-sixties, and still bench-pressing. "He's not expecting you."

"It's good for him," I said. "People who never get surprised stop developing. They might as well be rhododendrons."

"I'll have to ask." She started to close the door, looked down, and said, "Move your foot."

"When I'm inside," I said. "Then I'll move it to walk. Till then, it stays where it is. I don't wait outside for people."

"He's not going to like it."

I put the fingers of my left hand on the inside of my right wrist and took my pulse. "Looks like I'm okay with that."

Popsie said, "Shit," and opened the door. By the time I got through it, I was already watching her broad-shouldered back recede down the hallway. Her boots squeaked on the polished wood.

"Should I lock it?" I called after her. "There's no telling who'll turn up."

She didn't respond, just rounded the first corner. I closed the door and moved quickly behind her, looking into the first room

I passed, which had nothing but two picture windows with a lot of late-afternoon sun coming through them, and the second, which had windows of louvered glass, and the third, which had a couple of good old-fashioned windows that opened in the time-honored, burglar-favored way, with a lower pane you could raise. It was a quick detour to unlock one of them, just slip the semicircular latch that fastened the top pane to the bottom.

All the windows, including this one, were heavily alarmed, but I hadn't expected anything else.

I made up a little time, so I wasn't too far behind her when we came into the semicircular room where I'd met DiGaudio the night before. Popsie kept on going, heading right, down another hallway. The big white couch was heavily dented in the center where he'd been sitting, where he apparently always sat. A creature of habit. I figured, what the hell, and sat in the middle of the dent and waited.

There was music coming from somewhere in the house, basic fifties-simple, just drums, bass, guitar, and a keyboard of some kind, maybe an old-fashioned Hammond organ. The instruments weren't quite together, a little ragged. The guitar was carrying the riff, five notes in an ascending scale, which repeated three times. It sounded like an instrumental intro, the kind of thing record producers used to stick on the front of songs to give disk jockeys something to talk over. Then I heard a voice, mixed pretty far down, definitely not Pavarotti or even Bobby Vinton. Then the music stopped for a second, somebody said something, a pair of drumsticks clicked off the beat, and the instrumental intro began once more.

The music got louder as the organ riff rang out, and then a door closed and the level dropped again. A moment later, it got loud, and then it stopped completely. I waited, and patience was rewarded, sort of, when DiGaudio stalked into the room.

He was draped from head to foot in a black caftan that swirled around his bare feet as he came toward me, and he was holding a half-peeled banana. He didn't look happy.

"Business hours," he said. "You ever hear of business hours?"

"Sure," I said. "What do I look like I'm doing, playing forts?"

"Get out of my seat." He turned sideways and edged his way between the curved couch and the curved coffee table, and I scooted down to make room. "This better *be* something."

"Was Derek Bigelow blackmailing you?"

The question stopped him, although the caftan swung back and forth like a hoop skirt for a second. "Kind of bullshit is that?"

"Bigelow was a blackmailer. Was he putting a knife to you?"

"No, but what if he was? I didn't kill him, and your job is to prove I didn't."

"I can only do so much in the dark."

He sat down, looked at the banana, and dropped it on the table. "What could anybody blackmail me about? I'm, like, fifty years ago. Since the fucking Beatles ruined everything, I done nothing except gain weight. Who's gonna blackmail me, Jenny Craig?"

"You were, or are, mobbed up."

He shook his head slowly, like someone who's been asked the same question too often. "Like I said, you're forgetting why you're here. But just to close down this particular line, I was never part of the mob. J. Edgar Hoover spent hundreds of thousands of my tax dollars trying to pin me with that, probably because he wanted to meet some of my boys. All that money, all those FBI guys in bad suits hanging around, what did they find out? That the mob wanted to run me. Salerno, that pinhead, him and the other one, they both wanted in. Wanted in, as in *weren't* in."

"And what? You told them no?"

DiGaudio snickered. "Right, and I spit in their face, too. No, I didn't tell them no. I held them off as long as I could and then one night at four A.M. I got the hell out of Philly and took most of the kids with me. Came out here, got a couple of them into pictures, and waited it out while those dickheads ground each other into hamburger. Don't you know anything about Philly?"

"I know about the mob wars." And I knew that Salerno and Caponetto weren't the kinds of guys someone like DiGaudio could have "held off," not without a lot of help. Something to think about.

He spread his hands at the obviousness of it all. "Well, *yeah,* the mob wars. So they all blew each other away, and here we were, in Palm Tree Land, making records, making movies."

"I don't remember your clients making movies."

"No shit. How old are you?"

"Thirty-seven."

"Whadya think, you should remember it in your DNA or something? We're talking 1960, '62, in there somewhere. Your mom was probably thirteen then, ask *her.* Six movies, all dogs, I mean *peeeyuuuu,* but they all did okay moneywise. Little girls showed up. Brought all their friends with them. I had the kids appear at some of the shows. Put them on the road with a pickup band, and they did a live twenty minutes for maybe the first two, three days the picture was on. Packed the little girls in, didn't cost much of nothing. Kids traveled in buses, band played for cigarettes. Charged an extra four bucks for the live show, half a buck for an autograph. Some of those places, they sat two thousand people. Eight thousand for an hour's work. Multiply that times two shows a day, three days per city, ten, twelve cities, and you're talking about money, for those days, anyway. Wouldn't keep a rock star these days in Kleenex."

"Then what *did* Bigelow want with you?"

DiGaudio picked up the banana and took a bite. The smell bloomed beneath my nose. "None of your fucking business."

"Okay, he wasn't blackmailing you. Let's say he was looking for a story for one of the rags he sold to."

"Let's say you change the subject."

"Fine. Why was his body left on Giorgio's star?"

His lower lip came up and then went down and came up again. "Say what?"

"You didn't know? He was dumped on Giorgio's square yard of the Walk of Fame."

"No," he said, not so much a contradiction as an all-encompassing denial that the world could work like that. He looked past me at the wall, his mind obviously in high gear.

"Afraid so."

"No," he said again. He cleared his throat, and then he cleared it again. "No, how would I know anything about that? I didn't kill him, remember?" But he had beads of sweat on his forehead.

Might as well turn up the heat. "Who knew I was coming here last night?"

He looked back at me as though he'd forgotten I was in the room. "Nobody."

"Well, let's start with Cousin Paulie the cop, you, and Helga the house Nazi, or whatever her name is."

"Popsie. Her name is—"

"You and Popsie and Paulie and who?"

DiGaudio started peeling one of those little white strips from the inside of the banana peel, not looking at it, just fidgeting with his fingers. "Who cares?" He balled up the white thread and flicked it onto the table. "What's this about?"

"Last night, when I left, there was a Humvee waiting for me

outside. Tried to push me off the side of the hill, and then took a shot at me."

DiGaudio's chin fell onto his chest as though his head had suddenly increased in weight. He shifted his eyes around the room, licked his lips, and then dropped the banana back on the table. "Took a shot at you?"

I didn't say anything, just watched him. He was as pale as someone getting off a roller coaster.

"Nobody," he finally said. "Nobody else knew. I don't talk to many people." He pulled the sleeve of his caftan down over his left hand and used the cloth to blot his forehead.

"You talked to people about wanting to kill Bigelow."

"Yeah, I . . . I was dumb. I talked to a couple of people about, you know, doing him for me. And they talked to some other people. And then somebody goes and does him, and here I am, sitting out in plain view, big as a house, waiting for someone to pin it on me."

"Who'd you talk to about doing him?"

"Mmmmmmmmmm." His eyes were flicking back and forth, as though the question were floating in the air in front of him and he was trying to see past it. Finally, he said, "Stanley Hopper."

"*Stanley?* Stanley's a *patzer.* Let's say you lost a couple of books and the library's on your tail, that's the kind of thing Stanley can take care of."

"Stanley's who I talked to. And he talked to a couple guys, I don't know who."

"And Stanley didn't know I was coming last night."

"Uh-uh."

"So there's nobody you can think of who might have been sitting out there waiting for me."

"I said no."

"And you'd tell me if you *could* think of someone."

"Jesus," he said. "Get the fuck off me. You're all I got right now. You think I'd go through all this to get you here, and then ask somebody to cap you? What kind of crazy is that?"

"Vinnie," I said. "What's your secret?"

His eyes involuntarily flicked left, to the hallway the music had come from, but he brought them back to me, licked his lips again, and said, "Secret? I don't have secrets." He covered his hand with the sleeve again, but thought better of wiping away the moisture on his forehead. "Me, I'm just a guy. I got nothing to hide. My life is so open I might as well live outdoors."

**"That was quick,"** Ronnie said as I slid behind the wheel.

"I know when I'm not wanted." I eased the car into a three-point turn, brushing DiGaudio's azaleas, so I could head back down the driveway.

"Lookit," Ronnie said, regarding the miscellaneous assortment of vehicles pulled up to the house. "The man either has company or he collects crappy cars."

"I think he's got company. I heard some music playing." I reached down between the seats and came up with my notepad and the pen that's permanently clipped to it. "Take down those license plate numbers, would you?"

"I thought musicians made money," she said, jotting down numbers and letters. "What a bunch of junkers."

"Got them all?"

"Yeah." Ronnie dropped the pad, ran a finger over the dashboard, and looked at it as though she expected it to be covered in old phlegm. "Speaking of junkers."

"Were we?"

"Why are you driving this thing? You're in Los Angeles, where your car is sort of your astral projection, right? I've only been here six months, and I already know that by LA standards, this is a really crappy car."

I was still watching the mirror. "You think?"

"A white Toyota. I mean, please. With dents." She put a finger against the bullet hole in the window. "Not to mention this. And the one in the back window."

"I don't know," I said. "I think it has a kind of battered charm, a uniquely soigné sort of post-pizzazz distinction."

"I should introduce you to Donald. He could get you something nice."

"White Toyotas are the world's only invisible automobile. I could blow through a stop sign in this car, right in front of a cop, and not get ticketed. I have literally driven out of a dead-end street with a burglar alarm ringing in a house behind me, and sailed right past two private security cars coming the other way. They didn't even glance at me."

"If you say so." She drew a fingertip circle around the bullet hole. "Where are we going now?"

"I'm going to Tarzana to see my daughter, and you're going home, unless you want me to drop you somewhere else."

"Home, I guess."

We were on Sunnyslope, heading down toward Ventura. "Tell me what Derek was working on."

"If you're taking me home and dropping me off, you can damn well say please."

"Consider it said."

"I'll consider it said when I hear it."

"Okay. *Pleeeeeeeeeease?*"

"We didn't talk much, unless he was just totally jammed on powder. But then, he got jammed a lot. Said he had something going on Warren Wallace, you know, the actor. He'd been in a kids' Ku Klux Klan, like junior bigots, when he was twelve or something, and, let's see, *oh*, he was nosing around that Latina singer, somebody Lopez, he thought he had some stuff on her. And there was some big deal about singers from the fifties, people nobody's thought about in half a century."

"Someone was thinking about them. That's the one that got him killed." I explained about Derek's having been dumped on Giorgio's Walk of Fame star.

"But who'd care?" she asked. "Why would the National Trashbag, or whatever the paper's called, want something about those guys? Talk about *over*. They're probably all old and fat or even dead, and who cares?"

"Those are all good questions," I said. "And I'm asking them, too." I hung a left onto the Hollywood Freeway on-ramp. "Let's say for a minute that Derek landing on Giorgio's star is just a coincidence. Can you think of anything else at all that he was focused on?"

"Other than that actor and Lopez? Jeez. You know, sometimes when he was jammed, I was, too. He shared once in a while. Let me work on it for a minute." We merged into the traffic, which was miraculously in motion, as opposed to its usual state of total immobility. "He said one other thing, but it can't have anything to do with LA. He said he'd discovered the Loch Ness Monster."

**"You'll call me** later?"

She was leaning against the driver's door, head halfway into the car. The sun in her hair was almost blinding. This close, she smelled of talcum powder.

"Either later or tomorrow morning."

"Wake me up in the morning," she said. "I'd like that."

"Boy," I said. "This is serious."

"It's about *this* serious," she said, and she leaned the rest of the way in and kissed me, not a virtuoso, high-concept, ten-out-of-ten, Olympic-level kiss, just the kind of kiss that you think about when you think about being kissed, more sweetness than anything else, but with a shot of cayenne in it. Then she pulled back and grinned at me. She said, "I knew you'd taste like that."

"Like what?"

"Like you. Call me, or you're meat." She turned around and went into the apartment house, and I found myself studying the widow's backside in the faded jeans with a surprising pang at parting rather than the mild case of heat-friction I usually experience when I'm watching a well-shaped female backside. I was actually going to miss her. So I felt guilty when the door closed behind her and I picked up the phone to call Louie and tell him to get someone to watch Ronnie's apartment for the next twenty-four hours, and follow her wherever she went.

"I thought you guys were glued to each other," Louie said. "I figured you were talking baby names by now."

"Louie," I said. "What's the first rule of homicide?"

"Oh, yeah," Louie said. "Right. The spouse."

## 11
Lynching Souvenirs

The house sat back from the street, making room for a couple of lopsided orange trees that were still struggling to recover from an overenthusiastic pruning I'd given them five or six years back. I'd bought the place when Kathy and I got married, fifteen years ago. Energized by newlywed optimism, I'd painted the place, built the garage by hand, and dug most of the hole for the pool in back before coming to my senses and hiring someone. I'd removed the old, crummy front door that you could have knocked down with a blunt remark and replaced it with a very heavy one of solid oak, equipped with half a dozen good locks. Even though I'd resigned myself to the idea that the house was now Kathy's, I still thought of that door as mine.

So I was surprised when it was opened by someone I'd never seen before.

"Yeah?" he said.

"Yeah, yourself. Who the hell are you?"

He grinned, giving me a glimpse of several yards of silver wire woven through some crooked but soon-to-be-straight teeth. "You're her dad," he said.

"That takes care of one of us," I said. "Who are you?"

"Tyrone."

"And?"

"And? Oh, *and*. I'm Rina's friend." Tyrone was almost as tall as I was, but weighed maybe forty pounds less. He had a waist that was smaller around than my thigh and eyes the color of fallen leaves. He wasn't just black, he was on the far side of black, so dark the brown eyes looked almost beige.

"Really," I said from the center of a cloud of mutually exclusive feelings. "Where's Rina?"

"In the bathroom. Like girls always are." The smile, which was very broad, disappeared. "Oh, gosh. I'm in the middle of the doorway, huh?" He stepped back to allow me in.

"Thanks," I said. "So." I stopped and tried to figure out how to put it and then gave up. "What are you guys doing?"

"Your project," he said. "The Little Elvises. We've got some shit you—I mean, some *stuff* you won't believe."

"Really." I ran through ten or twelve possible responses and said, "Great. That's great."

"These kids, most of them, they were really hapless."

The word stopped me, and Tyrone gave me a victor's grin. "Hapless," he said. "As in, not possessing any hap."

"Is that him?" Rina called from the back of the house.

"Is that *he*," I corrected, mostly to get even for *hapless*.

"Yeah," Rina said. "That's him. Daddy, the guy who probably just scared you is Tyrone. Come on, I'm in my room."

"After you," Tyrone said.

I said, "Oh, for Christ's sake," and headed down the hall.

I hadn't been inside the house for a while, since I usually picked Rina up outside when we had our afternoons together. It wasn't that Kathy and I didn't get along. We just didn't seem to have much to say to each other, and after all we'd been through together, that made me sad. She was on her third replacement since the split, this guy Bill. Rina was right, there wasn't really anything wrong with Bill's nose, at least physically. The problem with Bill's nose was that he was sticking it into what I still thought of as my family.

I glanced into the master bedroom as I passed it, looking for, I don't know, a plaid wool shirt or a brace of recently shot ducks. According to Rina, Bill was an enthusiastic hunter, a guy who could head out into the nuclear winter with a gun over his shoulder and kill his family's radioactive meat. Whereas I'd go out and steal it, so I guess Kathy was moving up in the world.

The bedroom was reassuringly free of fresh game and it still looked pretty girly, and I felt my spirits rise. Bill hadn't taken up residence yet. I felt marginally better about not having knotted Ronnie Bigelow's hair in my fist and dragged her into Blitzen at the North Pole, which was what the part of me that's probably most like Bill had wanted to do. I had an unfamiliar sensation of holding the moral high ground.

"We've found more than you can imagine," Rina said at the door to her room. I put my arms around her and grabbed a peek over her shoulder at the bed, which was tightly made, without even the kind of wrinkles that would be caused by someone sitting on it, and there were two chairs pulled up in front of Rina's computer. Some spring somewhere underneath my heart uncoiled a little, and breathing got easier.

"More than she even had for her paper," Tyrone said behind me.

"Tyrone's in my modern media class," Rina said. "He did this amazing paper about lynching souvenirs. I'm frittering away my time doing little Elvises and he's doing lynching, like, *merchandise*. Did you know that towns in the south used to sell postcards of lynchings and little nooses and miniature signs that said stuff like NIGGER, DON'T LET THE SUN SET ON YOU IN THIS TOWN?"

I said, "Huh." Something more seemed to be called for, so I added, "How about that?"

Tyrone laughed. "Yeah. How about that?"

"Is that sick or what?" Rina said. "Like in the Middle Ages, with splinters of the True Cross, only even grosser."

"Only one True Cross," Tyrone said. "Lot of lynching trees."

"But your stuff," Rina said. "You're not going to believe it. It's like nobody's *obscure* any more. Whoever you are, if you ever did anything anywhere, there's whole cartons of stuff on you, and it's all available."

"If you know where to look," Tyrone said.

"Oh, come on," Rina said, and her dimples made a brief appearance. "You could have found it all."

"In a year, maybe."

"I hate to interrupt all this mutual validation," I said. "But maybe you could show me something."

"Sure." Rina stepped aside to let me get to the computer. "Who do you want first?"

"Giorgio."

"I knew it. What's that word, you know, when things work together and it's kind of an accident?"

"Synchronicity," Tyrone and I said together. Tyrone held up an open hand for a high five, and I blundered into a reciprocal gesture that couldn't have been clumsier if I'd been in a straitjacket. Tyrone grinned but had the good sense to keep his mouth shut.

"That's it," Rina said. "Giorgio was the only one I didn't really focus on in my paper, so he was the most fun to research, you know? 'Cause it was all new to me. So sit down and look at all this."

*All this* was a veritable blizzard of facts, hype, urban myths, statistics, photos, fan clubs, love letters, concert souvenirs, scrapbook pages, mp3 files of Giorgio imitating someone who was singing, everything except the kid's fingerprints and social security number.

"Here's the recap," Rina said, pulling a stack of pages out of her printer. "Born in 1943, in Philadelphia. Had a little trouble with the cops when he was twelve or thirteen or something, pre-shave, anyway. He got arrested for trying to buy liquor—boy, thirteen's pretty young to try that one—and he was in a stolen car another time, although he wasn't driving and it looked like he didn't know it was stolen. For a kid in that neighborhood, he was a good boy. Father was a roofer, mother, who's still alive, was a housewife. They'd probably call her a *homemaker* today."

"Your mother always called herself a housewipe," I said, "because—"

"Because she spent most of her time wiping stuff," Rina said. "That joke is still alive and well. Got a laugh out of Bill recently."

"Good," I said. "Glad to know Kathy's found someone who's easily amused."

"He actually laughs at the funny papers."

I suppose I said something, but in my head I was running a sort of equation: *funny papers=morning paper=Bill in my house at breakfast=Bill spending night while Rina is here=Junior kill-ing Bill.*

"Got discovered by that guy DiGaudio sitting on his front stoop," Rina was saying when I surfaced. She was looking at the pages in her hand. "Whatever a stoop is. He was sixteen, so it was 1959. DiGaudio seems to have driven around all the time— kind of creepy, huh?—just searching for kids who had a *look*, you know, that sort of Elvis thing? He'd promise them the moon and sign them up, and three weeks later they'd be on this show called *American Dance Hall* that I guess everybody watched back then, and a week after that they'd be on *Billboard*'s Hot 100. They'd get towed around the country, singing on a bill with half a dozen other acts."

"White acts," Tyrone said.

"Sure. It would have been cruel to put them onstage with black acts."

"Cruel to put Giorgio on a stage anywhere," Tyrone said.

"You don't get it, Tyrone," Rina said, sounding like her mother. "All he had to do was stand there. It wasn't like anybody could hear him. He just came on stage, and the girls screamed. I found a contract online that has what they called 'The Giorgio Clause' in it. It says that DiGaudio Enterprises has to turn over two hundred dollars from the ticket sales to pay for people to wash the seats after the show. Because so many girls peed themselves."

I wrenched myself away from the deep red zone of revenge on Bill to say, "For *him*? That lox? The kid I saw on YouTube?"

"Lox?" Rina said. "He was beautiful, even if he didn't have any talent. How often do you see someone who's really beautiful? Pretty, sure, cute, sure, but not beautiful. That's why he turned into a movie star."

My cell phone rang. "You just stay here," I said to Rina. "Here, in this parallel universe where there was a movie star named Giorgio, and I'll be right back." I put the phone to my ear and said, "Hi," as I went into the hall.

"Got a pencil?" DiGaudio the cop said.

"No *hello*? No *how you doing*?" I said, searching my pockets. "Hang on a second." I got out the pad and pen I'd brought in from the car, and put the pad against the wall. "Shoot."

"Current driver's license," DiGaudio said. "Issued three years ago. Lorne, with an *E*, Henry Pivensey."

"Lorne Henry what?"

"Pivensey." He spelled it. "First two syllables, *Piven*, like Niven as in David Niven, but with a *P*. S-e-y as in z-e-e. Pivensey."

"Got it."

"DOB 10/16/72. Height five feet six and a fraction. Brown hair and eyes. Got a tattoo on his right upper arm, says ABANDON HOPE."

"Who's Hope?"

"Funny. Why aren't you asking?"

"Okay, I'll ask. Since when do drivers' licenses note tattoos?"

"They don't. The tattoo is on his arrest sheet."

"Awwwww," I said, thinking about Marge. "How do I get into this stuff?"

"It's a bad sheet, too," DiGaudio said. "And I don't think this has anything to do with my uncle."

"Why not?"

"Mr. Pivensey is no danger to men. On the other hand, if you know a woman who's anywhere near him, you might tell her to move."

"Why is it that I never enjoy talking to you?"

"In 2001 Mr. Pivensey was sentenced to three years for beating up a seventeen-year-old girl. She said something unflattering about his shirt, and he broke her nose and one of her cheekbones. She damn near lost an eye. He got out a year and a half later, courtesy of all the periwinkle doilies on the parole board, and got arrested again seven months after *that* in the investigation of a disappeared waitress named, uh, waitaminute, Laurette Wissert. We never found her, couldn't make a case the DA would take, but we all knew he killed her. Last time anyone saw her was with him up in Twentynine Palms. She'll turn up in the desert someday. Some coyote will dig her up, but he'll never go down for it. And then last year, a couple people saw him try to run over a woman in a parking lot outside Ron's Market, you know Ron's, over on Highland?"

"Sure."

"Tried to hit her a couple of times. Peeled off onto the street, almost banged into a patrol car. So he got arrested, this being a nation of laws, but the woman was too frightened to press charges. We wanted to make a case for attempted murder, but the DA said no. Wouldn't hold up without a complaint. So your Mr. Pivensey got convicted for reckless driving, paid a fine, and walked. And, since we almost got him on those three, just think how many we don't know anything about."

"Why don't you guys just kill people like that?"

"There are those who claim that we do," DiGaudio said carefully. "And there are those who claim that we don't do it often enough. And if you're taping this call, I'm horrified at the idea of vigilante justice."

"You got a picture?"

"Sure. Got a nice little gallery of him holding up numbers."

"Can you send them to me?"

"Oh, sure. Cops send police records to burglars all the time."

"This guy may have been living with the daughter of someone I know. Now the daughter's not around."

"The police," DiGaudio said. "Remember us? The *someone you know* should call the police."

"I'll pass that along. But don't be a dick. Send me the pictures."

For a moment, I thought he'd hang up. But then he said, "Well, we haven't been doing too good with this guy, have we? It'll take me a couple of minutes to crop down to the face, get rid of the stuff that says *booking photo*. I'll send you two pictures. What email address?"

"Hold on. Rina," I called. "What's your email address?"

"Skyspirit at Bluepool-dot-com," she said.

"Great," I said. I gritted my teeth and passed the address to DiGaudio.

"Dot . . . com," DiGaudio said, obviously concentrating. It was hard not to picture him writing with the tip of his tongue plastered to his upper lip. "Okay, give me a few minutes. And, Bender, listen."

"I'm only sorry you can't see me, see how hard I'm listening."

"Two things. First, don't let this asshole Pivensey distract you from Vinnie's problem. And second, if you run across the little prick and the circumstances are right, do us all a favor. Punch some holes in him. And then, when he's dead, call us."

DiGaudio hung up.

**He'd done three** movies, Giorgio had, none of them likely to make the AFI's Twentieth-Century Classics list, but all of them apparently profitable.

"*Johnny Cool?*" Rina read off the screen. "That's *pathetic*. And then there's *The Boy with the Gold Guitar* and *Summer Star*. Which one do you want to watch?"

I said, "Watch?"

"Streaming," Tyrone said. "It's called streaming."

"When I want to hear a technical term, I'll ask for one."

Tyrone said, "Ooooohhhh," and pulled his hands up close to his chest, as though a badly made-up mummy had just staggered out of the closet.

"Is it legal?" I asked Rina.

"Who said that?" Rina said, looking around the room. "Whoever that was, did he mean, would we be *stealing* if we watched one of these?"

"Can't they track you?" I asked.

"Even if they could, I don't think people are spending much time protecting Giorgio's movies from being pirated."

"Call the White House," Tyrone said. "We got us another Giorgio thief."

"Okay, okay. Which one sounds least worst to you?"

"*Summer Star*," Rina said. "At least they can't screw up the season."

"Fine. *Summer Star* it is."

Rina was wrong. They screwed up the season. *Summer Star* was shot entirely on sound stages, apparently for about nine dollars. Bad lighting substituted for the sun, giving everyone three shadows when they were supposed to be outdoors, and painted backdrops substituted for the world. Giorgio substituted for a leading actor. He played identical twins, one good and one bad, although his performance gave new depth to the term *identical*. At one point, the good Giorgio (I think) was hit on the head, but not, unfortunately, fatally, and he went into a coma, which Giorgio did convincingly. And then the bad Giorgio (I think) pretended to be the good brother for some reason that never became clear, although it might have if I could have endured more than about twenty-three minutes of it.

But at minute twenty-three, he began to sing.

It wasn't that he was tone-deaf. It was more like what he heard in his head was music in whole new keys, keys that had never been played on earthly instruments. It was like the music of the spheres, if the spheres were large, wavering, formless, gelatinous globs of anti-music. And poor Giorgio knew it. His acting was awful, but when he was singing, you could actually feel the kid's pain. He knew exactly how terrible he was. I felt like I was looking at a dancing bear that had been forced to watch Fred Astaire movies just before he got shoved onstage.

"That's enough," I said. "So that's it? Three movies, and then Hollywood came to its senses?"

"You really don't know about this?" Rina asked.

"When he was doing whatever you call what he was doing, I wasn't even born yet. I didn't even know this scene existed."

"Well, he started a fourth one. Movie, I mean. *Boola Boola Hula*. It was being shot in Hawaii. But halfway through it, he didn't show up for the day's shooting. When they went to his hotel, he was gone. All his stuff was there, but he wasn't."

"Yeah? Is that the punch line? I mean, in that interview with DiGaudio, the lady asking the questions brought Giorgio up, and DiGaudio turned into a big nerve ending, but he didn't say the kid was dead or anything."

"I saw the interview, Daddy. What he didn't say was more interesting than what he did say."

"Textual elision," Tyrone volunteered. "Lotta times, elided material, the stuff that doesn't make it into a text is what's most important. Didn't make it because whoever wrote the text thought it was self-evident."

"Thank you," I said. "I'll keep that in mind the next time I'm trapped in a room with a primary-source document."

"So if you two are finished striking up a relationship?" Rina said. "Nobody could find him for about five weeks, and then he called the director and said he was through. Said he was sorry, but he wouldn't be acting any more. Or singing any more, or doing the star thing. He said he was finished, and he was. He never worked again."

"Shame they don't give a Kennedy Center Award for quitting," Tyrone said.

"And then, a few months later. . . ." She checked the paper in front of her. "On April 23, 1963, his house burned down with him in it. Smoking in bed, fell asleep."

Tyrone said, "I withdraw the comment."

"Dead?" I asked.

"Dead." She reached up and brushed a strand of hair out of her face. "Girls went into mourning all over the place. Bouquets of flowers stacked six feet high outside the fence around his place. About two thousand people at the funeral. It's kind of sad," she said. "That was how he got on the Walk of Fame. They only put him on because he died. It was like burning to death was a good career move."

"Awwww," Tyrone said.

"So one day, there was a star named Giorgio," Rina said. "And then, *pop*." She spread the fingers on both hands to mime a bursting bubble. "Pop, and he was gone."

Part Two

THE WIZARD OF WAS

# 12

## A Harmless-Looking Little Island of White

It was just a square of paper, folded into quarters and placed beneath the windshield wiper of my car, and it only had two words and a number on it, but those were enough to make me pop a sweat standing right there at the curb. The worst of it wasn't that it had been left for me. The worst of it was that it had been left for me in front of Kathy's and Rina's house.

The words were, CALL IRWIN. Beneath the words was a Beverly Hills phone number, a number that began proudly with the coveted 275 prefix. Whoever wrote the note had been aware of the weight of the prefix; he hadn't bothered with the 310 area code. Two-seven-five was Beverly Hills and nowhere but Beverly Hills, and it didn't need no stinking area code.

There were many places I could have gone just then and many things I could have done. I could have gone back to the North Pole to give Marge the bad news that she needed to get the cops involved in Doris's disappearance. I could have gone to Studio City to pick up one of my Glocks. I could have gone to Hollywood to pick up *another* one of my Glocks, since it was starting to feel like a two-Glock week. I could have gone to the Wedgwood, climbed into bed, and stayed there for six months. I could have gone back to Stinky Tetweiler's and threatened Ting Ting until Stinky gave me the names and addresses of the mugs who actually robbed the judge. I could have gone to the offices of *The National Snoop*, the paper Derek Bigelow had been working for when he got beaten to death, and asked whether he'd told his editor anything that might point to a motive for murder. I could have gone to the West Hollywood apartment building where the newly widowed Mrs. Bigelow was living with her grief, and attempted to comfort her. I could have done any of those things and a dozen more. But I knew, standing there with the note in my hand just outside the house inhabited by my ex-wife and my daughter, that there was one thing I was not, under any circumstances, going to do.

I was not going to call Irwin.

*Irwin* was the name Stinky had given me.

Irwin Dressler.

The Fixer, the biggest, fattest spider in Los Angeles. In his early nineties now, he had probably lost a little of the power he'd exercised so quietly for more than six decades, but that didn't mean he didn't have plenty left. Irwin Dressler was the *eminence gris* of Southern California. The power broker, the man who made things happen, the guy with the secrets. The Wizard of Was.

Except for the fact that he had managed to stay with us.

A lot of people, even a lot of crooks, don't know much about the Chicago Jewish mob. They know that "the mob" ran Las Vegas for a long time, for example, and they probably think of slick hair and double-breasted suits and names that end in a vowel, but they don't ask themselves why the mobster who started the whole thing was named Benjamin Siegel instead of something like Luigi Lasagna. He was named Benjamin Siegel, also called "Bugsy" (but not to his face), because he was one of the LA representatives of the Chicago outfit made up almost entirely of Jews who'd had the good sense to flee Russia, where killing Jews went in and out of fashion as the national sport. They were tough and smart, and they ran their own local rackets and got involved in Chicago politics and joined forces with Capone's Italian mob as lawyers and financial planners. *Without the Jews,* one Italian mobster famously told Congress, *we'd still be hiding money in mattresses.* Eventually, probably tired of having to explain things four and five times to the Guidos, they split from the Italians and went into business on their own.

In the thirties and forties, the Chicago mob came west, in the person of Siegel, Mickey Cohen, and some others, and the first thing they did was shove over a cliff the Italian mob, represented at that time by a thug named Jack Dragna. The Chicago guys were smarter than Dragna's bunch, better at long-range planning, more likely to use brains than machine guns and baseball bats, and they took one look at LA and saw the biggest piece of fruit on the national tree. Without too much effort, they picked it.

They ran most of the movie studios, the entertainment unions, the music business. The hotels and the hotel unions. The Teamsters. They started country clubs and banks and law firms. When the property of Japanese-Americans was confiscated after Pearl Harbor, the Chicago mob got one of their own, Robert Bazelon, named at the federal level to run the redistribution effort, and Bazelon made sure that millions of prime acres in California went to the family, so to speak. They ran the California Democratic party. They elected mayors. They elected governors. They elected presidents of the Screen Actors Guild. They played a key role in electing at least one president of the United States.

And slowly, over decades, they did what the Italians never quite succeeded in doing. They took their businesses legit. Gradually, they began to play by the rules, to declare their profits, to pay their taxes, to indulge in conspicuous philanthropy. But lurking back behind the white-shoe law firms, the big landmark buildings, the stock option plans, and the shiny, world-famous logos, behind all the apparent corporate rectitude, some of the roots still ran to Chicago, and by and large, they ran through one man, a lawyer named Irwin Dressler.

When there was a strike at a studio, when there was a strike in Vegas, when the Dodgers moved to LA and their opening day was threatened by a strike by the guys in the parking lot, Irwin Dressler stepped in. When the Teamsters Pension Fund had twenty or thirty million to invest, Irwin Dressler invested it. When a famous Italian-American singer, known for punching people, went ahead and punched someone, Irwin Dressler picked up the pieces. When an unsuccessful actor was named to head up one of Hollywood's top studios, and stars and directors all over town refused to work for him, Irwin Dressler made the peace.

And more to the point, where I was concerned, when guys got seriously out of line—mob guys or cops, it didn't matter—and then disappeared from view forever, Irwin Dressler's name was often whispered. And he'd done all this and a lot more, and made a massive fortune doing it, without ever having been formally charged with a crime. He'd been called to testify before Senate committees on organized crime more often than I'd been to baseball games, and at the end of his testimony, he was always thanked and praised for his cooperation, although you could probably spend years reviewing his testimony without stumbling over a single statement that was entirely true.

If the mob was an enormous black iceberg just inches beneath the surface of the sea, Irwin Dressler was the tiny tip, a harmless-looking little island of white in the middle of all that dark water. He might have been in his nineties, but there was still a *lot* of weight behind Irwin Dressler.

I wasn't about to call Irwin. Irwin and I barely inhabited the same galaxy.

So. Get in the car. Study the rearview mirror. Start the car. Drive up into the hills, into the remainder of the old Edgar Rice Burroughs estate that gave Tarzana its name, keeping one eye on the mirror. Head left up Willow Court and follow it slowly until it dead-ended at the iron gates of someone with more money than he needed. Turn the car around and wait as the sun did its daily descent.

Watch a coyote with a limp cross the street, tongue hanging out like pink ribbon, ribs like pleats beneath the scruff of fur, eyes all over the place. Coyotes in the wild are like dogs with an edge, but in civilization they're curs, always worried about the shotgun or the white truck that means their ass is over. I can identify with that, so I commune silently with the coyote until he's out of sight. Listen to a mockingbird, the Mozart of the animal world, run through a ten-minute medley of trills, chirps, riffs, bells, and whistles without a single repetition. Think about how to tell Marge about Lorne Henry Pivensey. Spend a minute or two looking at Pivensey's mug shots, fresh from Rina's printer, seeing a thin, short, nervous-looking nonentity with a receding hairline, a weak chin, and a wandering left eye. Pivensey didn't look any more dangerous than a paper cut.

But then, Irwin Dressler looked like a benign little old man with an extensive selection of plaid slacks. Like a man who never remembered to put batteries in the remote and had to call his kids when he wanted to watch TV.

Think about my reaction to Tyrone. I'd never seen myself as a racist. I had black friends and associates, I'd given ill-gotten gains to organizations that provided one-on-one tutoring to offset the weaknesses of inner-city schools. I'd voted for a black

man for president. I was an enlightened, unprejudiced resident
of the brave new multiracial world. Wasn't I?

So why had the hair on the back of my neck stood up when
it became obvious that Rina and Tyrone were, at the very least,
dancing around the beginning of a mutual attraction?

In William Gaddis's towering 1955 novel, *The Recognitions*,
which was the first book I had used to educate myself when I
decided that college wouldn't do the job, there is a character
named Otto. Otto is a fake. He pretends to be a writer but he's
not. He pretends to be an intellectual but he's not. He's a coun-
terfeit human, someone who continually tries to shape his life so
it looks enviable to others, without worrying about the fact that
it's all surface. It has no core. He occasionally looks at his expensive wristwatch, admires it, and then realizes that he forgot to
check the time. Otto thinks only about forging the next moment,
so he'll continue to be accepted as Otto.

But one sentence haunts him: *All of a sudden, somebody asks
you to pay in gold, and you can't.* Maybe Tyrone was that for
me, a moment when I had to pay in gold, when I had to cut
through the layers of bubble-wrap surrounding my core beliefs
and see what they really were. And I didn't know how to do it,
hadn't even thought I needed to until Tyrone opened that door.

Okay, later for that. Look through the damn windshield,
see whether death is in the neighborhood. Couldn't hear any
cars approaching, didn't see one appear around the bend. Either
nobody was bothering to follow me, or. . . .

Right. *Or.*

I got out of the car and ran my hands under the fenders, getting them good and dirty in the process. I had to lie down on
my back and stick my head under the car before I saw it, a little
black plastic box clinging like a limpet to the chassis of my car.

Well, I told myself, it was information. Neither good nor

bad, just something I probably wasn't supposed to know about, so my knowing about it was better than my not knowing about it, but on the other hand, it would be a *lot* better if I weren't in a position where people representing Irwin Dressler were sticking tracking devices on my car, wouldn't it?

Leave it on or take it off? That was easy: leave it on for the moment. It probably meant that I couldn't drive the car to the North Pole, since it was barely possible Dressler's people didn't know about the North Pole, but I could live with that. Park a quarter of a mile away and hike it.

I entertained the notion of yanking the limpet and moving out of the motel, but I had a feeling that Dressler could find me anywhere, and also that Marge was going to need me. And while I knew I was in trouble, I thought Marge was in more trouble than I was.

**"She's off the** lead," Louie said.

"Well, that's just great." I was doing big zigzags that took me south across Ventura, then a couple of blocks east, then back north across Ventura again, a few blocks further east, and so forth. No followers, although I wouldn't have expected one, what with the little radio station clamped beneath my car. But I learned a long time ago that it's usually exactly what you don't expect that pops up like the handle of a rake and splits your lip. "Who'd you have following her?"

"A girl. Usually pretty good."

"But our little amateur, our innocent, recently bereaved widow, shook her off."

"Yeah." Louie sounded defensive. "Did it pretty smooth, too."

"Define *smooth*."

"Came out, walked right past her car, like she was heading

for the Ralphs market a few blocks over, carrying one of those canvas shopping bags people use to save the earth from other kinds of shopping bags. So my girl, she decided driving real slow behind her wasn't such a great idea, and she went on foot. *Your* girl turned the corner and climbed into a taxi that she had waiting there, and my girl stood there and watched her drive off."

I said, "Hmmmm. And she's not really my girl."

"I'd say that's a good thing, considering."

"*Your* girl. You say she's good."

"Are you kidding?" Louie said. "*You* never saw her."

"What does that mean?"

"Means I put her on you for four, five days at the end of her training period."

"Shut *up*."

"God's truth."

"I didn't see her, but Ronnie Bigelow did?"

"Well, yeah."

I was at that very moment relying on my skill at spotting a tail. "The course of true love," I said, checking my rearview mirror more closely, "never did run smooth."

## 13

### Dickheads

I managed to interrupt a couple of early dinners, get snarled at by three hybrid dogs heavy on the Rottweiler/Doberman my-dog-can-kill-you bloodlines, and hissed at by one cat. The hour between 6 and 7 P.M. is not the best time for knocking on the doors of perfect strangers and asking questions about the neighbors.

Next door on the left and next door on the right, nothing. The residents were vaguely aware that there had at one time been people in the house that Lorne Henry Pivensey aka Lemuel Huff and Marge's wayward Doris had shared, although nobody seemed to know anything about them, and no one had any idea when they'd left. Good neighbors, LA-style. The folks next door could be waiting for the global premiere of their first movie or cooking up meth in the broom closet, and no one would know. The lady in the house to the right, a spectrally thin woman with jumpy eyes and a dull bruise on her left cheekbone, identified Pivensey from the mug shot and said, "Looked like a prick, so I didn't talk to him." She turned her back to me and raised her voice. "I don't got to go next door for pricks."

But across the street and one over, I got the person there's one of on every block. He was eighty, eighty-five, and so wrinkled it looked like he had enough skin for three people. His hair, white as processed flour, was an improbable match for the bristling, jet-black eyebrows beneath which two very bright blue eyes surveyed the world and found it wanting.

"*That* dickhead," he said after glancing at Pivensey's photo. "What is it with guys who have real thin necks? And a head that sticks way out in back, like a little kid's does?" He drew a curve, like a parenthesis, in the air. "They're all dickheads, every single one of them. Something in the genes is my guess: curved head, little neck, dickhead. Lee Harvey Oswald, remember? He was one of them. They're all right next to each other, those genes, there on that little curlicue ribbon. Just one-two-three. Probably holding hands. What's your name?"

"Junior."

"Guys named Junior, too. Dickheads, all of them. Maybe you're an exception, but if you are, you'll be the first."

"What can you tell me about them?"

"Dickheads? You haven't got enough time left on earth for—"

"No, I mean this guy and the woman he lived with."

"She was too good for him. A real pistol. He's one of those little guys who pushes women around, right?"

He took a breath to elaborate, so I said, "Right."

"Didn't get the extra four or five inches he thought he deserved, maybe got shorted down below, too, know what I mean? Plus he's got a neck that would barely stretch a rubber band. Wears one a those stupid baseball caps with the bill sideways like he walked into a wall, and a black leather biker jacket. Probably a kid's size. So he takes it out on the weaker sex, except that this one didn't put up with it. I'll bet her mom's a pistol."

"She is," I said.

This piece of information gave him pause. "Yeah? She attached?"

"She's a widow."

A speculative scratch at the neck. "Huh. Live around here?"

"In the Valley."

He gave it the back of his spotted hand. "Full of—"

"I know," I said. "Wall to wall."

He squinted at me, although it wasn't to see me better. He could probably read the newspaper from across the street. "So why you asking me about them? Those two," he said, glancing past me at the house across the street.

"The mother's worried. She hasn't heard from her daughter in—"

"Ahhhhh," he said. "The mother who should be worried is *his*. I seen her, a couple weeks back, lay into him with the garden hose. She's out there, watering that dead grass, and he comes home in his ratty little Jap car and starts yelling at her. And she takes out after him, swinging that hose like it's a bullwhip, water everywhere and that brass tip thing, you know, with the screw-marks on it where the nozzle—"

"I've seen hoses," I said.

"Dickhead answer," he said, "*Junior*."

"Sorry. I was just interested, and the tip of the hose was slowing down the story."

"Right. So she caught him one on the forehead, and he's all wet and bleeding, backing away with both hands out in front of him. Laugh? I like to pissed myself."

"How long since you've seen them?"

"Nine days."

"Not eight? Not ten?"

"Nine. Back when I was in school, you still had to be able to count."

"Nine days," I said. Pretty close to the time I moved into the North Pole.

"Aren't you going to ask if I saw them go?"

"Did you?"

"Maybe."

I said, "Maybe?"

"Does this pass as conversation out in the Valley?" he asked. "I say *nine days* and you say *nine days*. I say *maybe* and you say *maybe*. Don't invite me to any parties."

"I'll rephrase. When you say maybe, what do you mean?"

"Nine days back," he said, resting a shoulder against the edge of the door, "about eleven thirty at night, I saw him come out in that stupid cap and jacket, start up that little Jap car, and pull it into the driveway past the house. Got my attention, because they never parked behind the house. Let that little car sit out there night and day, dirty as hell, just an eyesore. Dogs peeing on the tires all the time. So I thought, *Huh.*"

I waited a moment and said, "I'll bet you did."

"You don't need to talk. When I pause like that, I'm just getting organized. Car sat back there, maybe half an hour, maybe a little longer. I can't see it because of the house, right? Just the tail end. But I can hear the back door to the house open and close four or five times, just *bang*, like a screen door that hasn't got one of those plunger things to slow it down, and the light comes on in the car's back window when he opens the doors and goes off when he . . . awwww, you know when it goes off. After a bunch of that, the engine starts and the taillights come on, and the car backs out and takes off. And that's it. Never came back, and nobody's taken up a collection to find out where he went. Dickhead."

"One person in the car, or two?"

He looked at me and then through me, pursed his lips for a moment, and said, "Two?"

"But you're not sure."

"Course not," he said. "It's not like I was paying attention."

o  o  o

**There was no** pneumatic arm on the screen door. I opened it and let it bang shut. Plenty loud enough to be heard from across the street. Just a detail, but details count when you're trying to decide whether what you've been told is the icy truth or an improvisation by someone who needed company.

I went to the door of the garage, backed up a yard to allow for the fact that Pivensey wouldn't want to run the car into the closed door, and then turned and paced off about fourteen feet, the length of an average-size car. And found myself looking at the house where Old Blue Eyes lived. So he *could* see the back end of the car.

It was about as dark as LA gets, which isn't very dark. There's always ambient city light, especially in a neighborhood like that one, with Sunset gleaming to the south and Hollywood Boulevard to the north. The house was a dark block raised against the sky, but enough light bounced off the walls to let me see the black rectangles of the windows. Even from out here, I could feel it. Something bad had happened on the other side of those windows, and I didn't really think I wanted to know what it was.

I'd been in the house, but not the garage. Knowing that I was being watched from across the street, I went to my Toyota—little dickhead Jap car, he'd probably say—and opened the trunk. From an exhaustive collection of Streamlight flashlights, the policeman's choice and *de rigeur* for the well-equipped burglar, I chose one that had a focused LED beam, a textured handle that made it harder to fumble, and enough weight to drop someone in his tracks if applied smartly to the side of the head. Holding it in front of me to keep it out of sight from The Ever-Open Eye across the street, I hiked back up the driveway, found the handle of the garage door in the dark, and yanked it up.

The door resisted at first and then swung up, counterweighted heavily enough to snatch the handle from my hand. Looking back to make sure I was out of sight from across the street, I snapped on the flashlight and played it around.

I wasn't expecting much of anything, and that's what I found. There was no internal drywall, just naked two-by fours over tar paper, liberally draped with cobwebs. A theme park for brown recluse spiders, *Death World*. Lots of what looked like black sand at the base of the two-by-fours. On closer examination, it turned out to be termite droppings. In the center of the cement pad was a large, shapeless dark spot, gunmetal gray at the edges shading to black in the middle, built up by God knew how many cars over the course of seventy or seventy-five years. It reminded me of the stains on the carpet at the North Pole.

At the far end of the space, someone who was probably dead by now had built a plywood shelf, maybe five feet off the ground, high enough to allow an old car to nose in beneath it. The plywood belled down in the middle, sagging beneath the memory of decades' worth of weight. Now, though, there were only a few black plastic trash bags and a couple of cardboard boxes, one old and one new, probably recycled decades apart from behind some supermarket.

I pulled my sleeves down over my hands to avoid leaving prints on the plastic bags, and opened one. It contained men's clothes, all pretty much worn out, and so did the second. The shirts were missing buttons or had a tear somewhere, the jeans were out at the knee or had a broken zipper. Discards, maybe, or maybe Pivensey was just frugal and he bagged these things up instead of throwing them away. Maybe figured some day he'd get the buttons, zippers, whatever, replaced. I pushed the two bags back to their original positions and passed on the third.

The first box I tugged toward me was the old one, and it weighed a ton. It had been packed to the brim with magazines from the 1940s, mostly devoted to movie stars. Perfect faces smiled from the covers, lighted and retouched with long-lost artistry. Probably worth something somewhere, since there is nothing that *someone* doesn't collect. I pushed it aside and pulled the newer box to the edge. It was much lighter.

It was a good-sized box and mostly empty. When I pointed the flashlight into it, metal glinted up at me, something silvery. A tangle of metal shapes, linked by shiny chain. Five—no, six—pairs of handcuffs.

Above the handcuffs was a broad strip of masking tape. Neatly lined up beneath it were six keys. The keys were evenly spaced beneath the tape, and there was room for three more, three that had in fact been there once and had left their impressions in the tape.

I changed my mind about the third plastic bag. I opened it and found more clothes.

Women's clothes. Some of them torn, some of them starch-stiff with the old rust of dried blood. When I opened the bag, the smell of fear escaped from it, saturated beneath the arms of blouses and sweaters.

Souvenirs.

The smell and the blood, I thought, might be all anyone would ever find of these women.

I pushed the bag back into place and closed the garage door behind me. When I started the car, I glanced across the street and saw one corner of a curtain drop into place.

## 14
### If You Stop Lighting Your Hair on Fire

"If she hears there's a cop looking for her," Marge said, "we'll never see her again."

"You're not listening to me. Pivensey is a bad guy." I hadn't told her about the handcuffs and the women's clothes, and I doubted I would.

"Honey," Marge said, lighting up. "I knew that the first time I looked at him. Pinky ring, weird-shaped head."

"Little neck," I contributed.

"That, too. That round head, sitting on that weensy neck. Looked like a balloon on a string. Wish I'd had a pin." She held up the jug of Old Igor's Private Reserve, tilted it to sight through it, and tightened her mouth at the results. "Where does this shit *go*?" she asked. "It evaporates right through the bottle."

Marge 'n Ed, back when they bought the motel, had knocked together two rooms on the ground floor and added a little kitchen, tiny enough to fit on a boat, in place of the second room's bathroom. We were in what passed as the living room, which was the unit with the kitchen. It had been furnished in sidewalk style; most of the furniture had the dejected patina of something that had sat in the open air for days. The room was as free of Christmas decorations as Ebenezer Scrooge's bedroom.

"You *need* to talk to the cops," I said again, moving from

one lump in the couch to another. "Don't take this lightly. They think Pivensey murdered one woman, and beat up some others. They can put a lot of people on this. I can't."

"What for?" Marge said. She was sitting on an aluminum beach chair across the warped coffee table. "She's been gone nine days, right? That's what the old man told you, nine days. The house was cleaned out. Whatever was going to happen, it's already happened. And, in spite of the way the world works, let's be optimistic. If she got away from him somehow and she finds out cops are involved, she'll never come home." She upended the bottle, getting about half a glassful out of it. "And if he's done something to her, there's not much we can do about it at this point." She dropped the empty bottle to the carpet, scrubbed her cheeks with the heel of her free hand, drank deeply, and lit another cigarette.

"You've already got one," I said, pointing at the ashtray.

"So what?" She defiantly lit a third. "I'll smoke the whole damn pack at once, if I want to. It's my house."

"I'm not really fond of cops," I said. "But I think you're making a mistake."

"Ed was a cop," she said. She puffed on the cigarette between her lips like a machine, without even lifting her hand to it.

Sometimes I have stupid spells. I said, "Ed?"

"Was a cop," she repeated. She knocked her knuckles against the coffee table. "You in there?"

"And—and what? Doris hates cops because her father was a cop?"

Marge shook her head, a gesture that was half disagreement and half weariness. "Ed got shot. He was breaking up an armed robbery, and he got shot. He killed the person who shot him, a Mexican with a record a mile long, and everybody went batshit. Community *activists*, you know, the vampires who make money by churning up poor people. LAPD did the normal internal affairs investigation and then looked out the window at all the people carrying signs that said BLUE MURDER OF BROWN PEOPLE, and decided that Ed was a small price to pay for peace in the streets. Drummed him out with the bullet still in him. He hadn't been in long enough for a full pension. It took every nickel we had to buy this place. He never got over it. Doris was her daddy's girl. Hates cops worse than he ever did." She knocked the cigarette against the edge of the ashtray, shaking loose a gray cylinder an inch long, then put the cigarette down and picked up one of the other ones. "So I send cops after her, and she'll smell them coming from a mile away. It's you or nobody. She'll never let a cop find her, and if one does, she'll be so pissed at me she'll never come home."

I thought it was highly unlikely that Doris would be coming home any time soon.

"And she's the only one I've got now," Marge said. She scrubbed her cheeks again. Her eyes were very bright. "If I've still got her."

"I'm sure she's fine," I said. It was pure reflex.

"You're a mensch," Marge said. "I've got some money—"

"No," I said.

"Why should you care? I'm just the old—"

"I'm not asking for—"

"—broad who owns the motel—"

"—money, so don't even—"

"—where you happen to be—"

We stopped talking at the same time and looked at each other. Then Marge raised a hand with a cigarette in it, a sign for me to shut up. "There's no reason you should help me," she said. "I had no right to ask you to do what you already did. You did it out of the goodness of your heart."

"I've got some left," I said. "And I haven't got anybody else to spend it on."

She turned away from me and studied the front door as though she'd heard something outside, as though Doris would push it open at any moment and come in, her arms full of packages and shopping bags, and I explored the lines of Marge's profile. A couple of hundred gallons of vodka and fifteen thousand cigarettes ago, Marge had been a thoroughbred. Hell, she was still a thoroughbred.

"I'll find a way," she said. "I'll find a way to thank you." She still hadn't looked back at me.

"But let's not kid each other," I said. "I'm not real optimistic. What I can do is try to track her down, track him down. And then we'll see what we see."

"That's what we'll see," Marge said. She brought up a hand to brush the hair from her face, but she was holding the cigarette, and there was a little frizzing sound and a smell of burning hair. She didn't even seem to notice.

"Names and addresses," I said. "All her friends, former friends, boyfriends, coworkers, anything you can think of. Likely or unlikely. Places she liked to go, places she might hide out if she just needed some time alone. Places from childhood, I don't care. Anything you can think of. And the newest picture you've got of her." Marge's hand came up again, and I reached across the table and pushed it down. "Make a deal," I said. "I'll do what I can if you stop lighting your hair on fire."

She looked back at me, and her eyes filled with tears. "You . . . you . . ." She stopped and swallowed twice. "You sound just like Ed."

**"Whaddya got?" demanded** DiGaudio the cop.

"Not much. Your uncle has something to hide, though, that's for sure." I was on the sidewalk of a small street, about a block east of Lankershim Boulevard. Hiking east, toward the rising moon, heading to the car. Going out to get something to eat. Like an idiot, I'd answered the phone.

"So?" DiGaudio said, and I could hear the sneer. "*You* don't have anything to hide?"

"Lots, but I'm not the issue."

"Like I said, whaddya got?"

Big plane trees had grown up on both sides of the street, and the car was parked in the dark spot beneath one of them. "We know Bigelow was a blackmailer. I think he was in the first stages of blackmailing somebody new, and I think it was your uncle." I opened the door of my car but the light didn't come on.

"You got anything to back that up?"

"Well, sure. His body was dumped on Giorgio's star."

Somebody was sitting in my car.

"Say what?"

"Bigelow's body. It was on Giorgio's star." I backed up, thinking about what Louie had said about lists. I'd let the day get away from me, and I hadn't picked up even one Glock.

"I don't know what you're talking about. Wasn't nothing about that in the report."

The person in my car hadn't moved. "Cop was probably too young," I said, backing farther away. "Probably never heard of Giorgio." I stopped. I'd backed into something that hadn't been there a minute ago. It breathed on my neck.

"Kind of crap work is that?" DiGaudio said.

"Standards," I said as a gun dug into my right kidney. "They've gone to hell."

He made a noise that sounded like he was shredding cellophane with his teeth. "Lemme get back to you."

The gun wiggled back and forth, just a little prompt for attention. I said, "I hope you can."

## 15
Nobody Wants to Dance with a Bear

"You didn't call," Irwin Dressler said.

"I didn't have much to say."

We were in a sunken living room, long enough to have goal posts. The furniture was white, the carpets were white, the walls were white. The hundred and fifty or so small carved objects on the white lacquered shelves on the far side of the room were a brilliant green, except for a few that were lavender.

The guys who had brought me were in the breakfast nook. Dressler had opened the door himself. He'd looked past me and regarded them with some affection. "Tuffy, Babe," he said. "You missed dinner. Eat, eat." Now I could hear utensils against plates and smell something that was almost certainly roast beef.

"You know," he said, crossing one plaid leg over another. He gave me a look that made me feel like he'd removed my skin, checked beneath it, and then put it back. "You have a reputation for being intelligent. Perhaps it's undeserved." He leaned back on his white sofa.

What was I supposed to do? Contradict him? I just sat there.

"You've got that look," he said. "In the last fifty, sixty years, I've seen a million guys with that look, says *I'm smarter than you, I'm one jump ahead*. Generally, they keep that look right up to the point when the bullet hits them. You know how they look then?"

He waited for an answer. "Dead?"

"Yeah." He passed a spotted hand over his chin. "But first they look surprised."

"I didn't come in here pretending to be smart."

"Maybe not. But I doubt you've done many things as stupid as not calling me when I asked you to." Dressler leaned forward again, literally taking a closer look. It was just as intimidating as he meant it to be. His shoulders were bent so far forward it looked like they were trying to meet in front, forming a line as curved as the wood on a bow, and he carried his head way back to compensate, so he could extend his neck farther than most people. His eyes, sunk deeply into the bones of his face, were West Point gray, set in yellowish whites. The skin on his face drooped downward as sharply as an astronaut's on liftoff, the gravity of age pulling the corners of his mouth into an inverted *U*. Age spots bloomed on his forehead, and his fog-gray hair was plastered down with some kind of hair tonic from the forties. I knew the smell, possibly from my father's hair. For ninety-something, he looked youthfully deadly. And he had an aura of solid steel.

"You know who I am." It wasn't a question.

"Yes, sir." The *sir* came without thought and was accepted without comment. Dressler pulled his head back, and what I saw was a snapping turtle making a feint before the fatal strike.

"I'm an old man," he said.

Another pause, so I tried for polite. "Not so—"

He held up a cautioning hand. "I assume that some day *you'd* like to be an old man."

"Um, sure."

"Well, Junior, right now, you're not on course." He blinked, so heavily I was surprised I couldn't hear it. "In my experience, people visualize old age as something very wide, as wide as the sea. Something there's no way around. Inescapable. Doesn't matter which way they go, they'll get there. But I'll tell you, the right way to think of old age is as a spot on a map. A small town." He put out an index finger and touched it, very precisely, to a spot on the tabletop. "A *dot*. In the Badlands, you know the Badlands?"

"By reputation."

"Just chasms everywhere. So your town, old age, it's in there. And there's only one road that'll get you there. Take a detour, make a wrong turn, you wind up under your car at the bottom of one of those chasms."

"That's a very vivid metaphor."

A stout Latina came into the room, black hair to the middle of her back, wearing a white nurse's uniform. She carried a polished wooden tray, which she put on the table in front of Dressler. It was piled with cheeses—Brie, Stilton, a crumbling, yellowish Cheddar, one of those goat-cheese log-things that's been rolled in dead herbs. A large baguette lay intact in the middle. Dressler told the woman, "The Margaux," picked up the baguette, and began to tear it into ragged pieces. His hands weren't shaky. "Another way to look at it," he said. "Nobody wants to dance with a bear, right?"

It didn't seem to be a rhetorical question, so I said, "Right," watching him rip the bread apart.

"But when the bear wants to dance with you, and you're aiming at old age, what's the smart thing to do? Turn around and run—hope you can run faster than a bear—or dance with him?"

"Well—"

"Good choice," Dressler said. He picked up a small silver knife, performed an incision on the wedge of Brie, cut off a thumb's worth, and spread it on one of the tatters of bread. "Here." He held it out to me. "Get a napkin."

I leaned over and picked up a yellow linen napkin. Dressler deposited the bread and cheese in the center of the napkin and dug the knife into the Cheddar. "Why do you think you're here?"

I'd known the question was coming, but that didn't mean I had an answer to it. "Jade?"

He waggled his head from side to side, a compromise between a nod and a head-shake. "Okay, jade. That's one way to get there. The judge got robbed by some idiots who overstepped their instructions. Got stupid. They hurt an old lady. So everybody's upset, and who can blame them? Violence is almost always stupid. There are so many ways to avoid it. Is that chair comfortable?"

"Sure."

"Because you keep shifting around."

"I have a lot of energy."

"Eat your cheese. Relax. You want to get old, you have to keep the blood pressure down. It's strange when you think about it. So many of the things that could keep us alive and guarantee us a peaceful, rewarding old age are under our control. They're simple. Diet, exercise, reduce stress. Happiness. You know, Abraham Lincoln once said he thought most people were about as happy as they made up their minds to be."

*Abraham Lincoln?* "Is that so?"

He picked up another piece of bread and tore it in half. Goat cheese this time. "Life is easy, if you just keep in mind how much of it you're actually in charge of. Eat right, get rest, don't stress out, be happy. Don't stand on the railroad tracks when a train is coming."

"The problem is knowing when you're on the tracks."

"That's not bad," he said, chewing. "I have to tell you, so far, this has been a disappointing conversation. I'd expected more. Jade, you say. Well, the jade is part of it. It's true that I have a weakness for jade."

The Hispanic woman came back into the room carrying a high-shouldered bottle of red wine, the cork sticking up an inch and a half. She put it on the table, took one of the linen napkins and pulled the cork, which came free with a soft pop. Then she put down the bottle, picked up a second napkin, and went to a glass-fronted cabinet, which she opened using one of the napkins. Then, with a napkin in each hand, she took two deeply-cut crystal glasses off the shelf, handling them only with the napkins. She brought them back, put them on the table, and took two steps back. She'd never touched the glasses.

"That's fine, Juana," Dressler said. "Have you chilled the salad plates?"

"Yes, sir."

"Good. Fifty degrees, no colder." He picked up the bottle and filled both glasses. "I won't be long."

Juana didn't bow, but she thought about it. A moment later, we were alone again.

"To our getting along," Dressler said. He picked up his glass.

I picked up my own. It weighed a ton. We clinked rims and drank. Every precious, pretentious, ridiculous, overblown thing I'd ever heard anyone say about wine went through my head at the speed of light. It was that good. The room took on the shimmer of perfection.

Dressler drank his like it was Kool-Aid and then picked up the bottle and refilled his glass. He held it out to me, but I shook my head. "It's too good to gulp."

"The men who pistol-whipped the judge's wife won't be heard from again," Dressler said in a matter-of-fact tone. "Not unless there's a terrific drought."

"A drought?"

"Long enough to empty a couple of lakes. So that's good for some people. They'll never get robbed by a couple of mutts who beat up an old lady because they enjoyed it. But for you, it's a problem, isn't it?"

That question called for another drink. I poured, downed half the glass and said, "You're well informed."

"Of course, I am. The way you were going to get out from under that fat cop's thumb was to bring in the thieves, with a case the most timid district attorney would see as a lead pipe cinch."

"DiGaudio."

"Of course. An Italian, naturally. When people talk about *a fine Italian hand*, I think they must mean penmanship. As far as plotting is concerned, they're klutzes, Machiavelli notwithstanding." He busied himself with the cheese again as though choosing the right one was the only important thing in the world. "He's got you by the short ones, doesn't he?"

"I don't know yet," I said. "I haven't spent much effort on working my way out of it."

The hand holding the knife stopped. "And do you think you can?"

"Not to sound immodest," I said, "but the day I can't outthink Paulie DiGaudio is the day I deserve to be in jail."

"You got that expression on your face."

"Sorry. But it's true. I could outthink DiGaudio with my left brain tied behind me."

"Then why haven't you tried?"

"Two reasons. First, I didn't know that the guys who stole the jade are going to spend eternity underwater. Second, I got interested."

"In what?"

"The whys and whats. Why Vinnie DiGaudio wanted to kill Bigelow, whether he did or not. What Bigelow had on Vinnie, because he had something, sure as hell. Why the killer called attention to Vinnie by leaving Bigelow's body on the Walk of Fame star that belongs to one of Vinnie's imitation Elvises. Why DiGaudio has a former female wrestler working for him when he seems like the type to hire ex-strippers and dress them in cellophane. And some other whys, too."

Dressler shook his head. "I don't care about any of those things. Here's what I care about. Nobody comes looking for the jade. And, for reasons of my own, I would prefer that Bigelow's death not be tied to Vinnie DiGaudio."

"You and everyone else."

Dressler held up an index finger with arthritic parentheses for joints. "Not quite. I know your cop wants you to prove somehow that it wasn't Vinnie. Well, if it *is* Vinnie, if it turns out Vinnie actually did it, then he did it. But I need to know before anyone else does. Right now, it looks like it was Vinnie, doesn't it?"

"More or less." I held out my glass. "More."

"More, *please*," Dressler said, picking up the bottle anyway.

"No. I mean it looks more like Vinnie did it. As opposed to less. More, please."

"Yes, that's the conclusion most people would draw." He was pouring. "I need you to do what you've been told to do, if that's possible. But if it's not—like I say, if it turns out to be Vinnie—I want you to give me some notice."

I knocked back most of it. The second glass was even better than the first. "That's peachy for you. But if it's Vinnie, and if there's nobody I can pin the Hammer robbery on, so I can get out from under DiGaudio the cop, I'm kind of screwed, aren't I?"

"On the contrary," Dressler said, looking genuinely surprised. "You will have done me a service."

"You'll excuse me if that sounds like a thin blanket for a cold winter."

The head-shake this time was just an irritated back-and-forth jerk. "Is *anything* I've been told about you true?"

"Depends on what you've been told."

"You've been described as intelligent and resourceful. Surely one aspect of being resourceful is being able to recognize a resource when you see it. Maybe it's just that you're young." He put down his glass and tugged at the pleats in his awful plaid slacks, then put his hands on his knees and leaned toward me again. "You will have done me a service," he said slowly. "I will owe you. Irwin Dressler will owe you."

"Oh," I said.

"That's something you can take to the bank anywhere in this state."

"How *much* will you owe me?"

He waggled a finger at me, side-to-side. "Uh-uh. Doesn't work that way. Let's see how much you want. When you decide you want it." He drained his glass and made a little *drink-up* gesture, wiggling his hand, palm up. "Finish it. Time to go."

I tipped the glass back and emptied it. I would have wrung it out if I could have. By the time I put it down Dressler was already standing.

"The guys don't need to follow you," he said.

"Not as far as I'm concerned. I mean, I always like company, but—"

"To make sure you're not going to hang around, keeping an eye on this place, for example."

"No," I said. "I've got a full datebook."

"Wouldn't want to detain you." He put a hand on my arm, stopping me. "We have an understanding, you and I."

"We do."

"Tell me what you think it is."

"In short, I keep looking at what happened to Bigelow, and

if it turns out that what happened to him was Vinnie, you're the first to know. And at some undefined point in the future, if I get my heinie in a crack, you'll help me pull it out."

"Exactly. Who knows? Maybe you *are* smart. Stranger things have happened." He was ahead of me, trudging across the carpet and then up the two steps that led to the entry hall. I took one last look at the little pieces of carved jade as I passed them. They were okay, but nothing I couldn't live without. I followed him to the door, which he pulled open. There was a man standing there, a finger half an inch from the doorbell.

I had first seen his face on a movie screen when I was maybe eight years old, and most recently about six weeks ago. There couldn't have been more than two or three actors in the history of Hollywood who'd managed to cling to the top rung as long as he had.

My mouth must have dropped open, because he mimicked it and then gave me a devil's smile, the devil's smile that had made him a star in the first place. He stepped aside to let me by, and then he went in and Irwin closed the door.

Irwin Dressler may have been ninety years old. His power may have faded away, may have been largely symbolic by that point. But in Los Angeles, it's always informative to see what segment of the list people hung with. Dressler was hanging with the apex of the A-list.

## 16

### Peligroso

Irwin Dressler. Little Elvises. Both DiGaudios. The Philly mob.
The missing Doris. Lorne Henry Pivensey, a possible serial killer.
Popsie, the Nazi Dustmop. Rina. Tyrone.

I needed time to think and a place to do it in.

There was no one behind me. Babe and Tuffy were probably
still chewing in Dressler's breakfast nook. Since I was on the
Beverly Hills side of the little crumple of dirt and stone called the
Santa Monica Mountains, I headed toward Koreatown, using all
the loops and dead-ends the neighborhood offered to make sure
I wasn't dragging anybody new.

By the time I hit Sunset, I knew I was alone. Sunset was flow-
ing pretty well. It was after ten P.M., most law-abiding people
were home, and it was a weeknight. Sunset follows the trail that
the Chumash Indians took to the sea when the basin got hot in
the summertime. I wondered, as I made a right onto Fairfax,
what they'd think of Sunset now—an electric canyon of light
that flows from the brown Hispanic blocks of downtown to the
bone-white suburbs of the Pacific Palisades and the wide blue
hard-line horizon of the Pacific. The sage and chaparral gone,
the sun-warmed stones and fresh springs gone, the cougars and
eagles gone. The land held at bay, the entire way paved with
money.

I took Fairfax south to Olympic and turned left, still keeping an eye on the rearview mirror, but mostly for form's sake. I
spotted a big green Dumpster at one end of the parking lot of
a typical Olympic Boulevard mini-mall—Cambodian donuts, a
Vietnamese nail shop, a Mexican taco takeout, and a tire store
of indeterminate parentage. I pulled in, bought a couple of apple
fritters, and put them on the passenger seat. Then I got under
the car, grabbed the magnetic limpet, and stuck it on the inside
of the Dumpster. I figured the Dumpster wasn't likely to go any-
place, and I could pick the thing up again when I wanted to.
Then, chewing on the first of the fritters, I pointed the Toyota
toward K-town.

The Wedgwood, the Lenox, and the Royal Doulton stand on
a corner just a few blocks north of the long stretch of Olympic
where all the signs are in Korean. The peeling facades of two
of the buildings face onto a street we shall, for the purposes
of this narrative, call Courtney Lane, and the third is directly
around the corner, facing onto Baltic Way. (Don't bother looking
on a map for either street.) Under the pretense of reinforcing and
reconstructing the buildings' basements, the Korean syndicate
who bought the buildings excavated an underground parking
lot beneath each of them. Many thousands of pounds of earth
were hauled out, and many building inspectors pocketed many
hundred-dollar bills during the process.

I pulled into the driveway for the apartment house that
faced onto Baltic, using a remote to slide open the iron bars
that blocked access to the garage. I drove all the way across
the big, echoing space, to the far side of the building above me,
and parked. Then I got out of the car, chose a key, and opened
a door in the wall that said, in large red letters surrounded by
lightning bolts, DANGER/PELIGROSO—HIGH VOLTAGE. The door
swung inward on well-oiled hinges, and I stepped through it into

the underground garage of the building next door. It took me about a minute to cross that and open a similar door on the far side, and then I crossed the third garage and turned the key that called the elevator.

If anyone had been following me, I was two apartment buildings away from the one they'd seen me pull into. And on a different street. I'd gone in on Baltic Way and I was now on Courtney Lane.

The elevator was dingy and sad. Its once glorious oak paneling now looked like something salvaged from a sunken liner, warped and scratched and written on. Its chandelier was dark and missing most of its crystals. The only light came from a cheap fluorescent ring stuck any old way on the ceiling. A bare wire ran across the ceiling from the fluorescent fixture and vanished into a hole that had been bored roughly into the paneling. Behind the hole, about two inches back so it would be hard to spot, was a little fish-eye lens attached to a closed-circuit camera that was monitored twenty-four hours a day by some very muscular Koreans. I waved at the camera.

The third-floor hallway, like all the hallways, was dark and disconcerting. The carpeting had holes in it. Water stains had been skillfully painted on the ceilings, and here and there the plaster was flaking away like industrial dandruff. Most of the light fixtures had burned out; irregular pools of light bloomed at odd intervals, usually above the worst stretches of carpet.

It took three keys to open the door to Unit 302, and not junk keys, either. And then I closed the door behind me, redid all the locks, and sighed into the dark.

**The window that** took up most of the wall at the far end of the living room was architectural art deco from 1923, a spiky tangle of thin black wrought-iron, holding irregularly-shaped pieces of glass: trapezoids, rectangles, triangles. Looking at it from the leather armchair, it reminded me of the geometrical nightmare that served as the floor plan of Vinnie DiGaudio's house. Since I was going to have to pay Vinnie a visit later that evening, I let my mind wander over what I remembered and what I'd conjectured about the parts of the house I hadn't seen.

People in the twenties understood that high ceilings promoted peace of mind. The ceilings at the Wedgwood were fourteen feet high, lighted at the edges by triangular brass sconces that threw light upward, turning the entire white ceiling into a lighting source. The sconces were the only lights I had turned on, and the illumination they produced was evenly distributed, practically shadowless. The oak floor gleamed, polished by the Korean cleaning crew that came with the building and who also functioned as spies to tell the syndicates whether any tenants were trashing the premises.

The skyline of Los Angeles' small, tightly bunched crowd of downtown skyscrapers glittered through the window. A skyline Irwin Dressler had helped to build, lending capital from labor union pension funds, bringing high-rollers to the city's new banks, initially money laundries but all legit now. Twenty years after he died, there would probably be a Dressler Drive somewhere down there.

There was room in the world for big money, big mobs, and small-time crooks like me. Somewhere in that continuum was the niche occupied by the predators like Lorne Henry Pivensey. While part of my mind was working my way through the upcoming creep of Vinnie's house, another part was laying out a roadmap that might lead me to Doris, living or—more likely—dead. How was I going to deal with Marge?

For that matter, how was I going to deal with the beautiful widow Bigelow? A woman who seemed not to have a thought to spare for her murdered husband, who essentially did a cross-country *dos-à-dos* from Trenton to Los Angeles, being passed from hand to hand, from one creep to another, like a scuzzball square dance. And now she seemed to like me. And I seemed to like her.

And what about Rina?

I got up and went into the kitchen, which was the only room I'd done anything to. The original marble floor, polished to a mirror surface, now reflected an eight-burner chef's stove, a Sub-Zero refrigerator, and other objects of hardware lust. If I was going to hide out here for a year or two, I was going to cook and eat well. And I was going to read; the apartment had a library, wall-to-wall walnut shelves, and they were jammed with books I'd picked up second-hand.

And, in two of those books, glued in between the thin boards of the covers, so someone could fan the pages without anything falling out, were the keys to a completely different life: a passport, social security card, birth certificate, and driver's license. Parked in the garage downstairs was a blue Toyota, this one registered to Silas A. Noone, my alter ego. The name was an almost-anagram for *alias no one*. In a locking, recessed niche four feet up inside the living room chimney was a steel box with almost eighty thousand dollars in it, plus half a dozen credit cards, all current and paid up.

If everything came down some day, I could pull into the driveway on Baltic Way as Junior Bender and, five minutes later, pull out of the driveway on Courtney Lane in a different car, as a different person.

And then I could disappear forever.

But it wasn't time for that yet. Things were tangled, but not terminal.

I took down a bottle of Glenfiddich and poured a one-and-a-half, since a double would have been pushing it. This was one of five bottles I had of the Glenfiddich produced in 1937, a bottle of which, billed as the world's oldest single-malt whiskey, had sold for about twenty thousand bucks in Hong Kong. Only sixty-one bottles had been produced. I'd liberated my five from the house on Carol Way, the one with the looping driveway that had let me dodge the Humvee. Glass in hand, I wandered the rooms of the apartment, just appreciating the workmanship and letting the high ceilings open my head up to relieve the pressure. Things *were* a tangle. Well, I'd been in tangles before, and I'd gotten out of them by applying an approach attributed to St. Francis of Assisi: *Start by doing what's necessary; then do what's possible; and suddenly you will be doing the impossible.*

What was necessary, at this hour of the night, was figuring out what was going on in Vinnie DiGaudio's house.

# The Ninth Circle of Pulmonary Hell

I made a quick stop at the mini-mall to reattach the limpet and then straightlined back to the Valley. It was a little after 1 A.M., and I had the roads pretty much to myself. After making the turn off of Ventura, I pulled to the curb, opened the trunk, grabbed everything I might need, and dropped it into the little black leather satchel I use for what I think of as house calls. Then I put the Toyota into gear and powered up the hill toward Vinnie's.

Virtually no traffic in the neighborhood, not many lights on in the houses. This part of the Valley is still more an early-to-bed community than, say, Silverlake or Venice, where a demographically significant number of people stay up well into the night. I took the last couple of turns with the lights out and pulled to the curb, careful not to let my tires squeal against it, grabbed the satchel, which was fairly light, and hoofed it up the driveway, steep enough to get me breathing hard. My cheap Chinese sneakers, which I'd dyed black long ago, were reassuringly soundless.

The windows I could see were all dark. Just to make sure nobody was up, nursing night sweats or whatever, I decided to make a complete circuit, trying at the same time to reassemble the puzzle of the floor plan in my mind's eye. From the front door I headed left, following the wall outside the rooms I'd glanced into from the long hallway. The window I'd unlocked was still unlocked. I kept going until I came to the long curved wall, but I could go only about two feet further than the edge of the window glass, because at that point the wall kissed the edge of a fifteen-foot drop, maybe a 70-degree angle, spiky with ice plant, that ended at the edge of a fenced yard below. The moon, dead center in a firefly party of stars, winked at me from the surface of a swimming pool.

So. Turn around and go back to the front door. Explore to the right of the door this time.

This was the side where geometrical whimsy had won the day. The first room I passed had triangular walls sloping up to a point, which I supposed made it a pyramid. Next came a concave wall, curving inward toward the middle, with another long window, the opposite of the one that bent out in the room where I'd talked to DiGaudio both times. These were the rooms I hadn't been able to look into. The black area on my burglar's map.

I ducked down as I passed the concave window, thinking as I did it that a piece of glass that size, cut to fit and custom-curved, had to cost a fortune. As DiGaudio told me himself, the only thing he'd done since 1960 was get fat. It was hard to believe that the stream of royalties from the Little Elvises was much more than a trickle, all these years later. Other than the occasional nostalgia CD hocked on late-night TV by a former member of Sha Na Na, the Frankies and Giorgios were a curiosity, a momentary lapse in taste, a fading echo in pop culture. It was hard to see where the money was coming from. Good investments? With a house like this, it was obvious that DiGaudio wasn't hoarding.

The next two rooms were rectangles, but they protruded from the side of the house like a couple of crooked teeth, with a V-shaped slice of grass between them like a green piece of pie.

Good-sized rooms, maybe bedrooms. Then I came to a long, unbroken stretch of wall, completely window-free. It took a moment for the penny to drop: this was the recording studio. So put one in the plus column—I'd located the studio—and one in the minus column: there was no way to know for sure that the Rolling Stones or Dion and the original Belmonts weren't inside, rocking up a storm. I sat down with my back to the wall for a couple of minutes and just let my ears explore the night. Heard an owl doing the ever-fresh *huu huu* number, heard something— probably a possum—crackle its way through the ice plant on the hillside below, heard the occasional *brrrrr* of an especially loud engine, far down on the Valley floor.

Heard no music at all. Heard instead the reverberations of a voice in my inner ear.

Irwin Dressler. A few hours back, I'd been in the same room with Irwin Dressler. Me, an obscure burglar who wouldn't deserve an asterisk in the long florid history of Southern California crime, having a one-on-one with The Dark Lord himself. The man with the plan, the geographer of local history. Famous and powerful men and women had been his hand puppets, acting out the plays he wrote for them. Business tycoons, Hollywood moguls, public faces, politicians. All navigating the intricate hopscotch pattern Irwin Dressler had chalked on the sidewalk of time. Erasing it behind them. Shaping the state of California.

An old guy in plaid pants. Looked as harmless as a skink.

And what he'd essentially told me was that I shouldn't worry about DiGaudio the cop. The inference was that he could take care of Paulie DiGaudio without even rolling over in bed. So worry about him, Irwin, instead.

This was not an improvement in my affairs. Paulie DiGaudio was the comic cut-out troll in a child's pop-up book compared to Irwin Dressler. When I'd unlocked the window in Vinnie's house earlier that day, it had just been a burglar's reflex, the way a shoe salesman might have glanced at a man's footwear. I didn't really have a reason to break into the house, since my job was to demonstrate Vinnie's innocence. Now, though, I had a new client, so to speak, and the assignment had changed.

There was absolutely no music coming from the house. I gave it another minute or so, hands cupped around my ears, but nope. I heard a woman laugh, a harsh, unamused laugh I was glad wasn't directed at me, from somewhere way down the hill, but nothing that demanded a treble clef.

So I reluctantly got up, a touch creaky from the cold ground, and followed the perimeter of the house until I came again to the ice-plant-covered drop. Passed several more windows, probably two more rooms, but no lights. Not so much as a candle.

Showtime.

The great thing about burglar alarms is that they're much more irritating to homeowners than they are to burglars. My sense of both Vinnie DiGaudio and Popsie was that they had extremely low irritation thresholds. I spotted a good hidey hole beneath the chassis of Vinnie's stately old Rolls Royce as I passed the front door.

I positioned myself under the unlocked window, opened the satchel, and pulled out a pair of black cotton gloves and a black ski mask. It took a moment to put them on, but it seemed to take longer because I was completely focused on listening for a voice, a door, a creak underfoot, anything to say that anyone inside was sentient and vertical. Nothing. I zipped the bag, looped the handles over my left arm so I wouldn't have to bend down to pick it up, and opened the window.

The alarm was shrill enough to abrade flesh. I eased the window back down until it was completely closed and scooted for the underside of the Rolls as the speakers tattered the night.

It took them long enough: they both must have been heavy sleepers. It was probably a full thirty seconds before I saw lights go on, and then something happened that I should have anticipated but hadn't—the area around the house was suddenly bathed in the kind of wattage that's usually reserved for major league night games. Even all in black, even underneath the Rolls, I figured that anyone who came through the front door would see me, as long as I could see them.

I hated to do it, because there are few things I dislike more than being hunted by someone I can't see, but I rolled to the far side of the Rolls. From my new position, I couldn't even see the bottom of the door. I was going to have to listen for footsteps and try to adjust my position. The nearest bushes were useless: they were azaleas, ten feet away and too low to hide behind. People look in bushes first anyway. I think it's some sort of animal holdover: if it can eat you, it's hiding in the bushes.

They finally shut down the alarm, and I heard the front door open and then slam up against the hallway wall. I recognized Popsie's velvet touch, and sure enough, a second later I heard her addressing her boss.

"Just check inside the fucking house like I told you. I'll take care of it out here."

An unintelligible response from DiGaudio, still inside. I couldn't make out the words, but it was clear that he wasn't returning any of the attitude. Kind of an interesting employer/employee dynamic, I thought, keeping my eyes on the part of the paved area nearest the front door.

And here she came, a pair of calves that would have raised eyebrows at a Mr. Universe pageant, her feet encased in what looked like live rabbits, but proved, as they came closer, to be beige fur slippers. Dangling to the right of her knees, which was as far up as I could see, was the shiny black double trouble of a shotgun barrel. Popsie was bad enough. Popsie with a shotgun was almost enough to send me home.

She went left, probably to take a look down the driveway, and I re-angled myself beneath the car so I was head-on to her. That way, if she caught sight of me as she came back, at least she wouldn't see a man-shaped silhouette. I watched the hem of her pink nightgown come into sight as she went eight or ten feet down the drive.

Okay, a bit of good news: she wasn't waving a flashlight around. She was depending on the exterior lights. So she couldn't just idly point a couple of hundred watts under the car. I stayed still, barely breathing, and watched her climb back up and then head around the other side of the house.

"Anything?" DiGaudio called from inside.

"Jesus Christ on a broomstick," Popsie said to herself. To him, she said, "Just handle your end."

He said, "Okay," sounding like he'd had his hand slapped. Then nothing happened for a minute or so, until Popsie reappeared and went to the chain-link gate that led to the pool. I heard it click shut behind her. By the time she came back, DiGaudio was standing in the doorway, although I couldn't see anything except a pair of bare feet.

"Everything's fine," he said. "Fucking alarm."

"Damn," Popsie said. "My sleeping pill had just kicked in."

"So take another one," DiGaudio said. "You got a thousand of them." The door closed.

A bit later, they snapped off the exterior lights. I pulled up my sleeve and looked at my watch, a Timex with that useful little death-ray-blue light that comes on whenever you push a button. I decided it would take twenty, twenty-five minutes for them to get resettled, for Popsie to drop another sleeper, and for the two of them to toddle off to dreamland.

Thirty-two minutes later, I opened the window again.

**The fourth time** the alarm sounded, around 3:40, they finally disabled it. It was hard to believe that Popsie was still walking, since she'd kept announcing her intention to take another of her little blue sweeties. I gave them forty-five minutes and then opened the window for the fifth time, unaccompanied by the siren this time, and climbed in. Once inside, I stood motionless beside the window for a slow count of two hundred. Then I eased myself into an armchair and removed my shoes. I didn't want the rubber soles of my sneakers making basketball squeaks on the hardwood floors.

I dropped the shoes into the satchel and then rummaged inside it until I found a penlight, not much thicker than one of Marge's cigarettes, with an adjustable-width beam. I pointed it at the floor, turned it on, and twisted the business end to narrow the splash of light as much as possible. Then I scanned the room once, located the doorway into the hall, and shut the penlight off. Once my eyes had readjusted to the darkness, I headed for the door.

The hallway was close to pitch black, but the darkness paled as I made my way toward the room with the big curved window. I went into it, waited a moment to listen again, and then turned on the penlight and did a sweep. Nothing interesting, nothing I hadn't seen before. Below, through the window, the Valley sparkled like the world's gaudiest, worst-shaped Christmas tree.

Acting on a burglar's compulsion, I went around behind the coffee table and opened the drawer from which Vinnie had pulled the five thousand bucks. It was stuffed with rubber-banded half-inch bricks of hundreds, stacked crisscross. Had to be thirty-five, forty thousand dollars. Maybe he was a big tipper. Closing the drawer without lifting some of the stash was a test of character. I failed. I counted down three stacks and pulled two or three bills out of each stack beneath those. I figured it would be weeks before he discovered it, if he ever did. With a diminished sense of self-esteem partially offset by twelve hundred dollars in my pocket, I put the intact stacks back on top and got up from the permanent dent Vinnie had made in the couch.

I hadn't seen the kitchen, so I pushed through the swinging door and found myself in a space bigger than both my rooms in the North Pole put together. Marble, or maybe granite, gleamed everywhere. What caught my attention, though, was the clutter. The place was a pigsty. Dishes tottered in precarious stacks. Smeared glasses and half-full cups lolled everywhere. Bits of food—bread, banana peels, half-eaten oranges—littered the counters and smooshed beneath my stockinged feet. The place smelled like a garbage disposal that needed a lemon run through it. So Popsie and Vinnie, whatever their good points might have been, weren't neat-freaks.

My penlight caught a glint in one corner: a stack of aluminum hospital trays, the kind with fold-out legs to fit over a person's lap in bed. Unlike the rest of the kitchen, they were spotless. Well-lubricated, too, as I learned when I picked one up and unfolded a leg. It moved easily, without a sound, snapping precisely into place.

Hmmmm. DeGaudio's kaftan, the abnormal thickness of the legs he could barely cross. Was he an occasional invalid? Popsie's muscles made a new kind of sense.

The kitchen had a second door, in the wall to the right. I figured it had to open into the hallway I hadn't been down yet, the hallway that led to the recording studio, the bedrooms, and whatever else was down there. Like the door I'd entered the kitchen through, it was a swinging door, meaning no noisy hardware to deal with. I turned off the penlight, put my ear to the door for a minute or two, and then pushed it open.

And once I was through it, I heard the burglar's favorite sound: snoring. It was in stereo, coming from rooms twenty feet apart. I stood outside the room from which the deeper snores came, trying to guess which one of them it was. As far as I could match up the inside of the house with the outside, the bedrooms were the two protruding teeth. To my right was the pyramid-shaped room, which was empty except for a fur rug dead center, a headache-inducing mandala on one wall, and something that looked like a mirrored disco ball but had probably been sold as an energy conduit. It hung from the apex of the pyramid, inert as far as I could tell. I tried to pick up on the room's spiritual vibration, but the snoring drowned it out. Maybe it *was* a disco ball.

Between the pyramid and the two bedrooms was a locked door. I tried it twice, as quietly as possible, but it wanted to stay locked, and I wasn't about to try to pick it. The room on the other side of the door had to be the one with the concave window, which made it the biggest room in this wing of the house, and I would have figured Vinnie would have staked it out as his palace of slumber, but apparently it served another purpose.

That left the two doors at the end of the hall, which had to lead to the recording studio. I opened the nearer one as slowly as possible, put my hand on the edge, and closed it gently behind me so it was open only by the thickness of my hand. Then I switched on the penlight.

An old-fashioned sound-mixing board, all sliders and round pots for volume control, leaped out of the darkness. Two wheeled office chairs were pushed up against it, and beyond it the penlight bounced off a window of what seemed to be smoked glass, undoubtedly allowing a view into the studio when the lights were on. I was in the control room.

I got my fingers out of the way and eased the door closed. Then I gave the room five minutes, long enough to learn that Vinnie was using eight-track tape, state of the art in maybe 1973, but neolithic in this age of ProTools and infinite hard drives. Little pieces of white surgical tape reflected light at various points along the paths taken by the sliders, obviously indicating a mix setting that had been satisfactory at the last session and had been preserved. In the middle of the console was a microphone with a button below it, to allow the producer to talk to the musicians on the other side of the glass.

A set of rough plywood shelves built into one wall held boxes of recorded tape, maybe the size of a dinner plate and about an inch thick. I counted fourteen of them. Someone with an enviably precise printing style had written titles in black marker on the spines of the boxes: *Candy Kisses*, *Pressed Flowers*, *Songs from Atlantis*, *Box of Light*, *Tomorrow's Shadow*, Rear View Mirror, *The Lost Album*, *Notes from Underground*, *Poison Pie*, *Black Beauty*, *Paw Prints on the Heart*. Song or album titles, I supposed. They seemed to reflect a changing sensibility, starting with early sixties sweetness and gradually turning a little fantasy-land, a little psychedelic, a little minimalist, a little Rimbaud, a little dark. I'd probably listen to an album called *Paw Prints on the Heart*.

A door to the left of the mixing board led into the studio. I took a last survey of the control room and opened the door.

Cigarettes had left their stale signature on the air. The penlight picked out half a dozen folding chairs set in an irregular semicircle. An acoustic guitar leaned against one of them, a squarish electric bass against another. On the scruffy carpet gleamed a couple of round film tins, maybe ten inches in diameter, each containing a mound of cigarette butts. Back behind the chairs, up on risers about eighteen inches high, was a drum kit, the sticks neatly crossed atop the snare drum.

Movable baffles—just upright wooden frames padded with soft material to absorb sound—stood here and there. The biggest one, about five feet high, had been positioned in front of the drum kit, probably to reduce leakage from the drums into the microphones for the guitar and bass, standing beside the folding chairs. In front of each chair was a black metal music stand with sheet music on it.

I chose a chair that wasn't supporting an instrument, sat on it, and thumbed through the sheets. On top was a piece called "Your Name on My Mind." Two-four time, written in D, the classic pop-song form: first verse, second verse, hook, third verse, and so forth. The composers were indicated in the upper right-hand corner: *DiGaudio/Abbruzzi.* Publisher was B.O.I. Music. The second song, "The Map to You," was also by DiGaudio/Abbruzzi. There were six songs in all. In the old days, a good session's worth. These days, it seems to take most bands a month to finish a single track, what with the depth of the contemporary creative process and all.

I put the sheet music back on the stand and let the penlight play over the room. On the wall behind the drums someone had hung a big whiteboard calendar. I was picking my way between the chairs to look at it when I thought I heard something. I killed the light and froze.

Whatever it was, it had been at the very threshold of hearing. I remained motionless just long enough to orient myself and then, with both hands in front of me, I felt my way toward the drums. In between them and me was the big padded baffle, and I edged around it and dropped down behind it. If the lights came on, I would be invisible from the control room. Not much, but something. I knelt on the floor and waited.

And for quite a while, nothing happened.

I asked myself whether I had really heard anything. The only safe course of action was to assume that I had, so I spent an increasingly uncomfortable ten minutes or so on my knees, listening.

Then there was a soft click, which seemed to come from everywhere at the same time, and something very odd happened. The walls of the room seemed to recede. I mean, they receded in my hearing; when you've spent as much time as I have working in the dark, you learn to hear walls. They're usually the nearest sound-reflective surface. I'd been in the studio long enough to get an ear's-shot estimate of the distance from me to all four walls, probably accurate within a foot or two.

But with that *click*, it was as though the walls had moved back somehow, and the room lost all shape in my head. If I hadn't been kneeling, I probably would have sat down.

And then, as my head cleared and the floor stayed solid beneath me, I knew what it was. Someone had pressed the button to turn on the microphone in the control room, with an audible click, and was holding it down. I was hearing, through the studio's speakers, the ambient noise of another room altogether. What I had heard first, the sound that made me turn off the penlight, had been the door from the control room to the hallway, closing on the other side of the pane of glass.

Someone in the control room.

The penlight had been on when I heard the door close. He'd seen me. Or *she*: I suddenly remembered Popsie's shotgun.

I still hadn't gone to pick up one, two, or all three of those Glocks. Hard to believe it was only that afternoon that I'd realized that I'd forgotten to do it. Felt like a week. But, of course, even if I'd retrieved all three of them, I wouldn't have one on me. As Paulie DiGaudio had taken pains to point out in our first chat, going into a house strapped is a whole new world of woe if you get caught. The cops and the courts are resolutely unamused by armed robbery.

So forget weapons. What I had on my side was years of experience, a good grasp of the house's floor plan, infinite patience, and my native cunning.

In other words, I was screwed.

A fingernail or something passed over the surface of the microphone, making a sound like a rockslide. In the silence that followed, somebody breathed.

And what a breath it was. It sounded as though it had been drawn through a wad of wet tissues, a gag of soaking Kleenex. It faded into a lower chest-rumble that came all the way from the ninth circle of pulmonary hell. It was difficult not to visualize thick ropes of drool.

My underarms released a pint of water each. I knelt behind the baffle, still as stone and newly wet, and heard another click as the mike button was released, and then—a minute or two later—the almost imperceptible sound of the control room door opening and closing again. I stayed where I was, running all sorts of doomsday scenarios through my head, for ninety minutes by my little blue-lit watch. Finally, when I figured sunrise was only half an hour away, I forced myself to get up, and then I felt my way at the highest possible speed out of the room, out of the house, and down the driveway, expecting at every second to see Popsie's shotgun blossom in the darkness. I didn't even stop to put on my shoes.

And when I pulled into the parking lot of the North Pole in the grayest moment of early morning, the first thing I saw was that the light above the door to Blitzen was out. The second thing I saw was the body curled up there.

## 18
### Dry and Wet

She didn't weigh much, and she wasn't much of an actress, either. Her eyelids did a telltale flutter when I picked her up, and one corner of her mouth lifted when I had to jam her inelegantly against the wall to get the card-key into the slot so I could open the door. So I toted her into the room, lifted her to shoulder height, and dropped her onto the bed.

Ronnie said, "Uuuhhhffffff," and opened her eyes. "You were doing so well, too."

"How long were you out there?" I thought about turning on the light but decided that the paling day through the window was appropriately bleak.

"Four hours? Five?"

"Just huddled like some refugee against the door. Being soaked by the dew and chilled by the wind and so forth."

She sat up and rubbed the forearm I'd scraped against the wall. "It was cold, yes. And your tone leaves something to be desired."

"It probably does."

"Well." She tugged down on her blouse, which had a pattern of small sunflowers on it. "The bloom came off the old rose pretty fast, didn't it?"

I went to the chair beside the table reserved for good elves and sat down. "Maybe we'd better start over."

"I think we already have."

"Why don't you fill me in on your day?"

She threw her legs over the side of the bed and let them dangle in their faded jeans. "And why don't you go to hell?"

"Let's start with why you were crumpled so dramatically against my door."

"How about this? It was cold, and I'd been standing there for hours." She straightened her arm at the elbow and bent it sharply, a demonstration. "You may have noticed that human beings are *hinged* here and there in a way that allows them to deviate from upright whenever they want. My feet got tired. I was freezing. I crumpled, as you so picturesquely put it, in order to try to get some sleep."

"And you were there in the first place because. . . ?"

"Oh, I don't know. I guess I was dumb enough to think you'd be glad to see me."

"Let's take it back a couple of steps. I'm still curious about how you spent the day."

"Just to keep us talking," Ronnie Bigelow said, "let's pretend you have a right to ask the question. If you did, I'd probably tell you that I did a bunch of stuff."

"Well," I said. "That's informative."

"If you ever turned your damn phone on, you'd know some of what happened today."

"Oh," I said. "Hold it." I pulled the phone out and powered it on.

"I can't believe this," she said to the room. "He's *checking* on me."

"I'm a crook. By now, with a whole string of us behind you, you ought to know we're not real trusting."

She rubbed lightly at the scraped arm. "And here I thought I was special, in my dowdy little way."

I had four voicemail messages. The first was from Ronnie, asking where I was and what I was doing. The next two were from Louie. First, he told me that Ronnie had returned to her apartment about 8 P.M., around the time I'd been getting hijacked to Irwin Dressler's place, and then he called back to say that the new person he'd assigned to watch the apartment house had followed her to my place, where she was just standing around outside the door. And then there was a message from Ronnie, telling me it was 2 A.M., and she was freezing her ass off outside my door, and that she was frightened to go home because she was being followed.

When I folded the phone, the room had brightened to the point where I could see her face clearly, and it wasn't friendly. And the new day wasn't the only thing that had dawned.

"It was *you*," she said. "You had those people follow me."

Sometimes I'm dismayed by how easily I lie. "I was worried about you."

She plucked up fistfuls of bedspread and let them drop. "We go out once, for lunch, you haul me to some—some *crime scene*—and you think you have the right to check up on me? To worry about who I'm seeing, what I'm doing?" She got up and made for the door. "Jesus, suppose we'd gone on a real date. What would you have done, fenced me in a yard somewhere? Put me on a leash?"

"Not like that," I said. "I was worried about your safety."

She had her hand on the doorknob, and her eyes were narrow. "Yeah? Why?"

"Your husband's been murdered. Nobody knows why. Nobody's sure what you do or don't know about his business. Suppose whoever killed Derek was after information, and suppose they didn't get what they wanted. Where would they look next?"

"That's not bad for spur of the moment." She turned to face me. "I don't believe a word of it, but I'm going to give you the benefit of a very slim doubt, and you can thank your landlady for that."

"Marge?"

"She came up twice. First time to see what I was doing, second time to bring me some rum and invite me down to sleep on her couch. I took the rum and passed on the couch. 'Oh, no,' I said trustingly. 'He'll be home any minute.' 'Sure he will, honey,' your landlady said. 'Whatever you say.' And then she told me it didn't matter what time you got home, you were worth waiting for. She said you were a keeper."

"Oh." I could feel my face heat up. "Well, she's prejudiced."

"Said motel owners had x-ray vision, and you were sterling."

"Sterling?"

"That was the word she used. Said most everybody is plated, but you're sterling."

"I guess that's flattering. Why don't you sit back down?"

"I reminded her that silver tarnishes," she said, going back to the bed and sitting primly on the very edge, ankles pressed together and feet flat on the floor. "She said that's what women are for, to keep men from getting too tarnished, sort of like the *beau ideal* of the knight and the fair lady, where her spotless innocence is a shining token of virtue as he ventures forth to chop people's heads off. She said the tragedy of being a woman was you could spend a lifetime polishing and then work your way through the silver plating. And there you are, you've given your life to a tin spoon."

"Marge?" I said.

She scooted her butt back to relax a little on the bed. "Sure."

"*Marge* prolonged that metaphor to that extent? *My* Marge?"

"Well," she said, wiggling one foot from side to side and looking down at it. "I may have embroidered on it."

"You very well may have."

She shrugged. "I may have made the whole thing up. Everything except sterling."

"Wouldn't surprise me."

She crossed her legs and cocked her head to one side. "What was the giveaway?"

"It's too wet for Marge."

"Wet? I'm wet? What the hell does that mean?"

"There's nothing wrong with it. Wet's okay. I divide the world into wet and dry. There's good wet stuff and good dry stuff. They're just different."

"Are you improvising? Like you were when you said you were worried about me?"

"Nope. Not that I wasn't actually worried, of course."

"Of course. Okay, examples. Wet and dry. Examples. Fast, no thinking about it."

"Music," I said. "Bach is dry and Beethoven's wet. Ravel is dry and Debussy is wet. Painting, the Flemish masters are dry, except for Bruegel, and Rembrandt's wet. Cezanne is dry and Renoir is wet enough to do dishes in. TV, CNN is dry and PBS is wet. Politicians, both Bushes were dry, Clinton was wet. Obama seems wet but he's actually dry. Pop music and rock and roll are dryer than soul and country."

I thought for a moment. "Classical Greece was dry, but Classical Rome was wet. England is dry and France is wet."

"Whole cultures?" she said. "Not exactly a nuanced approach, is it?"

"On *balance*," I said. "Cultures are wet and dry on balance."

"And Marge is dry but I'm wet."

"Actually, you're both dry, but Marge is dryer than you are. In my snap judgment, that is."

"Your effrontery is breathtaking."

"I never heard anyone say *effrontery* before."

"And this is the first time I ever said it. It seemed to call for a fresh word, one I hadn't worn out yet." She put a palm on one cheek, as though she'd been slapped, and moved it in a little circle. "And you? What about you?"

"On balance," I said, "I'm dry."

"Is there anyone we've both met who's wet?"

"Louie."

"Yeah," she said, pulling her knees up and settling in. "He's a sweet little man."

"And I'm not."

"No." She stuck out her feet, one after the other, and kicked off her shoes. Then she sighed. "No one would mistake you for a sweet little man."

"Well, good. I need to ask you some questions."

"Just hold on." She brought her wrist up, a couple of inches from her eyes so she could read her watch in the gloom. "It's five forty-three. Where the hell have *you* been?"

"I did a bunch of stuff. Wasn't that the formula?"

"That's okay for girls. We hold men to a higher standard."

"All right. Earlier in the evening, I was kidnapped and taken to the house of an old-time gangster who told me I was on the wrong road if I wanted to reach old age. I met a movie star on the way out. Then I broke into a house."

The look I got was rich in doubt. "Where's the swag?"

"Here." I pulled Vinnie's hundreds out of my pocket.

"Oh, fooey. That's just pocket money."

"Maybe, but until three or four hours ago, it was in somebody else's pocket."

"Kidnapped?" she said, catching up. "Old-time gangster? Which movie star?"

"Later. How the hell did you find this place?"

"Oh," she said. "Gosh, there's not much trust between us, is—"

"Nope," I said. "There isn't. I never told you where I was—"

"You left me in the car. When you went into that house? And I didn't have anything to do, so I—"

"You *searched* my—"

"And there it was, right on top of everything in the glove compartment, with little silvery sprinkles on it, a receipt for a week at the North Pole. Room number and everything."

"I can't believe you searched my car."

"Well, I can't believe you hired someone to follow me."

We looked at each other through the gloom. Then Ronnie said, "I win."

"Okay, here's your prize. You get to tell me everything you know, or think you know, about what Derek was doing."

"Derek," she said. "We're alone, in your room at the crack of dawn, and you want to talk about Derek."

"You told me about a couple of things he was working on. He'd just finished blackmailing Thad Pierce. He *had* finished, hadn't he?"

"So he said. And he never went back, remember?"

"Great. There's actually one person in the world I can rule out. Then there was Ms. Lopez."

"That was nothing," she said. "He was going to drop it. I just told you about it because you asked me to list everything."

"The Little Elvises."

"Yeah, although why anyone would be interested in—" She broke off and picked up a pillow, put it in her lap, and wrapped her arms around it. "'Judge Crater,' he said. Something about somebody named Judge Crater."

"Relative to the Little Elvises?"

She patted the bed, a prompt for me to come sit with her, and when I didn't, she shook her head and said, "Sure. That's what we're talking about, isn't it?"

"Why didn't you mention it before?"

"I didn't remember it. I'm surprised I remember it now. I don't even know who Judge Crater is."

"He's famous for being missing," I said. "Sometime in the thirties, I think, he left a restaurant in New York, got into a taxi, and disappeared without a trace. Nobody ever saw him again."

She gave the pillow a squeeze. "Who cares?"

I ransacked my mind for the name of the Little Elvis who disappeared, according to Vinnie in the YouTube interview, and came up with it. "Did he ever mention anyone named Bobby Angel?" I made a guess. "Or maybe Angeli? Angelico?"

"No. There was an Italian name, though. Vincent something."

"Any others? Think about it for a minute."

"I have thought about it. I talked to the cops, remember?"

"No other Italian names."

"This is a boring conversation."

"What about Giorgio?"

She spread her hands, palms up. "What about Leonardo? Michelangelo? Botticelli? Sophia Loren? Ferragamo? He didn't mention any of them, either. There are millions of Italian names he didn't mention. We could list them all day."

"Okay, okay. What was the Nessie thing? You said he was working on something about the Loch Ness Monster."

She shook her head. "The fact that Derek *said* he was doing something didn't necessarily mean he was actually doing it. Loch Ness is in Scotland, last I heard, and Derek hadn't been out of the States in three or four years. So how could he get a picture of Nessie?"

"He said he had a picture?"

"I just said that. If we *have* to have this conversation," she said, "it would be nice if we could avoid going over things twice."

"Did he seem particularly excited about the Little Elvises? About Nessie?"

"He was *British*, Junior. His idea of being excited was to open his eyes all the way." She put the pillow against the wall and lay on her side, one elbow bent and her head propped on her hand. "I'd say he smelled money. He talked about Nessie and the Little Elvises when he was loaded. When he was coking, money was pretty much the only thing he thought about."

"How much of this did you tell the cops?"

"All of it, except for Judge Crater. They weren't real interested, though. Asked me a few questions, like where I was when he was getting killed and who I thought might have killed him if it wasn't me. They poked around in the apartment for a while—without finding his stash, so how thorough was that?—and then went down and searched his car. Did a little of the *sorry to trouble you ma'am* thing and went away."

"Why weren't they interested? Cops usually get juiced about murder."

"Old Derek did some real reporting from time to time. Two of the stories he broke made the LAPD look bad. Shooting people who were handcuffed, stealing drugs from dealers and selling them, stuff like that. And then there was a sort of jurisdiction jibberjabber, between the cops from Hollywood who found the body and some fat cop who arrived from the Valley who. . . . Oh," she said, lifting her head off her palm. "The same name, huh? Vincent's last name, DiGaudio."

"Vinnie's nephew," I said. "Paulie." Something about what she had just said was bothering me but I couldn't put my finger on it. "Did they find his notebook? His camera?"

"I don't know." Her tone made it clear that the subject was closed. She rolled over and lay on her back. "I am so *stiff*. I was folded like a jackknife outside your door all night long, and you come home and interrogate me. Not a hug, not a kiss. I'm not even sure you said hello."

"I didn't. You were doing your Little Match Girl act, pretending to be unconscious."

"I *was* unconscious until you started fumbling around with me. Your landlady pours a big glass of rum."

"So you didn't see the cops with Derek's notebook or camera. He did use a notebook, right?"

"Aaarggghhh," she said. "Sure. A cheap little one with a metal spiral up one side. But he kept it in the car."

"Did you go down with them when they searched the car?"

"They made me. They wanted me to unlock it and then stand there while they looked through it. And, no, I didn't see the notebook or the camera. Maybe Derek had them on him."

"Not when he was found."

She slowly closed her eyes. "Maybe aliens snatched them. Maybe whoever killed him took them."

"And maybe they think you have them."

Her eyes opened again. "Gee. That's a nice thought."

I said, "That's why I had you followed."

"Not because you figured, it's always the spouse?"

"Of course not." I managed a tinge of injured irritation.

"Well, that's sweet," she said. "I take back all the things I've been calling you mentally for the last ten minutes or so."

"Bad things?"

She stretched her arms way above her, hands clasped into fists, and arched her back. Then she yawned. Around the yawn, she said. "Mostly. I have a problem with ambivalence."

"Ambivalence is a sign of intelligence."

"No, it's a sign that I only like guys who aren't good for me. Listen, you've been up all night and I've been sort of up all night, and we're both adults and we like each other, and there's this big bed in this terrible room, the only thing that doesn't look like Santa threw it away. Why don't you come over here and we'll get some rest. Or something."

I untied my sneakers. "Or something? Do I get a vote?"

"No. Just kick those things across the room and come here. Come on. You've been good once."

I went over there, and, sure enough, I didn't get a vote.

Forty-five minutes later, Ronnie was curled against me, the new light through the window making the gold hair gleam. Her skin was as warm as sunshine, and I was drifting toward sleep, despite a little tug of uneasiness about the conversation I was going to have to have with Rina.

"Final answer," Ronnie said without opening her eyes. "And you have to tell the truth now. One hundred percent level, understand?"

"Got it," I said. "You have my solemn word."

"You had me followed why?"

I leaned down and kissed her ear, making a mental note to ask Paulie DiGaudio where she'd told the cops she'd been the night Derek was killed. "I was worried about you," I said.

## 19
### How Few Tricks They Know

I was diving into clear blue water, arrowing down toward some shifting transparent green form, like a shapeless jellyfish but with light inside it, when Sam Cooke started to sing "A Change Is Gonna Come." I surfaced through the warm blue to the reality of the North Pole in the early afternoon, chilly light through the window, Ronnie Bigelow out cold with the blankets tugged down to her waist to display a shadowy gully of spine, and my cell phone blinking on the table where I'd left it.

I argued with myself while Sam went on about how he'd been running ever since, and lost the argument. I tossed the blankets, pulled myself up, and let Sam Cooke's voice guide my hand to the phone.

"Yeah," I croaked. I sounded like the last verse of "Old Man River."

"Your friend with the daughter," Paulie DiGaudio said. "She didn't call me."

"Um . . . what time is it?"

"Damn," DiGaudio said. "You're supposed to be working for Vinnie and you're asleep at this hour?"

"I was up all night."

"Breaking into some house, probably."

"Working on the thing with Vinnie."

"Yeah, well, get your friend into the station. Mr. Pivensey is now a person of interest."

I said, "Oh, shit," and sat on the edge of the bed. Ronnie mumbled something and threw out one arm. I looked at the curl of her fingers. "What happened?"

"We got *some* good cops," DiGaudio said. "They're not all like the clown who wrote up the report on Derek Bigelow. Yesterday up near Twentynine Palms, a Highway Patrolman saw a dog trot across the road with a bone in its mouth, and thought, that looks like a humerus from a human being. Humerus," he said thoughtfully. "Home of the funny bone—think that's a coincidence?"

I said, "Who gives a damn?" My stomach was cramping even though I knew we couldn't be talking about Doris; no way she'd be skeletal in nine days.

"Nobody, probably. Anyway, our cop stops the car but he can't catch the mutt, so he backtracks instead, follows a nice fresh set of prints in the sand, and about a quarter of a mile from the road he comes across some bones on the surface and a couple more sticking up out of a shallow hole, maybe two, three feet deep. Little bits of clothing around. The bones are pretty much scattered except for the wrists, which are still together, you want to ask me why?"

"Why?" I asked, knowing the answer.

"Because of the handcuffs. Anyway, it's a female Caucasian, our missing waitress. Same age, same height, they found a ring matches one the waitress wore, same break in the same place on the left leg, sounds like the same dental work in the remaining teeth. I think your friend with the missing daughter should come in."

"I'll talk to her. For all I know, her daughter's home by now."

"Then I want to talk to the daughter. She might be the last person who saw him."

"I'll give her a call."

"*Now*," DiGaudio said, with some snap to it. "We went to that house you asked us about, and you know what we found in the garage? A box of handcuffs, that's what. A bag of bloody clothes. I want to talk to your friend *and* her daughter now. I want a name and number before I get to five. One . . . two. . . ."

"You're breaking up on me," I said, and hung up. Within ten seconds, Sam started singing again. I turned off the phone and looked over at Ronnie, who had two pillows plumped under her chin and was regarding me with annoying clarity.

"Cops again?"

"Yes." I got up and grabbed my shirt. "Get dressed. You can shower first, if you want. I need to go down and talk to Marge."

"I'll skip the shower and go across the street and get you some coffee. Marge is behind the office, right?"

"Right. One and two, the only rooms with numbers on them."

"You're cute without pants."

"That's what everybody says."

She said, "Ouch. So how do you like it?"

I shrugged. "Pretty much the way you did it."

"I meant the coffee." She pulled the blankets up to her chin, shy by daylight, looking for her clothes. "Oh, right," she said. "I should have remembered. You take it black. Men always like it when women remember how they take their coffee."

"Men," I said. "We're so easy."

**"Nothing's changed," Marge** said. Her face was rigid with the effort it took not to let it cave in. "It's some bones in the desert, somebody's poor baby. But it's not Doris. We knew yesterday what kind of guy he was."

"I think you should go to the station."

"I know what you think. Want a drink?"

"What time is it?"

"Little after one."

"Early for me, but thanks."

"Sit tight," she said, getting up. She'd been on the couch and I'd taken the chair. "It was early for me, too, until a minute ago." She padded into the tiny kitchen and opened a cupboard to reveal a large water glass and six or seven bottles of Old Igor's. There was a knock at the door.

"I'll get it," I said.

"If anyone does, it'll be you." She pulled down a fresh bottle and waved it at me. "Sure about this?"

"Thanks anyway." I opened the door and Ronnie blew at me across the rim of an open cup of coffee. Just the smell made me feel better.

"You're a queen," I said. "Want to join Marge in a glass of vodka?"

"Sure, if there's room. Hi, Marge."

"Sweetie," Marge said, opening another cupboard and pulling out a second glass. "Heavy or light?"

"Same as you," Ronnie said, coming in and looking around the room. "Gee. No Christmas junk."

I swallowed hot coffee and said, "Decor. Down here, it's referred to as decor."

"It's junk," Marge said, pouring. "But Ed, old Ed really loved Christmas." She picked up the glasses and toted them into the living room. "Biggest day of the year for Ed was December 26. All the Christmas stuff went to half off, and he shopped all day long." As she handed a glass to Ronnie, she tipped the other to her mouth and knocked back a couple of good slugs. "If I got rid of it all now, it'd be like crumpling up Ed's memory and tossing it away."

"It's *cheerful* junk," Ronnie said, and then drank. She sat at the far end of the couch. "You know, we forget about the Christmas spirit most of the year, and seeing all that stuff reminds us—"

"You're a sweet little thing," Marge said, "but not much of a liar. Here's to a better tomorrow."

"No kidding," Ronnie said, and the two of them drank.

"What's your problem?" Marge asked her.

"Same old thing." She lifted her chin in my direction. "Men."

"Ahhh, *men*." Marge brought down an open palm, batting the topic to the floor. "I used to think that when I got older, I'd stop letting them upset me. But here I am, I'm older, and all I've learned is how few tricks they know. It's like having a dog. When you finally get through to it, you teach it to roll over and sit up, and you think *smart dog*, and then it's ten years old and it's still sitting up and rolling over, and you're thinking, *Why the hell can't it learn Spanish?* The big difference is that as you get older, you stop being pissed off about it and get bored instead."

"Speaking of men," I said.

She drank, and when she lowered the glass, her mouth was tight. "I don't want to talk to the cops."

"You're not listening," I said. "Pivensey's killed one. They found the—"

"Who?" Marge asked.

"Pivensey. Lorne—"

"That wasn't his name. You never said that name."

I tried to remember our last conversation. "I don't think I said any name. I just showed you his picture."

"Lemme see it again."

I was already fishing the folded printouts from my hip pocket. I glanced at them before I handed them to her. Sure enough, Paulie DiGaudio had cropped out the name and arrest number.

"That's the little pecker," she said. "No matter what he calls himself."

"Pivensey," I said. "Lorne Henry Pivensey."

"Lemuel Huff," she said. "No middle name, but I suppose Lemuel's more name than anybody needs."

"Can I see?" Ronnie held out a hand, and Marge passed her the pictures.

"There wasn't any a/k/a info on his sheet," I said.

"I don't give a shit," Marge said and glanced at Ronnie. "Sorry, honey, 'scuse the *Française.*" She came back to me. "He was Lemuel Huff to Doris, Lem for short, if you can believe that. Sounds like the guy you call to move the outhouse."

"Spelled like it sounds? H-U-F-F? Or H-O-U-G-H?"

"Who knows?"

"Marge, they're not going to leave me alone on this."

"He's got something," Ronnie said. She was studying the pictures.

"Who's not going to leave you alone?" Marge asked.

"The cops." I turned to Ronnie. "What do you mean, he's got something?"

Still looking down at Pivensey's picture, Ronnie stuck out her lower lip and shook her head. "In his face. There's something kind of sad and lost. I can see what some women would see in him."

"What could they possibly see?" This was Marge. "A wood shop project? Like a broken chair?"

"Your daughter," Ronnie said. "Was there any reason she'd be vulnerable to men who get, I don't know, damaged or something?"

"Oh, honey," Marge said, and suddenly tears were rolling down her cheeks. "Would she ever."

"Well," Ronnie said. "This is the guy who could bring that out."

"Oh, *balls*," Marge said, getting up so fast she almost knocked over the coffee table. She bolted into the bedroom and slammed the door behind her.

"What is it?" Ronnie asked.

"Cops found the bones of a woman who was probably killed by the guy who lived in that house. With Marge's daughter. *That* guy, the one you can see something in."

"Oh, no," Ronnie said. "Are they sure?"

Through the closed door, I heard Marge blow her nose, a sound like the honk of a waterfowl. "Yeah," I said. "And there are probably three or four more."

"I'm so embarrassed. Talking about my pishy little problems." She raised the glass and put an inch of vodka away. "Maybe I should just stay here and get drunk with her."

"In the name of charity."

"Well, sure. What are you going to do?"

"Marge was supposed to have pulled together a list of people who Doris might have talked to. If she's done it, I suppose I'll go find them. And think about poor sad Mr. Huff."

## 20
### What They Get Is an Anchor

"Kind of job is that?" Louie demanded around his cigar. "For a man of my skills, I mean."

"Then get somebody else to do it. Somebody who looks like a straight, who can use, say, twenty-five bucks an hour."

Louie tilted his head back and blew a cumulus cloud of stink that filled his car, which today was a 1995 Cadillac the color of an angry eggplant. We were parked on Sunshine Terrace in Sherman Oaks, just south of Ventura. After he'd emptied his lungs and taken a moment to appreciate the results, watching the smoke curlicue against the inside of the windshield like a Japanese painting of the ocean, he said, "Say thirty. Including travel time?"

"Sure." I pushed the button to lower my window, but the ignition was off, so I cracked the door. "It's a two, three-hour drive each way."

"I know who." Louie nodded in self-approval. "The girl your chick shook off. She looks like a librarian. Put her in glasses and one of those long skirts, she's Jane Plain."

"Fine. Think she can get up there and back without getting lost?"

"You want to be funny," Louie said, "hire a writer." He drew on the cigar.

"If you say she can do it, fine." I reached into my pocket and pulled out five of the hundreds I'd stolen from Vinnie DiGaudio. "She can take this up front and keep track of her hours."

"And she's looking for. . . ."

"Property transactions in Los Angeles and San Bernardino County. Anything that was bought by Lorne Henry Pivensey or Lemuel Huff." I gave him the alternative spellings. "And after that, parking and traffic citations in the same names."

"You don't think the cops'll do this?"

"They might or might not. But I don't think they'll do it for Huff. They don't know he used the name."

Louie nodded. "How far back?"

"Five years. Six, make it six."

"This is gonna take days."

"Good, she can get rich. Anyway it's all on computers now." I reached back into my pocket and handed him the other seven hundred. "Tell you what. She can slip one or two of these to the underpaid civil servants who'll be helping her. That'll speed things up. If she needs more, you can front it out of your ridiculously large share of the five thousand Vinnie gave me."

Louie tilted the cigar up at an optimistic angle and grinned around it. "Finally counted, huh?"

"You have no conscience."

"You're so wrong. I haven't slept a wink. What do you think you're going to get out of this?"

"The guy must have a place to go to ground. If he's really a serial, he might own a place where he plays with the victims before he puts them away. The woman the cops found was in Twentynine Palms, which is San Bernardino County. There's lots of nice, empty land up there. In fact, now that I think about it, she should start with San Berdoo and save LA for later."

"Makes sense, I suppose."

"Thanks for the enthusiasm."

Louie opened his own door and dropped the cigar on the street. It hissed in the trickle of water running along the curb. "What else you need? I figure you got about six hundred left on my meter."

"I talked to Irwin Dressler last night."

Louie's mouth dropped open. "You're shitting me."

"I was escorted there at gunpoint."

He nodded in grudging appreciation. "Irwin Dressler, huh? How'd he look?"

"Old and dangerous."

"What'd he need, a fourth at bridge?"

"He wanted to know about Vinnie DiGaudio." I gave him a summary of the chat.

"Junior," Louie said, "this ain't good."

"I'd worked that out for myself, actually. But why do you say it?"

"'Cause there's gotta be some sort of connection between Irwin and Vinnie, and Irwin, he wants to clean things up, cut the strings."

"And I'd be one of the strings," I said.

"Irwin is living a happy old age, all tucked away in Brentwood like that, wearing those ugly pants. He wants to stay invisible. That's what they used to call him, you know that? The invisible man."

"You made that up."

"Uh-uh," he said. "Irwin's never had a glove laid on him, you know? Stole like a billion dollars, set up hits, run the fuckin' state like his personal piggy bank, and nobody's ever made him. What a guy."

"What do you think I should do?"

Louie shifted his *tuchis* around so he was facing me. "Me? You're asking me?"

"Why not?"

"No reason. I'm just flattered. Nobody ever asked me what to do about Irwin Dressler before. It's like you just found out you got cancer and you say to me, 'Louie, what should I do?' and all of a sudden I feel like a doctor. Here's what you should do. Whatever he told you to do, plus a little more in the same direction. Listening around the words he said, sounds to me like he doesn't want it to be Vinnie."

"Pretty much what I thought."

"So," he said, fishing for another cigar. "No conflict of interest, huh? Paulie doesn't want it to be Vinnie, Irwin doesn't want it to be Vinnie. So, no problem."

I opened the door. "Unless it's Vinnie," I said.

"Yeah," Louie said, going to work on the cigar tip. "Then you're fucked."

**"I need four** names and addresses to go with some license plates," I said into the phone.

"And I need your friend and her daughter in here, now." The cooling-off period hadn't cooled Paulie DiGaudio off any.

"I can't give them to you. They don't want to talk to you."

"You're not listening. Those people come in here, or you do."

"Charged with what? Refusing to make an introduction? Losing my phone book?"

"How about obstruction of justice?"

"Sounds good. You want me to come in and give myself up? I'm sure you can find somebody else to work on Vinnie's problem. But I'll tell you that you'd better find somebody good, because he looks ripe for it."

Paulie put something crunchy in his mouth and chewed on it, and I held the phone away from my ear. "I could look like gold," he finally said. He was trying for wistful. "You bring these people in and we find Pivensey, I could look like gold."

"Make a deal with you. I'll do whatever I can to talk the mom into coming in—"

"You mean the kid's still missing?"

"That's what I mean. And all mom knows is that her daughter was living with him at that address in Hollywood. She's been gone nine days."

"And they left together," he said. So the cops had talked to the All-Seeing Eye across the street, too.

"Looks like it."

"What was her name?"

"The mother or the daughter?"

"Either."

"Neither," I said. "And be careful with your tenses. Far as we know, she's alive and eating three squares a day."

Paulie said, "And they're gonna put George W. Bush on Mount Rushmore."

"The license plates, remember?" With my free hand I unfolded the list of numbers Ronnie had copied off the junkers parked in Vinnie's driveway.

"What for?" DiGaudio said. He sounded like his feelings were hurt. "I mean, why do I want to do this for you?"

"I think one or more of the folks who own those cars might be Vinnie's alibi."

**While I talked** with DiGaudio I'd been sitting on the fender of my car, where it had been parked behind Louie's, up on Sunshine Terrace. Sunshine Terrace is rich in eucalyptus trees, and the November clouds had parted enough to allow a drizzle of diluted afternoon sunlight to turn the leaves five or six shades of green and tan, while a light breeze kicked up mysteriously and jittered them around in a picturesque fashion. The people who live south of the Boulevard can afford breezes.

Marge's list of people to talk to about the missing Doris was handwritten in purple ink on a notepad that had MARGE'S JOTTINGS printed across the top and was undoubtedly purchased for more lighthearted jottings. She had a child's big, careful handwriting, the vowels round and fat, with little circles hovering like halos over each lowercase I. She'd drawn precise five-pointed stars beside the names of the folks she thought Doris was most likely to have confided in.

The closest one with a star was an Amber Schlumberg in Burbank. The closest of my Glocks was also in Burbank. I pulled out a quarter and flipped it. When I took my hand away, I was looking at a bird, and for a disorienting minute, I had no idea whether that meant heads or tails. Then I couldn't remember whether the Glock had been heads and Amber had been tails, or vice versa.

I figured, the hell with it. Get the gun.

A little burglar boy has no better friends than his storage units. Scattered among them, my three contained guns, ammo, about twenty thousand in small bills, the *ne plus ultra* in illegal lock-picking technology, some hot jewelry being allowed to cool gradually, and two alternative realities in the form of forged documents: drivers license, Social Security cards, birth certificates, all bearing the names of males who would have been my age if they hadn't died in infancy. One of them even had a passport. They weren't as good as the set at the Wedgwood, but they'd do for short-time use.

Like all storage facilities, the one in Burbank smelled like people used it primarily to store dust. Within a minute of keying the three keyable locks and spinning the combination dial on the fourth, I'd sneezed twice and I had a nice, cold, slightly oily automatic jammed into the front of my pants and a couple thousand in twenties in my pockets. I grabbed two extra clips to give my pants that desirable *cholo* sag and relocked everything, then headed for Lankershim and followed it past the time-honored Warner Brothers lot, haunted even now by the shades of Bogey and Cagney and Bette Davis, Paul Muni and the Bowery Boys. Other studios were classier or more elegant or made flossier musicals, but Warner was the toughest and the grittiest. Crooks with taste like Warner Brothers best.

Amber Schlumberg lived in a little fifties stucco box crouched behind an ancient pepper tree that had killed the lawn, just burned it right down to the dark brown Valley dirt. A red tricycle, just like one I once bought for Rina, rusted in a far corner, looking like it hadn't been moved in a year or more. At some none-too-recent point, someone had started to put up shingles, trying to make the place look like a charming rural cottage. The shingles covered the front third of the house but gave out about four feet from the eaves. It looked like an eye-patch. Around and below the shingles, which had turned a dark woody brown with exposure, the stucco was the yuck-yellow of Dijon mustard.

The front door was yanked open before I could knock, and a woman, dimly visible through the dirty mesh of a screen, demanded, "What now?"

I said, "Always a good question." The air coming from inside the house smelled stale.

The woman's face came closer to the screen, a relatively nice face marred by an extremely unpleasant expression. "Who the hell are you?"

"I'm a friend of Doris Enderby's."

"Yeah?" Something guarded came into her face, and she reached up and wiggled something around inside the door. I heard the hook slip through the little eye that holds it in place. "How come I don't know you?"

"Karma? Kismet? The fact that almost eight million people live in Los Angeles?"

A tiny but decisive shake of the head. "I know Doris's friends."

"Well, I lied to you. I'm actually a friend of Doris's mother, Marge. Marge is worried about Doris, and she's asked me to talk to people, see if I can get some kind of fix on what's happening with her."

A beat, while she seemed to try to figure out what to say, as though there were a lot of possibilities. Then she licked her lips. "Worried why?"

"Either you know or you don't. If you don't, I can leave now."

She started the shake again but broke it off with her head angled away from me. Regarding me from the corner of her eye, she said, "You're not a cop."

"If you're Doris's friend, you know Marge wouldn't send a cop after Doris."

She looked at me long enough to take my pulse, her head still turned partly away as though she might decide to call over her shoulder for help. "I'll phone Marge."

"By all means."

Her mouth twisted to the right, and she chewed on the inside of her lip. Then she said, "Forget it. Ask your questions. But no coming in."

"Fine," I said. "I'll sit here." And I sank cross-legged onto her welcome mat.

She said, "Oh, for Christ's sake," and popped the lock.

**A big grandfather** clock beat time in the living room, one of the tall ones in dark wood with the brass pendulum, ticking loudly enough for us to hear it in the kitchen, or the kitchenette, or whatever you'd call it. The kitchen was almost as small as Marge's and much messier. Other than Amber's voice, the clock made the only sound in the house.

"Maybe two weeks ago, maybe a little more," Amber said. Across the kitchen behind her, the window over the sink offered a view of a dead-brown backyard. "Doris was—well, she wasn't happy. It was getting kind of old with Lem, although you'd think someone named Lem would remain ever fresh, wouldn't you? First time she told me about him, I said, 'What is he, Dodo? A leftover from *Deadwood*?' So after that I didn't hear from her for a while, you know how women are sometimes. If the old girlfriend doesn't like the new boyfriend, guess which one gets the ax?" She picked up a cup of herbal tea and blew on it, surrounding me in a cloud of cinnamon and mint. The phrase *fields of asphodel* ran through my mind, barefoot and trailing pastel gauze, even though I had no idea what asphodel was.

I said, "And?"

She chewed the inside of the lip again. "Yeah, right, old story. So we didn't see each other for a while. She felt sorry for him. He was such a sad little man. She said he reminded her of her father. You know about her father?"

"Yeah. Marge and I have had long talks."

"I'll bet they were long," Amber said. She leaned back in her chair, which was too banged up to be retro. It was just old— bent chrome, patched with rust in spots, with heavily taped plastic cushions that had hosted fannies since the fifties. I was in a matching number, facing her across a veneer breakfast table that looked like it was used for everything girly; it was littered with dirty, lip-printed cups, napkins that had been used to blot lipstick of many colors, a makeup mirror with a snowdrift of face powder, a day-book open to an empty week, a pencil diagonally optimistic across the page. At the edge of the table against the wall was a chipped ceramic mug filled with pens, and a hinged picture frame, open wide and facedown. Amber followed my glance to the frame, looked up to me, and said, "That Marge could talk the paint off the walls. That was one of the reasons Doris wanted to get out."

"Marge is lonely," I said. "Her husband's dead, and everybody she meets stays one night and leaves."

"Well, that's pitiful and all, but Doris got decades of it. Talk and vodka, vodka and talk. So when Lem appeared and needed so much *work*, Doris was gone like a shot."

"But then she called you—what?—a couple of weeks ago?"

Her eyes slipped from my face. "Something like that." She sipped the tea. Her hair was streaked unevenly, and the roots were dark and looked oily. The light through the kitchen window made sharp furrows out of the creases on either side of her mouth, the fan of crinkles at the corner of her eyes. The powder on her face was splotchy. Her T-shirt needed washing and her nails were not so much bitten as gnawed. We'd walked a path through a dusty living room to get here, and the house felt like most of its rooms had been unused for a long time.

It came to me with some force that she'd been abandoned. And although my departure from the house I'd shared with Kathy had been a mutual decision, it was impossible for me to look at Amber and not see Kathy.

I vaporized the image and said, "And she said she wanted to leave him."

She blew a wisp of hair from her face, and it promptly fell back. "Didn't take it that far. Said he was weirder than she thought. Said the house was getting way small and he was like everywhere in it all the time."

"Did she elaborate?"

"No. She's the opposite of her mom that way. Doesn't talk much. Just said he was—what's the thing about still waters?"

"They run deep." She sipped the tea again, her eyes on me, but there was no evidence of a penny dropping. "Still waters do," I said helpfully. "They run deep."

"Jesus, beat it to death, why don't you? I was just thinking that old Lem was about the stillest water I ever saw. Guy was practically a photograph. So what if they run deep? I mean, what's that supposed to mean?"

"Ummm, unexpected depths. Intelligence, some kind of hidden trait. It's generally a compliment."

"It wasn't when she said it. It was like the water was deep, deep, deep, and there might have been things swimming around way down there."

"In the dark," I said.

She made a little shiver, bringing her shoulders up practically to her ears. "We need a campfire," she said. "You could tell the one about The Hook."

"Mmmm."

She leaned toward me, her eyes tightening at the corners. "Where'd you go? What does *Mmmm* mean?"

"It means I don't know whether you're serious or not."

"Serious about what? Old Lem?"

"About being worried about Doris."

She looked down into the mug of tea and took hold of the string, pulled the teabag out, and then picked up a spoon. Said to the spoon, "I didn't actually say I was worried."

"Are you?"

She centered the bag on the spoon and then wrapped the string around the spoon and the bag a few times and pulled it to squeeze liquid out of the bag. "Naw," she said, watching the droplets fall into the mug. "She told me she was going away for a while. When we talked. Said she was going someplace, maybe to Vegas or like that, you know, someplace where she could have some fun."

I inhaled the mint and cinnamon. "So as far as you're concerned, there's nothing to worry about."

She gave the spoon a final shake and then painstakingly unwrapped the string. Then she got up and went to the stove to pour more water into the cup. Without looking back, she said, "Nothing. She'll be fine."

Keeping an eye on her, I picked up the hinged picture frame. The left-hand photo was a pleasant-looking guy with a low hairline and a square jaw. The one on the right was the same guy and Amber, and between them was a boy of three or four with a shadow of his father's square jaw. They all looked happy.

I put it down and pulled my hand away. "And that's how you felt after the conversation a couple of weeks ago, that Doris would be fine."

She turned to me and lifted the cup to her lips but kept her eyes on the floor, as though just noticing how badly it needed a mop. "Sure. Back then."

"She told you all of that then, about Vegas and so forth. You haven't talked to her since."

"No," she said. She grabbed a big breath and blew it out, then slid her slippered foot over the floor experimentally, back and forth. "Only that once."

"Well, thanks," I said. "You've been a big help." I got up and smiled goodbye and went through the dusty living room, with no sign of a child in it, and out across the dead yard and past the abandoned tricycle to my car. I sat there for a few minutes, exploring a tangle of emotions that included pity for Amber Schlumberg and a certain amount of guilt about Kathy, about my not having been able to work things out with Kathy. Something my mother had once said to me suddenly took on fresh meaning. *Women fall in love with a man thinking they're getting a ship that will take them somewhere,* she'd said, *but most of the time what they get is the anchor, and it drags them down.*

I caught myself sighing in imitation of Amber Schlumberg and banished the regret so I could try to figure out why she had lied to me.

Doris's second friend wasn't home. Her third was, but she didn't want to talk at all. The moment I said Doris's name, she said, "Oh," and brought the tips of her fingers to her mouth. Then she said, "Oh," again and closed the door in my face. The owner of the fourth starred name, the euphonious Melissa Simmons, lived over the hill, which is the term people in the Valley use to refer to the Los Angeles basin proper, and that people in the Los Angeles basin proper use to refer to the Valley. Either way, *over the hill* means a long, boring, bumper-to-bumper drive in a rich atmosphere of carbon monoxide at rush hour, which was what it now was.

I was toodling aimlessly north on Ventura through the darkening day, headed vaguely for Tarzana, when Paulie DiGaudio called with the info to go with the license plates from Vinnie's driveway. I pulled over to write it down. "Any of these guys got anything to shake Vinnie loose, you'll let me know, right?"

"Why wouldn't I? I've had more fun in Burglars Anonymous meetings."

"They really do that, you know," DiGaudio said. "In the joint. *Hi, I'm Junior and I'm a burglar.*"

"Thanks for the info," I said, folding the pad.

"Call me if you learn anything. And *get moving*. Sooner or

later, Vinnie's gonna get arrested. Right now, the DA's not sure they can make the case, but every day there's a little more pressure, know what I mean?"

"I'm on it," I said and powered off. I'd always wanted to say *I'm on it*, and now I had. I didn't feel much different. I checked the nearest address and pulled into traffic. If I were to keep drifting toward Tarzana, one of the guys who'd been parked at Vinnie's was just about half a mile out of the way, a few long blocks north of the Boulevard, off of Woodman. I checked the guy's house number to make sure, then looked at the name. I looked at it again, but it hadn't changed. Ace Rabinowitz. I thought about calling old Ace and then figured he'd either be there or he wouldn't, and I was going that way anyway.

Going, I now permitted myself to acknowledge, to check in on Kathy and Rina.

Amber Schlumberg was not Kathy. Kathy wasn't adrift and abandoned. Wherever Mr. Square Jaw had gone, he'd taken the kid with him, while Kathy still had Rina. For that matter, Kathy still had *me*, if she actually wanted me. Which, with Bill on the scene, didn't look likely. So Kathy also had good old Bill. Who laughed at the funny papers at the breakfast table early in the morning, sitting across from my daughter. Who was involved, or getting involved, with Tyrone. Who was so black it was as though he'd been set intentionally in front of me, a ring of fire through which I had to pass unburned in order to continue being the person I'd always thought I was instead of the boring middle-class bigot I seemed to have become.

All of this had happened in my absence. My self-imposed absence.

My mother notwithstanding, I hadn't been a ship for Kathy, or if I had been, I'd abandoned the helm. Or maybe that was exactly the wrong way to look at it. Maybe it had been Kathy's

ship all along, and she was steering it exactly where she wanted
to go. Maybe I was just ballast, no longer needed now that Rina
was aboard, just dead weight to be tossed over the side.

Or maybe, just *maybe*, the whole fucking world wasn't
about me.

I was so busy trying to keep my head above the dark and
bottomless pool of myself that I almost missed Woodman. I
angled sharply across the right lane, deeply satisfying someone
who'd been wanting all day to plant both elbows on his horn.
Ace lived on Burbank Boulevard, a street with so little character
it might as well have been a dry gulch, in one of several hundred
rectangular, two-story apartment houses set too close to the street.

I've always thought that one- and two-digit addresses have an
aristocratic *you don't live here* quality, while five-digit addresses
sound like shorthand for *trailer park with large dogs*. Ace Rabinowitz lived squarely in five-digit territory, at 12478 Burbank Boulevard, a two-story building designed by someone to whom the
French Quarter in New Orleans had once been described, badly.
Apartment five was on the second floor facing the street, with double doors opening onto a balcony so shallow the edge of the door
would have hit the railing before it was completely open. The day
was far enough gone that lights were on here and there, and as I
stood there, looking up, one snapped on behind Ace's windows.

I felt elephant-heavy going up the stairs. Maybe it was lack of
sleep, or maybe it was all the psychic weight from the chains of
shattered relationships I was dragging around. Whatever it was,
it made me want to fix my entire life somehow, to clear away
all the fragments and false starts and buried bones and broken
hearts, and start to redig the foundations, laying them true and
straight and deep.

It sounded like a lot of work. As an alternative, I pressed Ace
Rabinowitz's doorbell.

And was surprised to recognize the guitar riff from "Blue Tubes," a surf instrumental from the late 1960s that introduced me to the glory of the French horn when I first heard it in about 1985. I fell in love with the horn's sound and, because of it, the record, although it was just another attempt to cash in on the Beach Boys.

"Yeah, yeah, yeah," I heard from inside. It was a high, reedy voice, a kind of vocal clarinet, and it sounded harried. "Just stand there. Shift your weight from foot to foot. Sing 'A Hundred Bottles of Beer on the Wall.' Imagine a couple dozen doughnuts and fill in the holes. Be there in a minute."

Instead, I tried the knob and it turned. I opened it a couple of feet and watched a scrawny little guy with sparse gray hair hanging to his shoulders scurry around an over-furnished living room shoving evidence out of sight: mirrors with razor blades and straight white arctic lines of cocaine, decks of rolling papers, Ziploc bags bulging with marijuana, a brown golf ball that could have been opium. The little man was barefoot, dressed in faded jeans and a blue work shirt that had battered sequins sewed across the shoulders. The room reeked of pot and patchouli.

"Relax," I said. "I'm not the cops."

He whirled on me, one hand wrapped around a hookah holding a pint of water that had turned the color of something a big-league pitcher might spit. He was hugging the bong to his chest as though he expected me to snatch it away from him. A quick step back, away from me, brought his foot into contact with one of the room's many, many guitars. It had been propped in front of a battered brown leather couch, and when he kicked it, the guitar described a lazy sideways arc toward the floor. For a millisecond I saw in his eyes a glimpse of what hell must be like as he tried to choose between the guitar and the hookah, the hookah and the guitar. He dropped the hookah and grabbed the guitar, and the hookah hit the hardwood floor and exploded in a malodorous splash.

"Awwwww, *shit*," he said. He picked up the guitar and laid it down on the sofa, pulling the nearer foot away from the spreading, reeking brown lake. "Man's home is his *castle*, dude. Where's your fucking manners at?"

"Hey, Ace," I said.

He parted the hair in front of his face with both hands and peered through it at me, or just past me. He seemed to be having some trouble coordinating his eyes. He opened his mouth wide and worked his lower jaw from side to side. For some reason, this activity centered him, and his eyes settled on mine. "Yeah? Yeah? We know each other? Am I supposed to remember you from someplace?" He looked down at the floor. "*Look* at this shit, man. This is *messed up*."

"Sorry. Where are your paper towels?"

"Kitchen, man. Wait, *wait*, I didn't invite you—"

"No problem," I said. "Through here, right?" I angled through the tiny dining area into the kitchen of someone who intended to live forever. Fresh vegetables were everywhere, piled highest in the vicinity of an enormous juicer that sat in the middle of a thick pool of green stickum. Eight or nine big glasses stood in a line on the counter, each coated with a residue of green, except for one that was lined in a viscous, arterial red that might have been a coating of beet juice. If it wasn't, I didn't want to speculate on it. I pulled the entire roll of paper towels from the holder next to the sink and carried it back into the living room.

"I mean, seriously, man," Ace said the moment I came into sight. He was in the same place I'd left him. "Am I like supposed to know you? Is it in your head that we're like buds or something? 'Cause I gotta tell you, there's no bells ringing in here, where I keep the old bells." He was tapping his temple. "And I don't forget, man. Once it's in here, it's in here for good."

"Aww, Ace," I said. "Can't believe you forgot. Here." I lobbed the roll of towels underhand at him, and he turned his head and watched them sail slowly past. He seemed to enjoy the sight. I said, "How's what's her name?"

He blinked heavily, trying to assemble the question in his mind as the brown liquid spread at his feet. He had the air of someone with a selective hearing impairment that removed all the important words from a conversation. After a couple of false starts, he said, "Fine, man, she's fine."

"Beautiful as ever?"

"She's not—I mean, she's never been all that beautiful."

"Sure," I said. "But as beautiful as she was, she's about that beautiful?"

"Just about," Ace said. He turned to look at the paper towels, which had landed on the couch, beside yet another guitar, this one a blistered old Martin steel-string. "Almost hit old Marty," Ace said.

"Sorry, Marty," I said.

"Marty says it's okay," Ace said, apparently seriously. He turned back to me and his eyes slid past, braked, and came back as he tried to snap his fingers. "You're—I mean, you're—your name's not Freddie, is it?"

"Ace," I said. "You're amazing."

"I'm telling you," he said, tapping his temple again, "once it's in here, it's *in here*. Know what I mean?"

"It's in there," I said.

"*Way* in," Ace said. "So, ahhh, what brings you here?"

"Came to help you clean that up." I went past him and got the paper towels, pulled off a couple of yards' worth, folded them over, and dropped them onto the pool, then repeated the procedure until the floor was littered with sopping brown paper towels. Ace watched me with the concentrated attention of someone who hadn't seen motion in days.

"Cool," he said. "Don't cut yourself."

"Careful is my middle name."

"Really?" He nodded a couple of times. "Far out."

"Jesus," I said. "The water smells like it got a lot of use."

"Shame you can't smoke water," Ace said. "I tried a couple times, you know? Soaked tobacco in it, let it dry out, rolled it up, and made fire. Coughed so hard my ears fell off." He sat on the couch and picked up the Martin. He hit the strings once, then again, and then he struck a chord, and I glanced up at him as he sat there, head bent over the guitar, hair hanging in his face, and the chord turned into a chord progression, and his right foot began to tap, and as far as he was concerned I was no longer in the room.

I mounded the sopping towels, avoiding the glass, until I had a little sodden coffee-colored mountain, then wound a couple dozen towels around my right hand, wadded four or five into my left, and gathered up the whole mess. It dripped, but I got it into the kitchen. The big trash container was full, so I shoved the existing crap—mostly vegetable litter—down with my foot and then dropped the wet towels and glass on top of it. I rinsed my hands at the sink, dried them on Ace's last three towels, and followed the music back into the living room.

Ace's right hand was a blur, and the left was tiptoeing up and down the neck, hitting the frets with unerring accuracy. I stood there and listened for a couple of impressed minutes, and then sat next to him on the couch.

"Whoaaa," Ace said, sliding away, his eyes as round as quarters. "Where'd you come—"

"It's Freddie, Ace. I was in the kitchen."

"Oh, yeah. Did you have some juice?"

"Great stuff. What were you playing?"

"Riff. Just, you know, whatever was happening to me right then." He used his right hand to tuck the hair behind his ears. "What do you think about Bad Incision?"

"Sorry?"

"Or Vacancy. How about Vacancy?"

"They're both swell."

"The flower power stuff is dead," he said. It seemed to be news. "You know, no more, uh, Daffodils and Moonbeams, or StarHawk."

"The Pollen Children," I contributed.

"Yeah, all that's over. Edgy, that's what they want now. Floater, Sealed Tomb, that kind of stuff."

"How about Phantom Limb?"

"Ohhhh, *man*," he said. "Can I have that?"

"All yours. You got the band already, or you just working on names?"

"We're tight," he said. "Session guys, tight. Phantom Fucking Limb. We'll use that tomorrow."

"You guys playing tomorrow? Where?"

"Same place we play most days," Ace said. "Guy's home studio. Up south of Ventura."

"You changing the band's name?"

"Different days, different names. Guy who cuts us, he likes to act like he's putting all sorts of bands through the place, but mostly it's just the five of us. He always wants a name, so we just, like, tell him who we are that day and he writes it on the tapes. Dig it. He cuts on *tape*. Gotta be the only guy in America still cuts on tape."

I waited for a moment, but that seemed to be all he had on

his mind. "Cutting on tape, new names all the time. Not exactly business as usual, is it?"

"Not hardly. Hang on a minute." He did something very fast with the fingers of his left hand, walking them down the neck of the guitar, and brought the run to a close with a four-stroke strum that was faster than I could count. "Gotta finish it off, man. Otherwise it hangs around, makes the air thick. Can't get a new idea until you've tied a knot in the end of the last one." He reached over and pushed the STOP button on a cassette recorder that was jammed down into the couch cushions. "Smoke?"

"No, thanks."

"Good shit," he said, putting the Martin aside and reaching down to slide an ashtray from beneath the couch. An open cigarette paper bloomed in the middle of the butts and ash, and a miniature hedge of brownish pot ran down the middle of the paper. Ace rooted around in the butts until he came up with a ball of dark brown opium the size of a marble. He rolled the opium lovingly back and forth between his fingers directly above the pot, and the ball obligingly shed little brown flecks. I could smell the heavy perfume. "You sure?"

"Yeah, I'm on a program. Nothing but alcohol and airplane glue."

He looked over at me, weighing it. "Together?"

"It's amazing," I said. "*Great* headaches."

"Far out," he said, picking up the paper, expertly rolling it into a perfect cylinder and licking the gummed edge. "I'll try it sometime. But right now, my girl is Lady O." He lit the joint and inhaled a third of it.

"So," I said. "The band names. What's with the band names?"

"The man pay, the man get his way." Ace blew out the smoke, closed his eyes, and said, "Oh, *yes*, mama. The man pay, the man get—"

"But why? Why does he want a new name all the time?"

"Because he can. Rich guy, he can get what he wants. Who was that fat guy? With the fiddle?"

I said, "Got any more data?"

"Oh, come on, man, you know. Whole city's on fire, this tubbo's playing—"

"Nero," I said.

"That's the dude. So rich they didn't even give him a ticket. So the man up the hill, he wants us to be The Elbow Benders or the Pink Wrinklies, that's who we'll be."

"What kind of music?"

"Four chords, June Moon Spoon Tune. Verse, verse, hook, verse. Shit you could have heard fifty years ago on *American Dance Hall*." He took a deep hit and leaned back, closed his eyes again, and said, "Whoooo."

"You guys sing, too?"

"Oh, no," Ace said in a strangled voice, trying not to talk the smoke out. "The boys sing. He brings in one kid after another. They're all pretty, but. . . ." He exhaled a cloud of controlled substances. "But they blow. I mean, it's like the first round of *American Idol*, just one tone-deaf hood ornament after another. Some of 'em, they're so bad he doesn't even record the vocal."

"The pay okay?"

"Not as good as a real session, but, hey, it's five days a week." He carefully scraped the coal at the joint's end against the edge of the ashtray to shave off the ash. "No waiting for the phone to ring, hoping to get a call from some hot new band that can't play for shit, looking for something like the riff from 'Blue Tubes' so they can put it out and pretend they wrote it."

I remembered the doorbell. "You played 'Blue Tubes'?"

He pulled the hair in his face back with the hand that didn't have the joint in it, squinted at me, and said, "Your name—your name. . . ."

"Freddie."

"Shit, Freddie, we can't be buds if you don't know I was the fucking guitar player on 'Blue Tubes.' I'd probably be in the Rock and Roll Hall of Fame if I didn't have an unlisted number. You know how many times that riff's been bagged?"

"Who played the French horn?"

He shook his head; the horn didn't matter. "Some chick. Somebody's squeeze for the week. High school girl, played in the school band, showed up at the session in her band uniform. Wheeeooooowheeeooooowheeee. Of course, that was when you could look at a high school chick without wearing an ankle bracelet for the rest of your life. That's what rock and roll was *about*, man. Swear to God, I don't know why anybody learns to play the guitar any more. But it wasn't the horn on that record, man, it was the riff."

"It's a great riff," I said. "Classic."

He put the joint between his lips, picked up Marty, and did the high triplet that opened the riff. "Can't stop it, can you?" he asked. "Once it starts, it just finishes itself in your brain, right? Like somebody says *one, two*, man, you're gonna go *three* every time." He sucked on the joint without putting a finger on it, then hit the triplet again and exhaled over the dying ring of the guitar.

"The guy you're playing for."

"Yeah?" He was looking down at the guitar. His left hand hovered a quarter of an inch above the strings and went through a series of ghost-chords, moving down toward the soundbox and then back up again as the fingers curled in and out of the formations for G, C, D, and some others I didn't recognize. "Maybe," he said. "Just maybe."

"Maybe what?"

"Huh?" He looked up at me as if he were surprised to see me.

"It's me," I said. "Freddie."

"Yeah, yeah, yeah. Just—just, um. . . ." he did the progression again, pressing the strings this time and strumming lightly with his right. "Naahhh," he said. "Salad oil."

I said, "Salad oil?"

"Sure, man. We're all looking for the big one every time the music comes through, all looking to strike oil. And we do. Problem is, most of the time, it's salad oil."

"Ace," I said. "Five days ago."

Ace took the joint out of his mouth so he could give me his full attention. "Five days ago," he said.

"That would be Friday," I said. "This being Wednesday and all."

"Wednesday," Ace said.

"Friday," I said.

Ace looked past me a moment and then brought his eyes approximately to mine. "Next Friday?"

"No, Ace. Five days ago. Five days ago would be last Friday."

He nodded. Then he nodded again.

I nodded back.

"The Knuckle Dusters," he said.

"What about them?"

"That's who we were. Last Friday, I mean. I remember because it was the shittiest session of my life."

"Last Friday," I said, "you played a session at DiGaudio's house."

"As The Knuckle Dusters."

"What time?"

Ace said, "Friday."

"Ace," I said gently. "Friday is a day of the week. What *time* on Friday was your session?"

"*Friday.* The whole fucking day and most of the night. The songs were shit, we played for shit, the kid couldn't of sung 'Happy Birthday' if he'd had a year to work it up. Bad biorhythms, Mercury in retrograde, Year of the Dragon, the whole deal."

"You were there all day."

He eyed the remainder of the joint. "Who's smoking this stuff, you or me? All day. Say eleven in the morning till maybe one, maybe two A.M. Breaks once in a while for dope and munchies."

"Breaks how long?"

"Half hour, maybe a little more." He relit the roach, which had died from neglect, and sucked down pretty much everything that was left. "Why do you care about all this, anyway?"

"That's a really good question," I said. "Not much gets past you, does it?"

"Not old Ace."

"And the guy who owns the place, he was there all the time?"

"Stuck to the chair." He dropped the stub into the ashtray. "So why do you care—"

"Do me a favor," I said. "Play the 'Blue Tubes' riff for me again."

He pointed a finger at me, pistol-style, and grinned. "I *knew* it, man. Once you hear the beginning. . . ."

He was still playing when I left.

## 22

### We Just Add Color

"I need a perspective," I said into the phone as I neared the turnoff.

"Meter's still running," said Louie the Lost.

"Let's say you're suspected of murder."

"Whoa. *Way* out of my league."

"This is a hypothetical." The light in the intersection where I was going to turn went from green to yellow, and I slowed behind two massive SUVs, their owners doing everything in their power to ensure the future prosperity of Saudi Arabia. "So. Let's say you're suspected of murder. Let's say you *know* you're suspected of murder. Let's say you're sort of sitting around waiting for the cops to come and get you. You even hire someone to try to do something about it, try to get you off the hook."

"This has a familiar ring," Louie said.

"And now let's say that it turns out you have a perfectly good alibi."

After a beat, Louie said, "For?"

"For the murder. Let's say several people can place you at home the entire day when Derek Bigelow, your hypothetical victim, got made dead."

"How hypothetical is this?"

"Actually, not at all."

"This is like a word problem," Louie said. "Remember word problems? If Karen's on a train going West and Harvey's on a train going East and one of them's going fifty-nine miles an hour and the other one is doing eighty-three miles an hour, and Harvey's in the front car when the trains crash into each other, then how much did Karen weigh?"

I said, "It's like that? How is it like that?"

"It's like that because it doesn't make any sense. If Vinnie's got an alibi, why does he need you? Why doesn't he just tell his cousin he was busy?"

"Yeah. That's sort of the question I called to ask."

Louie went quiet for a moment. "Well, who were these guys? Were they assembling a suitcase bomb or something?"

"They were playing music. In a recording studio."

"Must have been awful, if he'd rather go down for murder than admit it."

The light changed. The SUVs accelerated, running interference against oncoming traffic, and I trailed in their wake, turning left off Ventura and heading south, toward the house that used to be mine. "It was crap, according to one of the guys who played it."

"But still," Louie said.

I said, "Yeah," again. I was getting the heaviness in the chest I always got when I made this drive, and the feeling forced its way out as a sigh. "I don't know what to do. I mean, if Vinnie would rather get arrested than use his alibi, and I've been hired to protect him, maybe I ought to just let him get arrested. If the alibi is somehow worse than the murder charge—"

"Then what you got to *do*," Louie said, and it was just this side of a snap, "is look at it different. If Vinnie has an alibi, then you know that he didn't waste Derek, so there's the big one out of the way. You just pretend you didn't find out about no alibi and get him off anyway. Since he didn't do it and all."

"I was afraid you'd say that."

"You want good news, buy yourself a greeting card."

"I can't. There's no category for self-pity. What's it going to say, *I'm sorry I'm feeling sorry for myself*?"

"Ahhh, lighten up. Worst thing that can happen is you get convicted on the Hammer robbery, Vinnie gets arrested, and Irwin Dressler has you killed in prison."

"By golly, you're right," I said. "I feel much better."

"Okay, *here's* good news: Our girl's in San Berdoo. Got some clerk burning oil all night to search property transfers in the names of Huff, spelled two ways, and Pivensey."

"And traffic tickets."

"And parking," Louie said. "Tickets and property are two different places. She barely made it up there in time to get into the County clerk's office. Tickets first thing tomorrow."

"Fine. Great. Peachy."

"Oh, and Stinky's pissed at you. He figures you ratted him to Dressler."

"I'm terrified," I said. "I can barely steer."

"Stinky may wear velveteen PJs," Louie said, "but he can hire heat same as anyone else."

"I'll put Stinky's heat on the list of people who are probably right behind me." My turn was coming up. "Talk to you tomorrow."

"Oh, good," Louie said. "A reason to live through the night."

**This time, Bill** opened the door.

"Ah," he said. He looked at me, and I looked at him. Once again, I had to admit that Rina was right; there was nothing wrong with his nose. It would have looked better broken in four or five places, but it was a perfectly good nose.

"Ah, yourself." I said. "Nice shirt. Territory Ahead?"

He looked down at it. "L.L. Bean."

"Everything for the fashionable duck hunter. If you'd step aside, I could get off this porch."

He blinked. "Does Kathy know you're coming?"

"I don't see how that affects you," I said reasonably. I waited a second or two while reason evaporated, my blood pressure tripled, and spots multiplied in front of my eyes, and then I said, "Let me put it more directly, Bill. Get out of my fucking way."

He was blinking again as he said, "Hold *on*," and I reached out and grabbed his shoulder. Then I kicked his right foot out from under him, spun him halfway around on his left, put my foot up against his butt, and shoved. He staggered forward into the hallway, and I followed him in fast, planning to tie his arms into a square knot.

And stopped.

The hall ended at an antique bureau that Kathy had bought and painted white and gold. Kathy liked white and gold. To the left was the archway to the living room. To the right was the hall that led to the bedrooms. As Bill engaged in a windmill collision with the bureau, I saw Kathy staring at me from the living room, and Rina, with Tyrone behind her, in the hallway. Rina was open-mouthed, and Tyrone looked appraising, like he wanted to see it again, in slow-mo.

I said, "Hi, everyone. I was showing Bill a trick. You okay, Bill?"

Bill looked at me and opened his mouth, and I let my left eyelid droop in the way that my father's did when he was furious, and Bill said quickly, "Fine. I'm fine."

Kathy said, "A trick." She was wearing a T-shirt and jeans, so the relationship with Bill was well past the let's-get-pretty stage.

"Since you've got him opening the door," I said, "he's sort of

your first line of defense, isn't he? And he can't always be bringing those duck guns to the door."

"Bill *does not hunt ducks*," Kathy said through her teeth,
sounding as though we'd argued about it a dozen times, but
Rina was trying, and failing, to laugh silently. "And it's not
funny, young lady. Your father is not free to burst in here any
time he wants and—and *manhandle* people."

"I'm fine," Bill repeated gamely.

Kathy said, "That's not the point." Bill's face suggested
that he thought it had been, but Kathy plowed on. "We have
an arrangement, Junior. You have specific visitation times, and
you're supposed to call in advance if you want to change them."

"I was. . . ." I said, and broke it off.

"Yes? You were what? Out of gas? In the neighborhood? Just
passing by?"

"Lonely," I said. "I was lonely."

Kathy's face softened for a second, but she shored it up from
inside. "Well, I'm sorry about that. But this isn't home base any
more. You can't come running in here every time you get tired of
your precious motels."

"I want to see him," Rina said.

"Of course, you do, honey," Kathy said. "It's natural for
you—"

"I mean now. I want to see him now."

There was an awkward silent moment. Then I said, "Well,
that makes two in favor. We only need one more for a majority."

Tyrone said, "Do I get a vote or am I disenfranchised?"

"This isn't the Electoral College, Junior," Kathy said. "And
you're trying to manipulate Rina."

"Why?" I demanded. "You're the only one who's allowed to
get lonely?" I glanced at Bill. "Not that you've got much room
for it."

"I am *not* discussing this," Kathy said.

"Fine. I'll go into my daughter's room and spend a few minutes with her, and you can go back to plucking geese or whatever you were—"

"And you're not funny. Rina, he's not, so stop laughing right now."

Rina turned and ran toward her room, and Tyrone ambled along behind her. Kid didn't have a stiff joint in his body. "I'll just go on in and chat with her for a little while," I said.

Kathy watched her daughter's receding back. "Fifteen minutes," she said. "We eat dinner in fifteen minutes."

"That's nice of you, but—"

"I'm not *inviting* you. I'm telling you she has to be in the dining room in a quarter of an hour."

"That's okay," I said. "I don't eat game anyway."

By the time I got to Rina's room, I was breathing regularly and the light fizziness of fury had left my limbs.

"You shouldn't get Mom crazy like that," Rina said as I came in. Tyrone had swiveled a chair around and straddled it, with his arms crossed on top of the back, his hands lying flat. He had amazingly long fingers.

"You play keyboards, Tyrone?" I asked.

"Horn," he said.

"Which one?"

"There's only one you just call *horn*. French."

"My favorite," I said. "You know a record called 'Blue Tubes'?"

"Daddy," Rina said. "Tyrone plays classical. He doesn't listen to stuff like—"

"Great record," Tyrone said. "But it was the guitar riff that made it."

"I just spent some time with the guy who played that riff."

Tyrone's eyebrows rose. "Yeah? How much time?"

"By my clock, about twenty minutes. By his, could have been thirty seconds or the entire Pleistocene."

Tyrone said, "How's that?" and then he said, "Oh. Kind of . . ." He wiggled his hand side to side and said, "Wuhwuhwuh."

"Exactly. Way too much wuhwuhwuh. Who's your favorite composer for horn?"

"Mozart," he said. "The concerti for horn are the top of the stack. But, you know, there's not that much material for solo horn. It's more of a color instrument. They just let us in to add color."

"Tyrone, stop it," Rina said. "Look at his face." She came over and hugged me, and I smelled the baby oil she used as a moisturizer. "Poor Daddy. Nothing's the way you want it to be. Did you really get lonely?"

"I'm so lonely I'm learning ventriloquism, just to hear another voice."

Rina let go of me. "I should have known better. I'm such a sucker for you."

"I did miss you."

"He did," Tyrone said. "Look at the man."

"He did," I said. "He really did."

"So you came by just to see me?" Rina asked.

I said, "Well, sort of."

The corners of her mouth contracted. "What's the rest of it?"

"I want you to check a couple more things for me."

"Fine," she said, not seeming particularly fine. She turned her back to me with a certain briskness and pulled out the chair in front of her laptop and sat down.

"But that's not the real reason I came," I said.

"Then what is?" she said, sounding quite a bit like her mother.

"It's—it's kind of hard to explain. I spent part of the day with someone, a woman whose husband left her in an empty house, and I just, well, I just started to feel, um, complicated."

She turned enough to give me an imperious profile. "Don't you *dare* feel sorry for us. We're fine."

I put up both hands in surrender. "I know. I know."

"Hey, folks," Tyrone said. "Start over. Everybody likes everybody, no reason to kick each other in the shins."

Rina filled her lungs and emptied them. "Right. Okay, I'm happy to see you, I really am, and is there anything I can help you with?"

"There is," I said. I pulled from my pocket the list I'd made of the names written on the boxes of tape in DeGaudio's studio. "See what you can pull up on any of these."

"Poison *Pie?*" she said. "Paw Prints on the Heart? What are these?"

"Either bands or album titles."

"Is this about the Little Elvises?"

"Whatever those are on that piece of paper, they're what the guy's been recording, the guy who drove around and discovered those kids."

"DiGaudio," she said. She banged a bunch of keys.

Tyrone said, "Try eMule."

"These are pretty obscure," she said. "But who knows? There's somebody who likes everything." More scrabbling on the keys. "Nothing for Paw Prints. Let's try Candy Kisses. Ho, look at this. Three songs. So it's a band."

I looked at the screen. The songs were called "Puppybreath," which provoked an inadvertent audible reaction, "Next Best Thing to Love," and "Most of Me."

Tyrone said, "'Most of Me?' Kind of creepy, isn't it? Where's the rest of him?"

"Can you play these?" I asked.

This time Rina gave me a full-out smile, rich in pity. "You really don't know anything, do you?"

"I'm learning to throw my voice."

"You have to download these before you can listen to them. And there are only three or four computers on the network that even have them, so it could take a while."

"What's a while?"

She shrugged. "Hours? Days? These people, the ones with the songs on their computers? They might not even be online right now. They might only be online a couple of hours a week."

"Try some of the other bands," I said.

She did and got zero on most of them. There were a couple of songs each for Tomorrow's Shadow and Notes from Underground, and she added them to the download queue, whatever that was. "Okay," she said. "Now that we've humored Tyrone by trying eMule, let's do the usual stuff."

For the next five or six minutes I stood around with my hands in my pockets while Rina batted the keyboard around and Tyrone looked at me, shifting his eyes away every time I tried to catch him. Finally, I said, "What?"

He sat up straighter. "What do you mean, what?"

"What are you looking for?"

"Oh," he said. "Rina. I was looking for Rina. I don't see much of her in her mom."

"Really?" Rina asked without slowing at the keyboard. "Mom's all over me."

"Not the way I see it," Tyrone said. "I see more of your dad."

"If you're trying to curry favor, Tyrone," I said, "you're doing great."

"Oh, this is awful," Rina said.

I went and looked at the screen. "What is it?"

"*Blender.com.* Look." She pointed at a corner of the screen, at a square graphic that showed a mermaid halfway out of a sparkling sea, surrounded by purple mist and singing into a 1940's big-band microphone. The type on the picture said *Songs from Atlantis,* and printed under the square were the words, *CD we didn't even open.*

"Is that as bad as I think it is?" I asked.

"It's the worst thing they can do," Rina said. "It's so *mean.*"

"Can you blow it up?" I asked.

"Sure," she said, and then she switched into a little singsong talk-to-yourself voice: "Right-click, save as jpg, import into Picasa, enlarge." She was doing things as she spoke, and when she was finished, there was the CD cover, bigger and a little dotty, but legible. In the lower right, it said, LARKSPUR RECORDS.

"Bingo," I said. "Larkspur Records." Larkspur was the street Vinnie DiGaudio lived on.

"Boy," Tyrone said. "Haven't heard anyone say 'bingo' in a long time."

"Is there a website?" I asked.

"Hold it." Rina did an online zigzag via Google and said, "Take a look."

I leaned over and found myself looking at a spiky blue flower, the words LARKSPUR RECORDS, and below that, THE FUTURE OF ROCK IS IN ITS ROOTS. I said, "Pretty."

"Pretty primitive," Tyrone said over my shoulder. "Static, noninteractive, no video, nothing. A picture and some buttons."

"Push the one for music," I said, and Rina did.

A vertical row of CD boxes populated the screen, ten or twelve of them. Above it was a sort of mission statement:

*Larkspur Records proudly releases music by artists who move the future forward as they embrace the roots of rock 'n roll.*

"Love the 'n," Tyrone said. "That went out with 'bingo.'"

"Kind of hard to move the future in any direction except forward," Rina said.

There were no pictures of bands on any of the CD boxes, just illustrations. I asked, "Can you make any of those things play music?"

Rina clicked on the CD boxes and roamed the screen with the cursor. "No. Maybe he's afraid of getting pirated."

"If the guy who plays the music can be believed," I said, "he's probably safe from pirates."

"Then why do you want to hear it?" This was Tyrone.

"The man's got a home studio, he's got a house band that he hires six or seven days a week, and he brings in pretty boys to sing, and half the time he doesn't even record the vocals. I'm kind of curious to see what the hell he's making."

"Time," Tyrone said. "Isn't that what they used to say, back when they said 'bingo'? *Making time*, right? Sounds like he just might possibly hypothetically probably have an unhealthy interest in boys. Look back at the man's life, that's about all he's ever done, nose around for boys."

"I don't know. If that's what he's after, why hire a band day after day? Why fill the place with witnesses? Why spend all that money? Why change band names all the time? He could hire the band once and have the kids sing to pre-recorded tracks for years, just him and them in the studio, nice and cozy."

"And look at these CDs," Rina said. "He's making *something*."

"Can you order them?" I asked.

"Probably. Sure," she said. "Here's a P.O. Box. No downloads, just the disks. Sixteen-ninety-five per, plus five dollars for postage and handling, whatever handling is."

"Order a couple."

"Fine," she said. "I've got nothing better to do with my

allowance." But she already had an order form on the screen. "Two, right? Any two?"

"Right. And here's fifty bucks, so you make a profit."

"Oh, no, you shouldn't," she said, turning to grab the bills. She shoved them deep into her pocket, as though I might change my mind and try to get them back. "Really, it's too much."

"Rina," Kathy called. "Tyrone. Dinner."

"I need one more thing," I said.

"Mom can get dangerous," Rina said.

"Information about the one who disappeared, the one called Bobby Angel."

I got the look teenagers reserve for adults who are beyond hope. "Did you read my paper *at all*?"

"Well, sure," I said. "It was great, really impressive."

She wasn't having any. "How *much* of it did you read?"

I said hopefully, "Most of it?"

"Where is it? Do you even know where you put it?"

"Sure," I said, but Rina looked at my eyes and shook her head in disgust. She grabbed some papers from the desk, folded them down the middle, and thrust them at me. "This is the last copy I'll give you. Go home and read the rest of it. Try to get past page five. Then, if you've got another question about Bobby Angel, call me."

"Rina," Kathy said, and this time she was standing in the doorway. "Dinner will get cold."

"Okay." Rina and Tyrone got up, and she turned to me and kissed my cheek. "Thanks for coming."

"Actually," Kathy said. Then she stopped, looked down, located a spot on the carpet, and said to it, "Actually, if you want to stay, Junior, you can."

"One too many at the table," I said, slipping Rina's report into my pocket. "But thanks."

"Bill's gone home," she said.

Rina emitted a puff of breath and said, "*Mom.*" She sounded like she was hurting.

"It's nothing," Kathy said. She pushed a smile into place. "Really, nothing."

I said, "I am such a jerk."

"Yes, you are," Kathy said. "But are you hungry?"

My cell phone rang.

"Hell," I said. The display said MARGE. "This will just take a second."

"You remember where the dining room is," Kathy said. "Come on, kids."

I waited until they were out the door and said, "Hi, Marge."

"You oughtta come home," Marge said. "Your girlfriend has had nine or ten too many."

I said, "My girlfriend?" and then shrunk eight or ten inches as Kathy turned back to look at me. Behind her, Rina's mouth was an O. "Is she okay?" Kathy shook her head and pushed past Rina and Tyrone, and the two of them followed her down the hall.

I said, to myself, not to Marge, "Idiot."

## 23

### Trank

Lights were burning in Blitzen, but that was to be expected if a vodka-sodden Ronnie was woozing around up there. Even drunk people sometimes prefer light. So I trudged up the stairs wrapped in the situation I'd just caused, and walked into an entirely new situation.

The look that greeted me when I opened the door didn't come from Ronnie. It came from the mirror over the dresser, and it belonged to the individual who was reflected there, a 350-pound white male genetic misfire with a badly shaved head and a nose that looked like it had been hit with a hammer until it was as flat against his face as a cricket's. He was shirtless and seemed to be fully involved in carving something into his stomach with a long, thin knife. A black case lay unzipped and open on the dresser, next to the festive bowl of glued-together Christmas-tree balls. The case contained four disposable syringes, all lined up like good little soldiers, and a couple of rubber-tipped vials. A fifth syringe lay beside the case. A tiny pool of fluid gleamed beneath the tip of the needle.

I pulled the Glock from under my shirt.

The monster in the mirror said, "Hey, Junior."

"Fronts," I said. There was a shapeless mound on the bed, covers pulled completely over it. "What did you do to her?"

"Her?" Fronts said. He was picking at his stomach with the knife's tip. "Oh, her. She's drunk." He looked up from his stomach and saw the gun. "That's funny."

"The world is full of people who should have shot you the minute they saw you."

"Uh-uh," Fronts said, focused on his work again. "The world *used* to be full of people who shoulda shot me. They ain't with us no more."

I stepped away from the door, leaving it half an inch ajar, and moved sideways to the bed, keeping the gun trained on Fronts, who was busy cutting himself. When I tugged the covers down, I found Ronnie looking straight at the ceiling through half-closed eyes. Her mouth was open so wide it looked like she was screaming.

"Stop shitting me," I said. "What did you do to her?"

"Just being nice. Suppose I have to kill you and she wakes up. This way, she'll never see me. She'll have a headache and she'll have to explain the body on the floor, but she'll be alive."

"What did you shoot her with?"

"Horse tranquilizer," Fronts said. "She was out cold when I came in, didn't feel a thing. If you live through this, I'm gonna want thirty bucks for the trank. Stuff's not cheap."

"I didn't know you had horses."

"I don't." He took a step back from the mirror, and I gripped the gun in both hands, aimed at the center of his body. "Whaddya think?" He turned to face me.

His chest had more stuff carved into it than a men's room wall. The fresh bright red letters on his stomach said, "*!iH.*"

"It's backward," I said.

Fronts looked down at himself and then turned back to the mirror. "Shit," he said. "I do that all the time."

"Kind of a painful way to learn about symmetrical letters."

He used his thumb and forefinger to pluck a fold of skin just above the bleeding word, pulled it out, and poised the sharp edge of the knife over it. "Don't hurt as much as erasing it," he said. He started to slice at himself.

I absolutely could *not* look. I turned my head a couple of inches, toward the bed with Ronnie on it, and there Fronts was, his arm clamped around my neck, the knife at my throat, and his lips peeled back from his speed-freak-brown teeth. "If I'd cut myself like that," he said, "think what I'd do to *you*."

I shoved the gun into his gut and tried not to choke on his smell.

"Knife's at your carotid," he said. "One little nick, you'll be down. You pull the trigger, think I'll die before I nick you? Are you *sure*? Also," he said, pushing the knife just a little harder, "you shouldn't forget that I don't care."

"Everybody says that." I could barely breathe.

"Junior," he said. "It's me. Fronts. You gotta know I don't give a shit."

"That's the plan? You're going to kill me?"

The door behind me opened, and Louie the Lost pushed through it, looked at the two of us, and turned white. "Oh, geez," he said, staring at Fronts. "You two guys, uh, you want some privacy?"

I gasped, "Thanks a lot, Louie."

Louie said, "No problem," and backed out, so fast he didn't even close the door.

"Friend of yours?" Fronts took his arm off me and took a step back, keeping the knife at my throat.

"You can never tell."

"Listen, Junior. If I wanna kill you, you think I'm gonna stand here, borrow your mirror, write on myself? Shit, DNA everywhere for the cops. Why not just cut off a finger, leave it here so they get a good print?" He took the knife away from my throat and put the edge against the index finger of his left hand.

"Please don't," I said. "Not in my room."

"It's a really shitty room."

I said, "Yeah, but I'll still have to replace the carpet."

Fronts turned away and went to the bed. He pulled the blanket down, checked to see that Ronnie was still doing her unconscious imitation of *The Scream*, and said, "Pretty girl, huh?"

"She's looked better."

"You might want to walk her around, throw her in some cold water. You never know, maybe the dose was too big. You got any speed?"

"No."

"Too bad. Oh, well, I ain't died from it yet. She smart?"

"Smart enough."

"Good, because she'll lose some brain cells. But I use it all the time, and look at me." He tugged the covers over her face again.

I said, "That's very reassuring," and then jumped a foot in the air as the door behind me banged against the wall, so loudly that it almost drowned out the sound of my gun going off as I accidentally yanked the trigger. The gun jumped once in my hand, and the bullet went through the outside of Fronts's upper right arm and slammed into the wall with a white puff of plaster. My ears were ringing like someone had clapped his hands over them. I turned to see Louie standing there with a shotgun.

Fronts said, "Ouch."

I said, "Sorry."

Louie, who had the shotgun trained on Fronts, said, "*Sorry?*"

"He shot me," Fronts explained. He pushed his index finger into the bullet hole.

"Please," Louie said, going even paler. "Stop that."

"Feels kind of cool," Fronts said. He pushed the finger

farther in and twisted it, and Louie's eyes went to the ceiling, and he crumpled as though his knees had dissolved. Fortunately, the shotgun didn't go off. Louie lay folded neatly over it, in the middle of one of the carpet's larger stains.

"You gonna shoot me again?" Fronts asked.

"No. I think I'm done."

Outside, I heard a door slam and then I heard the hard slap of shoes on the far stairway.

"Oh, no," I said. "Get into the bathroom. Now." I pushed my gun under the blankets next to Ronnie and grabbed the shotgun beneath the collapsed Louie, but it snagged on his shirt. I said something filthy, got a foot under him, and rolled him over to free the gun. I'd just slid the gun under the bed when Marge barged in.

"What the hell—" She stopped, looking across the room at Fronts, who hadn't moved an inch. "Who in the world are you? And who's he?" She pointed down at Louie, who was starting to come around, his eyelids fluttering like a moth's wings. She sniffed the air. "Who fired a gun?"

"No one," I said, but Fronts, the tattletale, said, "He did, Mom. He shot me." He grabbed the flesh around the bullet hole and yanked at it, as though he intended to hand it to her. "Here."

"Who the hell are you to call me Mom?" Marge took an aggressive step forward, her sequins glinting dangerously. "What are you, anyway, the human blackboard? If Junior shot you, he had a good reason." She looked down at his dangling hand. "Is that a boning knife?"

"Henckels Four-Star," Fronts said mildly, raising it to show it to her.

"About seventy-five bucks?" Marge said.

"Fifty-two-fifty," Fronts said. "Costco."

"Good price," Marge said. "But you don't go using it on a paying guest. Not in this economy."

"Sorry," Fronts said.

"And put your shirt on. You think this is Zuma? Wait a minute. Lift both your arms."

Fronts obeyed, displaying the four-foot-long, single scar that started beneath his left arm, ran all the way down to the top of his pants, crossed over beneath his belly-button to his right hip-bone, and traveled up to his right armpit. "Jesus," Marge said. "Looks like the hood of a car. Where'd you get that?"

"Around," Fronts said. He sounded shy.

"Who stitched you up, a sailmaker?" The stitches had left a red crisscross trail the full length of the cut.

"Did it myself," Fronts said, looking down at it critically. "It was hard, upside down."

"I'll bet. Well, this isn't your neighborhood, bub. Put your shirt on and beat it." She looked down at Louie. "Anybody shoot him?"

"He fainted," I said.

"Junior," she said, shaking her head. "I'm disappointed in you. If you weren't special to me, I'd throw your butt in the street for this. Shooting a man in Blitzen."

Fronts said, "Blitzen? Like the reindeer?"

"Don't tell me they had Christmas where you came from. Just get dressed and get out." Marge flicked a finger at the works on the bureau. "And take that filthy dope with you." She prodded Louie with her foot, and he groaned. "Present and accounted for," she said. "Where's Ronnie?"

"Taking a nap," I said, gesturing toward the bed.

"Girl can't drink," she said. "You might want to walk her around, maybe haul her into the shower."

"That's what I just said," Fronts said.

Marge didn't even glance at him. "I'm going now, but if I hear anything more, I'll be back with Ed's service revolver and shoot all of you."

"Okay, Mom," Fronts said.

"And don't call me Mom," Marge said, going through the door.

I went to the door and closed it behind her, and when I turned around, Fronts had the knife at my throat again. He reversed it and sawed with the blunt edge across the side of my neck, which was enough to loosen my knees. "This here is what I came to tell you," he said, his breath smelling like aged meat. "Stop."

I thought for a second. "Stop what?"

"I don't know," Fronts said. "But stop. If you don't, I'm gonna hurt you for a few hours and then open you up like—like, what did she say? Like the hood of a car."

"I can't stop if I don't know what I'm supposed to stop."

"That's your problem." Fronts turned the knife around and suddenly there was a stinging line on the left side of my throat. "Right about there, but deeper," he said. "You got any Mercurochrome?"

"I guess." My fingers came away with blood on them.

"You oughta use it. You don't wanna get infected." He licked the side of the knife. "Stop everything. Next time you see me, you're going to hurt until you're dead."

Louie groaned and opened his eyes.

"Squeamish little guy, aren't you?" Fronts said, letting go of me and leaning over him. He wiggled his index finger and aimed it at the bullet hole again. Louie closed his eyes. "Your sidekicks," he said. "A guy who faints and an old lady in sparkles."

"I didn't notice you giving her any lip."

"Tell you what, Junior," Fronts said. "Whyn't you just shoot me? Then you won't have to worry about nothing."

"Marge will kill me," I said.

"No, she won't," he said. "But I will." He put the knife on the bureau and stuck his arms into a plaid short-sleeve shirt the size of a tablecloth. "Fashion tip," he said, buttoning it. "If you're probably gonna bleed, wear plaid."

"Should have told me before you cut me." I watched him zip up the case full of syringes. "Take the empty," I said. "Who sent you?"

"Doesn't work that way." He picked up the used hypodermic and shoved it point-first into the pocket of his jeans. I felt myself wince. Fronts said, "Ow."

"Be careful or it'll break off."

"Yeah?" He made a ham-size fist and swung it against the pocket with the needle in it. "Whaddya know?" he said. "It will." He headed past me, toward the door. When I stepped aside, he grabbed me again, and out of nowhere, there was a hypo pressed into the skin just below my left eye. "Don't point a gun at me again, Junior," he said. "Not unless you're gonna shoot me. Now ask me to move the needle. And say please."

"Move the needle, please."

Fronts gave me a tombstone grin. "Which way?"

"Away from the eye."

"You got it," he said, and he lowered the needle to my cheek, shoved it in half an inch, and pushed the plunger. "That's just a touch," he said, pulling the needle out and showing it to me. The plunger was only about a quarter of the way down. "Should give you an interesting few hours."

My cheek and jaw were suddenly ice-cold. "Shame shtuff?" I heard myself ask. "Shame ash you gave her?" My tongue felt like a cork.

"Yeah." He jabbed the needle into the inside of his elbow and hammered the plunger home.

"Course, I'm used to it. You and sweetie over there, it'll all be bright and shiny new. Gimme forty bucks."

I said, with considerable difficulty, "You shaid shirty."

"That was before I gave you some. Ten bucks more."

"I need to si' down," I said. I felt as though I'd spent several hours with my head and shoulders stuffed forcibly into a freezer.

"Money, money, money." Fronts wiggled his fingers at me. "Gimme. Then I'm gone."

I pulled money out of my pocket and held it out while the floor tilted, and then I watched Fronts dwindle as I stumbled back, away from him, until the backs of my legs hit the bed. I bounced to a landing beside Ronnie, who didn't even grunt.

Fronts grabbed the money. "Forty," he said, counting. "Okay?" He held up a few green rectangles of paper with numbers of some kind on them. "Nod, if you can move your head." I couldn't, and he said, "Okay, let your jaw drop." That I could manage, and he threw the rest of the money into my lap.

"One more time," he said, and I realized I'd gone someplace while he walked to the door. "One word, Junior. *Stop*."

He closed the door and I folded forward, fell off the bed, and landed on my face on the carpet.

It seemed to me that I studied it for quite a while, trying to decipher the code that was hidden there, before I gave up and went somewhere dark and full of ripples.

## 24

### Num Num Num

"Drink it up," Louie said. "Just num num num."

"I'm a grown-up, Louie." My watch said 11:30 P.M., so I'd been gone for a while.

"Num num num always worked with my daughters," Louie said. He gestured, palm up, for me to tilt the cup and drink.

I gulped it and scalded my tongue. Good. Feeling was returning.

"Careful, it's hot."

I stuck my tongue out as far as I could to let the air cool it. The shower made shower noises in the bathroom, but I was listening around it for the sound of a body hitting the tiles. Ronnie had still been several stations beyond wasted when I finally got her under the cold water.

"More, more," Louie said.

"In a second," I said. "That meat you smell cooking is my tongue."

"Don't be a baby." Before I'd staggered into the bathroom with Ronnie over one shoulder, Louie had gone across the street for coffee and then he'd darted into the bathroom and come back with a wet facecloth. As I sat on the bed, waiting for the coffee to cool, he was wiping every washable surface in the place.

"What are you doing? Getting rid of prints?"

"Getting rid of Fronts," he said without looking back at me. "Guy leaves slime everywhere he goes. Mopping it up gets my heart back under control." He was scrubbing at the spot where the hypodermic had drooled on the bureau. "Drink your coffee."

"Thanks for coming in with the shotgun," I said. "That took guts."

"I don't wanna think about it," Louie said. "Musta been crazy. Fuckin' Fronts, he could take both barrels and not even limp. Guy's so dumb he'd probably rip you apart before he realized he was dead."

"You know him from before?" The coffee was getting drinkable.

Louie shrugged, bringing both hands up in his one and only Italian-looking gesture. "Know who he is. Everybody knows who he is, with those scars. He's like the Last Tax Audit. Guy shows up, it's so over it's not even worth arguing about it." He shook the facecloth open, primly refolded it to get a clean surface, then started wiping again. "You figure it was Stinky sent him?"

"No. Fronts told me to stop, right? What Stinky's pissed about has already happened. I already talked to Dressler and that's what got Stinky in an uproar, so there's nothing there for me to stop. I figure it's whoever did Derek. In fact, when you think about Derek, pretty much crumbled like an animal cracker, it sort of sings Fronts."

"I fucking hate animal crackers," Louie said. "I always got elephants. Wanted lions or tigers, but I always got elephants."

"Poor kid. No wonder you turned to crime."

"Think he was in the Humvee?" Louie said. "The one that chased you—"

"Could be. There aren't many cars Fronts would fit in, but a Humvee is one of them."

"'Cause if it's about Derek," Louie said, "then Vinnie's alibi don't mean so much. If he hired it done, and all."

"Hold the thought," I said. "I need more coffee before I try to think about anything."

"Take your time," Louie said. "Fronts probably won't come back or anything."

"Don't worry. He's home by now, carving the *Times* crossword into his chest."

"Hard to imagine Fronts having a home except maybe in the roots of a tree. What about the other thing, the thing with Marge's daughter?"

"What about it?"

"You don't figure Fronts—"

"No. Pivensey or Huff, whatever you call him, he's a solo, a freak but not a pro. He kills girls and moves along. Somebody like Fronts would terrify him."

"So it's Derek," Louie said.

"What's Derek?" Ronnie said from the door to the bathroom. She was wrapped in a towel, her hair dripping water onto her shoulders and her eyes at half-mast. I hadn't heard the shower shut off, so I was still in slow-learner mode.

"The man who isn't here," I said. "The one you slept through."

"I didn't sleep. I was hit with a block of cement." She reached up, grabbed her hair, gave it a bunch of twists, and wrung it out.

Louie said, "Ouch."

"Doesn't hurt," she said. She slapped herself experimentally on the cheek. "I don't think anything will ever hurt again."

"That's what I said after my divorce," I said.

"Awwww," Louie said, "that's sadder than my elephants."

"Who was he?" Ronnie asked, and then she took a little side-step just to remain upright.

"A hit man named Arthur Love Johnson," I said. "Used to

be called Algae on account of his initials, until he discovered the joy of carving things into himself. Since he can't turn his head all the way around to the back, he concentrated on his front. So now they call him Fronts."

"How colorful," Ronnie said. "What did he want with you?"

"He was cautioning me to stop looking into Derek's murder."

"We think," Louie said.

"Well, so stop," Ronnie said. "You're more important to me alive than Derek is dead."

I said, "That's sweet."

"Got you some coffee," Louie said, popping the plastic top from a paper cup. "While you were, um, freshening up."

"You're right," Ronnie said to me, taking the cup. "He's wet. And thanks."

"Wet?" Louie asked.

"Never mind," I said. "What brought you here, anyway?"

"Her," Louie said, lifting his chin at Ronnie. "I got a call that she was looking really drunk when she came out of Marge's, and . . ." He broke off, sucked his lips in, and made a defeated little squelching sound with them.

"You," Ronnie said to him, narrow-eyed, but then she turned to me. "I mean, *you*. You're still having me followed."

"And look what happened," I said immediately. "A hit man, a guy who—"

"He came after you, not me. As far as I can tell, *my* throat didn't get cut."

"It doesn't hurt that much," I said, although it did.

"I don't care," she said. "Well, I do, but that's beside the point. You actually think I had something to do with Derek's—"

"Don't be silly," I said.

"He worries about you," Louie said, demonstrating loyalty for the second time in a single evening.

Ronnie wrung more water out of her hair. "He's not worried about me. He *suspects* me. I can't believe it. I'm nice to him, I get *lonely* for him, I drive over here when he's not home and sleep outside his door, I let him fumble at me and bounce all over me, I keep his landlady company, and he—he—"

I said, "Fumble?" and then the penny dropped. "You drove over here," I said. "The *car*." It had only taken me twenty-four hours to figure out what my question had been, back when she was telling me about the cops' search.

It stopped her for a second, and then she said, "What about the car?"

"You said the cops searched Derek's car."

"They're cops," Ronnie said. "He's dead. That's one thing they do. They search things."

"He was out working," I said. "When he got killed, he was—"

She took a good gulp of coffee, waving me to stop, and said, "And?"

"And his car was there. In your parking space."

"Sure, it was. Like I just said, I drove it here."

"But why was it there?"

"Oh." The towel started to slip, and she tucked the coffee under her chin and rewrapped the towel as Louie, ever the gentleman, turned his back. "Why was it there when he wasn't? Good question."

"Got a good answer?"

"Sure. When he was working on something that involved surveillance or tailing, he'd change cars. Get a new one every day or two." She turned to Louie. "Something you ought to try once in a while."

Louie said, "Mmmph," like somebody catching one in the gut.

"Where did he get the cars?"

"He was British," she said. "That means he hated to spend money. He got them at Cheap Wheels."

"Those are *wrecks*," Louie said with what seemed like actual, physical pain. "How could anybody drive a—"

"Put some clothes on," I said. "Let's go."

Louie said, "You're in no shape to drive."

"Maybe not," I said, "but I've got a friend who's a driver."

"LA's a big town to look for one car in," he said, but he'd already reached into his jacket pocket for his driving gloves.

"Only two places to look," I said.

**We started with** the theory that Derek had been followed home and then grabbed after he parked, so we began the search directly in front of the apartment house and did concentric circles around it, then went all the way up to Sunset and zigzagged back and forth down to Santa Monica.

"It'll be a heap," Louie said for the fourth or fifth time. "Got CHEAP WHEELS on the license plate frames."

"We know," I said.

"It's just, you know, you look at a couple thousand cars, it's easy to forget what you're looking for."

"Thank you for the reminder," Ronnie said. "Again." She was still talking more slowly than usual, thanks to the trank.

"Just saying," Louie said.

"Well," I said, "if a junker would stick out anywhere, it'd be here. I never saw so many clean cars in my life."

"Gay guys," Ronnie said. "They take care of things. This is the carpet-shampoo-and-clear-fingernail-polish capital of the world. These guys pick up their dogs' poop."

Louie said, "Eeeeewww."

"Better than leaving it there for some nice girl like me to step on. I'll tell you, nobody in Albany picked up their dog poop."

"I thought it was Trenton," I said.

She turned to look out the window for a moment and said, "It was. Look, there's one."

"Naw," Louie said. The car she'd pointed out was an eggplant-colored Plymouth coupe from about 1948, gleaming beneath the streetlights. "That's vintage. Somebody put a stack of money into that."

"Trenton or Albany?" I asked.

"Who cares?" Ronnie said. She waved her hand in front of her face as though to dispel the question. "They're both pissholes in the snow."

"They may be," I said, "but you're from either one or the other."

She turned to give me both eyes, neither friendly. "I lived in Trenton *and* Albany, and nobody scooped the poop in either of them. Okay?"

"Leave her alone," Louie said.

"You skipped Trenton when you told me your life story."

"I skipped fifth grade, too."

"Actually," I said, "you didn't skip Trenton. It was Albany you skipped. Quick. What was the name of the guy who drove you to Chicago?"

"John Doe," Ronnie said. "I'm loaded, remember? And are we taking this conversation in the direction I think we're taking it in? The Ronnie-the-suspect direction?"

Louie said, "Fronts probably did Derek."

"But obviously somebody hired Fronts," Ronnie said. "And you're having me followed, and you're cross-examining me while I'm under the influence of drugs, and it's always the spouse, right?"

"Not all the time," Louie said comfortingly.

"Turn right," she said. "The light coming up. Turn right."

Louie took a look. "We been up that street."

"I don't care. Turn right."

Louie turned right and lead-footed the car uphill a couple of blocks.

"Here. Stop here." Ronnie already had her door open an inch.

"Don't be childish," I said.

"How is this childish?"

"Your car is at my place, and you're jumping out here."

"Where my car is is my concern. I choose not to spend the evening with somebody who thinks I order hits on people."

"He don't mean it," Louie said. "He just acts dumb sometimes."

She opened the door the rest of the way. "Is that right, Junior? Do you act dumb sometimes?"

I said, "Trenton or Albany? Who was that Michelangelo in the desert, the one who painted neon?"

Ronnie said, "Goodbye," and got out of the car.

"You *are* dumb," Louie said, watching her go. "Girl like that don't land in your hand every day. And how would she know Fronts? Whaddya think, they met at a party? A fund-raiser, like for chamber music?"

"I'm not in the mood to be lied to. Let's go."

Louie muttered something and put the car into first, but I said, "Wait a second."

I watched as she keyed the gate to get into the complex and kept my eyes on her until it was closed again. "Okay," I said. "Hollywood."

"Talk about a mixed message," Louie said at the top of the hill, as he hit the turn indicator to go right on Sunset and slowed for the stop. "Why couldn't you ease up on her? So she told you a couple. What chick doesn't?"

"Skip it."

"Oho," Louie said, making the turn.

I waited. "Is that it? Oho?"

"That's it. Sometimes *oho* is enough."

"Well, whatever it was meant to suggest, you can roll down your window and throw it into the street."

"Oho," Louie said again. "And you can't force *me* out of the car, because I'm driving."

"I didn't force her out of—"

"You could of just made a mental note, you know? Sort of wet your finger and made a *one* in the air to remind you that there's details that don't fit together. Maybe a little fib here and there. Instead, you give it to her right in the face. What city? What name?" He braked to a stop at the light in front of the Chateau Marmont. "Girls don't like that, you know? They feel like they got a right to make up the past. Old Alice, for about twenty years I believed she was the youngest sister, and it turned out Ora and Gladys were both younger than she was."

I didn't say anything, just watched a knock-kneed, rickety-looking white girl in a short coat and calf-high yellow patent leather boots stand between parked cars and troll the oncoming traffic.

"But that's not it, is it?" he said.

"What's not what?" I asked, against my better judgment.

"It's not about her, Ronnie, I mean. It's about Kathy and your kid. You've got the guilts."

A car slowed to window-shop the woman in the yellow boots, and she leaned down to give the driver a better look, but the car accelerated and sped away. The girl offered it a parting middle finger and turned back to fish the traffic stream.

"Has it occurred to you that you're asking a personal question?"

Louie said, "Personal shmersonal."

"One of the things I like least about crooks," I said, "is that they don't have a subconscious. They say pretty much everything. They expect everybody *else* to say pretty much everything."

Louie said, "Don't change the subject. You *shtupped* her, right? And you got this no-lies policy with your kid. So one big talk, coming up."

"It's worse than that." I told him about the *my girlfriend* slip in front of Kathy and Rina.

"You're as fucked as Custer," Louie said. "You can't even have the old heart-to-heart, break it to her your way. And you know women, they're both back there turning it into the crime of the century. Planting it in a little garden in the center of their hearts and watering it with *feelings*. *Talking* about it, *sharing* it. You're a cheat, you're a heartbreaker, you're like a museum exhibit, Everything That's Wrong with Guys."

"And in the meantime," I said, "Kathy's sleeping with this survivalist, Mr. Twelve-Gauge Wilderness. Plaid shirts and ankle traps. Venison jerky. But that's supposed to be okay. It's like there are two sets of rules."

"Alice says, sure, two sets of rules. Men and women need different rules on account of how they're not anything alike, what with women being all admirable and so forth."

We were most of the way to La Brea now, and I told Louie to aim for the 6000 block of Hollywood. You can tell Louie where you want to go as long as you never suggest a route. Professional drivers regard choosing the route as a nonnegotiable prerogative.

"Argyle," he said at once. "Flows nice. Stop signs where it needs them. It'll take us right there. What's there?"

"Giorgio's star. Where they dumped Derek."

"Don't make sense," Louie said, hitting the turn indicator for a left. "What do you figure, they killed him and then drove him there in his own car, dropped him off, parked the car, and walked home? I mean, would anybody do that?" He made the left and said, "Well, okay, Fronts might. He's that dumb."

"Actually, I kind of like it *because* it doesn't make sense," I said. "Nothing else makes sense, either. I've got a suspect with an airtight alibi he won't use, a recording studio where expensive session musicians come in six days a week to cut tracks for singers who can't sing and whose vocals aren't even recorded half the time, a bunch of band names that nobody's ever heard of, and some sort of beast that breathes water."

Louie almost rolled through a stop sign. "Say what?"

"There's somebody in Vinnie DiGaudio's house who pretty much caught me inside last night but instead of shooting me, he breathed at me. Through a microphone."

"Breathed at you." Louie stopped for the light at Hollywood Boulevard.

"From the bottom of a swimming pool is what it sounded like." I put a hand on his arm. "Get across the boulevard and pull over wherever there's a streetlight. I need to read something." I patted my pockets until I located the folded copy of Rina's paper. I pulled it out, waiting for Louie to find me some light.

"Forget a parking space," Louie said, crossing Hollywood Boulevard. "Every doper in town is shopping the sidewalk, and they're all parked back here. Just open the dash compartment and read it on your lap. Should be enough light."

I popped the dash, and a twenty-watt bulb put out a squint's worth of yellow light. I opened the paper and flipped through it until I got to page six, and there it was.

**Bobby Angel** (Roberto Abbruzzi) was the least typical of the Little Elvises. For one thing, he looked like
an accountant with a weight problem. All the other
boys DiGaudio discovered had a slight resemblance to
Elvis Presley. They looked like Elvis's cousins, with dark
hair and plump faces. Most of them learned to sneer.
But Bobby Angel was tubby and so near-sighted that he
looked at the wrong camera all the time when he was on
TV. The other thing that made him different was that he
could sing. His records are the best of all the DiGaudio
productions, even better than Fabio's and Eddie Win-
ston's. He was so good he almost made up for Giorgio.
Bobby Angel was the only one of the Philadelvises who
had real talent. He disappeared in Philadelphia on April
19, 1963. He left the house he shared with his parents,
saying he'd be back in a few hours, and was never heard
from again. There were theories that Angel was killed
by the Philadelphia mob as a threat to DiGaudio, but
DiGaudio had already been in Los Angeles for a year
by then.

"Abbruzzi," I said. I refolded the paper, seeing in my mind's
eye the sheet music on the stands in DiGaudio's studio. It had
been written by DiGaudio and Abbruzzi. *What the hell?*

"Nice town, Abbruzzi," Louie said. "Good wine, too. We
looking for this car, or what?"

"Yeah. Yeah, sure. Let's cruise."

"Got a lot more heaps here," Louie said, making a turn onto
some anonymous little street that paralleled Hollywood Boulevard. "Harder to spot one here than in Boy's Town."

And it was. Every third or fourth car qualified as a junker,
and we had to check the license plate frame on every one of

them. By the time we'd stopped and looked at a couple of hundred of them, Louie was yawning, and I was catching it from him.

"Time is it?" he asked.

"Coming up on two thirty."

"And you're not tired?"

"I had a nap," I said. "Although it feels like three days ago."

"Half an hour with Fronts will do that to a guy. I gotta tell you, I don't think old Derek's car is gonna be here."

"I'll defer to your judgment. Let's pack it in."

Louie worked his way via back streets to the Cahuenga Pass and then dropped down on the other side of the hill onto Ventura, made a right onto Lankershim, and let me out at the North Pole. He waited, just in case, while I went upstairs, but there was no need. For the first time in what seemed like weeks, there was no light on, no mourning motel owner, no sleeping beauty, no self-mutilating hit man. I had Blitzen to myself.

It almost felt lonely.

## 25
Orange Boot

Thirty minutes after I'd turned the light off, I turned it back on and got dressed. Because obviously, there weren't only two places where Derek's Cheap Wheels heap could have been.

There were three.

I was still feeling kind of fuzzy from Fronts' trank, but at least traffic wasn't a challenge. At 3:20 A.M., Ventura Boulevard was almost deserted. I had clear sailing all the way, watching the lane lines very carefully and braking at every yellow light, until I got to the turn that would take me south of the Boulevard, up into the exclusive neighborhood of second-string TV stars, screenwriters, pornographers, Van Nuys slumlords, and such upstanding citizens as Stinky Tetweiler and Vincent L. DiGaudio. Despite the old saying, lots of people who live in glass houses more or less throw stones for a living.

It took me about eight minutes to find the car, which was parked a couple of blocks uphill from DiGaudio's house. It would have been hard to miss even if I hadn't been looking, because a forged-steel, bright orange boot had been clamped to the front wheel on the driver's side, the city's greeting card to people who have been parked for too long and whose cars suggest that they'd be more at home in a different kind of neighborhood.

And, in fact, among the little Porsches and the big Escalades, whatever those are, Derek Bigelow's rented wreck looked like an artichoke in a bowl of roses. Rusted, dented, crumpled like tinfoil in places, it was a pea-green Ford Falcon from the American automotive nadir of the late sixties, when the Big Three rolled out one piece of crap after another as the Japanese slid in below the radar with cars that actually worked and didn't require a gallon and a half of gas to get from the garage to the curb.

For the second or third time, I reflected on the unusual level of sloppiness in the police work around Derek's death: no Giorgio in the notes from the murder scene, the car sitting right here. Then I shook my head and called myself a mildly unpleasant name. It wasn't sloppy. It was Paulie DiGaudio, steering the investigation away from Uncle Vinnie. Giving me room to get killed in.

I had a slim jim in my hand, ready to slip it between the driver's window and the door, but I didn't need it. The lock was broken, a first for me. I had no idea that car locks ever actually stopped functioning, but here we were: Detroit had staked out yet another frontier.

The front window on the passenger side had been lowered about four inches, letting out a smell like the trolls' locker room, courtesy of too much time spent in a small space by a man who took too few baths, plus an open, jumbo-size, wide-mouth grape juice bottle full of piss. The grape juice bottle is a popular solution to a stake-out man's most pressing need, but it's usually kept tightly capped when it's not in use. The cap to Derek's bottle was on the passenger seat, and the bottle was on the floor in front of the passenger seat. Hard to imagine anyone driving off with an uncapped bottle of urine in the car.

So he hadn't had time to cap the bottle before he got yanked. Or else he'd never gotten back to the car from DiGaudio's house. And back home, the little woman wasn't exactly pacing the floor, waiting up for him.

The thought of Ronnie produced a complicated emotional wince, an interesting mixture of desire, warmth, and guilt. It was remarkable how many of my life's current tangles had one end of the string knotted into my short acquaintance with Ronnie: Kathy's disappointed face, the excruciatingly awkward situation with Rina, the problem of Derek and Fronts, and my own growing affection for a woman who shook off tails like a spy, lied like a senator, and bounced from one partner to another without any visible second, or even first, thoughts. Precisely the kind of relationship I needed least, and yet I remembered, with a pang, the sight of the gate to her apartment complex swinging closed behind her.

I went around to the curb and opened the passenger door. The car exhaled malevolently at me. I took the precaution of grabbing a napkin from a half-eaten Whopper, still in its grease-spotted Burger King bag, and using it to pick up the bottle of piss. I put the bottle on the curb, where I couldn't accidentally knock it over as I searched, and went to work.

Nothing in the glove compartment and nothing under the gummy floor mats. Crawling further into the car with my breath held, I pointed my penlight down between the seats and saw a small spiral-bound notebook jammed under the emergency brake. It took a couple of minutes to wiggle it free, meaning that I had to breathe several times. As soon as I had it, I backed out into the fresh air and gave it a flip. Only the first few pages had been written on, so I grabbed another deep breath and crawled back in to look for an earlier notebook, without success. Either Derek had stashed it somewhere when he'd filled it up, or the people who killed him had found it and taken it with them.

Nothing beneath the front seats, nothing on the backseat. A

lot of nothings. I opened the trunk and found a flat spare tire and a few greasy tools, plus a couple of days' worth of fast-food wrappers and some dispirited French fries. I was trying to move the tire out of the way to look beneath it when I heard the vibration of a car coming up the hill. I slammed the trunk and ducked around to the passenger door to shut it, killing the interior lights just as headlights swept the opposite curb. I dropped to my knees on the sidewalk and held my breath.

The car slowed and then stopped. I could hear the static-ridden back-and-forth of a police radio. A spotlight beamed through Derek's car's dirty windows and lit up the hillside behind me. A breeze delivered a sharp whiff of cigarette smoke, so Officer Somebody was breaking the rules. The door of the police cruiser opened, and I listened to the scuff of heavy cop shoes over asphalt. There wasn't much I could do other than listen, since there was nowhere to go. The smell of smoke got stronger. As near as I could figure, the cop with the cigarette was heading for the front of the car. A moment later, a sharp metallic *bang* confirmed it: The cop had swung something hard, probably his flashlight, at the orange boot.

"Aw, come on," called the cop in the car. "Nobody can get those things off."

"When're they gonna tow this piece of crap?" asked the smoker.

"Oh, who knows? After a few more complaints, probably. Let's go."

"If I lived here," said Officer Nicotine, "I'd complain every time I saw this thing."

"If you lived here," the other cop scoffed. "You wanna live here, get transferred to vice or narco."

"Car really stinks," the smoker said. He played his flashlight into the windows and then started to come around the front of the car. I backed away, crablike, and my foot hit something hard. It took me, conservatively speaking, one one-hundredth of a second to realize what it was and how much noise it was going to make if it fell over. I got my hand back there somehow and caught it half an inch before it shattered against the curb. Unfortunately, I caught it by the top, and a pint or two of piss flowed out over my hand and down the curb and into the gutter. I squatted there, enveloped in stink, and watched it wind down-hill in a darkly shining stream. All the cop in the car had to do was look. "Jesus," said Officer Nicotine. "Smells like every cat in the neighborhood's been using it for pissing practice."

"And this appeals to you why?" asked the cop in the car. "Come on, I'm hungry and I want to stay that way."

"Okay, okay. Just doing the job, right?"

"I'll put you in for a decoration." Shoes on asphalt again, then the slam of a door. "Dental hygiene, maybe, the way you work on your teeth. Sound good?"

"The Golden Floss Award," said Officer Nicotine, and the car pulled away.

They'd gone uphill, and I couldn't be sure they wouldn't come down again, so I yanked the rear door open again as fast as I could, ran my hands between the seat and the seatback, find-ing a couple of quarters and a military-looking button with an anchor on it. I was sweating with tension and my hands smelled like they'd been marinated in a urinal. Finally, I grabbed the backseat and yanked it free.

And there, nestled in a graying snarl of extremely unwhole-some litter, the decaying scut of a decaying civilization, was a small silvery digital camera.

I drove home with the windows open to dissipate the stink on my hands.

The holiday lights blinked festively in Blitzen's window, and try as I would, I couldn't ignore them. My irritation threshold had been eroded to zero by tension, lack of sleep, and a jolt of horse tranquilizer. I suddenly realized that it didn't matter whether the plug for the lights had been glued into place; I could unscrew the bulbs. I got up with the brisk resolve of someone who's solved a longstanding problem and did it, burning my fingers in the process. It was worth it. The blinking stopped, Christmas floated away as the clog was at long last cleared from the stream of time, and I went back to the bed and Derek's notebook.

Page one said, *DiGaudio* and then *Abruzi*, so Derek was on the track of something, even if it wasn't a gold star for spelling. Beneath that were the words, *insurance policy?* Beneath that, *carrier? beneficiary?*

Then, *double indemnity??????* I counted the question marks. Then, BHPD?

And beneath that, a sort of a timetable:

> *January 7 '62*
> *December ? '62*
> *April 19*
> *April 23*

I was willing to venture a guess that the latter two dates, the ones without a year attached to them, referred to 1963, since I recognized both of them. Beneath the dates was a rough schematic, more a diagram than a map, with arrows leading from a box that said *Philly* to a box that said *Chicago* and then to a box that said *LA*. Then a line in a different color linked *LA* to a box that said *Hawaii*. There were little arrowheads on the lines, presumably to show the directions in which people had traveled. The arrows between *LA* and *Hawaii* went in both directions. There was also a single two-way line between *Philly* and *Hawaii*, with a question mark drawn above it. The lines between *Philly*, *Chicago*, and *LA* went only in one direction, west. Then there was one more line, from *Philly* direct to *LA* without connecting through *Chicago*, and it too went only west. So: travels.

*BHPD* was obviously the Beverly Hills Police Department.

Then a cryptic equation: *Sal = ID*? I parked that for later consideration, but I didn't like the look of it.

On the next page, Derek had written *NESSIE* and drawn a heavy black cube around it. A wreath of dollar signs surrounded the cube. Centered on the page beneath the cube were the words, *which is which*?

Then, all alone on the next page, *$350,000*. Wishful thinking or a demand?

The last page that had any writing on it contained a shopping list, and I doubted it was in code because it said *stoli, coke, cigs, white bread, mayo, salami, new ball point*. Given its position between Stolichnaya and cigarettes, I doubted the coke was made in Atlanta and came in a can.

The whole thing gave me a rancid feeling: This was the legacy of a man's life. Peeping, lurking, sneaking, smoking, coking, drinking, eating crap food, pissing in bottles, sniffing out secrets, looking under the rocks in people's lives, finding pain points and the stains of shame, trading them for money. Day in day out, sneak, cheat, betray, steal, get loaded, sleep. How did he get up in the morning? What were his first thoughts when he opened his eyes to the bright new day? Who will I hurt by nighttime? Whose trust will I violate? How fucked up on junk can I get?

It his own subterranean way, I thought that Derek was worse than Fronts. Fronts was a top-of-the-line, designer-label sociopath who half-hoped he wouldn't live through the day, who inhabited a dim expectation that somebody would shoot him or he'd finally slip over the far edge of an overdose. He'd kill me in a minute for a few bucks, and he'd dutifully hurt me for a while first if that were part of the job, unless there was something good on television, in which case he'd hurt me during commercials. But it wouldn't be personal. And if push came to shove, he'd just as soon kill himself as me. Fronts was a nightmare wrapped around a void; if you peeled his skin off in a spiral, as you might an apple, there'd be nothing underneath it. A little darkness, a few dead moths, some sour-smelling air. All of it gone in seconds, dissipated like a musty odor when you open a closet door.

But Derek was something else. He was plausible. He functioned in the world just like a real person, someone with a moral code and a soul. He'd hoodwinked Ronnie into marrying him, and no matter how drunk she was, she wouldn't have done it unless he'd been able to present some alluring surface, some convincing imitation of a human being. To be able to do that, he had to be able to project himself into others, to see what they wanted and cared about. He had to understand what they would see as good and desirable, what made them smile, what they would open their hearts to. *A guy,* he'd said to her, *who was worried he couldn't write convincingly from a woman's perspective.* He'd figured she'd be open to that, and then he made himself into it.

So he knew the difference between good and evil, between truth and lie, between human and beast. He just didn't give a fuck.

It would never even occur to Fronts to pretend to be human. He had no more moral awareness than a cancer cell. You either got it or you didn't, and it didn't matter to him one way or the other. He wasn't going to waste any time trying to look like anything he wasn't.

If I had the two of them in front of me, I thought, with a gun in my hand and an ironclad guarantee that I'd walk free if I shot one or the other of them, I'd have popped Derek without a moment's reflection.

I wanted to call Ronnie. But at 3 A.M., when she was already furious at me, that probably wasn't a productive idea.

The battery in Derek's camera was dead, and I didn't have a charger that would fit it. I pushed on various bits and pieces until a little slot popped open to reveal the flash memory card. I fished it out and said, "*Voilà*," since nobody was around to criticize my accent. The card was the same size as the one in my own camera, and I had a little reader I could slide it into and then plug the whole thing into my laptop through a USB port so I could see the pictures on the screen. I did it all without breaking anything. Rina would have been proud of me.

For a journalist, Derek hadn't been much of a photographer. The first five or six shots were of something very pink and very blurry that I eventually identified as his index finger, which was partially covering the lens. Then there were three pictures of his lap and one of his feet, about as interesting as they sound, and undoubtedly taken accidentally with the camera hanging by its strap around his neck.

The next five were of Ronnie, and for just a moment I felt a little softening toward Derek.

She was asleep, the sheets bunched around her bare shoulders, the cotton as softly crumpled as an angel's robe in a Flemish painting. Soft light flowed through a window to the left, and he'd shot without the flash so he wouldn't wake her up. He'd moved in close, catching the heartbreak curve of cheekbones and the perfect line of her nose, the upturned corners of her lips, so pronounced that she seemed to be smiling even in sleep. The last shot was an extreme close-up: a luxuriant tangle of hair, almost an abstract, looking like the swirling grain of a cypress or a whirlpool of spun gold, all curls and whorls and vortexes set off by the slant of light through the window. So he'd cared on some level. He'd at least been able to recognize beauty, and for the space of a few snapshots, he'd risen to its challenge. He'd actually felt something, even if it was just a spark of desire to keep some tracery, a two-dimensional miniature of the woman who would ultimately leave him. Ultimately, I was certain, everybody left him.

And then, in the next eight or ten shots, he went back to being Derek. A steep driveway that I recognized as DiGaudio's, shot in broad daylight, then a close-up of the mailbox with the address clearly readable. The house, photographed from a hill above it, its asymmetric geometry staggering through the azaleas and across the lawn, the pool a blue kidney behind it. From the slant of the shadows, it was early afternoon. Cars pointed every which way in the parking area, so a recording session was in progress, and I wondered what Ace and the guys had been calling themselves that day—Foot of the Nameless? Cyanide Chapstick?

Then the house at night, windows ablaze, the camera shaky from being hand-held for a long exposure without a flash. He'd moved in closer to get a blurred shot of the room with the curved window where I'd spoken twice with DiGaudio. In the center of the room, a ghostly apparition was in streaky motion, heading away from the couch. DiGaudio from the bulk, but it was hard to tell; the exposure was probably half a second, the hand holding the camera was jittery, the lens had auto-focused on the surface of the window, and the person inside was moving.

But it was DiGaudio. Nobody else in that house was that big. And I couldn't see legs, so he was probably wearing a kaftan.

The door was open behind him, the door to the hallway that led to the bedrooms and the recording studio. The doorway was a dark rectangle, but there was something framed in it, back there in the gloom of the hall, something pale and formless. It was too far back to catch the splash of light from the main room, amorphous as a puff of steam.

I clicked to enlarge, but there wasn't enough detail, and what I got was a bigger blur. About the only thing I could tell for certain was that it was short. Even allowing for the fact that it was a few feet back in the hall, it barely reached the doorknob. Not a child: too wide, too bulky. A very wide dwarf, perhaps.

Or a very tall mushroom. From all I could tell, it was a wandering piece of furniture.

The next shot showed DiGaudio going through the door to the hallway. He was pressing himself to the wall, so whatever was in the hall was relatively wide, although it didn't have to be all *that* wide, since DiGaudio was pretty wide himself. He had his head tilted downward, either looking at whatever it was, or else—

Of course. Talking to it.

Derek had tried to zoom in on the next shot, but whatever he'd seen, it had been clearer to him than it had to the camera. I could just make out a deeper darkness that was probably Vinnie DiGaudio in black-kaftaned retreat down the hallway, now on the far side of the pale blur, which was, if anything, even less resolved. But its shape had changed. Before, it had been vaguely rectangular, and now it was shaped a little like a lowercase *h*. It reminded me of something, although I couldn't say what.

I hit the space bar to navigate to the next picture, and the hair stood up on my arms. I was looking at Popsie, who was standing in the middle of the room, frowning as she stared out the window, her eyes fixed on at a spot to Derek's left. Even the mole on her chin bristled with suspicion. She'd heard or sensed something, but he was apparently far enough out of the light that she couldn't see him. It wasn't hard to imagine him frozen there, not daring to move, as Popsie's eyes raked the darkness. The next shot was just a dim blur of motion with something that might have been a foot at the bottom of the frame, probably another accidental shot as Derek hauled ass away from the window and Popsie.

And then, paydirt.

First, a blinding star of light reflected in the glass of a window—Derek finally seeing something worth risking the flash for, but forgetting to angle the camera away to deflect the light's bounce. He got it right in the next shot, the camera pointed down, catching the bottom edge of the window, and the flash bringing a flat, grainy face out of the darkness, a face no more than four feet off the floor to judge by the height of the window, a face that looked like a watercolor that had been left in the rain so the colors ran down the page and the shapes drooped irregularly, or maybe a face glimpsed underwater, distorted by the ripples on the surface, one eye fixed in wide alarm on the camera and the other fully closed, closed so completely that it looked as though it had been sealed in that position.

The face was so low that I realized that the shape in the hallway that I'd seen as a lower-case "h" was actually a chair, someone in a chair. Most likely, a wheelchair.

I heard again that amphibious breathing.

I said, "Nessie."

**Part Three**

**NESSIE**

## 27
### Lick and Stick

I slept until almost ten A.M., and when I woke up, I didn't even go get coffee before I reached for the phone and dialed.

"Yeah?" Joanie White was short on social skills but long on information retrieval. She was a PhD candidate in the social sciences at UCLA, the daughter of an acquaintance—a bookie to the stars who had the idyllic family life straight people never think crooks enjoy, including a pair of great kids. I'd paid Joanie for research on a few occasions before Rina turned into the Mistress of the Internet.

"The World Wrestling Federation," I said. "And its predecessors."

"That's the worst conversation opener of the year," Joanie said. "Pardon me while I yawn in your ear."

"Five hundred bucks."

"You're approaching my frame of reference," Joanie said.

"I need to find out everything there is to know about a former wrestler," I said, "and I'll pay five hundred dollars to the person who locates the information."

"What about the whiz kid? I thought I'd been permanently replaced."

"She's at school at this hour. Plus, we're at a delicate stage in our relationship," I said.

"Really. A father and a daughter? At a delicate stage? Call the *LA Times*."

"Interested in the money?"

"Sure. Got a name?"

"Sort of. Hilda, the Queen of the Gestapo."

"Oh, well," she said. "At least there's probably only one of them. How long do I have?"

"A couple of hours. Let's say noon."

She said, "Let's say two."

I said, "Let's say three hundred fifty."

"Noon it is," she said. She hung up, and I dialed another number.

The man who picked up the phone said, in a voice with a rasp like a match being struck on a zipper, "Don't waste my time."

"Nobody says hello any more. This is Paul Klee."

"Hey, Paul. Still painting?"

"With these petroleum prices," I said, "who can afford to work in oils? You want to make a call for me?"

"What I live for," Jake Whelan said. Whelan had been one of Hollywood's top producers until his unerring nose for a hit was permanently numbed by several tons of cocaine. These days he lived in baronial splendor in a fourteenth-century French chateau that had been reassembled in Laurel Canyon, where he passed his days hoovering white lines, working on his tan, ordering up tag teams of hookers, and enjoying a large private collection of mostly stolen art. He thought he owed me a favor, and apparently he hadn't yet found out that he actually didn't.

"The Museum of Television and Radio," I said. "I need the kind of access you'd get."

"When?"

"Maybe this afternoon."

"Okay. What do you need to look at?"

"Don't laugh."

"I haven't laughed since they wheeled Cheney out of the White House."

"*American Dance Hall.*"

"Oh," he said. "Sure. You want me to send a woman with a whip, too? Maybe a scourge and a hair shirt?"

"I don't think I'll need them. I want to see whatever they've got with two of the Little Elvises from Philadelphia, Bobby Angel and Giorgio."

"I'm gonna have to get somebody else to make the call," Whelan said. "No fucking way I'm gonna have people think I want to look at Giorgio."

"I'm surprised you even remember him."

"Ahhh, well. Somebody came to me a few years back with a screenplay about those kids. Idea was to get a bunch of really pretty, minimum-wage boys and do the story on the cheap, cut a CD, promote the whole thing on MTV, make a reality show out of the casting. The whole shmear."

"What happened?"

"You mean, aside from the fact that the idea sucked?"

"Since when does that matter?"

"You should be in the business. Sure, it sucked, but I figured it was good for some development bucks. I mean, it'd never get made, but I could probably have pried a million, million and a half out of one of the blow-drys at the studios. But the fatso who discovered all the kids said no way."

"DiGaudio."

"That's the guy. Jeez, what a schmuck. I make one call, just a polite feeler, and all of a sudden I got lawyers on the phone. You'da thought I was suggesting a prequel to Genesis."

"Protective."

"You could say that. Like he had something to hide."

"I'm pretty sure he does," I said. "Listen, I'm not certain I'm going to need you to make the call. I'll let you know in a little while if I do."

"Oh, well," Whelan said. "I'll just put my whole day on hold."

**It seemed like** a good time to be careful. I wasn't *stopping*, in spite of what Fronts had said, and I'd already been shot at and had my throat nicked. So I paid a lot of attention to the rear-view mirror as I drove over the hill to try to chat with Melissa Simmons, the next of the names Marge had starred as being one of Doris's special friends.

Even with one eye in front of me and the other on the mirror, it was hard not to think about Vinnie DiGaudio and the various ways his little secret could kill me. I was pretty sure I had sixty percent of it figured out, but the remaining forty percent was probably all sharp edges. *Which is which?* had been the best question in Derek's notebook, and the difference between Possibility Number One and Possibility Number Two was yet another murder.

People who are trying to hide a murder can get touchy.

Derek had been puzzling it through, both chronologically and geographically, and he'd figured that it was worth a lot of money—$350,000 counts as a lot of money to me—but I didn't think he'd gotten any closer to the real answer than I had. He'd gotten close enough to get killed, though, so I was obviously out on the end of the plank myself, with Fronts behind me, holding the sword to my back, and the sharks circling below.

The question was, who were the sharks?

Or were there any? Was Fronts the only weapon aimed at me, or was there another, one left over from a murder a long time ago? One threat or two?

*Sal = ID?*, Derek had written. I knew who Sal was and I was afraid I also knew who ID was.

So, safer to figure two. Or even more. I started watching the side mirrors, too.

**Melissa Simmons had** spent a fortune on not aging, and she hadn't. Instead of moving forward with the rest of us, towed in the wake of time's arrow, she'd gone sideways, into a parallel universe where people's faces morphed monthly, lips plumping, cheekbones swelling, chins clefting, noses shrinking, muscles relaxing to the point of paralysis, neck skin stretching as tight as a drumhead.

"Yes?" she said, thinking about smiling. You could see traces of the expression around her eyes, trying to push its way out.

I said, "Doris Enderby."

"Oh," she said, the ghost of her smile replaced by the ghost of concern. Beneath the concern, she looked at me the way a wolf would look at a pork chop. "Poor Doris."

She was standing in the open doorway of a small house in the flats of Beverly Hills, a semi-modest rococo excrescence that, even at today's fire sale prices, would probably fetch, as the real estate agents like to say, about four million. She had tilted her body away from me at a forty-five degree angle as though inviting me to push past her. I got a definite feeling that she was considering offering me more than I was there for. She'd first seen me about thirty seconds ago, and it smelled a little desperate. The plastic surgery suddenly looked like a plea for attention by someone who had stopped getting any.

These women—Amber, Melissa, and Doris—had been friends since high school. It was enough to make me wonder what was wrong with our lives: Two decades after swearing undying allegiance as optimistic high school students with a whole world of primrose promise in front of them, Amber lived alone in her run-down, childless house, Melissa was sculpting her face in Beverly Hills and hitting on strangers, and Doris had stayed home with Mom, surrounded by the bargain-basement glitter of the North Pole, until she eloped with the Big Bad Wolf.

Nevertheless, I said, "Why poor?"

"Sad, lonely little soul," she said. "It makes one ask oneself about her past lives. That mother and that awful little man."

"You met him?"

"Forty-five minutes was all I could stand. I made my excuses and just *fled.*" She accompanied the verb with a sideways sweep of her hand, noticed some imperfection in one of her long, lac-quered nails, and glanced down at it. When she'd either diag-nosed the problem or dismissed it, she looked back up at me and said, "I felt guilty about it, but I'm not responsible for Doris's choices, am I?"

Along with the facial restructuring, Melissa had had surgery on her vowels, which sounded like she'd spent her childhood as a prisoner in a BBC serial before escaping to Brooklyn. She put a hand on the door jamb and I caught a glimpse of a diamond the size of the doorknobs at Versailles.

"How long ago did you see them?" She kept looking at me, so I said, "Doris and Huff."

"Ages." She closed her eyes to think and then managed to open them again. "Three months? Four? It's hard to keep track when one's life is so full."

"What didn't you like about him?"

She tightened her mouth enough to make her look like she was sipping through a straw, then relaxed it again. "What was there to like? He was small in the wrong way." Her eyes tracked me from head to foot, apparently seeking reassurance that I was a proper size. "Some small men have a sort of fierce energy, don't they? They want to get even with the world, I suppose. It can be attractive. But Doris's awful man was small like those little metal statues people used to put on lawns, the ones that once were black. African-American, I mean. Holding a lantern. He had a cowlick. It made him look like he'd escaped from Appalachia. And slippery eyes. Every time I looked at Doris, he would stare at me, and then, when I felt his gaze, he'd look away. At anything, the door, the rug, a fork on the table. And then he'd look at me again. There was something *humid* in the way he looked at me. It gave one the creeps."

"How did she seem?"

"Like someone who's just bought something expensive she's not sure of. A Louis Vuitton bag, maybe, and you suddenly notice that one of the seams runs through the logo."

"That's bad?"

She put a hand, fingers open, in the center of her chest. "It's disaster. It means you've got a fake."

"You think he was a fake."

An economical shake of the head. "Don't be so literal. He was all too real. No one would pretend to be like that. No, one came away from the meeting with the feeling that under all the obvious disagreeableness, there was something even more disagreeable."

"Still waters," I said, thinking of Amber.

"I suppose." She was losing interest in the topic. She stepped a little further aside as though to prove to me that the house was empty behind her. She said, "It's cooler inside."

"Looks cooler," I said. "Have you seen Doris, or heard from her, since?"

She looked from one of my eyes to the other and back again, which I'd never seen anyone do except in the movies. In the movies, it usually meant a kiss was on the way. "You haven't told me why you're asking me these questions, have you?"

"No. I haven't." I smiled at her.

"Then I don't see why I should answer them." Despite the words, she made no move to close the door. She was now far enough to one side to let me walk in without even turning sideways. "It's not that I doubt your motives, you understand. You're modestly attractive, and something about you inspires trust."

"I've been told that."

She did her best to raise an eyebrow. "But, after all, who are you?" She put out a single finger and touched it to the tip of my chin. "Popping up on one's doorstep in the middle of the day like a pizza, asking all these questions."

I pulled my head back an inch or so. "I'm just someone who's worried about Doris."

"Yes, well, we're all worried about Doris." She lowered the hand and rested it on her hip, a stance with a certain amount of banked impatience behind it. "Or we were, at any rate."

"You were, but now you're not?"

She blew out a perfunctory puff of air. "An enviably concise way to put it."

"Then you *have* seen Doris since—since whenever it was you met her with Huff?"

"I didn't say that," she said. "Doris is *on her own path.*" She made the statement forcefully, as though she thought I might have difficulty following it. "It might not be the path I would choose, but perhaps she had fewer alternatives than I've had." She turned her head from side to side, looking past me at the front yard, surveying her alternatives. "But, to tell you the truth, I have far too much to think about in my own little life to waste much time worrying about the directions other people take."

"I understand. Other people's lives are so sloppy."

Her chin came up an inch or so, and I knew I'd lost a little more favor. "You're making me sound unsympathetic. One always wants the best for others, I'm sure."

"And Doris? One wants the best for Doris, too, I assume. You say you're not worried about her any more. Does that suggest she's changed paths, so to speak? Does it suggest that you know where she is now?"

She stepped back and put a hand on the door, but this time it wasn't an invitation. She was barring the way. "In Seattle," she said.

"Why Seattle?"

"Oh, who knows?" Melissa Simmons said, just barely not curling a lip. "Maybe she wanted to wear plaid shirts. She said Seattle, and I saw no reason to question her."

"Who else would you talk to, if you were trying to find her?"

"You mean, someone who might be keeping track of Doris? Not a soul in the world. Please step back."

She closed the door in my face.

**"A parking ticket,"** Louie the Lost said on the phone. "Six days ago. You wouldn't think it'd be in the system that fast, but they got these little electric tablet things now, the cop writes the ticket on the screen and pushes a button, and the ticket goes up into the sky and comes down in the computer."

"Really," I said. I was on Maple Drive, just around the corner from Melissa Simmons's house, watching my mirrors.

"How the hell we supposed to get away with anything any more?" Louie's tone was querulous. "All this information floating around in the sky."

"Where was he parked when he got the ticket?"

"Twentynine Palms. Bunch of sand and rocks. Snakes all over the place. Up near Joshua Tree."

"Well, that's nice. He's in a small town."

"Anyway, that's the good news."

"I hate it when people say that." A Beverly Hills Police Department car came into my rearview, saw me, and slowed as it approached.

"Yeah, me, too. Here's the bad news. No property sales involving any male named Huff or Pivensey. Maybe he's renting."

The cop rolled past in slow-mo, looking over at me. I gave him a little wave, pointed at my phone, and made a *yack-yack* sign with my hand, just a law-abiding citizen obediently pulled over to talk on the cell phone. He nodded and kept going, but I figured he'd be back. Beverly Hills is the only place in Los Angeles where a white Toyota stands out. "Could be renting, I guess," I said. "It was worth a try. Did your girl get printouts?"

"Printouts? Of something there isn't?" Louie was trying not to sound like someone talking to an imbecile, and he was almost succeeding.

"Of any transfer involving anyone with names *like* Hough or Huff or Pivensey. In fact, have her look under Enderby, too."

"She's already driving—"

"Then tell her to turn around. Tell her to get the printouts for any pages that have those names, or names near those in the alphabet. Just the pages of records that those names would be on alphabetically, plus one page on either side."

"Gonna cost you."

"Like I expect anything to be free," I said, and hung up. The phone rang immediately.

"No," Joanie White said.

"Is that the full report? I'm paying two hundred fifty dollars a letter?"

She slurped something through a straw, obviously emptying

the bottom of the glass. "No, there's no Hilda the Queen of the Gestapo. Or Helga the Queen of the Gestapo. Or Hilda the Bitch of the Gestapo. There isn't now and there never has been. The only two wrestlers ever to use *Gestapo* in their names were men. Do you want to know about them?"

"No. I've had enough useless information for one day."

"Oh, come on," Joanie said.

"I'd love to hear about them."

"Bruce of the Gestapo, who came into the ring in a chenille sundress and ripped it off to reveal black leather *lederhosen* and a swastika tattoo on his chest, and Gestapo Gus, the Nazi Cowboy, who used a bullwhip in the ring."

"And they say American creativity is dead."

"Bruce of the Gestapo's swastika tattoo was a press-on—you know, a lick-and-stick. He shaved his chest so it would take. He teaches third grade now. Worth five bills?"

"To the extent that something absolutely worthless can be."

"Good. Send me a check. In the mail, right?"

"Soon as I can find my stamps," I said.

I pulled away from the curb and drove the streets aimlessly for a few minutes, looking at the big houses where movie stars did or didn't live. Geographically, I was maybe a mile below Irwin Dressler's off-white mansion, but metaphorically, I had no idea where the hell I was. It seemed relatively certain that both Amber Schlumberg and Melissa Simmons knew, or thought they knew, something about Doris, and it seemed possible that Doris had told them to lie about it. Either that or she'd lied to both of them. Las Vegas and Seattle were unlikely stops on any single itinerary.

Of course, Pivensey could have made her lie to them. For all I knew, Doris had talked to her girlfriends on the telephone while Pivensey stood over her with his gun pressing a cold circle into her forehead.

But then why hadn't he forced her to call her mother? If anyone was going to make a fuss, it was her mother. If Pivensey were going to worry about Doris's girlfriends, why not worry about Marge?

*Stupidity* presented itself, with a little curtsy, as a possible reason. This was, after all, a guy who attempted to run down a woman in broad daylight in a supermarket parking lot. Barely animate. But, still. The simple desire for survival usually confers a certain minimal level of animal cunning, and skipping the call to Marge didn't measure up to it.

But I couldn't stay focused on Doris, however much I might want to. No Hilda the Queen of the Gestapo. That opened up a number of questions, none of them welcome. But I might as well ask them. If Fronts was going to be stalking me between bouts of carving *Bartlett's Quotations* into his chest and stomach, I probably ought to deserve it.

*Which is which?* That was the issue. I thought I ought to take a look at the two nominees.

So I called Jake Whelan back, and ten minutes later got a call from someone at the Museum of Television and Radio who managed to sound both young and starchy at the same time, and who told me that the Museum would be delighted, institutionally speaking, to make available a private viewing room and the program material—as she described it—that Mr. Whelan had asked about, but they'd appreciate ninety minutes or so to pull it together because it was infrequently requested. I told her I could well believe that, and she said that she'd see me at three.

"Make it four thirty," I said. "I need to bring my expert with me."

## 28
### Beauty Spot

"The thing was," Rina said around her fishburger, "it wasn't just the guest stars."

"What wasn't?" I was still watching the mirrors.

"*American Dance Hall,*" she said, sounding like she'd been asked the question eight or ten times. "Are you the person I was talking to a minute ago, or some cloud of alien shape-shifters who take turns inhabiting my father's body?"

I glanced over at her, avoiding looking at the fishburger. "Did you make that up?"

She licked the exposed edge of the dead-white patty and I got prickles in the small of my back. "The shape-shifters? No. They're all over online games. They're great avatars because no one knows who you are."

I said, "Avatars."

"Never mind," Rina said.

"So if it wasn't just the guest stars," I said, "what else was it?"

"The kids. The ones who were dancing. It was like the first reality TV, if you don't count the news."

"Nothing realistic about the news."

"Did you just change the subject?"

"No," I said. "I'm being open and unpredictable in my responses. Trying to be an interesting avatar."

"As I was *saying*," Rina said, "part of it was the kids. They were just regular old Philly kids, and at first the people who put on the show let in different ones all the time, but after a while they figured it out. The kids at home liked watching the kids on the screen. They wanted to see the same ones all the time. It was like they all knew each other. Like a national clique. They kept track of who was dancing with who—"

"Whom," I said.

"Thank you for sparing me a lifetime of humiliation. So there was this whole parallel soap opera going on in the studio, and at home kids were calling each other to talk about it all. There were even some stories in *TV Guide*. Did Kenny break up with Arlene or vice versa? Is Eddie cuter than Jack? Didn't it look like Betty had been crying? And is Corinne really a tramp, or is it just the way she does her eyes?"

I said, "A tramp?"

"This is the late fifties, early sixties," Rina said. "Girls who got around were tramps."

"Whereas today," I said, "they're empowering themselves."

"God, you're old," my daughter said. "Do you want to hear about this or not?"

"Sure. It's one reason I brought you along. Your expertise."

"And the other reason," she said, "is your girlfriend." She put the remnant of the fishburger into her mouth and said around it, "And it was really nice of Mom to let me come with you, all things considered."

"It was," I said. "How are things with her and Bill?"

"Better."

"Good," I said. "That's good."

"You are *such* a liar. Do I have mayonnaise all over me?"

"Only the bottom third of your face."

"Not so bad."

"And your neck."

"Do not." She reached up and swiveled the rearview mirror away from me. "Phooey," she said. "I'm immaculate." She looked out the window and said, "Beverly Hills, huh? Guess what. It's possible to spend a fortune and still live in a dump."

I repositioned the mirror.

"Who do you think is behind us?" She turned back to check. "The paparazzi?"

"My fan base."

"The Junior Burglars' League?"

"So," I said, "the kids in the audience were watching the kids on the show."

"You know, we're going to have to talk about this thing sooner or later."

"Later sounds good."

"*Your girlfriend*, you said."

"I did," I said. "But it was the way I said it."

She cocked her head. "And the way you said it was what?"

"I was confused. It was something that popped out because I heard something I didn't expect, and it confused me for a second. It was a—a blurt."

"Keep going," Rina said. "Because so far it doesn't make any sense at all."

"Okay," I said. "Here's an example. Let's say you're on the phone and somebody says about Tyrone, 'Hey, I just saw your boyfriend,' and you'd say 'My *boyfriend*?'"

Rina didn't reply. She was folding the bag the fishburger had come in, creasing it into quarters.

"Well, I mean, wouldn't you?"

"No," she said.

I said, "Oh." We covered a block of Santa Monica Boulevard

and eight or ten acres of jagged emotional moonscape. "Were you ever going to talk to me about this?"

"About *Tyrone?*" She sounded like she couldn't believe the question.

"What do you think I mean?"

"Daddy," she said. "It's not the same thing as your girlfriend, and you know it."

"It certainly isn't. You're thirteen years old."

"Have you—you know—" She fluttered her left hand in the air. "—with her? Have you?"

"*Later*," I said. "Later is sounding better by the moment."

The hand fell into her lap. "Then you have. Oh my God, you have."

It was my turn not to say anything.

"And you're telling me she's *not* your girlfriend? I mean, speaking of tramps. And I'm not talking about her." She pushed the button to lower her window and then raised it again. "Take me home."

"Just once," I said.

"Oh, *once*. Well, that makes everything fine."

"And she's the only one. In all this time."

Rina tore the burger bag in half and said, "I think I want to cry."

"I don't know her very well yet," I said. "But I like most of what I know about her. And I'm telling you the truth. I've never been with anyone since your mom and I—"

"Okay, okay. You're a great guy. You've been completely faithful except for this *stranger*—"

"Faithful?" I said. "Rina, I'm not married any more. And she's not a stranger."

"Yeah? How long have you known her?"

"Umm. Two days."

"Wow. Two whole days. I take it all back."

"It's not. . . ." I said, and then I stopped, since it was the blindest of blind alleys.

Rina pounced on it. "It's not what? It's not important? It's not *serious*? Do you think that makes it better?"

"It doesn't make it anything," I said. "It may be important or it may not be. I don't know yet. It happened, and I can't make it unhappen."

"But you don't think of her as your girlfriend."

"I don't know how to answer that. She might be. Eventually."

"I give up," Rina said. "You don't even know how you feel."

"You and, um, you and Tyrone—"

"Oh, don't be silly," she snapped. "I'm thirteen."

I said, "Sorry."

"Yeah," Rina said, cracking her window open again and facing away from me as though she desperately needed fresh air. "Me, too." She put the window down the rest of the way and stuck an arm out, trailing her fingers through the car's slipstream. "I'm thirteen," she said again.

"Yeah, I registered that."

"Going on fourteen."

"That's the traditional sequence," I said. "And you'll still be too young at fourteen."

"You don't have a clue, do you?"

"I was fourteen once. I wouldn't do it again for all—"

"Fourteen is the year I get to choose," Rina said.

I looked over at her. "Choose?"

"Who I live with."

"Whom," I said, and stopped dead in my mental tracks. "Whom you *live* with?"

"You," Rina said. Then she shook her head, brought her arm back inside, and put up a *slow-down* hand, beginning over. "I'll point at you to make this easier to follow, okay?" She tilted her index finger at me. "You," she said, and then she thumbed over her shoulder, more or less toward the Valley. "Or Mom."

An icy wave broke over me. "The agreement."

"Gee. You do remember." Kathy and I had decided that Rina, when she turned fourteen, could decide whom she would live with.

"You mean—you could decide to live with me?"

"I mean that I'll be entitled to make that decision." She put the window back up and looked at her lap. "Assuming you'd want me, I mean."

"Well, of course, I'd want you—"

"To live in motels," she interrupted. "With you and your girlfriend. Or succession of girlfriends."

"That's not fair. There's been no succession—"

"I suppose I could get used to the motels. I mean, you'd have to get an extra room, and I'd *really* want a nonsmoking room. Do they have nonsmoking rooms in motels? I don't spend much time in motels."

"That's good," I said, trying desperately to catch up with the conversation. "I mean, motels—"

"They're okay for you," she said, gathering speed. "I suppose. I'd have to sort of weed my things down to a suitcase or two, and you'd have to buy me a laptop to replace my desktop, and you'd have to stick to motels pretty close to my school, at least when it's in session. And you'd have to pay my cell phone bills so Mom could get in touch with me no matter where we are. Where are you now?"

"Um . . . the, the North Pole." Never until I said those three words had I seen the sheer breadth of the gulf between the way I lived and the way Rina lived. It yawned wider than the Grand Canyon. "It's not for you."

A pause almost too narrow for daylight. "Does she stay there, too?"

"She? Oh, her. No. No, she's got an apartment. I don't stay with anybody."

"What about me?" Rina asked. "Could you stay with me?"

I rolled straight through a yellow light. "I, uh—what I mean—"

"That's okay," Rina said. "Are we almost there?"

"It's just a big change—"

"Sure. Sure, I understand. I mean, Mom *said* you'd—"

"My life, the way it is right now, it's not right for you. I'd have to make a lot of changes, find a permanent place, maybe change a bunch of other things, but—"

"But you like your life the way it is. That's why you left in the first place, isn't it? You don't want the little white house and the fence and the, the kid you have to look after all the time. No, the North Pole sounds great. And your girlfriend. Sounds great. How much farther *is* it?"

"Right up here. We're not finished talking about this."

"We are for now," Rina said, and she sounded exactly like her mother.

**The room was** small and intensively air-conditioned. It contained two rolling black leather office chairs and a style-free black-and-chrome table, topped by a flatscreen TV hooked up to a DVD player. Rina took the chair on the right without a word, provoking a curious glance from the young woman who had ushered us in. Rina gave the glance back with compound interest and then turned to study the wall to her right. We hadn't spoken since we parked the car.

"We pulled everything that came up using the search terms Mr. Whelan gave us," the young woman said. "Our collection of

*American Dance Hall* isn't anything like complete. Some of the kinescopes have disappeared, some haven't been digitized, and Art Clay hasn't made others available to us yet. But we found three appearances by Giorgio and two by the other boy, Bobby, um, Bobby Angel."

"That's great," I said, all hearty enthusiasm.

"I'd never seen any of it until I dug these out for you," she said. "Gosh, Giorgio was handsome, wasn't he? Whatever happened to him?"

Without turning to face us, Rina said, "He died in a fire." She barely seemed to be in the room.

"How terrible. He was so beautiful. I was surprised I hadn't heard of him before."

"Did you listen to him sing?" I asked.

"Oh, well, yes," she said. "That. Still, he could have made movies."

"He did," Rina snapped. "Isn't this supposed to be like a research facility or something? He made three movies and quit acting halfway through the fourth."

The young woman took a step back. "I see. Well." She handed me a DVD in a plastic sleeve. "It's all on here. Just leave it in the player when you're finished." She backed out of the room and closed the door.

"New friends are like stepping stones in life," I said.

"Who cares? This place looks like it cost a trillion dollars, and there's more information in *Wikipedia*." She put a foot on the white wall, removed it, and looked with satisfaction at the print of her shoe. "Which is free, as you might remember. This is so *old-world*. Everybody getting rich preserving stuff that's already getting preserved for free. And most of it's junk anyway."

"Speaking of junk," I said, sliding the DVD into the player.

"What am I supposed to tell Mom? About your girlfriend, I mean."

"Oh, Jesus. I don't know. Nothing, don't tell her anything. It's not going to make her happy."

Rina said something rude under her breath. Aloud, she said, "She's already not happy. I don't know how a lie is going to help."

"It's not a lie. I don't know yet whether this is important. You could get your mother all upset and three days from now, it'll be over."

"And then there's me."

"We're not through talking about you."

"Says you. Maybe I say we are."

"You're too smart for that."

Rina slid her chair four inches away from me, closer to the wall. "Not everything is about smart."

"Do you think I don't know—"

"So, about the girlfriend," she said, "I suppose you want me to keep quiet until you decide whether the woman is *worthy* of you."

"That's not the issue. She's not a box of crackers. She's got something to say about it, too."

"Glad to hear it. But what's already happened, that's going to cut Mom up, you know?"

"An excellent reason not to tell—"

"You probably think, because of Bill—"

"I'm not talking about Bill."

"No," Rina said. She'd been sitting forward in her chair, and now she leaned back. "You've been really good about that. I keep waiting for you to bring Bill up, and you keep not doing it."

"Listen." I paused and tried to find words that wouldn't crank things up again. "You living with me, that's a different discussion. We'll have it after I think about how I can create a space, any kind of space, that would be good for you. But about the other thing, it's—look, if you were out in a car with some friends, and somebody else drove into, I don't know, the rear fender of your friend's car, and the car got kind of dinged up but nobody was hurt, I mean everybody is absolutely okay, not a scratch, just some damage to this other kid's car, would you tell your mother?"

She shook her head slowly. "Is that like supposed to be a metaphor or something?"

"That's exactly what it's supposed to be."

"So what you seem to be saying," Rina said, "is that it doesn't matter what you do with your body. It's just sort of unimportant, like an accident where nobody got hurt."

"Not *your* body," I said. "What you do with your body matters a lot."

"You're not being real consistent, are you?"

I pushed PLAY and then PAUSE. "I don't have to be consistent. I'm your father."

She slapped both palms against her thighs. "I *knew* we'd get to this point sooner or later. It's such a bogus argument. Especially when you don't even want me to live—"

"I didn't say that. I said I have to think about how to make it work. And don't be so quick to call the argument bogus, because you're going to get stuck with it yourself when you're a parent."

"And in the meantime, while I let you get away with being Mister Adult, I'm also supposed to decide what's best for Mom. Me, Miss Kid."

"No," I admitted. "It's not real consistent."

"No shit," she said. "And don't tell me to watch my language, because I needed to say that."

"I hate that you're in this position," I said. "But you're

not exactly an ordinary kid, Rina, and that's not flattery. I'd worry a lot more about Kathy if you weren't in that house with her."

After a moment, she said, "I know." She put her palms together and squeezed them between her legs. "Could it be any colder in here?"

"So I guess you have to do what you think—"

"Bill's okay," she said, sounding like we'd been discussing it all day. "He's kind of basic, you know? Like, like Ajax Cleanser. There's nothing fancy about him, but he sort of *works*. If he says he'll fix the sink, he fixes the sink. Things in the house don't squeak any more. He doesn't make Mom feel stupid. You always kind of made her feel dumb, did you know that?"

I had to turn to look at her. Kathy had held the moral high ground so effortlessly throughout our time together that it had never occurred to me that there was another index in play, one on which she came in second. "No."

Rina nodded and turned her eyes back to the road. "Well, you did. You still do. And he doesn't. He asks her for advice. And he takes it. You never did that. And it's not like she gets to give me much advice, I mean, besides telling me to eat my vegetables and get a lot of sleep, Mom 101 advice. And if you think *you're* confused about Tyrone, she spent the first two dinners he ate with us talking about Bill Cosby and, jeez, Louis Armstrong. She kept bringing up Oprah. She was so rattled she forgot Barack Obama is black. I wanted to hide under the table."

"You wouldn't do that, though."

"Neither would Tyrone. I didn't know how much I liked him until I heard him talk to Mom. It was really . . . pretty, the way he handled it. I know that's an odd word, but that's what it was, it was pretty."

She broke it off and sat there, looking down at the hands clasped between her legs. "Okay," she said. "I won't tell her."

"I think that's smart."

"Don't sound so relieved. There's a deal involved."

"This is not a complete surprise."

"What's her name?"

"Ronnie. Short for Veronica."

"I like Veronica better."

"Me, too."

"Well, if *Ronnie* is still around in a week, I want to meet her."

"Fine."

I got a sidelong look. "Does she know you have a daughter?"

"She does. And she knows I tell you everything that matters."

"So you were going to tell me about—"

"I was. I just wanted to do it my way."

"Huh," Rina said. "We'll be looking at each other pretty hard. All this information."

"Just to get this straight in advance," I said, "I will refuse to leave the room. I won't go out for a walk, I won't even go get anyone a glass of water. There will be no girl talk, no heart to heart. I'll be there the entire time. Like a, a lifeguard."

"The sure sign of a guilty conscience."

"Read it any way you want."

"Okay," she said. "That's how I'll read it." She sat up and looked around the room. "Why am I here again?"

"I want to borrow your eyes. You've seen pieces of *American Dance Hall* on YouTube, right?"

"Are you kidding? I've seen more of it than they've got here."

"Well, we're looking for anything that sticks out. Anything that's out of the ordinary. Anything that reminds you of something that maybe wasn't in your paper. And just explain things to me."

"There's a lot of stuff that wasn't in my paper. I barely wrote about Giorgio at all."

"Let's go, then." I pushed PLAY again, and the screen flickered and then stuttered a few black-and-white frames before settling into something coherent.

"Here's somebody I know you're going to like," said Art Clay, who had built his local Philadelphia TV show into a national phenomenon and then made it the basis of an enormous production company dedicated entirely to mediocrity, all the while staying miraculously clear of payola charges. And here he was, baby-faced and slick-haired, holding a microphone the size of a blackjack. "He's one of our own," Clay said, "but he's riding the rocket to national stardom. Let's hear it for Giorgio."

Fade to black for a moment to build the expectation level, and then the lights went up on the stage in the corner of the studio, and Giorgio stood there like someone frozen on the train tracks. His hair was plastered back and triple-combed, except for a long comma that had been trained forward to fall over the left half of his forehead and bisect his eyebrow. He licked his lips nervously, waiting for the music to start. The camera tracked left to provide some movement, since Giorgio wasn't supplying any, and the kids came into the shot, and Rina said, "Freeze it."

I looked down at the remote, which was complicated enough to fly the space shuttle. It had buttons, wheels, arrows, sliders, everything but an ashtray. As I stared helplessly at it, Giorgio's music came out of the TV speakers, *chunk, chunk, chunk*, three major chords.

Rina said, "God, just give it to me."

I handed it to her without even bothering to protest, and she played a quick Chopin polonaise on it with her thumbs, and the picture on the screen froze just as Giorgio opened his ridiculously perfect lips to sing.

"That's great," I said. "No sound on freeze-frame. We don't have to listen to him."

"Look," Rina said, and she backed up the DVD at about quarter-speed, and there, as the camera reached the farthest extremity of its track to the left, you could see the edge of the set and Art Clay over Giorgio's shoulder, and standing next to Clay, whispering in his ear and apparently believing he was off-camera, was a pudgy, mustachioed Italian guy in a loose, boxy suit.

"DiGaudio," Rina said. "In his late twenties, probably. Doesn't he look like a gangster?"

"I think that was just the neighborhood style. The FBI files make it pretty clear that the Philly mob wanted him, not that they had him."

Rina said, "*Daddy.*"

Something in her tone made me look over at her.

"My footnotes," she said. "All those footnotes at the end of my paper? The footnotes I spent so many hours on?"

"I saw them," I said, knowing I was in trouble. "Very professional looking. Very, uh, scholarly."

"The Philly mob wanted DiGaudio," she said. "But not because he wasn't a gangster. You didn't read them."

"I think I can honestly say that I've never read a footnote in my life. I skip them. They're the linguistic equivalent of pimento. That was the main reason I educated myself mostly out of novels. Most novelists don't use—" I stopped and replayed what she'd said. "What do you mean it wasn't because he wasn't a gangster?"

"He *was* a gangster. He just wasn't a Philly gangster. The Philly gangsters wanted to get him away from the gang that was running him."

"The gang that was—" I said, and stopped. I felt like someone had broken an egg over my head. "Los Angeles," I said. "He came to Los Angeles." The page from Derek's notebook swam into view, supplying the next piece right on cue. "And he came by way of Chicago."

"As you'd know, if you'd read—" Rina began.

"So *Sal=ID* was wrong," I said over her.

"Sal equals ID?" Rina asked. "What's that supposed to mean?"

"It's a speculation," I said, "made by someone who's no longer with us. He was wondering whether Eddie 'The Moose' Salerno—"

"Right, the Philadelphia mob guy who got cooked in that restaurant."

"—whether Salerno was partners with Irwin Dressler, here in Los Angeles."

"Irwin who?"

"Dressler. Irwin Dressler. The LA presence for the Chicago mob."

"The mob that was running DiGaudio's company," Rina said.

"Right, and I would have known that earlier if I'd read your footnote."

"Or a few more of those FBI files I linked you to."

"It creeped me out, being on the FBI's site," I said. "I had a feeling they were looking back at me."

She crossed her legs and returned her attention to the television screen. "They probably were."

"But he was wrong, our dead guy. Salerno didn't equal Irwin. Irwin and Salerno were rivals."

"If this Irwin was Chicago," Rina said, "his guys probably started the war that got the Italians in Philadelphia to eat each other for dinner."

"What year was that?"

She turned back to me and looked doubtful. "Nineteen sixty-four? Sixty-five?"

"That works," I said.

"Works for what?"

"For a time line. And now I understand why Irwin wanted to know—" I broke it off, but it was too late. Rina was staring at me as though I'd just spontaneously burst into flame.

"Irwin?" She looked horrified. "You're talking to this guy Irwin?"

"You know," I said airily. "You meet all kinds—"

"This mob guy? This mob guy who must be, what, two thousand years old? This is all forty-five, fifty years ago. But still—"

"He's old and harmless now," I said. "Just an old guy in plaid slacks."

"I suppose this is something else I shouldn't go talking to Mom about."

"Let's watch our nice show."

"You drive me crazy," she said, and she hit PLAY and cranked up the volume as Giorgio made his noises. I had my fingers in my ears when she slowed the disk again. There was a camera behind Giorgio, and it caught the kids dancing in front of him and looking up at him, the girls with awe and the boys with a kind of irritated tolerance.

"That's Corinne," she said, freezing the frame and leaning forward to touch the face of a girl whose eye makeup had been inspired by Elizabeth Taylor's in *Cleopatra*. "Lots of guys thought she was hot. She's dancing with somebody whose name I don't know, but later she took Kenny away from Arlene and then dropped him, and everybody got all vengeful about it, like she should have to wear a scarlet letter."

"Kind of a waste on black-and-white TV."

"You know what I mean." She tapped the screen again. "See

how she's pushing that broomstick she's dancing with toward Giorgio? One of the reasons girls hated her was that she had such an obvious case on Giorgio."

Corinne had piled her hair into a beehive high enough to conceal a highway safety cone. The black lines around her eyes were as thick as jet trails, and she'd also put some kind of beauty spot on her chin.

Rina pushed PLAY and used her index fingers to identify other regulars as they danced through the reverse shot over Giorgio's shoulder, and then the camera was back in closeup on Giorgio's perfect face, and once again I had the sense that he was terrified.

"This poor kid," I said. "He should never have been up there."

"No. He never looked like he enjoyed it."

"Well, he was terrible. It's like watching a stool try to tap dance."

"There are lots of terrible singers," Rina said. "Although you're right, there weren't many as bad as Giorgio. And look, he's a little fat on this show. The poor kid gained weight real easily. See under his chin? He's got maybe five, ten pounds on him that aren't there in his movies."

"Maybe he wanted to be fat," I said. "Maybe he figured if he got fat, everybody would leave him alone."

"Maybe," she said. "He was apparently really fat when he was making the movie in Hawaii, the one he walked off of. They had him like living on lettuce."

"How much longer does this song go on?"

"Wait a minute," she said. "It just seems long. Got another audience shot coming up, when he bows."

And sure enough, the song actually did end and Giorgio stopped lip-synching, and the kids screamed dutifully while he kind of ducked his head, looking deeply embarrassed. The kids flocked around him, with the tramp, whatever her name was—Corinne—in the lead, gazing up at him with a kind of manic adoration. It looked like she was going to lean forward and take a bite out of his thigh. And then they changed camera angles to shoot over the kids' heads at Giorgio, and DiGaudio was standing about four feet from him, at the edge of the stage looking like he expected his star to bolt.

"That's one eerie guy," Rina said.

There was a brief glimpse of a commercial for Clearasil, and then the DVD skipped to the next track and Art Clay, all slick hair, narrow tie, and blackjack microphone, introduced Bobby Angel.

I sat forward.

Bobby was square-featured and pudgy, and the shiny white, oversize shirt with the puffy sleeves didn't do much to disguise it. He had the loose, ultra-cool, left-hand finger-snap thing down pat, and even before he started to lip-synch, I knew what I was in for: late-period, pallid, third-generation Sinatra, via Bobby Darin, modest swing vocals with a hand-me-down ring-a-ding-ding attitude, and that's what I got. But the kid had a decent voice and despite the extra pounds, his body language was rhythmic and economical. And he looked like he was having fun.

"Embryonic lounge singer," I said.

"That's probably what he would have been, if he hadn't vanished." Rina said. "I kind of like him. He looks, I don't know, *nice*. He looks like someone who thought he'd always be the little fat boy in the corner, and instead he's standing up there with all the girls looking at him."

"Not exactly drooling, though."

"No." The audience was back on camera, and Rina hit PAUSE. The kids were dancing, paying more attention to each other than to Bobby, but they were obviously enjoying themselves. "Kenny and Arlene," Rina said, tapping a nail against the screen. Two perfectly ordinary looking kids, except that Kenny had the ghostly ambition of sideburns, just shadows now but a style choice that would probably have gotten him into trouble at school in a week or so. "They were off and on, off and on." Rina sat back. "Like a soap opera. It's hard to believe anybody was interested."

"Where's Corinne?"

"Who knows? Giorgio's not on, so she's probably in the bathroom, putting burnt cork on her eyes."

We watched Bobby Angel work the song, making a real effort to look like he was singing live. Rina was right: There was something endearing about him. He was a schlub who couldn't believe his luck, and it was impossible not to enjoy it along with him.

"How tall were they?" I asked.

"You mean Giorgio and Bobby? I have no idea."

"We don't get to see them standing next to anybody, do we?"

"I think Giorgio was around five-ten," Rina said. "In the movies, he looks just, you know, *kind of* tall. He's not towering over everybody, but he's not standing on a box, either."

"Here he comes again," I said as the DVD moved to the next track. This time, Art Clay waded through the crowd of kids, microphone in hand, doing a tease intro: "One of the brightest new stars in American music, a young man who's on his way to Hollywood—"

I was halfway out of my chair before I said to Rina, "Stop it. Freeze it right there."

She did, stranding Art Clay with his mouth open, all the kids around him looking at him except the Egyptian-eyed Corinne, who was staring off to her left, where Giorgio had presumably taken his place on the stage. I looked at her and said, "Holy shit."

Rina said, "I'm obviously missing something significant."

"The mole on her chin," I said. "That's not a beauty spot."

## 29
### Looking for the Groove

"We're going home," I said, starting the car.

"So what?" Rina demanded for the fourth time. "So what if it wasn't a beauty spot?"

"It would take me half an hour to explain it to you."

"Remember rush hour?" she said. "From here to the Valley, we've only got like the rest of our lives."

"I need to think." I put the car into reverse.

"You need to look behind you, too," she said. "You're going to back into that Hummer."

"A Hummer," I said, putting the car back into park and resisting the urge to rest my forehead on the steering wheel and close my eyes. The Hummer sat square in my rearview mirror, not going anywhere. I couldn't see who was driving without adjusting the side mirror, and I didn't want to give him the satisfaction.

"Listen to me," I said. "And I mean listen one hundred percent. Are you with me?"

"Right here."

"Okay. If you go left in the alley at the end of this lot, it'll take you to Brighton Way. If you go right on Brighton Way and then left at the first cross street, that will take you straight down to Wilshire."

"And?"

"And when you get a light to cross, because there's a lot of traffic, you can go into the Beverly Wilshire Hotel."

"That's really interesting," Rina said, "but I'm not the one who's driving."

"I'm going to get out of the car now. At the count of three. When I say 'three,' you open your door just a crack, at the same time I do. Hold it so it doesn't open further. I'll leave mine open so the light in the car stays on."

"Why do we want the light in the car to—"

"Shush. If I hit the trunk or the fender hard, twice, that means you open your door the rest of the way and take off running as fast as you can. Left into the alley, right on Brighton—"

"You're scaring me."

"Good. Because you need to run like there's a fucking bear after you. Right on Brighton and left at the first—"

"Got it. Into the hotel, if I can get there." Rina's face was pale. "Then what?"

"Wait ten minutes. If I don't show up, call your mom."

"Oh, boy." There was perspiration at her hairline.

"You're okay. At the count of three. One. Two. Three."

I opened the door and climbed out, and I felt, rather than heard, Rina's door pop off the latch. I got out, and was surprised to see the Humvee move forward. Once it was out of the way, it stopped and the door opened, and Fronts clambered out and said, "We gonna need to move that car, I think."

"You should have moved Derek's."

"I forgot. Let me see your hands, Junior."

My hands, unfortunately, were empty. I have a policy of not being armed when I'm around my daughter, so the Glock was in the trunk. I thought for a second about going back and popping the trunk but the automatic hanging straight down beside

Fronts' leg changed my mind. I wasn't sure he even knew he had it in his hand, and I didn't want to remind him.

"Beverly Hills," Fronts said, nodding ponderously. He was the color of library paste, the color of someone who has voluntarily had every drop of blood drained out of him, the dead, long-term floater-white of Rina's fishburger patty. He wore a pair of horrifically stained painter's coveralls and a white T-shirt, and the T-shirt was translucently wet, hanging heavy with sweat despite the cool day. There was a wide bandage wrapped around the upper arm I'd put the bullet through. Carved into the forearm below it, his right, in gouges still fresh enough for the meat to be red, was the word LEFT.

"My kind of town," I said. "All this glamour."

"Always with a chick," Fronts said, squinting through the back window at Rina. "I don't have all these chicks."

"You want to find a girl who really needs something to read."

"You're fuckin' up," Fronts said. "I thought I was kind of plain about it, but here you are, looking at old TV. That's what people do in there, right? How's the other one?"

"The other what?"

He winced for a second, and I mistook it for pain until I realized it was the sheer effort of trying to remember what we were talking about. "The other chick. The one in bed."

"Fine," I said. "She woke up."

He nodded. "It's better when they wake up." He let his eyes drop to the pavement. His body swayed to the left, but he stepped to the side before he went down. "Hey, look," he said, still studying the pavement. "The hell with moving the car. I'm going to have to kill you."

"You're screwed," I said. "I know everything, and I'm not the only one who does. You kill me, it's going to point straight at you. You're going to get an extra death sentence. What you ought to do is get the hell out of here. Go tell her you did it, tell her I'm dead, get your money, and get out of town."

It took him a moment, but it eventually brought his head up. "Her," he said.

"I know it all, Fronts. And, like I said, I've shared it with some people. If you do me, there's only going to be one suspect."

I watched him process it, watched his eyebrows come together and his lips move, and then he shook his head heavily and brought up the arm with the gun in it until it was pointed straight at my chest.

"Uh-uh," he said. "Sorry, Junior."

I was backing away. "That's your right arm," I said.

"What is?" The gun was as steady as a hypnotist's gaze.

"The one you carved LEFT on."

"It's a joke," Fronts said, and he closed one eye to sight more precisely, and I took two more steps back, and the car roared into life and jerked into reverse with a shriek of rubber, missing me by about an inch and knocking Fronts a good five feet. I caught a glimpse of Rina's enormous eyes, her head craned all the way around, and then I sprinted around the back of the car and found Fronts, looking confused, trying to push himself to his knees. I snatched the gun out of his hand and pasted him across the side of the head with it. He emitted the peaceful sigh of a man whose sleeping pill has finally kicked in, and went back down. I got both hands under him and rolled him back like a rug across a dance floor, giving Rina enough room to back the car the rest of the way out, and then I got in as she slid across the seat and huddled against the passenger door, which swung open under her weight. If I hadn't grabbed her arm, she'd have fallen sideways out of the car. She closed the door and put on her seatbelt, moving like a robot and breathing shallowly through her mouth, and I drove decorously away, heading for the parking kiosk, where the attendant was looking everywhere at the world except at me. He opened the gate as I pulled up, flapping both hands at me and saying, "No charge, no charge," and I turned right onto Canon.

"I didn't know you could drive," I said.

"I'm not so good at going forward," Rina said, and there was something spidery and insubstantial in her voice, as though she'd run three miles but didn't want it to show, and then suddenly we were both laughing. Then she stopped laughing, as abrupt as a film cut, and said, "He was going to shoot you."

"He was thinking about it," I said. "In his own way."

"I *ran over him*." She put her hand over her mouth, fingers pointed up, looking like she needed to keep the next words from escaping, as though that could somehow derail the thought behind them. "He might be. . . . He might be—"

"He isn't," I said. "He barely felt it. This is a guy who irons himself for fun."

"But the car—it felt like I hit a tree."

"You knocked him ass over elbow," I said. "But he wasn't even unconscious, or at least no more unconscious than he usually is. I had to slap him with this to put him out." I took the gun off my lap and put it on the seat between us. She scooted away from it until she was plastered to the door again.

"Lock that thing," I said. "If you're going to lean on it, lock it."

"You're worried about a *car door?*"

"I'm worried about you. Lock it."

"Who was he?"

"He was—is—a guy named Fronts. He kills people."

"And he—I mean, you—" She broke off and turned to look at me for the first time since I'd gotten into the car. "Why do you *live* like this?"

I said, "It keeps me young."

"You're crazy. My father is crazy. You want to know what Mom sees in Bill? *This* is what she sees in Bill. There isn't any of this with Bill."

"I don't know," I said. "Suppose the ducks decide to get even."

Rina said, "It isn't funny."

"It might as well be. Since it has to be something, it might as well be funny." I made a sudden right onto a smaller street and pulled into a red zone. "Hold on a second," I said. I got out of the car and ran toward the sidewalk and bent over with my hands on my knees and threw up. Then I threw up again. I stood there like that, all bent over with my guts in spasm, until Rina's window went down and her hand came out with two sticks of gum in it.

"Here," she said.

I said, "Thanks," and took it. I let the wrappers flutter to the pavement and chewed for a moment, feeling the clean spearmint replace the acidic taste of vomit. Then I went around the car and climbed back in. I put both hands on the wheel and just sat there, shaking, for what felt like a couple of minutes.

"I suppose," Rina said, "that you don't want me to tell Mom about this."

I started to laugh again, and a second later, Rina laughed, too. She said, "Yeah, maybe you need to make some changes before I move in," and the two of us laughed harder.

I pulled into traffic, and her cell phone rang. She was still laughing, kind of a high-pitched, breathless laugh, as she dug the phone out of her purse, opened it, caught her breath, and said, "Hello." I caught an undertone in her voice I'd never heard before and turned to see her sitting with her head inclined forward, curled protectively over the phone, one hand cradling it as though it were the Koh-i-noor Diamond and the other hand shielding her mouth as if that would keep me from hearing her end of the conversation, and I stopped laughing and it felt like a part of my heart broke off and sank.

I said, "Tyrone?" and she nodded.

"It's my dad," she said into the phone. She wiped at her eyes. "You won't believe what just happened. What's up?" She sat up. "Really? What's it sound like?" To me, she said, "One of those records of DiGaudio's just finished downloading." She said to Tyrone, "Sure. Right now, I can believe anything. Play it for me." She used her free hand to cover her other ear and listened for a few moments, and her eyes widened, and she turned to me and said, *Daddy*," looking like she'd just seen someone rise from the dead.

And I said, "I know."

**Since I've been** looking into things, so to speak, for other people, I've learned that there comes a point in every case when the rock begins to roll downhill. What you do at that point depends on whether you're behind the rock, trying to see where it's going, or in front of it, trying not to get smashed flat. I was unmistakably at the point where the rock has started to roll. The question was whether I was behind it or in front of it.

Or, since I was doing two things at the same time, whether I was both behind it *and* in front of it.

In either case, the only thing to do was run. So, as I drove east on Ventura, away from Kathy's house, I took the first steps to get out of the way on at least one front.

"He didn't murder Derek Bigelow," I said into the phone. Traffic was crawling. The sun was touching the horizon, and it was about to get dark. "But the person who did is very close to him, and Vinnie's going to get splashed."

"Splashed," Irwin Dressler said. "How bad?"

"Bad enough. It's all going to come out, the whole story. And I have to tell you, he's going to have at least an accessory charge against him."

"What's going to come out? No, never mind. You said a splash, not a charge."

"Not a charge on Bigelow. Somebody else."

"For *what* with somebody else? Kidnapping? Rape? Murder?"

"Murder. As I think you already know."

"Pretend I don't. Who?"

"I don't feel like pretending. But I'll tell you, if I were you, I'd do whatever it takes to cut the strings."

"Yeah."

"You're welcome," I said. "And you owe me." I hung up.

**With my Glock** in one hand and the stubby Sig Sauer P226 I'd taken from Fronts in the other, it would have been awkward for me to finesse the hardware on Vinnie DiGaudio's door, but I didn't have to. It was standing wide open.

I'd hiked up the driveway, figuring I'd give them as little warning as possible. It had been a waste of energy. There were no cars in the parking area, and the front door was all the way back against the inside wall that Popsie—or, rather, Corinne— had kept slamming it against.

I went in quietly anyway.

The house was darkening and silent, no lights on that I could see, and there was a strong scorched smell, familiar somehow and kind of homey. All I could hear was the occasional creak of wood as the air outside cooled and bits and pieces of the house contracted and settled. I slowly worked my way down the length of the entrance hall, my back brushing the wall on the right, and checking each dimming room as I went. Nobody in either of the first two rooms. Nobody in the big room with the curved window, just the dented cushions in the center of the couch and, in front of it, an open and empty drawer where DiGaudio had kept his cash. I checked to make sure. Nothing but four rubber bands, all twisted up in that kind of agonized tangle rubber bands sometimes achieve when they've been triple-stretched around something and then rolled off.

The smell in here was sharper and heavier at the same time. Definitely something burning.

Standing in the middle of the floor, I turned toward the window. I was right on the spot where Corinne had been when she sensed Derek. It wasn't hard to imagine him out there, frozen in the darkness, with no idea that he was minutes away from making his final discovery, peeking under his final rock, firing off the flash that would bring Fronts into his life

The door to the hallway, the hallway where Vinnie had been photographed chatting with Nessie, was closed. I went instead into the kitchen and turned on the light to reveal the familiar mess. The charred smell in here was almost strong enough to make me sneeze. A covered pot sat atop a back burner with a low flame beneath it. I tucked Fronts' gun under my left arm to free up a hand and lifted the lid. Smoke escaped from the browned, dried-out rice inside, so I put the lid back and turned off the fire. Missing money, burning rice, no lights on: All seemed to signal a hurried departure, and not long ago, before the sun had sunk. Fronts had obviously recovered enough to make a phone call, or maybe even to drop by.

I flipped the kitchen lights off and was about to open the swinging door into the hallway when the music started.

I froze.

It was your basic eight-bar intro, nothing special about it.

Variations of it had been used to open tens of thousands of records over the years. Nothing unusual about the instruments, either: just the classic rock configuration of lead guitar, rhythm guitar, bass, and drums. Ace Rabinowitz was probably in the mix somewhere, drilling for oil and coming up with Mazola. The progression repeated, and then it repeated again. Then it repeated again. It sounded like the tape had been allowed to run unattended as the musicians noodled around with the intro, ran through it over and over, making little changes, trying to crank up the groove, trying to get it right.

The lead guitar suddenly dropped out. A second later, the bass went mute, and then it was as though the strings on the rhythm guitar had been snipped with scissors, and all that was left was the drum track. It got louder and louder. It filled the house, until it was loud enough to make the swinging kitchen door vibrate under my fingers. I probably could have fired the Glock without being heard over it.

There didn't seem to be much point in tiptoeing. I shoved open the door, and the drums thundered down the hall, two-four on the offbeat: snare, high-hat cymbal, double-kick on the bass pedal. It got even louder.

The hallway was dark, but light fell across the carpet and up the wall opposite the open door to the control room.

I was being invited down.

Since an entire mechanized division of the old Soviet Army could have mobilized, sputtering and clanking behind me without my hearing a thing, I decided to check my back. I took a look into the pyramid room, which was still empty and not conspicuously alive with spirit, and the two bedrooms, both unoccupied. Closets full of clothes, but no one lurking inside. Bathrooms rifled—drawers open, stuff on the floor—but unpopulated. The door that had been locked on the night I broke in was standing wide, and I looked into a big room with a king-size bed in it. Hanging from a frame above the bed was a dark blue canopy of some sort of glittering midnight cloth, as fey as the decor in a Disney cartoon. It looked like birds might have swooped in and hung it there while the princess slept. Other than the ornate bed, there wasn't much else in the way of furniture: a small table beside the bed with a lamp and a couple of books on it, a desk with a computer. No chairs, which wasn't a surprise.

The walls were almost completely covered with posters. Different titles, different venues, different costumes, different dates, but always the same face, shot from every possible angle, the same name, over and over again. It hadn't been much of a career, but it had been extensively photographed.

I went back into the hall and approached the open door of the control room. I stood beside it for a moment, grabbed a breath, brought both guns up, and stepped into the doorway. There he was. He'd turned the wheelchair around, putting his back to the console so he could look up at me. He reached behind him and pulled down a slider on the board, and the drums mercifully stopped.

I said, "Hi, Giorgio."

He weighed three hundred pounds if he weighed an ounce. The left side of his head was bald, the border between bare scalp and graying hair as irregular as the edge of a splash of water. Below the baldness, the left half of his face was a liquid smear of skin that looked like something done to modeling clay by a willful child. The left eye was fused closed, but the right one glittered up at me. He had a violet blanket folded across his lap and one hand underneath it. There was something in the hand.

I wiggled the two guns, just claiming his attention, and he smiled with the right side of his mouth.

"I told them," he said, and he drew one of those fluid-filled breaths. "I told them you'd figure it out."

"I'd have known earlier if all that sheet music hadn't said 'Abbruzzi.' What was the point?"

"Vinnie always thought we'd have a hit." He made a noise like someone tearing wet paper, and I realized it was a laugh. "He had a vision of us on top of the charts again. I never bought it, but if it happened, I wanted the money to go to Bobby's family."

"Blood money."

"I guess. Kind of academic, though, isn't it? We never sold anything."

"The night you caught me in here. Why didn't you raise some sort of alarm?"

"We'd had enough alarms for one night. That was pretty cute, the thing you did with the alarm. And I figured, why bother? Sooner or later, you know. It had to come sooner or later. It's already lasted way too long."

"Why are you still here? Why didn't you go with them?"

He shrugged. "Same reason. Didn't want to. Too much trouble. Anyway, why bother? What am I going to do, melt into the crowd? Grow a mustache, wear sunglasses? I've had enough. It's terrible about Bobby, terrible he had to die, but I'd trade places with him."

"Too bad you didn't realize that before you killed him. It was you, wasn't it?"

"And Corinne. It was Corinne's idea. She told Vinnie to get him to come out here, tell him it was a secret, not to tell anybody anything. Told him it was about the movies." The laugh again. "I guess it was, sort of." Laugh or no laugh, he couldn't hold my eyes. His gaze dropped to the floor between us.

"Your movie in Hawaii. What happened?"

He sighed. It sounded like resignation; there was no way out of the conversation. "Salerno. It was plain old stupid revenge.

He didn't even want Vinnie's business any more, not with the Chicago guys on the scene. He just wanted to hurt somebody. So he sent a couple of guys to Honolulu, just a pair of thugs. They knocked on my door, told me The Moose had sent them and to say hi to Vinnie, and poured acid on me. Then they cut the tendons behind my knees and left."

"It never made the papers."

He sat bolt upright in the chair, gaining a couple of inches in height. "Look at me," Giorgio said. "I'm hideous. I'm half-blind. I can't walk. This hurt like nothing in the world has ever hurt. I was *not going to be in the newspapers*. I was not going to be the freak of the year, the hole the world poured pity into. That was all I had left. It was the only thing I could control." His voice had tightened until it was almost shrill. He stopped, drew a deep breath, and brought his eyes back up to mine. "So." He paused and ran hit tongue over his upper lip. "Vinnie hauled me out of there wrapped from head to foot in sheets, someone in Chicago arranged for a doctor to wash everything out, disinfect it, do what he could do. It wasn't much. Then Vinnie and Corinne and I got on a freighter and came home. The press doesn't meet freighters. The people on board had never heard of me—they were too old. Vinnie and Corinne pushed me right off the boat in a wheelchair and took me home, and nobody even glanced at us."

"But sooner or later," I said, "people would have begun to wonder where you were. They'd have come looking for you. Sooner or later, it would have been *poor Giorgio*."

"With the vermin milking it," he said. "Magazine covers. Guest experts. Hack psychiatrists. Sob sisters. 'How does it *feel* to have half your face wiped away?' *Hideous* Giorgio, *tragic* Giorgio, a modern-day Phantom of the Opera, we feel so *sorry* for him, that'll be three-ninety-five for the magazine, your thirty-second commercial will run you a hundred thou." He moved the hand beneath the blanket, and I tapped the door frame with the barrel of the Glock. He stopped moving the hand. "And they'd trot me out on Halloween or during slow news weeks. Art Clay would have made a fortune out of it."

"So there was Bobby. You'd gained weight, you were about the same height. What did you use?"

"Ether. It dissipates faster than barbiturates, which was pretty much all there were in those days. Doesn't leave much of anything in the respiratory system that a fire wouldn't account for. I soaked a napkin with it and knocked him out. Corinne put him in my bed and lit a cigarette. Then she poured ether on the sheets and dropped the cigarette into the middle of it. Went up like that flash paper magicians use, just *fwoooosh*. Ether's so flammable it ignites at a hundred eighty degrees, did you know that?"

"I haven't had much need for the information."

"I found out later. Read a lot about it, over the years. It became one of my topics. So anyway, Bobby was in the part of the house that burned longest, my height, my weight, my bed, and we knew Vinnie would be called to make the identification. No DNA then, and neither of us had fillings, so no dental work to check. Oh, we gave Bobby a bracelet I wore, a big clunky thing with my name on it. An ID bracelet, remember ID bracelets?"

"Not really."

"You've worked out the rest of it, probably."

"I suppose. You here, safe and sound. Corinne to take care of you, Vinnie to support you. The band coming in to cut records. Kids singing, but the idea was always to pull their vocals—if the vocals were even recorded—and put you on later. And my guess is that the kids were all good-looking because Vinnie was looking for someone commercial, somebody who'd look good when it was time to lip-synch to the records, if it ever came to that."

"Imagine," Giorgio said. "Someone willingly pretending to have my singing voice."

"You hated singing, you hated performing. I saw you. You hated every minute of it. Why would you let them go through all this?"

He looked over my shoulder, and I almost turned to check it out, but then the open eye came to mine. "It was the only thing I could give them. I didn't have anything else for them. Look at all they'd done for me. They'd ruined their lives for me. Vinnie, Corinne. Maybe Corinne most of all. Because they loved me. They thought it would make me *happy*, having more hits, being a star again, even if some other kid's face was on the record. They thought I enjoyed writing the songs. They thought. . . ." He relaxed his neck suddenly and his head dropped forward, his chin on his chest. Slowly he brought it back up and turned it from side to side. It obviously hurt. "They thought it made me happy. How could I tell them it didn't?" The hand beneath the blanket moved again. "If I'd said no, if I hadn't let them do it, what would they have had? All they wanted was to make me happy."

"Love," I said.

I got the half-smile again. "Weird, isn't it."

"So here you are—what?—forty-five, forty-six years later, something like that? And all that time you've been buried in this house, and somebody finally got sloppy, and there was Derek Bigelow."

"One of the musicians," Giorgio said. "He and the reporter— Derek, I guess that's the name—were coke buddies. So, naturally, they talked. And talked, and talked. And the reporter figured out something, I don't know what, exactly, but that there was some sort of monster in Vinnie's house, and he did a lot of research and he took that picture. And then he came to Vinnie for money."

"Three hundred fifty," I said. "Here's the thing I can't figure out. Why dump Bigelow's body on your star? Of all the places in the world, why there?"

"Ah," he said. "That was the result of a little tiff."

"A tiff."

"Between Vinnie and Corinne. Vinnie was going to pay. Talked about killing the guy, even put out a feeler but then he pulled back because Vinnie's soft. Decided to pay. Thought Derek would take the money and go away, and we could all go back to being the happy family we'd been before. But Corinne, who has a forceful personality, said, essentially, *fuck that*, and hired that human potato with the cuts all over him to take care of the reporter. She had him left on top of me—on that part of the sidewalk, I mean—as a warning to Vinnie. Like a statement: No negotiation, ever. Problem was, Vinnie's cop nephew got you involved." He shook the ruined head. "Terrified Corrine so bad she set it up so the potato would kill you when you left. But it didn't work, and then you told Vinnie that Bigelow had been dropped on my star, and Vinnie figured it out, figured it had to be Corrine. But what was he going to do by then? Try to call you off?"

He rocked back and forth in the wheelchair, his weight producing a squeak. "It was so dumb. Vinnie had an alibi and everything, but he figured if he used it—you know, *recording session; musicians*—it would point at me somehow, especially after where the body was found. And, of course, if it pointed to me, then who's buried in my grave? See? Murder one way or the other." He sighed deeply, and the heavy shoulders drooped. "So here we are, and I've had enough. More than enough. This was never fun, but now it's just not worth doing any more. I wouldn't do it even if I could."

"Where'd they go?"

"Who knows? Vinnie grabbed everything valuable he could get his hands on, tried to take me with him, and ran. He couldn't exactly pick me up and carry me out. Corinne said to me, *Hold tight, sweetie, it's not over*, and left with the potato. Oh, yeah, and she kissed me," he said. "Right about here, she kissed me," and he brought the hand out from under the blanket and touched the barrel of the gun to his right cheek and said, "Right here," and pulled the trigger.

He was thrown back against the console, shoving the slider back up, and the drums boomed out again. They chased me all the way out of the house. I could still hear them at the bottom of the hill, the same simple pattern over and over again, snare, high-hat, double bass pedal, twenty, twenty-five, thirty times.

Looking for the groove.

# 30
## Forty Miles Uphill

Nobody was happy with me. Paulie DiGaudio wasn't happy with me because Vinnie was hanging out there in the wind somewhere, Irwin Dressler wasn't happy with me because ditto, Marge wasn't happy with me because I didn't have anything to tell her about Doris except that Pivensey might be in Twentynine Palms, and Rina and Kathy weren't happy with me, for a whole handful of reasons.

And of all of them, I was probably the least happy with me. I should have seen it coming the moment I registered the blanket in Giorgio's lap. The moment I saw him sitting there, alone in that house, suicidally overweight, disfigured, crippled, abandoned, waiting for nothing.

Sitting on the edge of my bed at the North Pole, I couldn't stop seeing the kid in those black-and-white images from half a century ago. The Philadelphia street kid who'd been kidnapped from his front stoop and shoved into the light. Who couldn't sing, couldn't act, couldn't do much of anything. Trapped behind that beautiful face. Frightened all the time, terrified as he hung from his lucky star, far too high. And he'd been right to be terrified.

I should have known what he was going to do the moment I

saw that there was something in his hand. I should have known he didn't intend to use it on *me*.

In search of an appropriate outlet for my feelings, I took off one shoe and went over to the dresser. I gripped the shoe by the front end and used the heel to hammer at the glued-together Christmas-tree balls until every single one of them was pounded to fragments. When the dresser was covered with shards of glass, multicolored and shimmering like the shattered shells of phoenix eggs, and there were half a dozen small cuts on my knuckles, I threw the shoe at the bowl the balls had been in, breaking it in half. Then I went to the bed, sat down, picked up the phone and dialed.

"I'm sorry," I said when she answered.

She said, coolly, "You have good reason to be."

"I know who killed Derek."

"Excuse me if I don't gasp with surprise. I thought we knew yesterday who killed Derek."

"I know who hired him."

"I see," Ronnie said. "And you're calling to inform me that it wasn't I."

"Something like that. It was someone you've never even heard of."

"Well, that's a relief. I may not have lived an exemplary life, back there in Trenton or Albany, but it's good to know I didn't have my husband murdered."

"I don't care where you used to live. I don't give a shit."

"That may be the nicest thing you've ever said to me."

"And I meant every word of it."

She said, "Are you smoking?"

"I don't smoke."

"If you did, would this be the kind of conversation you'd smoke during?"

"Nonstop."

"Then it must matter," she said.

"I think it does." I listened to the sound of her breathing for a second, and then I said, "I told my daughter about—well, *about*."

"Lord almighty," she said. "I won't ask how she took it. Want me to come over?"

"Would you?"

"Instantly. Or I could come over there."

"Wait a minute," I said. "I've kind of totaled this room. Let me check the other one. If it doesn't look worthy of you, I'll go to you."

"What do you mean, you totaled the room?"

"Just finding a creative way to express my self-loathing." I was up and walking.

"Self-loathing? This is the kind of problem women are *for*. I'll be right there."

"Wait," I said. I had the door to Prancer open, and there was a thin stack of computer printouts dead-center on top of the table. Louie had made use of his key. "I need to call you back."

"I'm coming over," she said. "You can hang up, but I'm coming." She disconnected.

Nine sheets of paper, clusters of property records centered on three letters of the alphabet: *P* for Pivensey, *H* for Huff and/ or Hough, and *E* for Enderby. Just as I'd asked, Louie's young woman had pulled the sheet with each of those names on it, or the sheet on which they would have fallen alphabetically, plus the one on either side of it.

There were no Pivenseys, neither male nor female. There was one Enderby, but his name was Edgar, and anyway, he was a seller, not a buyer. There was nobody named Huff. There was nobody named Hough.

But there was a Hoff. A Doris E. Hoff. *E*, at a guess, for Enderby.

A sixteen-acre parcel, probably snipped from a 19th-century 640-acre homestead, the parcel described as having a cabin, a legal easement, and an official hookup to city electric and water. Within the city limits of Twentynine Palms.

Right where he'd gotten the parking ticket.

So he'd married Doris—something Marge didn't know—and bought the property in her name, staying off the official records. Probably told her he was putting her name on the title so it would always be hers. Like a gift. Undoubtedly painted her a picture of a secluded refuge, away from the craziness and dirt of the city, someplace they could live the good, simple life. Someplace with clean air, big skies, warm days, crisp nights. Maybe a wood-burning stove and a big front porch looking out over the otherworldly beauty of Joshua Tree.

Someplace with lots of room for a grave.

He'd introduced the typo into the record at some point in the process, or maybe he just had the luck of the wicked, and Marge had heard him wrong: Huff instead of Hoff. Doris E. Hoff. It might have kept him safe for decades, once she was out of the way.

Which she almost certainly was by now.

The deed listed the property by parcel number, but even better, there was a street address. 1772 Sunrise Drive. It took two minutes on the Rand McNally website to map the whole thing out.

I grabbed the extra magazines for the Glock and checked the Sig Sauer, which was full. The bluing was worn away in places, so the gun had seen a lot of use, but the P226 is a solid, if ugly, piece of machinery and when I popped the clip and racked the slide a couple of times, it was as precise as a Rolex, no burrs or glitches. It dry-fired more easily than I expected; I could have pulled the trigger with an eyelash. Seemed way too light a pull for someone as jittery in his approach to life as Fronts, but you never knew. He might have been a savant where guns were concerned.

My flashlights were already in the car. I owned a pair of night-vision goggles, but they were in storage. I put both guns and the extra clips into a briefcase and toted it down to the Toyota, where I laid it on the floor in front of the passenger seat. The case would be visible to cops, but they'd need probable cause to open it, and I didn't want the weapons locked away in the trunk. I'd had enough of that in my most recent interaction with Fronts.

I opened the trunk and chose a flashlight. I also selected a knife from a small assortment I keep under the spare tire, a razor-sharp, bone-handled buck knife in a leather sheath that it only took a moment to slip over my belt. I hate knives, but I hate the idea of dying more.

I got behind the wheel, started the car, and called Ronnie.

"I'm ten minutes away," she said.

"I have to leave."

A pause. "This better be good."

"I think I know where Doris is."

"Okay," she said. "That's good."

"Can you spend some time with Marge without getting hammered?"

"If I really, really try. What's my excuse?"

"You came to see me but I wasn't home. Stop somewhere and pick up a bottle of vodka, something good, not that formaldehyde she usually drinks. Tell her you were bringing it to me and thought she might like it."

"How long are we talking about?"

"If I drive fast and don't get arrested or killed, you mean?"

"Yes. Especially not killed."

"Two and a half, three hours. By then I'll either know something or I'll be in the wrong place."

"Or dead."

"There's that. But if I'm not, and I know something, then I think Marge had better have someone with her."

"Okay. Not to sound like a girl, but are you going to be careful?"

"Stealthy," I said. "I'm going to be stealthy as hell."

"You'd better be. If you get yourself killed, don't come nosing around for sympathy."

"Take care of Marge," I said.

It was almost nine o'clock, and the Hollywood Freeway was clear all the way to the 10. Los Angeles slid by flat and glittering, the only real spike in the horizon the high-rise downtown skyline to the left. A fat moon, yellow as a smoker's teeth, cleared the horizon through my windshield as I sped east at about seventy-five miles per hour. I was keeping pace with the other traffic, sticking pretty much to one lane, neither the slow lane nor the fast lane, driving my invisible car as invisibly as possible.

When and how had Corinne managed to find her way into Giorgio's life? Obviously it was pre-Hawaii, because she'd been on the scene in Honolulu to help DiGaudio get him home. That was only a few years after DiGaudio decamped to Hollywood, taking most of his boys with him. She was still in her teens then, still dancing on the television show. How could a girl that age—

Oh, for Christ's sake. That eye makeup. That faux-Egyptian raccoon mask. No other girl wore makeup that extreme. Everybody else was groomed for Sunday school, and there she was, looking like the doorwoman to a pyramid. Why was she allowed to look like that? Why did she dance with different guys all the time? Why were her eyes glued to Giorgio every moment he was onstage?

Because the rules didn't apply to her. Because Corinne was Giorgio's girlfriend.

She came to California with him. It was a lifelong love. For both of them, I figured, both DiGaudio and Corrine. They were both in love with the boy with the impossible face. The absolutely, resolutely unremarkable boy who was trapped for life, first behind the accident of his beauty and then inside the ruin of that beauty. Beauty means nothing, it just is, but we pour our feelings into it and demand that it means something, and eventually it does. It means whatever we wanted to see in it. And Corinne and DiGaudio had poured themselves into Giorgio until he was part of them. The three of them, sharing their nightmare Eden as a *ménage à trois* until the serpent appeared in the form of a junk journalist with a camera.

Not knowing that there was a murder back there.

And they were a family, of a kind. And they weren't willing to be ripped apart. So, hello, Fronts. Bye-bye, Derek.

I was working to keep my eyes and my mind on the road, but there was no way I could keep myself from seeing that gun come up from beneath the blanket, arc through the air and finish its journey *right here.*

On the kiss.

And then, of course, there was the *other* tragedy, the forgotten tragedy: Roberto Abbruzzi, Bobby Angel, sacrificed to prevent the very thing Derek was threatening to expose. Bobby Angel, who could actually sing, who actually had a modest talent. In a different world, Bobby would have been more important than Giorgio. But this is the world we have, and the people who live in it don't live or die for a modest talent. They'll live or die for beauty, though. And poor Bobby wasn't beautiful.

Thoughts and recriminations tumbled around in my head, and when I spotted the turnoff for Highway 62 coming up, I realized I was doing almost ninety. Not a good policy with two guns in a briefcase on the floor and a knife on my belt. I slowed and took the long lazy loop that put me onto 62.

62, also called the Twentynine Palms Highway, is essentially forty miles uphill. It begins on the ancient seafloor where Palm Springs and Desert Hot Springs bake in the year-round heat, and it ascends: up, up, and up some more, all the way to the high desert. As I climbed, the air cooled and cleared, and the stars popped into sharp relief. The moon whitened and grew colder looking.

It was a pretty big moon, bigger and brighter than I'd have requested if I'd been consulted. It was the kind of moon that casts shadows. The kind of moon that makes motion obvious even to those who aren't on the lookout. A killing moon, if my luck was bad.

I couldn't get killed. Rina wanted to live with me.

And look where I was, just a few hours after our confrontation with Fronts, look what I was doing.

*Why do you live like this*, she'd asked, and I'd said, as though it were a joke, that it kept me young. But it wasn't a joke, or at least not completely. I lived like this because I enjoyed it. I liked to flip coins, I liked not knowing whether I'd win or lose, and I liked it when the stakes were high. I liked breaking into houses, I liked stepping into the maze of a puzzle, more complicated than the floor plan of DiGaudio's house, not knowing whether there was a Minotaur inside.

It made me feel alive.

But so did Rina. In a completely different way. What would I be giving up if she lived with me? What would I be giving up if she didn't?

Long ago, Kathy had told me I was two different people, and I'd said it was okay as long as I could hold it to two.

Wrong again. I was wrong so often, you'd think I'd be used to it. It seemed like all I did was make mistakes and drive. What I needed was an inflatable therapist, a fatherly vinyl figure in a tweed jacket I could blow up and put in the passenger seat. I could work through my issues as I drove.

The highway rose, here and there slicing between steep walls cut through stone, but more often just rolling across trackless sand. Occasionally a narrow road, usually unpaved, bisected it at a perpendicular and dwindled to a point in the distance. Here and there, I caught the glitter of one of the desert's mysteries: a shiny, metallic ribbon of cassette tape, unspooled and fluttering across the road's surface, knotted into a bush or snagged on one of the reflectors that have thoughtfully been posted every few hundred yards to provide some sort of margin that might prevent the half-hypnotized driver from drifting off the road and onto the deceptive smoothness of the desert. I found myself wondering, as I always did when I made this drive, who the hell listens to cassette tapes any more? Long-haul truckers? High-desert Luddites unwilling to be dragged into the age of the mp3 file? Aging hippies wedded to their 40-year-old mix tapes?

Once in a very great while, a yellow rectangle of light defined a distant window. Somebody's life, out there in the silence.

Almost 11:30. Any minute now.

I'd already passed through Joshua Tree, basically a big sign announcing a small town. I'd reached the outskirts of Twenty-nine Palms, long a rest station on the Utah Trail, now a military town that serves a Marine base.

The terrain rose to the left of the road and rolled downhill to the right, south toward the untouched and protected desert of the Joshua Tree Monument. Most of the development, such as it was—the new dirt roads, the occasional block of stucco houses—were up to the left, rising toward the foothills of some modest, prickly-looking mountains, nameless to me. Street signs began to appear, some of them reflective and official, others hopeful, just names printed in black on white fiber board, marking the way to some developer's optimistic grid scratched into the sand, or perhaps the refuge of some desert rat, solitary as a trapdoor spider.

From the description on the deed to Pivensey's parcel, the cabin he'd bought as Doris's last address had been one of those, a spider's lair. The only structure in a square of sixteen acres, probably surrounded by square miles of nothing, somewhere up there on the slope.

The terrain was populated now by Joshua trees, the kings of the high desert, essentially variants on the yucca that mimic trees with their branches upraised to heaven, the prayerful silhouette that led the Mormons on the Utah Trail to give them their name. The sandy stretches between the Joshuas were broken by patches of scrub: ocotillo, mesquite, cholla cactus bristling with barbed spines that bite into the skin and break off when you try to pull them out. And here and there rose the massive boulders, glacier-dragged and then slowly broken into geometric piles by million years of heat and erosion. The moon, now about a third of the way up, caught the southeastern surfaces of the giant rocks, coating them in white chalk and creating enormous shadows, holes in the moonlight, on the opposite side.

Even though I was driving slowly, the little sign that said FELDSPAR LANE bloomed in my headlights almost too late for me to make the left, and the rear of the car swung wide as I cut the wheel. According to Rand McNally, I'd follow Feldspar for a little more than a mile and then make another left onto Sunrise

Drive. After another two-fifths of a mile, Sunrise Drive led to the access road to Pivensey's dream cottage.

And it was uphill all the way, with nothing between me and it except a few piles of rock and some Joshua trees. There was more moonlight than I wanted, but at least it meant I could turn off my headlights. I got far enough off the highway that I felt reasonably secure I wouldn't draw the attention of the Highway Patrol and doused the lights.

Feldspar Lane, two compact vehicles wide, was slightly banked on either side, just ridges of the sand that had been bull-dozed aside to create a smoother surface, and the ridges caught the moonlight and turned the lane into a sharp-edged crayon line scrawled over the desert. Easy for me to follow, easy for someone else to see from above, even with no headlights.

I slowed without tapping the brakes—not eager for the blink of red lights—and leaned over to grab the briefcase from the floor. With one hand on the wheel, I popped the two snaps that kept the case closed and felt around until my hand hit the reas-suringly cold and solid surface of the Glock. I put it in my lap and then located the Sig Sauer and put it on the seat beside the briefcase. Finally, I pulled out the two full clips and dropped them into my shirt pocket. They were amazingly heavy. Then I pushed the briefcase back onto the floor and located the Sig by touch once again. Put my hand back on the wheel and found the Sig once more. Then I did it again and again, until I could hit it first time every time, with my hand right on the grip.

I passed a little turn-off, no sign, just a track across the sand that led toward one of the rock monoliths.

I used the flashlight to check the odometer. Eight-tenths of a mile since I turned off the highway. About three-tenths left, and then the left onto Sunrise. And I was seeing nothing on either side or ahead of me that looked like a plausible alternative destination: no houses, no bar, no rundown motel. Anyone sitting on the front porch of Pivensey's house would have to figure I was on my way to drop in.

And there was no way the house didn't face south. South was where the view was.

Sound carries in the desert. He could hear me, too.

I said, "Hell," and pulled the car over. I got the right front tire up and over the little ridge of sand at the edge and cut the wheel left as hard as I could. No way to do this without the brake lights coming on, but what was the alternative? Feldspar was so narrow that it took me several back-and-forths, with a lot of blinking red lights, before I'd managed a three-point turn to point myself back down the road. I let the car coast until I came to the track I'd just passed, and then I turned onto it and followed it to the rocks. As I'd hoped, it swung around them, and I stayed on the track until my car was out of sight from the slopes to the north. Then I stopped and turned the engine off. And sat there.

I decided to give it an hour. After an hour, whoever saw the brake lights would be bored enough to do something else.

Maybe.

## 31
### A Sort of Plateau

Once you get outside Palm Springs, desert land values have remained low, and I had a lot of opportunity to appreciate the reasons for that as I hiked toward Pivensey's property. The desert is dull and featureless for long stretches, and when it suddenly isn't, it's because you've just walked into a bunch of things that can kill you. Even the plants bite. By the time I'd gone halfway, I'd been spiked several times, I'd heard a couple of probably poisonous life forms slither away from me, and I'd turned my ankle on a rock that nature had abandoned to sulk all by itself in the middle of nowhere.

The moon was almost halfway across the sky when I encountered yet another reason to hate the evening. Although it hadn't been visible from the highway or from Feldspar Lane, the area around *chez* Pivensey was comparatively hilly. Erosion had cut gullies through it, and mounds of sand, topped with thorny stuff, rose up all over the place. While the rolling terrain might help me stay out of sight, it would also complicate the search that was my first order of business.

I was keeping Sunrise Drive to my left as I walked. I figured I had to be getting close, so I slogged up to the highest of the rises and found myself looking across three or four other small hills to the straight white line of a roof, the white probably chosen to reflect the sun and cool the house, to whatever extent that was possible. The burglar's Eternal Question came to me, somewhat belatedly: are there dogs? Not much I could do about it at this point if there were. I took the Glock out of my belt, put my finger on the trigger guard, and moved quietly in the direction of the house.

I topped the hill closest to it and took a longer look. It was at least fifty years old, a basic clapboard rectangle of three or four rooms, maybe 1,200 square feet. A narrow, south-looking porch ran along the side of the house I was facing, and a chimney sprouted from the near left corner of the roof, announcing the location of the living room. Looking down at the roof, I visualized a plausible floor plan. The front door, which I could see, opened from the porch directly into the living room. The kitchen would be straight back, and the bedroom and bathroom would be off to the right, linked by a short hall, with perhaps another, smaller bedroom or storage room behind the front bedroom. Rudimentary but big enough for two people.

Or, of course, for one.

There were no lights in the windows.

Sixteen acres isn't all that big. From where I stood I could see the driveway to the house, just an economical, straight sand track that went past the structure and disappeared from sight. I figured I could use the driveway and the house as reference points to let me walk a grid of parallel lines across the property, so I hiked on down the hill, heading toward the point at which the driveway intersected Sunrise Drive. It took me about five minutes, with only one serious slip, when my feet went out from under me and nearly dropped me into a patch of cholla, but I got there.

It seemed unlikely that anyone would dig a grave any closer to the property line than thirty yards, so I measured off thirty long paces from the beginning of the driveway and then turned left. I blundered up and down the little rises for ten minutes or so, walking as straight a line as possible and taking a sighting of the house's roof whenever it was visible, to keep me on track. When I figured I was close to the edge of the property—assuming that the driveway and the house were roughly centered on it—I made a right that took me about ten yards closer to the house and then turned again in the direction I'd come, and hiked back to the driveway, keeping my eyes on the ground as much as possible, looking for anything out of the ordinary. Then I went ten yards back up the driveway until I was exactly opposite the point at which I'd gone left, and this time I went the other way. After nine or ten minutes, I did the ten-yard zigzag that took me closer to the house and hiked back to the driveway. I continued with that pattern: go as straight as possible from one probable property line to the other, then get ten yards closer to the house, and go back again, scanning the ground as I went.

One of the very few good things about the desert, at least for my purposes that evening, is that it's relatively smooth. It's where God put all the sand left over from the beach, and there's a lot of moving air. The air makes the sand flow like a very slow liquid, smoothing it, even creating ripples like the ones you'd see in a photograph of moving water. Among all that smoothness, irregularity stands out: rocks, brush, the decaying skeletons of Joshua trees and cholla plants, the littered scree of small stones in the bottoms of temporary stream beds. Here and there I saw a hole surrounded by a fan of loose sand where a coyote had gone subterranean, digging after some burrowing prey.

I'd crossed the plot of land four times now, and still hadn't alerted a dog, so there probably wasn't one. The house was getting pretty close. I changed my pattern and started moving in a squared-off U pattern, beginning about forty feet from the house. I went around the sides and the back of it, always maintaining my distance, then moved another ten yards away and repeated the U in the other direction.

By now, I had theories. If I were going to bury someone in the desert, I'd avoid the flash-flood gullies for the obvious reason that the water would bring whoever it was to the surface sooner or later, possibly scattering bones for a conspicuous mile or five across the desert as storm followed storm. Steep slopes were out because of wind erosion and the possibility of sand slides opening the grave. No, if I wanted to bury someone, I'd either look for a relatively flat patch of high ground, or I'd dig on the downwind slope of a gentle hill.

My eyes began to go automatically to those areas, and on the fourth U, maybe fifty yards behind the house, I saw it. A level area, a sort of plateau. Its surface was broken and irregular. A hole had been dug and something had been put into it, something with significant volume, because there was a lot of sand left over. Three piles of it, not yet smoothed, streamlined by the wind.

I dropped to my knees and, with profound misgivings, began to dig with my bare hands.

The hole was recent. The sand hadn't settled. It was still loose and easy to scoop out of the way. It was easier than I wanted it to be. I wanted resistance, I wanted difficulty, I wanted anything that would delay the moment when my fingers found the hand.

I stopped, popping goose bumps so pronounced I felt like a cactus. I didn't want to look at it, but I dug further down, eyes raised to the moon, until I could grip the entire hand. It was a small hand and a cold one. And now I could smell it.

I stood up so quickly I got dizzy. Without even knowing I was doing it, I took three or four steps back, away from the grave. Then, not wanting to, I looked down.

Five fingers protruded from the hole I'd dug. They were spread wide and slightly curled toward the palm. It looked like the hand of someone who'd tried to claw back to the surface, back to the air and the moonlight and the spangle of stars. I knew I was imagining that, knew he wouldn't bury anyone who wasn't dead, because—well, because sand is soft. I was sure his imagination was sufficiently vivid to allow him the vision of someone digging free, staggering up out of the hole. Coming for him.

But that's what the hand looked like. Someone trying to dig out. Someone small.

I was glad that Marge wasn't alone.

And it occurred to me that it would be a good idea to kill Pivensey.

I'd seen the car parked beside the house, so he was there. With the moon at its high point in the sky, there were no obscuring shadows now, but it didn't worry me. There had been no lights on in the house the first time I saw it, forty or fifty minutes ago, and there still weren't.

Odds were that he'd be in the front bedroom. The door at the rear of the house led into the kitchen if my mental floor plan was accurate. The back door was farther from the bedroom than the front door, so the back door it was. It had a lock I could have opened with a toothpick. In about ten seconds, I took the step up into the kitchen, which was right where I thought it would be.

Even though a skilled burglar gets in and out as quickly as possible, it's always a good idea to spend the first minute or two in a house just standing still and listening. I was breathing through my mouth with my tip of my tongue against the roof of the mouth, which is the quietest way to breathe. The moonlight through the windows spread itself over a spotless kitchen. A day's worth of dishes for a single person—three plates, a cup, a couple of glasses, and some silverware—gleamed in a drying rack next to the sink. A dishtowel had been folded into smooth quarters and placed beside the rack. A painted wooden shelf a couple of feet above the counter held big sealed mayonnaise jars full of what looked like sugar and tea and coffee beans and flour, plus smaller containers of herbs and spices. A boxy white refrigerator from the 1950s, barely shoulder high, hummed against the wall next to the door that led to the living room. On top of the refrigerator was an old wooden breadbox.

It was all pretty homey.

The kitchen floor was wood, with too much space between the uprights to which the floorboards were nailed, and it creaked. I slid my feet over the surface, moving slowly and transferring my weight as smoothly as possible, the Glock loose and comfortable in my right hand. I crossed the kitchen with a minimum of noise and paused at the door to the living room. The fireplace, made of river stone, took up much of the wall to the right. Facing it was an old couch, covered in corduroy or some other napped fabric that ate light without giving any back. A pale pine coffee table, rough-hewn and a couple of inches thick, sat in front of the couch. Magazines were fanned out over its surface, tidy as the selection in a dentist's office at the beginning of the day. Smug, glossy women looked up from the covers: *Cosmopolitan, Harper's Bazaar, Glamour.* Doris's leftovers, dreams between covers.

The only other furniture in the living room was an armchair covered in scarred leather, one of those ones with the brass nailheads on the front of the arms to make it clear that it's one hundred percent guy furniture. Beyond the armchair was a dark rectangle, the opening into the hallway leading to the bedrooms.

After the kitchen, the living room was a breeze because a rug covered almost the entire floor. It was a cheap oriental nine-by-twelve in a dark pattern that might have been mainly red in daylight, and it was thin, but it was a lot quieter than bare wood. The front wall of the living room was mostly a big window that let in plenty of moonlight, but the hallway was much darker. As I stood beside the entrance to the hall, I could see a soft rectangle of cold white moonlight falling through an open door on the right, the door to the front bedroom. Other than that, the hall was dark enough to make me nervous.

For all I knew Lorne Henry Pivensey was standing somewhere in there right now, breathing as quietly as I was, gun in hand. Maybe the open door was an invitation. Maybe he was behind the mostly-closed door on the opposite side of the hall, waiting for me to edge my way to that open door and stand in it, my back to him, silhouetted in moonlight, presenting my spinal column for a nice, clean shot.

Most people aren't very good at remaining completely still for long periods of time. I'm an exception. I stood to the side of the hall entrance and counted mentally to a thousand, even though I knew much sooner than that—knew by the time I got to three hundred—that there was someone inside the bedroom with the open door, knew that the person in that room was taking the slow, even breaths of sleep. Still, I stood there, unmoving, waiting for anything to suggest the presence of another person in the house.

And didn't hear, or feel, a thing.

So I inched my way down the hall and looked into the bedroom and listened to the sleeping person, watched the covers rise and fall, and then leveled my gun and switched on the light so the little prick would see it coming, and squinted against the light as Doris Enderby sat bolt upright in the bed and screamed her head off.

# 32

## Two Graves, a Car, and a House

"There he is, the little shit," Doris said, looking down at the protruding hand. "Jesus, when that light went on, I thought he'd come back for me."

We were both sipping coffee, possibly the worst I'd ever drunk. Doris was very thrifty with her coffee and very generous with her water. As far as she was concerned, a little caffeine went a long way. But it seemed to steady her.

"How did you do it?"

"He's on top of somebody," Doris said. "That's why he's so close to the surface. Some poor girl is already down there. For a year, maybe."

"That wasn't actually my question."

"He had a game he liked to play." She blew on her coffee, even though it was already cool. "I'm assuming he was the same with all of them—all of *us*—because, well, you know, pathology. My guess is, it was like one-two-three every time. So anyway, first he swept them—no, let's say *me*—off my feet. Found somebody lonely and pathetic and maybe a little resentful. Like me, in other words. Treated me like he'd been alone on a desert island his whole life and the goddess of love had appeared. I was perfect. I was smart and funny and beautiful and everything he'd ever hoped for."

She kicked sand, quite a lot of it, in the general direction of the protruding hand. "Okay, so I'm not so beautiful and I'm apparently not very smart, either, but I'd been stuck in that motel with my mother ever since my father died, and I was ripe for somebody like Lem. So we take off and get married, and I move into the house, I mean the house in Hollywood, and it's just honeymoon time. After a week or so, he brings me up here, shows me this hideaway he'd been renting, and explained it was for sale. He'd buy it for me, and we could escape up here whenever we wanted. Just honeymoon all day and all night. Except that after a little while it isn't, because I begin to *disappoint* him. That was always the word, disappoint. Things weren't perfect after all. Now that I look back on it, I can see that he was working himself up. This was his one-man play, he'd probably performed it in front of half a dozen women, women who had no idea what their role would be. It went on like that for a few weeks, just kind of downhill, until we were barely speaking." She crossed her arms and hugged herself a little, as though she was cold. "We had some real fights, too. I hit him with the garden hose once. He came home and I was watering the lawn, and he accused me of running up the water bill, and I just did a short-circuit and went after him with the hose."

"Somebody told me about it."

"Gee, I wonder who that could have been. Mister Neighborhood Watch, I called him. He made Lem *really* nervous, although I didn't know why at the time. Obviously, or I'd have been out of there. But I wasn't, because nobody ever really believes the person they're with is a complete nightmare lunatic. I was thinking, 'Wow, his mom must have been hard on him,' and he was thinking, 'Maybe I'll hang her by her ankles for a few days and then kick her head in.'"

"No," I said. "That wouldn't occur to most people."

"Didn't to me, anyway. And then one day I came home a little later than I'd said I would, and that was the trigger he'd been waiting for. He grabbed me by the hair, punched me in the face, kicked me around a little, and then handcuffed me. That was when the fun really began for him, because what he enjoyed most was frightening me. Just plain terrifying me. So he had me cuffed on the kitchen floor, one cuff around my right hand and the other around the plumbing trap under the sink, and he pulled up a chair and got comfy and told me about all his girls."

"The ones who disappointed him."

"Did they ever. Do you have a cigarette?"

"Sorry."

"Oh, well. I lived through him, I can live through a nicotine attack. A couple of hours of scaring the shit out of me, telling me about all the girls sleeping in the sand, made him hungry, and he wasn't about to let me get a hot frying pan in my hands, so he went out for Chinese. Asked me if I'd prefer Thai, if you can believe that, there I am, punched out, bleeding, cuffed to a pipe, and half-crazy afraid, and he's asking whether I want pad Thai or kung pao chicken. Just a total raving barker. I told him Chinese because the Chinese place he liked was farther away than the Thai place."

"And."

"And he didn't know that my dad had taught me everything there is to know about handcuffs, working with good cuffs, LAPD cuffs. And Lem's cuffs—I mean, they were junk, and don't forget, I had a hand free. I waited until he left the house, and then I got out of them and went into the garage, where he'd gone to get the first set, and I got two more pairs. When he came home I hit him with the chair he'd been sitting on, so hard I knocked one leg off it. Then I cuffed his hands and his feet, so tight he could never work his way out of them, and took his gun and moved the car around to the side of the house and cleaned the place while I waited for him to wake up."

"That must have been a twist for him."

Doris turned her head slowly, as though she were seeing the landscape for the last time. "He didn't have any way to deal with it. Just *gaped* at me, like the steak he'd been eating had suddenly taken a bite out of his tongue. I got him into the car and drove him up here, hands and feet cuffed and another pair of cuffs holding those together so he was folded in half, right? And all the way I'm telling him I'm just going to deliver him to the sheriff's office up here, and he's a cinch for the death penalty or life in prison, whichever it is these days. I tell him he's only got two choices. He can show me a grave and prove he hasn't been bullshitting me, and I'll think about how to handle it, or I can take him straight to the cops and we'll let *them* dig the place up. And, I mean, he knew I was still going to turn him in, but any chance was better than none, so we got up here and he hopped to the house and got a shovel, and he dug with his hands still cuffed until he was knee-deep and I saw some cloth and some bone. And then, since he was already standing in a grave, I shot him with his own gun."

"Good for you."

She nodded. "I figure that vengeance is the Lord's unless it takes him too long."

"But why stay here? And what's with calling Amber and Melissa?"

She lowered the coffee cup, which she had raised to her lips. "Have you been paying attention? I murdered somebody. Oh, sure he was overdue, but come on. I hit him with a chair, handcuffed him, drove him all the way up here, shot him, and covered him with sand. Does that sound like a self-defense plea? Can you spell *premeditation*? It's not just something you can walk away from. So I told a few people I was going various places so nobody'd come looking for me, and then I stayed here and tried to figure out what to do." She tossed the remainder of her coffee onto something thorny. "*Tried* is the operative word."

"What would you like to do?"

"Well," she said, "in the best of all possible worlds, I'd make Lem's body disappear from the face of the earth, and then I'd arrange for the girls who are buried here to be found so their families could stop wondering what happened to them, and then I'd go home to Mom without leaving a trace that I'd ever been here."

I said, "Okay."

"Sure," she said. "Fine." She nodded carefully. "Glad we had this talk."

"Do you know how many girls are buried up here?"

At first, I didn't think she'd answer. She was looking at me as though I might suddenly sprout claws. But then she said, "Two. The one Lem's on top of and another one about twenty feet from here, over by that dead Joshua Tree."

"Go get your stuff. Everything that belongs to you."

"Yeah? I mean, you think we can just take a stroll into a new world? There are *bodies* here. I killed one of them."

"Somebody owes me a favor," I said. "How's cell phone reception up here?"

"It's good. What else are they going to use all this dirt for? They put cell towers on it. Are you kidding me? About being able to fix this?"

"You can listen in," I said, and I dialed Irwin Dressler's number. He answered on the first ring.

"Here's where we find out how much you owe me," I said.

"Vinnie's under control," he said, whatever that meant. "Thanks to you. So I owe you pretty good."

"I'm going to give you an address in Twentynine Palms. When your guys get here, they'll find two graves, a car, and a house."

"Yeah?"

"The graves will have white flags over them, dishtowels on sticks. One of the graves has two people in it. The one on top is a male, and he's relatively fresh. He's material for one of those lakes you told me about. Nobody should ever be inconvenienced by tripping over the remains and maybe spraining an ankle. Not ever. The other two are women he killed. They're skeletal. They should be dug up and re-buried someplace eight or ten miles away, and then tips should be called in to the cops, so the families can find out what happened to their daughters."

"The guy murdered the girls?"

"And some others."

"You're having an interesting evening. Is that all?"

"No. The car will have keys in it. It needs to disappear forever. The house needs to burn down."

"This is getting kind of complicated."

"Two guys—what are their names? Babe and Tuffy?—or three at most, a couple of hours, what's complicated? The only tricky part is the reburial. Everything else is just gruntwork. Drive the car off, send it to Mexico to get chopped. And the house will go up like a box of matches. And then we're even."

"I'll think about that," Dressler said. "Maybe even, maybe not. Maybe you'll owe me."

"Tonight," I said.

"Don't push. Okay, tonight, but forget even." He hung up.

"Come on," I said to Doris. She had taken a couple of steps away from me as she listened, and her mouth was halfway open. "You've got to get your stuff, and I've got to make those flags."

"Who the hell *are* you?" Doris asked.

"Oh, that reminds me," I said, punching a new number into the phone. I listened until it rang, and then I handed it to her. "Say hello to your mother."

**An hour and** a half later, Doris and I toted a suitcase and three plastic trash bags full of stuff around the big rock I'd parked behind, and I opened the passenger door. As the light from inside the car struck Doris, Fronts said, "Jeez. You can even find a chick in the desert."

**33**

Cutters

Doris said to him, "Do you smoke?"

"Naw," Fronts said. He ambled into the light. His left arm was all scraped up from hitting the pavement, but other than that he looked the same as always, which is to say terrible. The bandage over the bullet hole in his arm was filthy. He had another Sig Sauer in his hand. Brand loyalty. "I got some other stuff if you want it. Junior, leave your hands there."

"Where?"

"Where they are now. Don't think about the guns. Hey, is one of them mine?"

"Used to be," I said.

"For Christ's sake," said a woman's voice. "Just shoot them and get it over with."

"Hey, Corinne," I said into the darkness.

"Like what?" Doris asked.

Fronts said, "Whaddya mean, like what?"

"You said you had other stuff. Like what?"

Fronts scratched his head with the barrel of his gun. "Melaril, which is like a tranquilizer for people in the electric chair. Got some opium, got some Xanax, at least I think I got some Xanax. I took a handful a while back. I got some horse trank, you could ask Junior about it."

"I don't recommend it," I said. "It was you, wasn't it, Corrine? You're the one who put the transmitter on the car."

"Second time you dropped by." I heard her scuffing over the sand before I saw her. Still in black, chewing gum like she was angry at it. Now I could see the rectangular silhouette of the Humvee behind her. "What the hell are you waiting for, Fronts?"

"I saw Giorgio," I said. "He told me you kissed him goodbye."

She broke stride for a moment, but picked up the pace again. "It wasn't goodbye," she said. "I'll see him again. I'll always see him again."

I said, "I'm sure you will."

"You know, Mom," Fronts said to her, "you didn't say nothing about shooting no chick."

Corrine said, "Who cares? Shoot one, shoot two, what's the difference? And don't call me Mom, dammit."

"You shoot everybody who asks you for a smoke?" Doris said. She was ignoring Corinne completely, and I was liking her better by the minute.

"Chicks are extra, Mom," Fronts said. "On account that I don't like shooting them."

"I've paid you a fortune," Corinne said. "And so far it's been one fuckup after another."

"You don't look much like your mom," Doris said.

"Thanks," Fronts said. He was looking at her with interest. His eyes were on her forearms. "You a cutter?"

"When I was a kid," Doris said. "After my father died." She held out her left arm, which had a series of fine-ridged scars cross-hatched into it. "It kept me going."

"I do it two-handed," Fronts said. "I'm ambidextrous."

"Yeah?" She studied him. "You can write with both hands?"

"In a mirror, too," Fronts said. His eyes came to mine for a moment, and he looked embarrassed. "Sometimes I get it backward."

"I quit after a few years," Doris said. "You should stop. Infections are the shits."

"I don't get infected," Fronts said. "I just take antibiotics all the time."

Doris shook her head. "Antibiotics are bad for your stomach."

"This is *enough* of this," Corinne said, and there was a small gun in her hand. To Fronts, she said, "You're not getting paid to stand around discussing your psychoses. Just get it over with so we can get out of here."

"She's the only thing that ties Derek to Irwin Dressler," I said to Fronts.

"You shut up," Corinne said, and she pointed her gun at me, but Fronts put out a hand in a lazy gesture and shoved her shoulder, and she stumbled sideways and almost went down.

He said, "Say what?"

"Irwin Dressler. He was connected to Vinnie and Corinne, and he'd be happier if there weren't any links around. You know, he just wants to lead a peaceful life."

"Irwin Dressler," Fronts said. "The old guy."

"That's the one."

"Shoot him, or I will," Corinne said. Her voice was getting shrill. "Just do your fucking job."

"And he's interested," Fronts said. "Irwin is."

"Like I said."

Doris said, "You wouldn't shoot another cutter."

"You're a nice girl," Fronts said. "But just so you know, Junior has a lot of girlfriends."

"That's it," Corinne said. "Bunch of morons." She held the gun at arm's length and aimed it at my head, and Fronts reached over and plucked it from her hand.

He said, "Sorry, Mom," and tossed the little gun into the darkness.

Corinne jumped at him and grabbed his shoulder. "I am not your mom, you stupid freak retard, if I were your mom I'd have a retroactive abortion. Give me that gun, you dumb fuck, you fat, disgusting—"

Fronts put his free hand around Corinne's throat. He was so big his fingers almost met. Corinne's voice went up a few squeezed notches, but she kept grabbing at him, clawing at his arm with her nails.

Fronts said, "Irwin Dressler."

"Doesn't want any links," I said.

Corinne emitted a strangled scream and kneed Fronts between the legs, and he turned to her, looking irritated, and the gun in his hand went off with a bang that rebounded immediately from the rockpile behind us and then spread out over the desert floor. Corrine was flung back until she slammed against the side of the Hummer. She slowly slid to a sitting position, her eyes wide, a stain spreading out from the center of her chest.

Fronts said, "Oops."

There was a silence of ten or twenty seconds. I heard Doris swallow. Then Corinne made a rattling sound.

I said to Fronts, "We've got a shovel."

## 34

### Candy-Cane Points

At ten in the morning, my cell phone rang. I had to reach across Ronnie's bare back to get it. She didn't even stir.

I said, "It's early."

"You're breaking my heart." It was Paulie DiGaudio. "Try working a real job sometime."

"No, thanks."

"Vinnie's in Costa Rica," Paulie said. "The guy who told the Hollywood cops that Vinnie was going to hire him to do Derek Bigelow now says he made the whole thing up. Says he was just trying to get attention. He's needed attention his whole life, he says."

"Well, there you are."

"But there's also that new dead guy in Vinnie's house, the wheelchair guy, so I'm not completely happy."

"Who is, these days?"

"So okay, the new guy is a suicide. But I don't have anybody for Derek. And you remember, that was the other part of the problem: One, get Vinnie off the hook, and two, nail somebody for Derek,"

"Derek had a lot of enemies. I wouldn't be surprised to learn somebody hired a pro."

Paulie said, "Oh, some other people changed their minds,

too. Turns out you *do* have an alibi for the night the Hammers got robbed and old Mrs. Hammer got knocked around."

"See?" I said. "Sooner or later, the truth always comes out."

"Just kind of interesting, don't you think? In one night, everybody changed their story. Your buddies remember being with you even though I put some pretty good weight on them to forget it, and the guy who fingered Vinnie suddenly tells us he just needs a lot of attention. It's like they all talked to somebody, you know?"

"The Ghost of Christmas Past," I said.

Ronnie said, "How can you talk so *early?*"

"You're not alone," Paulie said accusingly.

"Emphatically," I said. "I'm as far from being alone as it's possible to be."

"You got a sleepy dame talking in your ear and I'm sitting here at this cheap desk looking out at the smog. There ain't no justice, is there?"

"Actually, there is," I said. "We were talking earlier about someone, someone you sent me pictures of."

"Yeah. Your friend's daughter. The guy who had your friend's—"

"He doesn't have her any more. She's home, safe and sound. And he's nothing you have to worry about, not ever again."

I heard paper rustling: Paulie was unwrapping a Tootsie Roll. "How sure are you?"

"Several bullets and fifteen or twenty feet of lake water sure."

"See, this is interesting, too," Paulie said. "Because we hear the Sheriffs in San Berdoo got some calls this morning about girls. In the desert. Dead girls, I mean."

"Boy," I said. "What a night."

"Okay," Paulie said. "Okay. Hope I don't see you for a while." He hung up.

Ronnie stretched, her arms fully extended in a high V, and

the sunshine through the window caught the fine golden hair on her forearms and turned it into liquid light. "That was wonderful last night," she said. "I think I cried more than Marge did. I don't think I ever saw anyone so happy. That's the difference between men and women. Women cry at love."

"Yeah? What do men cry at?"

"The World Series."

"Love's funny," I said. "Seems like everything I've been doing for the last few days has been about love in one way or another, and a lot of people got killed for it. And all the love doesn't make them any less dead."

"Well," she said, "love can make you feel more alive, too."

"My God," I said. "Is that a compliment?"

The phone rang again, and I looked at the display.

"Why don't you go for a walk?" Ronnie said. "Take that thing with you."

"Hello, Rina," I said. "Aren't you at school?"

"Sure, I'm at school. I'm in between classes. I read about Giorgio this morning. Was that you?"

"No. It was Giorgio."

"Well, I know that. But you—I mean, did you have anything to do with it?"

"No. They'd been living in a pressure cooker for years. It was going to blow up sooner or later."

"Honest?"

"Honest."

"Does anybody know where Corinne is? Wow, imagine her following him all the way from Philadelphia."

"I was just saying, there's no way to know about love."

"Just saying to who? *Whom*, I mean, just saying to whom?"

I looked down at Ronnie, who gave me a small smile with a large charge behind it.

"Ronnie?" Rina said. "Is Ronnie there?"

"She is."

"I want to talk to her. Come on, let me talk to her. I've only got a minute until I have to be in class."

"Rina," I said into the phone, "meet Ronnie."

Ronnie took the phone and said, "You're the only thing your father talks about."

Somebody knocked on the door.

"Why don't we just move to the bus station?" I said. I got up and went into the bathroom and wrapped a towel around me, listening to Ronnie laugh at something Rina had said, and then I went to the door and opened it.

Marge's eyes were so swollen I was surprised she'd been able to find the door, but she looked almost weightless, transparent with joy. She'd put on a blouse the color of a dubious pumpkin, with a sequined yellow chrysanthemum dead-middle. The chrysanthemum glittered as though there were a light source in the center of her chest. She held out a sheaf of brightly printed cards.

"For you," she said, and sniffled.

"Thank you," I said. I took the cards and found myself looking at hundreds of little peppermint-striped canes.

"That's fifty thousand candy-cane points," Marge said. "It's our frequent sleeper program. That's the highest level. It means you can stay here anytime you want. For free, I mean."

"Oh, no," I said, with complete sincerity. "I couldn't. Really, I couldn't."

"You can even have Donder."

Behind me, Ronnie was whispering into the phone.

"This is too much," I said to Doris. "And I'll tell you a secret. I think my daughter might be moving in with me, and I don't think a motel—"

"No," Marge said, taking the candy-cane points back. "Your

daughter. How wonderful. You'll have to make her a proper home."

"Tell you what. Let's all have lunch in a couple of hours. We can talk about it then."

"Lunch is on me," Marge said. "You name it. Denny's, El Torito, anywhere." She was tearing up again. "Doris loves El Torito."

"El Torito it is," I said. "See you at noon."

I closed the door and turned to the bed. Ronnie said something into the phone and then closed it. She put it on the table beside the bed. "You phony," she said.

"How? How am I a phony?"

"Mister Tough Burglar. Mister Soft-Touch Find-the-Missing-Daughter Burglar. Mr. Daddy-of-the-Year-Worry-About-Your-Daughter's-Boyfriend Burglar. You cream puff."

"I may be a cream puff," I said, climbing back onto the bed, "but there's a very hard candy at my center."

"If there is," she said, "I'll find it. And then I'll melt it."

"That could take a while."

"No problem." She unknotted the towel. "I don't have to go back to Trenton for a long time."

"Or Albany," I said.

She wrapped her arms around my neck. "Or Albany," she said.

Author's Note

**For those of** you who are either too young to remember the sixties or who have the instinctive taste and discretion to avoid early sixties, post-Chuck Berry, pre-Beatles rock music (one of the most dire periods in the history of Rock & Roll, if you exclude the wonder of Motown), there really were "little Elvises" who were "churned to the surface in the wake of Elvis Presley," to use Rina's phrase.

Some of them were country and western stars who combed their hair into pompadours, learned how to sneer, and were either temporarily or permanently repurposed as rock stars. Others were just good-looking kids with loose hips who made one or two records and then went back to selling shoes or, for all I know, completing doctorates in astrophysics.

And it's also true that a number of them—some of the more successful, as it turned out—came out of Philadelphia and were managed and produced by an Italian-American guy whose name, like Vincent DiGaudio's, ended in a vowel. The primary purpose of this page is to state emphatically that, other than those two similarities, none of the characters in this book is intended to represent either that music producer nor his prodigies. Their existence gave me the book's title and an idea for the story, but that's all there is to it.

Books come out of the ether. I'd been contemplating for some time the tendency of American pop culture to stamp out little tin duplicates, often scrubbed and sanitized, of the relatively small number of genuinely individual breakthroughs. For years I lived in a house on Venice Beach next to one of the great songwriters of the 20th century, Jerry Leiber. With his partner, Mike Stoller, he wrote "Hound Dog," Stand By Me," "Spanish Harlem," "Love Potion Number Nine," "Up on the Roof," "Is That All There Is," and dozens—hundreds—more. I also wrote songs (dismally) for a while, and I saw whole schools of songwriters trying and failing to match the Leiber/Stoller magic. Didn't work, any more than any of the people who were billed as "the next Dylan" worked (although some of them, such as Bruce Springsteen, outgrew the hype to make it on their own merit). Now, of course, following "American Idol," every fourth show is a talent competition judged by members of that increasingly amorphous group, celebrities.

So I wanted to play with the idea of media imitation and also the way fame can destroy people who aren't equipped for it. The title appeared in front of my eyes while I was taking a morning run, and that determined everything that followed.

I want to say that I deserve combat pay for this book. Music is an essential component of my writing environment, and for this book I downloaded—and *listened* to—days' worth of so-called rock recorded between 1959 and 1963. I like to think that my musical tastes are broad, but this experience brought me smack up against my limitations. It was like walking into a glass door. In the vast and flowered meadow that is 20th century popular music, the years between 1959 and 1963 are crowded into a tangled, dusty patch of thorny and noxious scrub, "an unweeded garden," as Hamlet says, "that grows to seed things rank and gross in nature."

Yeah, I know, there *were* good records—mostly country music transplants such as the Everly Brothers, Marty Robbins, Patsy Cline, and the astonishing Roy Orbison; brilliant R&B from, among others, Sam Cooke, Jackie Wilson, Ray Charles, and Lloyd Price; plus some amazing girl groups, including the Shirelles and the Marvelettes; and then there was Motown. Most of the rest of it was mayonnaise, and I say pfui to it. I had to listen to it.

Anybody who's got any obscure masterpieces from that period is invited to send them to me at timothyhallinan.com and if I haven't heard them, I promise to listen. For at least ten seconds.

Thanks to my wife, Munyin Choy, who disagrees with me about some of this music, and to my editor, Juliet Grames, who probably hasn't heard much of it but who edited this book in an absolute marathon frenzy and made a big difference.

And thanks to you for getting this far.

Continue reading for a sneak preview from the next
Junior Bender Mystery

# The Fame Thief

# 1

My business plan calls for long periods of inactivity

Irwin Dressler crossed one eye-agonizing plaid leg over the other, leaned back on a white leather couch half the width of the *Queen Mary*, and said, "Junior, I'm disappointed in you."

If Dressler had said that to me the first time I'd been hauled up to his Bel Air estate for a command appearance, I'd have dropped to my knees and begged for a painless death. He was, after all, the Dark Lord in the flesh. But now I'd survived him once, so I said, "Well, Mr. Dressler—"

A row of yellow teeth, bared in what was supposed to be a smile but looked like the last thing many small animals see. "Call me Irwin."

"Well, Mr. Dressler, at the risk of being rowed into the center of the Hollywood Reservoir wired to half a dozen cinder blocks and being offered the chance to swim home, what have I done to disappoint you?"

"Nothing. That's the problem." Despite the golf slacks and the polo shirt, Dressler was old without being grandfatherly, old without going all dumpling, old without getting quaint. He'd been a dangerous young man in 1943, when he assumed control of mob activity in Los Angeles, and he'd gone on being dangerous until he was a dangerous old man. Forty minutes ago, I'd been snatched off a Hollywood sidewalk by two walking biceps and thrown into the back seat of a big old Lincoln Town Car, and when I'd said, "Where's your weapon?" the guy in the front said, "Irwin Dressler," and I'd shut up.

Dressler gave me a glance I could have searched for hours without finding any friendliness in. "You got yourself a *franchise*, Junior, a *monopoly*, and you're not working it."

I said, "My business plan calls for long periods of inactivity."

"That's not how this country was built, Junior." Like many great crooks, even the very few at his stratospheric level, Dressler was a political conservative. "What made America great? I'll tell you: backbone, elbow grease, noses to the grindstone."

"Sounds uncomfortable."

Dressler had lowered his head while he was speaking, perhaps to demonstrate the approved nose-to-the-grindstone position. Only his eyes moved. Beneath heavy white eyebrows, they came up to meet mine, as smooth, dry, and friendly as a couple of river stones. He kept them on me until the back of my neck began to prickle, and I shifted in my chair.

"This is amusing?" he said. "I'm amusing you?"

"No, sir." I picked up the platter of bread and brie and said, "Cheese?"

"In my own house he's offering me cheese." Dressler addressed this line to some household spirit hovering invisibly over the table. "It's true, it's true. I've grown old."

"No, sir," I said again. "It's, uh, it's. . . ."

"The loss of American verbal skills," he said, nodding, "is a terrible thing. Even in someone like you. I remember a time, this will be hard for you to believe, when almost everyone could speak in complete sentences. In English, no less. What have I done, Junior, that you should laugh at me? Get so old that I don't frighten you any more?"

"I wasn't—"

"I bring you here, I give you cheese, good cheese—is the cheese good, Junior?"

"Fabulous," I said, seriously rattled. This had the earmarks of one of Irwin's legendary rants, rants that frequently ended with one less person alive in the room.

"Fabulous, he says, it's fabulous. What are you, a hat maker? Of course, it's fabulous. The Jews, you know, we're a desert people. The two gods everybody's killing each other over now, Jehovah and the other one, Allah, they're both desert gods, did you know that, Junior?"

"Um, yes, sir."

"Desert gods are short on forgiveness, you know? And we Jews, we're the chosen people of a desert god and hospitality is part of our tradition, and now I'm going to get badmouthed for my cheese by some *pisher*, some *vonce*—you know what a *vonce* is, Junior?"

"No, sir."

"It's a bedbug, in Yiddish, great language for invective. I'll tell you, Junior, I could flay the skin off you using Yiddish alone. I wouldn't even need Babe and Tuffy in the next room there, listening to everything we're saying so they can come in and kill you if I get too excited. My heart, you know? A man my age, I can't be too careful. Someone gets me upset, better for Babe and Tuffy just to kill them first, before my heart attacks me."

"I'm sorry, Mr. Dressler. I wasn't thinking."

"But *thinking*, Junior, that's what you're supposed to be good at." He reached out and took some bread off the platter, which I was apparently still holding, and said, "Down, put it down. Did I offer you wine?"

"Yes, sir." He hadn't, but I wasn't about to bring it up. I put the tray in front of him on the table. Inched it toward him so he wouldn't have to lean forward.

"I still got arms," he said, tearing some bread. "What were we talking about before you got so upset?"

"My franchise."

"Right, right. You may not know this, Junior, but you're the only one there is. You're like Lew Winterman when he—did you know Lew?"

"Not personally." Lew Winterman had been the head of Universe Pictures and long considered the most powerful man in Hollywood, at least by those who didn't know that the first thing he did every morning and the last thing he did every night was to phone Irwin Dressler.

"When he and I thought of packaging, we had to get horses to carry it to the bank, that's how much the money weighed," Dressler said. "You know packaging? *You can have Jimmy Stewart for your movie, but you also gotta take some whozis, I don't know, John Gavin. And every other actor in your picture and also the cameraman and the writers,* and he represented them all, Lew did. For about a year after we figured it out, he was the only guy in Hollywood who knew how to do it, and he did it ten hours a day, seven days a week. You know how much he made?"

"No, sir. How much?"

"Don't ask. You can't think that high. So you're like that now, like Lew, but on your own level, and what are you doing? Sitting around on your *tuchis,* that's what you're doing. That whole thing you got going? Solving crimes for crooks? And living through it? You got Vinnie DiGaudio out of the picture for me with every cop in LA trying to pin him. You helped Trey Annunziato with her dirty movie, although she didn't like it much, the way you did it. When four hundred and eighty flatscreens got bagged out of Arnie Muffins's garage in Panorama City, you brought them back, and without a crowd of people getting killed, which is something, the way Arnie is.

You're it, Junior, you're the only one. And you're not working it."

"Every time I do it," I said, "I almost get killed."

"Ehhh," Dressler said. "You're a young man, in the prime of life. What're you, thirty-eight?"

"Thirty-seven."

"Prime of life. Got your reflexes, got all your IQ, at least as much as you were born with. You're piddling along with a franchise that, I'm telling you, could be worth millions. Where's the wine?"

I said, "I'll get it."

"*You'll* get it? You think I'm going to let you in my cellar?" He picked up a silver bell and rang it. A moment later, one of the bruisers who'd abducted me and dragged me up here came into the room. He was roughly nine feet tall and his belt had to be five feet long, and none of it was fat.

"Yes, Mr. Dressler?"

"Tuffy," Dressler said. "You I don't want. Where's Juana?"

"She's got a headache." Despite being the size of a genie in *The Thousand and One Nights*, Tuffy had the high, hoarse voice of someone who gargled thumbtacks.

"So mix her my special cocktail, half a glass of water, half a teaspoon each of bicarbonate of soda and cream of Tartar. Stir it up real good, till it foams, and take it to her with two aspirins. And get us a bottle of—what do you think, Junior? Burgundy or Bordeaux?"

"Ummm—"

"You're right, it's not a Bordeaux day. Too drizzly. We need something with some sunshine in it. Tuffy. Get us a nice Hermitage, the 1990. Wide-mouthed goblets so it can breathe fast. Got it?"

Tuffy said, "Yes, Mr. Dressler."

I said, "And put on an apron."

Tuffy took an involuntary step toward me, but Dressler raised one parchment-yellow hand and said, "He just needs to pick on somebody. Don't take it personal."

Tuffy gave me a little bonus eye-action for a moment but then ducked his head in Dressler's direction and exited stage left. Dressler said, "So. People try to kill you."

"Occupational hazard. I'm working for crooks, but I'm also catching crooks. If I solve the crime, the perp wants to kill me. If I don't solve it, my client wants to kill me."

"Nobody's really tough any more," Dressler said, shaking his head at the Decline of the West. "You know how we took care of the Italians?"

I did. "Not really."

"Kind of a long way to say *no*, isn't it? Three syllables instead of one. So, okay, the Italians came out to California first, and when we got here from Chicago it was like Naples, just Guidos everywhere, running all the obvious stuff: girls, betting, alcohol, unions, pawnshops, dope. Well, we were nice Jewish boys who didn't want to make widows and orphans everywhere so you know what we used? Never mind answering, we used baseball bats. Didn't kill anybody except a few who were extra-stubborn, but we wrapped things up pretty quick. See, *that's* tough, walking into a room full of guns with a baseball bat. Ask a guy to do that these days, he'd have to be wearing Depends."

I said, "Huh."

Dressler nodded a couple of times, in total agreement with himself. "But let's say the people who want to kill you, give them the benefit of the doubt, let's say they could manage it. And all that nonsense with a different motel every month isn't really going to cut it, is it? What's the motel this month? Valentine something?"

"Valentine Shmalentine," I said, feeling like I was drowning. "In Canoga Park."

"Valentine Shmalentine? Kind of name is that?"

"Supposed to be the world's only kosher love motel."

"What's kosher mean for a love motel? No missionary position?"

"Heh heh heh," I said. He wasn't supposed to know about the motel of the month. *Nobody* was, beyond my immediate circle: my girlfriend, Ronnie; my daughter, Rina; and a couple of close friends and accomplices, such as Louie the Lost. But, I comforted myself, even if word about the motels had leaked, I still had the ultra-secret apartment in Koreatown. Nobody in the world knew about that except for Winnie Park, the Korean con woman who had sublet it to me, and Winnie was in jail in Singapore and had been for seven years.

"So the motels don't work," Dressler said, "not even taking the room next door like you do, with the connecting door and all, to give you a backup exit. It's a cute trick though, I'll give you that. So I'll tell you what you need. Since you can't hide, I mean. You need a patron, so people know you're under his protection. Somebody who's got the kind of weight that people wouldn't kill you even if they caught you playing kneesie with their teenage daughter, and you know how crooks are about their daughters."

"What I need," I said, "is to quit. Just do the occasional burglary, like a regular crook."

"Not an option," Dressler said. "You agree that everyone, even a schmuck like Bernie Madoff, has the right to a good defense attorney?"

I examined the question and saw the booby trap, but what could I do? "I suppose."

"Then why don't they deserve a detective when some *ganef* steals something from them? Or tries to frame them, like Vinnie De Gaudio? You remember helping Vinnie Di Gaudio?"

"Sure. That was how I met you."

"See? You lived through it. You got told to keep Vinnie out of the cops' eyes for a murder even though it looked like he did it, and you kept me out of the picture so my little line to Vinnie shouldn't attract attention. This was a job that required tact and finesse, and you showed me both of those things, didn't you? And now you're eating this nice cheese and you're about to drink a wine, a wine that'll put a choir in your ear. So quitting is not an option."

"What *is* an option?" I held up the platter, feeling like I was making an Old-Testament sacrifice. "Cheese? It's terrific cheese."

"You can lighten up on the cheese. I know it's good. You thought this dodge up all by yourself, Junior, and I respect that. Something new. Gives me hope for your generation. Like I said, a patron, *patronage*, that's what you need. And an A-list client, somebody nobody's going to mess with."

"A client and a patron," I said. "Two different people?"

"That's funny," Dressler said gravely. "You gotta work with me here, Junior. I've got your best interests in mind."

"And don't think I don't appreciate it. But I—"

"I *do* think you don't appreciate it," Dressler said, "and I don't give a shit."

I said, "Right.'"

"And also, I gotta tell you, this is a job I wouldn't give to just anybody. The client, for example—"

"I thought you were the client."

"Literal, you're too literal. I'm the client in the sense that I'm the one who chose you for the job and the one who'll foot the bill. But think about it, Junior. Am I somebody some crook's going to hit?"

"No."

"How stupid would anybody have to be to hit me?"

"Someone would have to be insane to take your newspaper off your lawn."

"Not bad. Sometimes I get glimpses of something that makes me think maybe you're smart after all. No, the client, in the sense that she's the one who got ripped off, the client is—are you ready, Junior?" He sat back as though to measure my reaction better.

I put both hands on the arms of my chair to demonstrate readiness. "Ready."

"Your client is . . . Dolores La Marr."

There was a little *ta-daaa* in his voice and something expectant in his expression, something that tipped me off that this was a test I didn't want to fail. So I said, "You're kidding."

"Dolores," he said, nodding three times, "La Marr."

I said, "Wow. Dolores La Marr."

"The most beautiful woman in the world," Dressler said, and there was a hush of reverence in his voice. "*Life* magazine said so. On the cover, no less."

*Life* ceased publication on a regular basis in 1972, which I know because I once stole a framed display of the first issue, from 1883, paired with the last, both in mint condition. I got $6,500 for it from the Valley's top fence, Stinky Tetweiler, and Stinky turned it around to a dealer for $14 K. A year later it fetched $22,700 at auction while I gnashed my teeth in frustration. So it seemed safe to ask Dressler, "What year was that?"

"Nineteen fifty. April tenth, Nineteen fifty. She was twenty-one then. Most beautiful thing I ever saw in my life."

The penny dropped. Dolores *La Marr*. Always referred to as "Hollywood starlet Dolores La Marr" in the sensational coverage of the Senate subcommittee hearings into organized crime at which she testified, reluctantly, during the early 1950s.

I said, "She'd be what now, eighty?"

"She's eighty-three," Dressler said. "But she admits to sixty-six."

"Sixty-six?" I said. "That would mean *Life* named her the most beautiful woman in the world when she was four. I know journalism was better back then, but—"

"A lady has her privileges," Dressler said, a bit stiffly. "She's as old as she wants to be."

"Well, sure."

"I gotta admit," Dressler said, "I didn't expect you to know who she was. What're you, thirty-eight?"

"Thirty-seven," I said again.

"Oh, yeah, I already asked that. Don't think it's 'cause I'm getting old. It's 'cause I don't care. But you know, you're practically a larva, but you remember Dolly."

"Dolly? Oh, sorry, Dolores. I remember her because I'm a criminal. I read a lot about crime. I pay special attention to that, just like some baseball players can tell you the batting averages of every MVP for fifty years. I read the old coverage of the Congressional hearings into organized crime like it was a best seller."

Tuffy came in with an open bottle of wine and a couple of glasses on a tray. To me, he said, "Say one cute thing, and you'll be drinking this through the cork."

I asked Dressler, "You let the help talk to your guests like that?"

"Tuffy, be nice. If Mr. Bender and I don't reach a satisfactory conclusion to our chat, you have my permission to put him in a full-body cast." Dressler looked at me. "A little joke."

I waited while Tuffy yanked the cork and poured. Then I waited until he'd left the room. Then I waited until Dressler picked up his glass and said, "Cheers." Only then did I pick up my own glass and drink. An entire world opened before me: fine dust on grape leaves in the hot French sun, echoing stone passageways in fifteenth-century chateaus, the rippling laughter of Émile Zola's courtesans.

"Jesus," I said. "Where do you get this stuff?"

"Doesn't matter," Dressler said. "They wouldn't deal with you. Tell you what. You take care of Dolores, and I'll see you get a case of this."

"And a case of the one we had last time," I said. "I've thought about it every day since I drank it."

"You drive a hard bargain. Done. If you can fix things for Dolores. If not, I'll let Tuffy pay you."

"I don't need threats," I said, feeling obscurely hurt. "If I say I'll do something, I'll do it. And I'll do it the best I can."

"That's fine," Dressler said. "But I might need better than that."

# OTHER TITLES IN THE SOHO CRIME SERIES